For Such a Time as This

A NOVEL

Peace— Love— Joy

Madestella

MADESTELLA C. HOLCOMB

ISBN 978-1-0980-2797-1 (paperback)
ISBN 978-1-0980-2798-8 (digital)

Christian Faith Publishing, Inc.
832 Park Avenue
Meadville, PA 16335
www.christianfaithpublishing.com

Printed in the United States of America

Also by Madestella C. Holcomb

Therefore Choose Life

He who loveliness within
hath found, all outward loathes.
For he who color loves, and skin
Loves but their oldest clothes.

—John Donne,
Songs and Sonnets

PROLOGUE

I am Darius Paul Deavers, and I am White. My soon-to-be-wife, Ariel Sage Copple, is Black.

I believe in trees.
I believe that trees breathe. I believe that trees communicate.

The time is December 1946.

My attraction to Sage Copple began when we were only five years old. Oil had been discovered on her family's farm in Riggs, Oklahoma, and my father, Reverend Michael Paul Deavers, representing the New Western Oil Company, went to purchase the land. He took me with him because he wanted me to have an introduction to Black people, despite strong objections from my mother, who detested Black people. I was born in New England, and for the first five years of my life, all the persons in my life were White, and I am an only child.

I remember being immediately attracted to Sage. I thought, *She's a pretty little green-eyed girl, and I like her.* Her smile let me know that she liked me too.

The sale of their oil-rich acreage made Sage's father, Mr. Isaac Columbus Copple, a very rich man; but being uneducated, he soon lost all his money and died a hopeless alcoholic. Sage's mother, Mrs. Mary Jane Copple, also uneducated, was hired as cook and laundress in our house because as she told my father those tasks were where she was skilled. Sage came along with her, and they lived in our servant's quarters, a small apartment above our garage, and I was allowed to play with her.

When I was told that Sage could not go to school with me because she was Black, to me, that meant her blood was Black. I wanted to be what she was, and I wanted her to be what I was so that we could go to school together, so we pricked our fingers with one of her mother's sewing needles, and we held our fingers together to exchange our blood, thinking that would make us the same. We were seven years old.

When Sage's mother saw the community violence created by my insistence that Sage attend school with me, which was impossible in segregated Oklahoma, she quit her job as our maid, and she and Sage went to live in the Black community.

At age twenty-five, I graduated from law school in Massachusetts. I passed the bar examination and received my license. I worked one year at a prestigious law firm in Boston, and then I was drafted, and I served one year in the US Army at Fort Lewis, Washington. I came in contact with Sage on several occasions during our growing-up years, and our love for each other was evident in our adulthood. And when I proposed marriage, Sage said yes. But the miscegenation laws forbade Black and White to marry in Massachusetts, where I worked, and in Oklahoma, where we lived, so I professed my blackness because the one-drop rule in the United States says that if you have one drop of black blood in you, you are Black. My father said to me, "Darius, don't try to be something you are not. You are White, and you can't change that, and there is no such thing as black blood and white blood. All blood is red."

The thing that I now know and had to know in order to survive and not jump into the river someplace and drown myself is that I do honestly and truly love Sage Copple, and she very necessarily has to love me in order for us to keep going as if we were normal people, which we are. It's just that our lives are not controlled by normal, ordinary people. We fell in love at a time when local law and custom mandated racial separation.

Sage's sister and her aunt decorated my father's ranch house, and we planned to have a "mock wedding ceremony" there in Oklahoma for our families and friends, the same as a real ceremony, but not legal. Then some evil segregationists set fire to the ranch house, and all of our beautiful wedding paraphernalia was destroyed in the fire. My mother, bless her heart, offered our beautiful home as a place to have the ceremony. We then planned to move to the state of Washington where the miscegenation law no longer exists and could be legally married there.

I also believe in God, and when I listen, I can hear his voice from the trees, speaking to me, telling me to stay strong and don't fragment myself, half White and half Black, but to be whole in who and what I am. Yes, I am a human being, and like trees, I am one of God's creations, but I am White.

Part One

1

Friday, December 27, 1946, was the date of their *mock wedding ceremony*. It was held in the Deavers' home in Proctor, Oklahoma, which was one of elegance, beauty, and charm. A huge Christmas tree, with its many colored lights and gold and silver tinsel, stood in a corner of the living room. A large lighted star was at the top of the tree. Paper flowers had been strung on a cord and laid at the edge of the carpeting, and fresh-cut red roses filled the vases, which were placed all around the room.

List of Characters in This Room

- Reverend Michael Paul Deavers, Darius's father (White)
- Mrs. Lucy Deavers, Darius's mother (White)
- Mrs. Mary Jane Copple, Sage's mother (Black)
- Burnett Copple, Sage's brother (Black)
- Kay Lee Copple, Sage's sister (Black)
- Sophronia Martin, family friend (Black)
- Charles Williams, Darius's friend from college (Black)
- Iola Lewis, Sage's friend from college (Black)
- Beth and Paul Porter, Reverend Deavers's friends from Colorado (White)

Darius was wearing a beautiful white silk tuxedo. Sage was wearing Mrs. Lucy Deavers's beautiful white wedding dress as the one her mother made for her was destroyed in the fire. Today, for some reason not known to her, Sage was drawn to the chirping of a little bird that could be heard from outside, even though it was December. *Yes*, she thought, *it's a winter day, and you're singing as if it were summer. You're singing because you're happy, and I'm happy, and the world around me is happy. We may seem to be out of place on this cold winter's day, but we're not. We're precisely where we belong, for it is where God wants us to be.*

After the ceremony, before the guests left to go to their respective homes, they all gathered on the front porch. The outside lights had been turned on, and the occasion became more festive: the golden artificial candlesticks, the small manger scene, silver lights on the real trees flashing red, green, and blue lights on the edge of the roof.

They all joined hands in a circle, and Reverend Deavers said, "Repeat after me. Go in peace. Go in joy. Go in love." As they said the words with joy in their hearts and happiness on their minds, they tried not to think of what was ahead for the couple, one Black and one White, as they had to move away from their homes just only in order to live together as man and wife.

It was nearing the midnight hour, and the elder Deavers had gone inside. Everyone had departed except Iola Lewis and Charles Williams. Darius turned around, his face beaming, full of the charm of the evening, to suddenly realize he hadn't been able, because of time constraints, to spend any time with his friend Charles.

"I'm really glad you could come, and I wanted so very much to be able to spend some time with you, but as you see, things have moved in a different direction from how they were planned."

"Oh, I do understand," Charles said, knowing his friend's true feelings toward him. "And you don't need to apologize. I'm just happy for you and Miss Sage." He turned and smiled at Sage. The use of *miss, missus,* or *mister* being a trait of his Southern culture.

"I'm sorry," Darius said, "but you haven't been formally introduced." He took Sage by the hand, his face shining with utter happiness as he loved her so deeply, and made the introduction.

"This is my lovely." He beamed.

"And you're so right, she is lovely," Charles said, taking Sage's other hand and kissing it. "I feel honored to meet you up close.

Darius has talked about you so much that I feel like I kinda know you already."

"Thank you," Sage said, smiling her beautiful smile, which always seemed to light up the area around her. And turning to her college friend, she introduced her. "This is my friend, Iola Lewis."

"Yes," Darius said, shaking her hand and holding it, but she didn't feel warm about him. "You were Sage's roommate at college, and she tells me that your home is also right here in Proctor."

"Yes. Small world, huh?" She knew that even though they had lived most of their lives in the same city, inevitably their paths never crossed.

"What is your occupation here?" Darius asked.

"My sister and I own and operate a school," she said, proud that she could represent herself in a positive way. "It's a preschool and kindergarten. We teach the children early so when they enter first grade, they'll already know the alphabet and the numbers and how to write them, which makes learning to read and count much easier."

"Congratulations," Darius said. "It seems that you and Sage have a common interest in teaching children."

"We do," Iola said, smiling toward Sage.

"And this is Charles Williams," Darius said to Iola. "He and I attended law school together, and we were in the same graduating class."

"It's good to meet you," Iola said, smiling at Charles. "Where do you live, and what, may I ask, do you do? Your work, I mean."

"I'm from Georgia, but right now I'm trying to decide where I want to live and, actually, what kind of work I really want to do. In other words, I'm not presently employed."

"Well, you have a law degree," Darius said. "And I'd think your prospects would be very good along legal lines."

"I don't know about being a lawyer in my hometown. I do really think that I have to get out of the South. It's pretty prejudiced down there, and I don't know what kind of help I could be to my people. It looks rather hopeless right now, so I was thinking of driving up north. I hear that Chicago is pretty friendly for us, but I don't know if it's any better than down South. Boston wasn't."

"I was thinking that maybe you would like to come to BeachSide, and we could be law partners," Darius said.

"That sounds like a good prospect, so I'll surely think about it," Charles said. "I'm also very good in diving and swimming, even boating."

"Well, there's plenty of water in Washington."

"Maybe you could find something here," Iola said.

"Yes," Sage said. "My brother is a lawyer, and I'm sure he would be willing to help you with your career."

"How long are you planning on being here?" Iola asked.

"I will most likely leave on Monday. I have to get out of that motel."

"If you would like to stay here a little longer and get to know Sage's brother and check out the situation here, we have a small cottage next to our school where we sometimes stay overnight if we have to instead of going home. It's quite comfortable, and you're welcome to stay there while you're in town," Iola offered.

Obviously, Iola had eyes for Charles, and as he turned and looked at her—seemingly seeing her or looking at her or paying attention to her for the first time—a sort of liking seemed to show in his being.

"I might very well take you up on that," Charles said.

Sage and Darius looked at their two friends, and they thought, *Do we have a budding romance here? And wouldn't that just be a kick in the head.*

"Well," Darius said, breaking the silence as they looked at their friends, "we don't have to stand out here in the cold. Let's go inside and have some hot chocolate."

Hmm, Sage thought as they walked inside, *the ice has been broken to allow the two races to comingle in this White neighborhood, in these White people's home.*

After having a cup of hot chocolate with their friends, tiredness overtook them, and they bade Iola and Charles good-night. Iola took Charles to his motel, and as they sat in the car, she presented her feelings to him about Sage and Darius.

"I just think Sage is making a huge mistake, and although you admire Darius, you're Black, and you should prefer Black men for Black women."

Charles, however, was true to his friend. "I don't really think that my friend sees color when he looks at Sage, and knowing him like I do, I know that he loves her with his whole heart and soul."

"But she'll face so many problems," Iola continued her argument. "As a matter of fact, she's already defied some of her family—and the law." She sighed deeply and put her hands over her face as if to shut out some evil spirits. "And he's so...so...he's so rich," she said as if that would also present a problem for Sage.

"Well, it's a new day," Charles said. "And it's time things changed, especially for our race. I've lived in the South all my life except when I went to law school, and I've seen the way we're treated. That's why I joined the Black Student's Movement when I was attending college in Boston. We had hoped to bring about changes in our educational system for Negroes. You know that if we were educated, a lot of other things would be better. Better jobs, thus better housing and a better life all around. And you do know that Darius joined the group. I know he's White, and I know he's rich, but he's..." He paused as if searching for the proper words to describe his friend. "He's always honest. He's always for real, and from what I've seen and also heard from him, his mind and his heart have told him that he truly loves Sage, and she is the one he will marry."

"Yeah, people think that love conquers all, but that's not always true. This might only be a passing infatuation which won't last. I just hope Sage knows what she's getting herself into." Then she turned and changed her position from looking straight ahead to facing Charles. She also changed the gist of the conversation. "Anyway, I want her to enjoy herself while she's here, so I'm thinking of having her and a few of our former school friends over for food and drinks and some games, like cards or checkers. You know, let her have some fun."

"That does sound like a good idea, so let me know if I can help you."

Iola had already set her sights on Charles Williams as a permanent part of her own future, and responding to his offer of help, she put her arms around his neck and kissed him on the cheek. Charles responded cordially and went out into the night, but some uncertainty took hold of him, and he decided it would be better if he didn't accept her offer for a place to stay.

Without consulting anyone else, Iola began planning for her social gathering, as she called it. She would invite some eligible bachelor friends whom she knew, and maybe Sage would like one of them, and then she would be discouraged from marrying Darius. Iola's mind took her to Fred Hunter. He graduated from high school with Sage and Iola, and he also graduated with them from the University in Missouri, and he was now a successful businessman, having taken over his father's drugstore, one of only two such stores in the Black community.

She thought, *Hmm. Instead of inviting a larger number, we can make it a foursome. Charles and me. Sage and Fred. Yes.*

Darius and Sage spent Friday night together in the place they had first established what their future would be, although they didn't know it at the time. It was in the little servant's quarters above the garage behind his parents' house where they pricked their fingers in the act of exchanging their blood, thus wanting to become the same. And now, having the same feelings of love and admiration for each other, love now pricked their hearts, and the blood of love flowed from one to the other through veins of passion and the lifelines of peace. "Till death do us part," they promised. Again.

A small seed of love had been planted in a garden of hope, and it had been watered with longings and fed by the sunshine of endurance. It had grown into this young sapling and had weathered the fall season when leaves of despair had fallen, the winter seasons of cold hate, and now it was growing stronger, the spring with its warmth; and now a beautiful sapling of togetherness was here, one day to become a sturdy tree. Perennial, hopefully continuing to live and grow from year to year.

Time had passed, and their love and togetherness was flourishing, and they spoke it.

"I will always love you, Sage."

"I will always love you, Darius."

They decided: since this was the first time they said "I do," their anniversary date should actually be celebrated at Christmastime, the birth of the Christ and the birth of their becoming one.

On Saturday, Sage and Darius spent the day with Darius's parents, Reverend Paul and Mrs. Lucy Deavers, and they shared dinner and prayers. Saturday night, Darius took Sage home to her mother's house.

On Sunday morning, Sage went to church with her family, and Darius went to church with his parents. Sage would not be allowed to worship with Darius in the White church.

It was decided that Darius and his father would drive to Washington to make preparations for Sage's coming, finding a place for them to live and a place for Darius to work. Besides, it would be difficult for Sage and Darius driving across country together, stopping at gas stations with all eyes on them, hateful eyes, and Sage needing to urinate and not being able to use the restroom, not being able to eat at restaurants or stay at motels. Sage would stay in Proctor with her mother, and she would travel by train to Washington, hopefully in no more than two months.

Sunday evening, Reverend Deavers and Darius went to bid "so long," not goodbye, to Sage's mother and to receive her blessing as they traveled. Mrs. Mary Jane Copple's heart was warmed by the sight of them, so obviously aware that the beautiful love liaison between Sage and Darius had allowed his family to shut out the worldly oppositions to this young mixed-race couple's love.

Mrs. Mary Jane Copple read to them the prayer of Jabez from the first book of Chronicles:

> Oh that thou wouldst bless me indeed, and enlarge my coast, and that thine hand might be with me, and that thou wouldst keep me from evil, that it may not grieve me.

"And the Word says that God granted Jabez that which he requested, so you all go in peace, love, and joy, and with my blessing and with God's blessing."

And their hugs and kisses were genuine.

2

Early Monday morning, Darius and his father began the motor trip across country from the state of Oklahoma to the state of Washington. They drove all day Monday, and they rested at a motel Monday night. They drove all day Tuesday, and they rested at a motel Tuesday night. Arriving in BeachSide, Washington on Wednesday afternoon, Darius and his father took a suite in a modern upper-class hotel; and after settling in, giving thanks for a safe trip, they rested.

After resting, they got dressed and went downstairs for dinner. People were celebrating New Year's Eve in the main dining room, and noticeable was the fact that there were no Black faces. Even the hired help, the servers, cashiers, hostesses, cooks were White.

Both men knew that Sage would not be able to reside in this hotel, and she would not be allowed to eat in this dining room.

"Well," Darius said, "we're here, and I guess this is as far as I was able to get in my thinking, except to look forward to Sage's coming." He breathed a sigh. "So what should we do now?" he asked.

"Well," his father said, ignoring Darius's sigh and smiling, showing the peace that existed in his mind, "first things first. First, we need to get a good night's rest, and then in the morning, we can focus on where you and Sage will live."

"I think I should look for a nice place to rent, and then when I get settled in a job, I can consider buying a home."

"Your mother and I have already talked about that. When you graduated from law school, she gave you a new automobile for your graduation present, which was fine with me. And now I'm going to give you and Sage a house for your wedding present. You'll have enough to worry about with other things, so being comfortable in your own home will mean a great deal."

"Oh, Dad, you and Mom have been so good to me, but I don't want to be a burden on you forever."

"You're not a burden, Darius, and we know that you're not a lazy person, and so you will certainly figure out how to make it on your own, and you'll be led, somehow, to find your true place in life, but we'll always be here to help you."

Darius lay awake long into the night deep in thought. He thought of his father's words: "You'll figure out how to make it on your own, and you'll be led, somehow, to find your true place in life."

Hmm. I have never really and truly been on my own. Not in the sense of being responsible for my sustenance. My meals have always been served to me, my clothes have been laundered for me, and money has been given to me to purchase them and whatever else I needed. Oh me. What have I gotten myself into by planning on marrying Sage? What have I gotten Sage into? How difficult will it be for me being responsible for my own household? How difficult will it be for us to live together being an interracial couple?

Those were his questions, but he answered them himself: *I will figure out how to make it work. There is, of course, no alternative. I know that there is always uncertainty how to proceed when one arrives in a new place with a new wife. We can eat at home more than eating out. I will ask Sage to teach me how to cook. I never had to cook my own meals. How long does one boil an egg anyway? Or bake a turkey? Hmm. Am I assuming that Sage knows how to cook, or am I following the existing opinion that all Black people know how to cook? Well, whatever we need to learn, we can do it together, and of course, I will hire a cook and a housekeeper. And where is my true place in life, not only mine being White but mine with Sage, her being Black? Oh my!*

Then he realized that his body was tired from the long trip, and his mind was tired from so much trying to figure things out. He told himself, as Oblonsky's valet told him at one of his life crises, *Never mind. Things will shape themselves.*

He was able to relax in the peaceful mood where he placed himself. He called Sage, and they each shared their activities of the day, and they ended their conversation with loving words.

"I love you, Sage Copple, and I miss you."

"I love you, Darius Deavers, and I miss you."

He went to sleep in peace.

Reverend Deavers also lay awake thinking, *My son is of the opinion that his life is unique, that his mixed marriage is his major hurdle to overcome, but I am compelled to smile for I know that all marriages come with hurdles to overcome. In the movies, the couples come together, they declare their love, kiss, and then they walk off into the sunset, and that's the end of the movie. It suggests that life is easy breezy from that time on and forever after. Not true. Rich, poor, old, young, Black, White—all live with marital problems of some kind, and if they're going to abide by till death do us part, as they promised in their wedding vows, it will require some give and some take, some compromise, and above all, a lot of love. I thank God for Sage. It was her loving-kindness that softened and melted even my wife's hard heart. I feel very confident that Sage will bring the same loving-kindness to their life in Washington. And I thank God for Mrs. Mary Jane Copple. Her faith in God and her ability to weather the storms in her life gave strength and confidence to Sage.*

He called his wife, and they each shared their activities of that day.

"I know you're helping Darius, but I'll be glad when you get things settled so I can come out there for the real wedding." Lucy sighed.

"I'm praying for God to bless all of us." He slept.

The next day, Darius and his father paid a visit to the City Hospitality Center to seek information about the city of BeachSide and the state of Washington, and they wanted to find a lovely, spiritual place for Darius and Sage to have a legal marriage ceremony performed.

They received a free visitor's packet that gave this information about the state: Washington is the only state named for a president.

It was named in honor of George Washington. The state lies in the northwestern part of the United States. Seattle is the largest city of the Pacific Northwest, and it is the headquarters of the Northwest fishing industry, including the rich Alaska salmon fisheries. Puget Sound is a large irregular body of water in the northwest corner of the state, and it is a leading American shipping center. The Puget Sound is 80 miles long and covers an area of about 2,000 square miles. The largest ships can steam into any part of the Sound as its depth is from 180 to 925 feet. It is one of the most beautiful bodies of water in the United States. The city of BeachSide is noted for its hills; some of which rise as high as 514 feet above sea level. Located across from the city are the Olympic Mountains. To the east rise Mount Rainier, one of the highest peaks in the United States.

The visitor's packet included a brochure describing a place called the Peace Arch. It was described as a beautiful and scenic park, and they considered it as a good place for the wedding. In Darius's mind, however, was always the question: do they allow Blacks there?

Also available were city tours. They chose one. They saw the beautiful campuses around the University of Washington, Seattle University, and the Central Community college. They passed the Boeing Plant, which was involved in making planes. They passed the beautiful Puget Sound and the mighty Coulee Dam, which is considered to be one of the engineering wonders of the world.

"One of our features of this tour is a stream that we call the Wishing Water. Take this path to the bottom of the hill and check it out. It's very interesting," their tour guide said.

Following the path, they came to a rippling stream. There was a large wooden sign with instructions on making a wish. The sign read, "Place a coin in the box at the bottom of this structure and then take the 2×2 card from the slot. Write a one-word wish on the card and drop it through the designated opening to the stream. The claim is that the water has magical powers, and as the water is always flowing downstream," the guide continued, "your wish is carried down to the home of the wish genie. The genie will grant you your wish. Of course, it's a money-making thing, but if you believe that wishes do come true, it leaves you with a pleasant thought for the day."

Reverend Deavers wrote on his card the word *grace*. Darius wrote the word *mercy*.

When they were back at the hotel, Darius remembered the friendly relationship he had had with his commanding officer, Major Marvin Hawthorne, when he served his year in the army here in Washington. Darius felt sure he could get a better perspective of the city and its racial climate from him. Darius called and was able to make an appointment to see the major on Friday.

In high school and college, Marvin Hawthorne was a good student; and even though he was really very smart, he disliked having to sit quietly at a desk and listen to what seemed to him a monotonously endless spay of words coming from the mouths of his teachers, so he'd spend the time drawing pictures—of women. He liked looking at women, all the different shapes and sizes; and even though he was White, his repertoire included women of all colors. They all had some interesting feature which he liked. He also drew pictures of clouds. Clouds, he thought, are like people: different shapes and colors, coming and going, and thought-provoking.

After college, Marvin Hawthorne joined the United States Army. Because of his aptitude for learning, his agility in the routine drills, he received several promotions; and after attending officer training school, he reached the rank of major. He spent a part of his service overseas, some time at a base in Georgia, and at a base in Oklahoma; and now retired, he had an easy desk job at the veteran's hospital in Washington as a public relations guidance counselor. In that position, he dealt mostly with military families who had little money and unusual medical problems.

Major Marvin Hawthorne had a handsome, bright appearance, dancing brown eyes, and a head full of thick dark wavy hair. He smiled a lot and chewed gum a lot, saying it was good for his teeth and that it helped maintain the muscles in his neck and face.

He dressed very fashionably with everything matching and coordinated. He was charming in many ways, and he loved people and thus had friends from many walks of life. Friday night sports, drinking beer with the fans at their favorite bar were some of his usual activities.

He and his wife, Alicia, were married at ages 30 and 32 respectively; and after five years of marriage, they were still childless. Alicia Hawthorne had been pregnant three times, and each time a weakness in her system produced a miscarriage. They tried artificial insemination, but the result was the same. For one year, they cared for two foster children, becoming very attached to them and applying for adoption, but the female parent somehow got herself stable and was able to reclaim the children.

After much thought, Marvin put their names on the adoption list at the hospital where he was assigned, and Alicia was happy when news came to the major of a pregnant mother who opted to give her baby up at birth. And Marvin was willing, without the knowledge of his wife, to pay a sizeable amount to a coworker who illegally saw that the child would be given to Major Hawthorne and his wife. He also used his position and his knowledge of the procedures at the hospital to obtain a birth certificate that listed him and his wife as the birth parents. One stipulation of the father to the adoptive parents was that if the child was a girl, she must be given the name of Miriama Imani, and if a boy, he must be given the name of Adama Pascal.

When their beautiful girl child was born, Alicia thought the letter *a* at the end of the name was a mistake, and she removed it. Their newly acquired daughter was given the name *Miriam Imani*.

On Friday, Darius and his father drove to the veteran's hospital, which was a large six-story building inside the main gate, about half mile from the entrance. They entered and stopped at the reception desk.

"I'm Darius Deavers, and I'm here to see Major Marvin Hawthorne," Darius said.

"Yes," the receptionist said with a smile. "He's expecting you. Come, I'll show you the way. It's easy to get lost in this building with its long crisscrossing halls and many offices."

They arrived at the major's office, and the young lady smiled again and opened the door for them.

"Have a good day," she said, turning to leave them.

"Thank you, and the same to you," Darius said, acknowledging her kindness with a handshake and a smile. Inside the room, there were several rows of desks occupied by civilian workers. The major's desk was at the back of the room facing the entrance, and Major Hawthorne, recognizing Darius, stood up and moved from behind his desk with a wide grin on his handsome face.

"Captain Deavers. How good to see you again," Major Hawthorne said good-naturedly as he approached Darius. They greeted each other with an army salute, but not really satisfied with a salute, Darius took the major's hand and drew him closer, giving him a friendly hug.

"I'm a civilian now, so just call me Darius. I'm happy to see you again, and I still have a great amount of respect for the uniform."

"Thank you."

"This is my father, Reverend Deavers," Darius said, turning toward his father.

"I'm happy to meet you, sir," the major said. He exuded such a pleasant impression that both men felt comfortably at ease.

"Well, we don't have to stand here all day. Let's go into my private office," the major said, leading the way.

Major Marvin Hawthorne was obviously on familiar terms with all of his office employees, smiling and being greeted with return smiles as he walked through. He led his guests to a large room, richly and tastefully furnished with lounge chairs, a leather sofa, end tables with lamps, and a large mahogany desk. Behind the desk was an upholstered leather chair. The room had three large windows with draperies that matched the wall-to-wall carpet. Darius remembered that the army officers' lives, their living quarters and accommodations, were lavishly different from those of the enlisted men.

"I'm just so very glad to see you," Major Hawthorne said as they sat in the comfortable lounge chairs. "So how are you doing, Mr. Civilian? And what brings you to this part of the country? A vacation?"

"No. This isn't a vacation. We're moving out here to live."

"You and your father?"

"No. Me and my wife."

"Don't tell me you're married."

"Not yet. That's one of the things I want to talk to you about."

Major Hawthorne, of course, was older than Darius; and when Darius was in his unit, Major Hawthorne was always amazed and appreciative of Darius's willingness to work and his aptitude for adjusting to the army ways. Watching him now, Major Hawthorne sensed a problematic tone in Darius's voice, and he detected a little embarrassment in the flush on his face.

"Well, all right, why don't we sit down and talk about it."

Darius wanted to ask him about the racial climate here, but he couldn't somehow. What he wanted to talk about was so personal and so close to his heart, and he didn't want to experience the shock he imagined his revelation that Sage is Black would evoke.

"Thank you," Darius said. Then after a moment's thought, he spoke, not mentioning Sage. "I wanted to ask if you know of a nice place where we can say our marriage vows. We don't want to go to a justice of the peace as my father can perform the ceremony, but we'd like to have it someplace that's nice and private."

Major Hawthorne's first thought was of the chapel on the base, but he didn't think that Darius wanted a military setting. Then suddenly brightening, as if he'd only just thought of it, he smiled.

"I certainly do, and I highly recommend this place. It's called the Peace Arch, and it's a beautiful park, close to the Washington-Canadian border. Yes. Go by the Hospitality Center, and they'll give you a brochure that will tell you all about it."

"Thank you, but we already have one in our visitor's packet, so we'll certainly look into it," Darius said.

"When is your intended coming?"

"Well, she'll have to wait until we find a place to live."

"Where are you staying now?"

"My father and I have a suite at the Downtown Brighton, but we're looking into finding a house for me and my wife to either purchase or rent, and of course, to decide on my employment. We have a lot to do coming to a new city."

"Well, I'm sure I can help you, and I can enlist the help of my wife and my daughter and her husband. My daughter, she'd be about your age, Darius. So call me, I'm at your command." He smiled and gave a salute.

Darius felt a bit more comfortable with the major, but still not enough to tell him that Sage is Black.

After the departure of Darius and his father, a struggle seemed to be going on within the major's mind. When he asked Darius his reason for coming to Washington, Darius said he came to get married, and he needed a special place for the ceremony, he needed a place to live, and he spoke of earning a living. Major Hawthorne knew that before his enlistment, Darius had been employed with a very high-class law firm in the East, and when his year of enlistment was up, he went back to the same position because it had been held for him.

He couldn't help wondering, what had brought Darius here with no job, no house, and no prospects? And why did he leave his hometown in Oklahoma? *Oh, just forget it*, he thought. *If he needs me, he certainly knows where I am, and he'll contact me.*

But the more he tried to forget about the former captain, the more thoughts of him took over. *Oh hell*, he said to himself. *There is probably no cause for anxiety.* Yet he kept thinking that something out of the ordinary had happened to his friend.

So now the major's feeling was that Captain Deavers was not saying what he was thinking, and he was not acting in the way he really felt. It was as if he was holding something inside him that he couldn't release, or there was something he didn't feel comfortable talking about. Was he in trouble? Why was his father with him? Was his father running away from something, and he needed his son's help? Or was Darius trying to escape from something, and his father was supporting him? Was the girl he intends to marry pregnant? Was he gay, and he was marrying a man? He said his intended's name was Sage. He'd never heard the name *Sage* before, except as a seasoning for the turkey dressing. Could Sage be a man's name?

He tried to busy himself with all the papers in his in-basket, his to-do things, trying as hard as he could to take his mind off Captain Deavers and Reverend Deavers and whatever their problems might be. Then his thoughts just seemed, without his trying at all, to turn and focus on the reverend. Major Hawthorne knew from Darius's army statistics that his father was an Oklahoma oil executive, which meant he was quite wealthy, and Major Hawthorne noticed how richly he was dressed. He knew that Darius drove an expensive automobile, which had been a graduation gift from his parents, so evidently he wasn't having money problems. Hmm. Maybe Reverend Deavers had gotten his money illegally.

After some serious thinking about it, he came up with the conclusion that he could help by being a guide. *I can take them to check out the Peace Arch, and I can take them through the upper-class residential areas, and I can help the captain research the overall prospects of a job. Does he want to involve himself with law? Practicing? Teaching? I'll offer my services. He can accept or refuse.*

He picked up the phone and left a message at their hotel inviting them to dinner at his home on Sunday, and then he felt better and more at ease. Major Hawthorne was not a very religious man, but he always said that his life was led and guided by his "little green man." He leaned back in his big chair, folded his arms behind his head, thanked his Little Green Man for an answer, and he breathed a sigh of relief.

3

On New Year's day, Sage stayed in Proctor with her mother, and the Copple family always shared the traditional New Year's dinner for Black folk consisting of chitterlings, candied yams, collard greens, black-eyed peas, corn bread, pound cake, and home-made ice cream. The myth was that these dishes would bring good luck for the entire year to those partaking.

As she had previously promised, Sage went on Thursday to spend some time with her future mother-in-law, Mrs. Lucy Deavers. Why? Because she asked her to. Sage was not totally comfortable, and a little whiff of anxiety remained on her presence because everything was different being in the Deavers' house as part of the family. The hired help—the cook, the housekeeper, the chauffeur—all knew that she was here, and they were somewhat confused about how to relate to her. They had never been compelled to provide service to a Negro.

Sage thought to herself, *I can control my own mind and not that of the servants, so if they have a problem with me, it's their problem and not mine.*

That night, Mrs. Deavers showed Sage to the bedroom that she would occupy. It was such a beautiful room, and even though it spoke of luxury, money, and cleanliness, Sage wondered if these were the things that created happiness. Of course not, for when she was in her room at home, not nearly so much money having been spent on its furnishings, she had the same warm feeling of contentment. Yet she was in Mrs. Lucy Deavers's house now, and this was the house where her mother had worked as a maid.

31

So much had happened in the last few days, even months, that had drained Sage's mental and physical being and had depleted her energies on both those levels. Now the warm lilac-scented bubble bath—oh dear, oh dear, each bedroom has its own private bathroom—and the soft calf-length nightgown that Mrs. Deavers had placed on the bed helped her to get a feeling of comfort.

As usual, since their engagement, any time he was away from Sage, Darius called and talking with him gave her some comfort, some hope, and some peace, and they always ended their talks with some loving words.

"I love you, my Sage, and I miss you."

"I love you, my Darius, and I miss you."

The fact that decisions had been made and events and minds changed, love now filled every corner of Sage's world and surrounded her. A conversation of thanks to God helped her to relax during her mother-in-law's hugs and wishes that she sleep well. She went to sleep in this lovely house, between these lovely matching sheets, and she was at peace.

The next morning, Sage awoke to the smell of coffee, and she felt the warmth of the comforter over her, and a soft knock on the door and the soft calling of her name brought her fully awake.

"Sage, are you awake?"

"Yes, I am."

"May I come in?"

"Of course. Good morning," Sage said as Mrs. Deavers entered. She sat at the side of the bed and patted Sage's exposed hand. It was such a meaningful gesture, full of the words *I really want you to like me.*

But her presence there, and her hand there brought back memories of this formerly forbidden set of rooms. When she was living in the servant's quarters as a child, she was not allowed to come up here. She was familiar with the basement area, the kitchen, and the backyard, but she had never been upstairs. Sage now had to reconnoiter her mind to receive this lady, very nearly a stranger, here in her house. Being here for the Mock Wedding Ceremony was different. It was just that: a place for their ceremony.

Now she was actually sleeping up here as if this was her house and her bedroom. She had to become the adult Sage that she was and the daughter-in-law of this woman who was White. She had to erase the idea of White from her mind and allow Lucy Deavers to be her relative.

However, when she went downstairs for breakfast, being among the maids and servants, she suddenly felt like that little seven-year-old girl again; but like the script of a movie or a play, with a few strokes of the pen in her brain, she grew her up. Even back then, she had not felt inferior. She was in an inferior place, but she wasn't inferior. Then and now, she considered herself an equal.

This grown-up Sage sat down at the breakfast table and allowed herself to be served. Situations and climates change, and the racial situation and climate had changed in this house.

Then it was Friday, Sage Copple's second day at the Deavers' house.

"I want to take you shopping today. We'll go to Martinique's. Is that all right with you?" Lucy Deavers asked when she and Sage had finished eating breakfast.

"Mrs. Deavers—" Sage began, but Lucy Deavers cut her off right away.

"Sage, why do you insist on calling me Mrs. Deavers? It's so formal."

"It's formal, yes, but it's what will be accepted when we're out among other people, and I'd rather not draw undue attention to us by calling you mother or mom."

"But that's who I am."

"I know who you are," Sage said, looking at Lucy and at the same time feeling her dilemma.

"And I know who you are, Sage," she said after a moment, like a fresh cup of coffee you've just tasted, only a sip to see if it's too hot or too cold or have just the right amount of sugar and cream. "You're my daughter, and that's what it is."

"That's what it is to us, and regardless to how we think, it isn't how the world thinks, and certainly not the White world of Proctor, Oklahoma," Sage said.

All the while they were putting on their coats, getting into the car, and beginning the drive to the downtown section of town, Sage was thinking, *This is a mistake*, as she remembered the mistake that was made when Darius's father, Michael Deavers, mistakenly adhered to the deep desire of his young White son, Darius, in wanting his young colored friend Sage to attend school with him. Mr. Deavers, Darius, and Sage, this trio, had gone to the school with all the strength that the oldest of them could muster. However, it was not the time of day, nor was it the time in history when it could happen. There was cursing and running, screaming and crying, and there was hate and ugliness. All this because of one little colored child who should have been as entitled to attend this school as any White child.

Sage remembered that day as if it was today, and she could feel it and hear it, and she was quite aware that there was still racial segregation in schools, in churches, at water fountains, in parks, on buses, and in department stores.

"We really shouldn't go to Martinique's," Sage said, not wanting a replay of that ugly school scene.

"Why not?"

"They won't allow me to shop there," Sage said *me* rather than *Negro* or *Black* or *colored* to bring attention to the fact of those words.

"They'll allow you if you're with me. They'll have to. I have an account there, and I've spent a lot of money in that store. As a matter of fact, I've spent enough money there to buy one of the departments."

"No. They don't have to allow it. Their hate of my color is stronger than their love of your money."

"All right. I'll say that you're my..." She paused, and Sage smiled.

"Your maid?" Sage knew what she was going to say. You see, this closing of doors, barring of entrances, had arisen in Sage's life many times, but it was new to Lucy Deavers. She'd never even had to think about not being able to go into places where she wanted to go, and she thought, as her husband had thought about the school, that her presence and her request would make it happen.

"No. I'll say you're my personal assistant."

"It still means that I'm a servant in your employ, and I can't be that. I'm not that. Maid or personal assistant means I'm something beneath you."

"But we'll know differently, and damn it, this needs to change," Lucy said.

"I want you to remember that I've been placed with you by being engaged to marry your son, but my place in the world hasn't changed." Sage reached over and squeezed Lucy's hand.

And as Sage had predicted, Mrs. Lucy Deavers's determination to have her shop at Martinique's proved to be unsuccessful, and Sage's awareness that it wouldn't be allowed proved to be correct. And back in the car, as Sage looked over at her, she saw that Mrs. Lucy Deavers was crying.

"You want to buy me some things, so we'll go to Fosters," Sage said. "It's one of the two department stores downtown where we're allowed to shop. The merchandise is nice, but not as expensive as at your store."

To Mrs. Lucy Deavers, it was an impossible situation, like being pregnant and never having had sexual intercourse. When they went to Fosters, of course, everyone in the store just automatically determined that Sage was this White lady's maid or her maid's daughter, going back to that Black university, and this White lady was buying the colored girl some clothes for school.

The next day, rich White Lucy Deavers went back to Martinique's and shopped. She now knew Sage's size and her color preferences. Sage didn't want her to do it, but she realized that sometimes you have to let people display their benevolence. Sage did need all the things Lucy bought, and Sage's receiving them with a hug of thanks made Lucy happy. But Sage smiled, for the experience caused her to think of all the places she would be barred from entering with Darius when they were married, and Sage's smile spoke words. *I will be all right. Darius and I will be all right. With our love to sustain us, we will have to weather whatever storms that come.*

The Wise Counselor said: "And they will come. And as the storms come and go, so will acquaintances, friends, and enemies."

On Sunday, Sage made the bed, washed in the attached bathroom, went downstairs, sat down at the breakfast table, and allowed herself to be served.

Later, after lunch, knowing they would not be attending either the Black or the White church, Sage suggested that they dismantle the Christmas tree. It was something usually done by the maid or housekeeper, and it was something Lucy Deavers had never done; and as she carefully took down each bulb and put it in the box it came out of, she smiled a happy smile and thought, *This is so nice.* She had always enjoyed the finished product of the Christmas tree, but she had never thought of all the work that went into either putting it up or dismantling it.

Lucy was thinking, *Yes, this is more than dismantling a tree. We're at the same level. I'm not above or below, and neither is Sage. This is an activity we can share without shifting. I really feel, at this moment, like a totally different person.* She now thought of all the many things others did for her, and she decided she could do something in her house besides giving orders for someone else to do it.

The maid and the housekeeper who had been accustomed to carrying out this job looked on in amazement. But the overall feeling was that this was different, but it was nice. Sage seemed always to exude friendly karma to all around her, and they couldn't feel any animosity toward this lovely brown girl who was here because of her love for Darius and the love of this family for her.

Sage hummed, and Mrs. Lucy Deavers joined in, and their working and humming put a pleasant layer of warmth all around. As Lucy Deavers looked at Sage and saw her welcoming smile, it told her not to waste any pity on Sage because of her race. Sage was aware of the biases but content. Aware but strong. Strong and determined.

They spent the next few days sorting, unwrapping, and making a list of all the wedding gifts, writing thank-you cards, and mailing them.

Friday night, Darius called, and his voice gave Sage an added breath of calm. She was at peace. They ended their conversation as usual with words of love.

"I love you, my Sage."

"I love you, my Darius."

On Saturday morning, Sage asked to be taken to her mother's house. They rode all the way to Mrs. Mary Jane Copple's house in silence. Passing through the south end of town, Sage was sure all the White people just thought it was a nice White lady taking her maid home.

When they arrived at Sage's mother's house, Lucy came in also, and she was happy that the wall had been torn down, and Sage could see that here in this room in this house at this moment, Lucy and Mary Jane had become equal. It was no great river to cross for Mary Jane Copple because she'd always been there in her mind. But Lucy Deavers had had to step through so many brambles and mud and rocks of the Negro scene because she was limited for so long by looking only on the outside of Mary Jane and Sage, if she looked at them at all. She was forced through the years, however, to look at Sage when Darius, her only son, desired so strongly to be Sage's friend, and an epiphany had happened when Lucy Deavers realized that if Darius had been made to choose between her and Sage, he would have chosen and did choose Sage. She had to look hard at Sage and Mary Jane and think a little deeper about them as a people, and she was proud of herself that she could now see Sage's whole family as people. Real people. Mary Jane knew that Lucy had come so far on the path, and it helped when Lucy was able to look inside Mary Jane. Perhaps she could do so because Mary Jane Copple was so transparent. She was good all the time, receptive and accepting, not very changeable in mood or thought, believing in God and knowing that God is love. Expecting nothing. Giving everything. Everything that another could receive.

Lucy Deavers thought about this equality when she sat down in Mary Jane's house. *We're equal here in this house, but there are many things that we can't do together as equals outside this house in the maddening crowd of biased bigots.*

"I want to thank you again for letting Sage wear your beautiful wedding dress. It was so sad that the dress I made got destroyed in the fire," Mary Jane said.

"That was a terrible thing, and I know that the dress you made for Sage was very pretty. You should be a professional seamstress and sew for other people," Lucy said.

"No, I just sew for my family, and sometimes I get together with the church ladies, and we make quilts."

"Make quilts?" Lucy asked.

"Here, I'll show you," she said, taking Lucy into her sewing room. "We cut the cloth into blocks, and we sew them together by hand. Then we use this quilting frame, and we put some soft padding in the middle and some cloth on the bottom, and we sew it all together, also by hand. Then we have a beautiful quilt."

"How interesting," Lucy said, not ever having thought of how quilts were made.

Mary Jane took Lucy into the backyard and showed her the garden. She showed her how to pick winter squash and string beans. Inside, Sage had made sandwiches and lemonade, and she served lunch. Sage smiled inwardly because she was serving as a friend, not as a maid.

What happened here this day and the previous day, was something that took Lucy Deavers out of being Ms. White Boss Lady and into being Ms. Friend. But when Mrs. Lucy Deavers was back in her car driving to her house, her neighborhood, she involuntarily became her White self again. She could not deceive herself into thinking she would try to integrate her bridge club by asking Sage to play, and she now knew that she couldn't take Sage or her mother to Martindale's tea room. She could enjoy Mary Jane's company in Mary Jane's home, not trying to go to church or prayer meeting with her. And she thought, *I will still keep my minority employees, my maid, and my housekeeper. When in Rome, do as the Romans do*, she said.

Is it possible to be these two people? she asked herself, and then she answered herself. *I am White, and I cannot change that, nor do I want to. But I can live by the needs of both environments, mine and theirs. I can become that quasi-chameleon and change as change is needed but still be true to the person I am. This whole scenario with Sage and Darius has been a trial for me and for Mrs. Mary Jane Copple. She learned some things about me, and I learned some things about her. I learned, above all else, that she is a nice Black person, and she learned that I am a nice White person. Sage's liaison with Darius strengthened that.*

The Wise Counselor agreed:

> Be what you is,
> And not what you ain't.
> Because when you're what you ain't,
> Then you ain't what you is.

4

On Sunday morning, Reverend Deavers and Darius visited one of the Baptist churches which was close by and discovered that it was a Black congregation. They were the only White people there, and Reverend Deavers knew that Sunday morning in the United States was a very segregated time, but he also knew that if Darius and Sage truly wanted to worship together, they'd have to find a way. It wouldn't be easy.

At five o'clock on Sunday afternoon, Darius and his father arrived at the home of Major Marvin and Mrs. Alicia Hawthorne. It was a cool, cloudy day, and cars were parked in some driveways beside well-kept lawns. The houses, with trees in the yard, some decorated around the bottom with white rock, were large, some two-story, and some ranch style. The affluence of the residents in this part of the city was evident. It reminded Darius of the restricted areas in Massachusetts where he went to school and the south side of Proctor where he had lived with his family.

They walked up the sidewalk, which was inlaid with colorful slabs of rock. Darius rang the doorbell, and it was answered by a colored lady, but this was not new to him as there had always been colored help in his home.

After having their coats taken by the servant, they passed through a small entrance hall and stepped down a couple of steps onto the soft carpet of a beautiful large living room. They were warmly greeted by Major Hawthorne, who came forward from inside the room.

"Hello there. I'm glad to see you again. Come on in," he said, shaking both their hands and leading them into the room. The draperies were open, revealing a patio lit with Christmas lights, and tiny white lights were on every branch of the trees outside in the yard.

"My wife always enjoys the Christmas decorations, and she spends a lot of time putting them up."

"They're beautiful. My wife likes to decorate quite lavishly too," Reverend Deavers said.

"Meet my wife, Alicia," the major said, turning to the slightly attractive tall lady who rose to meet them. "Alicia, this is a former captain of mine, Darius Deavers," he said, patting Darius on the shoulder. "And this is his father, Reverend Deavers."

"How nice to meet both of you," Alicia said, her face brightening into her usual put-on smile, seeming always to have a smile on her face. She was full-bodied, not fat, but with a look of health. "Have a seat. Dinner will be ready in a few minutes," she said.

"You'll get to meet our daughter, Miriam, and her husband, Bertram, and our grandson, Timmy," Major Hawthorne said. "They're also coming for dinner."

"Miriam volunteers once a week at a charm school for young girls ages eight through twelve," Alicia said. "She's so talented, and I'm quite proud of her." It was obvious that Alicia worshipped Miriam.

A charm school, Reverend Deavers thought, and he remembered that his niece had gone to a finishing school, and he knew the name *charm* and *finishing* meant money. And as his niece's school only included rich White children, he was sure Miriam's did too.

"Oh, here they are now," Alicia said, looking out the window.

Darius and Reverend Deavers stood to greet the three as they came into the house. The young family took off their coats, and as they turned toward them, Darius looked at Miriam, and he couldn't take his eyes off her. It was as if Sage had come into the room and was standing before him. Miriam so much reminded him of his intended—her willowy frame, her straight well-rounded legs, her long hair, and her half-smile. Even though her hair was light brown and her skin was a creamy white as compared to Sage's dark curly hair and her brown skin (and Miriam's eyes were light brown compared

41

to Sage's green eyes), he was mesmerized and not really listening to the introductions.

"This is our daughter, Miriam," Alicia said.

Miriam was a beautiful aristocratic-looking woman. She is tall for a girl, five feet eight inches, nicely built, weighing 150 pounds.

When Miriam smiled and reached out her hand to shake his, Darius wanted to take her in his arms and say, "Hello, my Sage."

"I'm very pleased to meet you," he heard his voice saying, and he was jolted back into himself and into the real world.

"This is her husband, Bertram Withers," Alicia said, continuing the introductions. "He is head professor of the law department at the university, but my hope is that he will one day seriously consider a run for mayor."

"Good evening," Bertram said. "My mother-in-law likes to put that thought about becoming the mayor into my head, but I have thrown my hat into the ring as president of my university." He exuded a stilted dignity and a somewhat distant self-pride.

"And this is Timothy, my grandson," Alicia said, beaming. "I just love this little man, and he's his grandmother's sweetheart." She kissed him on the forehead.

"Timmy is six, and he is spoiled rotten," Major Hawthorne said. "Of course, by both of us." He turned and pointed to his wife, as if not forgetting to include her.

"I'm quite looking forward to becoming a grandparent myself," Reverend Deavers said. "I'm sure Darius and Sage will have children. More than one, I hope, as an only child is both spoiled and lonesome. Darius is an only child."

"You're right," Alicia said, kissing Miriam on the cheek. "Miriam is an only child, and she is spoiled, and so is Timothy. And hey, it doesn't matter how many they have, I'm sure I'll spoil them all." She kissed Timothy again.

"We always have a cocktail before dinner. I hope that's not offensive to you, Reverend," she said as she directed them to a soft leather couch. "Marvin is the bartender."

"That's quite all right," Reverend Deavers said. "We do the same at our house."

"Good," Marvin said jovially. "What'll it be? My wife and I prefer a gin martini, but we have wine, whiskey,—whatever you prefer. I keep my bar well stocked." He laughed.

What a happy couple, Reverend Deavers thought. "A little glass of sherry for me, please," he said.

"The same for me," Darius said.

"I'll have my usual," Bertram said.

"I know," Marvin said. "Vodka and cranberry juice."

"Yes, and straight cranberry juice and seltzer water over ice for my baby," Bertram said, indicating Miriam.

"Captain Deavers, Marvin tells me you're here to stay," Alicia said, taking a sip of her martini and turning to Darius.

"You can just call me Darius. I'm no longer in the service, and yes, my fiancé is coming later, and we plan to make BeachSide our home."

"Congratulations," she said. "BeachSide is a pleasant place to live. And Reverend, what is your...?" She searched for the proper word.

"I'm Baptist," he said, knowing what she was asking.

"So you'll be looking for a church."

"No, I'm not staying. I only came to help Darius with the drive out here, and then I can help him find a nice home for him and his wife."

"Too bad, you're not staying." Alicia said. "You'd probably like BeachSide too."

"I probably would, but I've learned that the churches are mostly, uh"—he paused as he was thinking of Darius and Sage—"they're mostly segregated."

This surprised Alicia as she wondered why that would be of concern to him, being White.

"Well, of course, the colored people, they have their churches, and we have ours, and we don't have any problem with the coloreds. As you see, our maid is colored. We love Mamie. She's been with us nine years, and she's like family. And you know, those people, they're happy living their lives, and we live ours, and never the twain shall meet," she said. She evidently didn't consider the maid as a real person to be included in such a thing as a meeting. A part of the twain.

Darius knew that this was not the right time to tell them of Sage's race, but he knew he'd have to tell them later, but not now because, at this moment, he felt his Whiteness more than ever in the presence of this White family and this Black servant. Oh Sage. He thought of her with tenderness and pleasure, and although he felt sure of his love for her, he had to question her fitting in here.

Mrs. Hawthorne's words stayed with him and caused him some unease: "They live their lives, and we live ours, and never the twain shall meet." But it was a grave untruth because he and Sage had met and come together in love and in spirit and would soon come together—so the definition of *marriage* says "as one." And he was somewhat comforted that there were other mixed marriages here in Washington.

"Darius also asked about a place to get married, and I recommended the Peace Arch Park," the major said, breaking the pause in the conversation as he noticed Darius's unease, and he determined that maybe it was because he was among strangers.

"Oh yes," Miriam said. "It's absolutely a lovely place to get married. It's located up at the border of Washington state and Canada, and even the trip up there is a scenic ride, and there's a special train that goes directly there from Seattle, which is only a fifteen-minute drive from our city. Oh, you'll be happy about that park."

"We have a brochure, but I haven't read it yet. We'll be sure to do that."

"Say," Marvin said, as if having a sudden revelation, "why don't I take you on a tour of the city, you know, through the best residential neighborhoods, and we can also check out the park, and you can decide if it's the right place for your wedding."

"We wouldn't want to cause you any extra trouble," Reverend Deavers said.

"No trouble. We can plan that for one day next week. At your convenience, because I can take off from work any time I want."

"Thank you. I'll call you when we have a definite time," Darius said.

"You know, Darius, you should also take a tour of the university," Marvin said. "Since you'll be looking for a job, you might want to think about being a law professor, and I'm sure Bertram could put in a good word for you there."

"So you have experience in the legal profession?" Bertram asked.

"I am a licensed attorney, and I'm hoping to establish my own law firm," Darius said.

Marvin said, "I think you'd be a good professor, and a good lawyer too. Uh-huh." Turning to his family, Major Hawthorne asked, "Why don't you all come with us on the tour? We'll make it a family day."

"I'll have to see what day you're planning," Miriam said. "You know Mom and I have our water exercise at the recreation center every Wednesday, and I volunteer at the charm school on Friday, so if it's on Wednesday or Friday, I can't go. But perhaps you could plan on going with them, dear," she said to her husband.

"Sorry, but I have quite a busy schedule, and I couldn't possibly fit it in," Bertram said, looking at his daybook. "But let me know, Darius, if you are serious about a position at the university. I'm sure that I can be of assistance."

"Thank you," Darius said, but he didn't get the same friendly feeling from Bertram and Alicia as he did from Major Hawthorne and Miriam.

It was a beautifully arranged table and an enticing aroma came from the kitchen. The food was delicious, and the conversation centered on the state of Washington and how it compared to Oklahoma and Massachusetts.

"Why did you choose Washington?" Bertram asked.

They waited for Darius to answer, but there was a noticeable pause, and those present couldn't help noticing something peculiar in Darius's expression.

"Well, let's just say that I fell in love with the city—as a matter of fact, the whole state—when I was stationed here, and we wanted to get away from our hometown and just start out anew someplace else."

"From what I've seen so far," Reverend Deavers said, wanting to rescue Darius, "I think it's a good place to live. I pray that they'll be happy here, you know, find some friends and a place to worship."

The rest of the evening went well, and Darius was relieved when they finally left. Reverend Deavers could feel the anguish and uneasiness in Darius's body, and he tried to comfort his son.

"Stop worrying so much, you know that it doesn't help. Think of the serenity prayer. Lord, give me the serenity to accept the things I cannot change, the courage to change the things I can, and the wisdom to know the difference."

Well, Darius was thinking, *I can't change Sage's color, and I can't change loving her. The unequal laws need to be changed, but I wonder if I have the wisdom and the courage to try that?*

They rode the rest of the way in silence, and Darius accepted his father's words and became calm. He smiled as he thought of Sage, and he wished she was here. He could hear her saying, "Don't worry, Darius. It's going to be all right." He missed her so much.

Yet he knew he had not been wholly honest in answering when Bertram asked, "Why Washington?" As he looked at Bertram, he hadn't felt comfortable enough to tell him, but he chastised himself, *I should have looked him in the face and boldly told him that it's because Sage is Black, and we'll be allowed to marry here, which we couldn't do legally in either Massachusetts or in our hometown.*

But he'd have to tell the major, despite the words that his wife had said, "never the twain should meet." Regardless, sooner or later, they'd have to know. Oh well!

Darius and his father each made their nightly phone call, Darius to Sage, and Reverend Deavers to his wife, each one expressing the love for their mate.

5

After Lucy Deavers left Mary Jane Copple's house, Sage showed her mother all the things that were the result of her shopping trip with Lucy Deavers, and Mary Jane smiled. They picked the outfit Sage would wear to church tomorrow, and Sage sat with her mother, drinking tea and eating home-made cookies; and when she looked over at her mother, she smiled. Even though Sage thought of it sometimes as her mother's house, she knew that anywhere her mother is, is home, for home is where the heart is. Her heart was with her mother, for through all the difficult years of her childhood, her teenage years, and now in her adulthood, her mother's presence was with her, and Sage had learned from her mother how to live in order to stay strong and to endure, for Mary Jane told her that endurance produces strength.

My mother, she is me, and I am her.

On Sunday morning, Sage and her mother arrived at church, and they were joined by the family, Charles, and Iola. At the podium was the same pastor who had so adamantly advised Sage not to marry a White man, but his words today belied his innermost feelings.

"We're so blessed this morning to have the Copple family with us, and we all wish the greatest blessings for Miss Sage, on her proposed marriage, and we pray that the Lord will bless and keep you and that he will make his face to shine upon you and give you peace."

After church, it was a happy and congenial group at Mary Jane's house for dinner. Seemingly, some of their interests were the same. Iola related to Kay Lee's and Sage's interest in education. Charles related to Burnett's interest in the legal profession. Sage smiled as she watched Charles and Iola become closer acquainted and seeming to like each other in a more intimate way. Wishful thinking, perhaps, as she wished the best for them, each of them being special in their own way to her and Darius. She watched her mother just naturally becoming the matriarch, all of them becoming her children, and she was happy.

After the meal, there were some private conversations. Kay Lee, who had been opposed to the marriage, spoke to Iola. "I suggested to Sage that she should continue teaching here."

"Yeah, I wish Sage was staying here too," Iola said. "You know there's a need for Black teachers here. She would have no problem getting a position here." The word *here* was repeated seemingly for emphasis.

"That would be nice," Kay Lee said. "But she and Darius wouldn't be allowed to marry here or live here together because the law forbids it."

"That's my point. I never ever wanted her to marry Darius, you know, since it's out of her race. Seems like just asking for trouble."

"I guess that makes two of us. I was against it too, but she is determined, bless her heart, so we just to have to hope that it works out."

"Well, it hasn't happened yet. I wish she would meet some nice Black man, you know, and avoid all the trouble she's going to have in a mixed-race marriage."

Kay Lee agreed with her, but she felt that Sage was family; and even though Iola had been Sage's roommate at college and was considered to be a close friend, she wasn't family. Thus, Kay Lee became uncomfortable being negative about Sage with Iola.

"Well, as I said, we just have to hope that she'll be happy," Kay Lee said. Thus ended that conversation, but Iola hadn't changed her mind.

There was also a conversation between Burnett and Charles.

"So you studied in Boston? It was mostly White, huh?" Burnett said, smiling as if joking with Charles. "But I know it's a good school," he added.

"Yes, it is."

"So what are your present plans?" Burnett asked, thinking that maybe he could help this young man in his pursuit of the legal profession.

"I don't have any definite plan yet, but I'm working on it. Sage tells me that you're pretty well established here in your own law firm."

"Yes, I am. After I graduated law school and I got my law license, I was hired as the first Black court-appointed attorney, but I wasn't happy in that position, dealing with mostly White folk. I wanted to help my own people, so I quit that job. I bought two pieces of property: a small house, which I made into my office, and a little larger house, which is my place of residence. And here I am. I have my own law firm, Burnett Copple, attorney at law. Slogan: I CAN HELP YOU.

"I see where Sage got her confidence, and I feel fortunate that I've met you all." Charles was impressed with Burnett's professionalism yet with his very friendly demeanor. He liked him. He liked the whole family.

Charles never had many close friends, and his family had been extremely poor. His mother worked very hard both outside and inside the home. His father worked as a field hand, but his work was seasonal. His older brother ran away from home when Charles was twelve, so Charles practically took care of himself. His uncle, his father's brother, was the only one in the family to finish high school, and he was a little better off financially, so with assistance from the White family he worked for, he was able to obtain a scholarship for Charles to attend law school.

"How long do you plan on being here?" Burnett asked.

"I had planned on leaving pretty soon, and I haven't decided on a place, but I definitely have to get out of that motel. I might just have to go back home."

"Well, I do know how expensive motels are, but as long as you're here, my house is available for you, so you're welcome to stay with me, if you would like."

"That's very kind of you," Charles said, showing how surprised and appreciative he was that Burnett had invited him, having felt uneasy with Iola's invitation. "I might take you up on that, if you're sure I wouldn't be in the way."

"No, I plan to put you to work," Burnett said, smiling. "Really, since you have a law degree and you haven't practiced anywhere, helping me for a while could give you an idea how a small-town Black lawyer works."

"Gee, your whole family has been so good to me I wish I could do something to repay you," Charles said to everyone.

"We've enjoyed having you," Mary Jane said.

"Yes, any friend of Darius is a friend of ours," Sage said, patting him on the shoulder.

"So it's a deal. You can plan on moving out of that motel tomorrow, if you like." Burnett knew how lost he had felt when he first received his law license, and he was fortunate to have had his family, and Burnett liked Charles and also appreciated the fact that Charles and Darius were friends. Burnett also liked Darius.

Kay Lee was sitting beside Sage at the dinner table, and after Burnett's invitation to Charles, she reached over and, taking Sage's hand, invited her to spend the week with her at her school. Kay Lee graduated from Tuskegee in Alabama, and she was employed as a teacher in the small Oklahoma town of Lancaster, not far from Proctor. She had a house there, but she came to Proctor on most weekends and stayed with her mother.

Why not? Sage asked herself. *If I'm going to pursue a career in teaching, maybe I can learn some valuable things about it from my sister.*

Sitting here with her family and with Iola and Charles, it suddenly struck Sage that, as it had been her whole life, everyone was Black. She never had a White classmate or a White teacher, except at the school in Colorado. She had taught at an all-Black school, and now she was thinking that if Darius were here, he'd be the only White person.

Then she began to wonder what it would be like in Washington. *Will my environment necessarily be White since my husband is White? How well will I be able to adjust to that?* A little dark cloud of doubt appeared over her.

As they said their goodbyes, Charles going with Burnett and Sage going with Kay Lee, Mary Jane smiled to see them being so friendly with each other, but she felt a little sad seeing that Iola would be going home alone.

She gave them each a motherly hug and sent them out with a parting message: "I know that we are all hoping for a smooth transition for Sage and Darius as they leave all the places and all the people who were in their lives, and you're probably wondering what you can do. Well, what we can do is to pray because I know that prayer changes things. Think about things that are good, and good will prevail, and I feel confident that Sage and Darius will be all right."

Darius called, and he and Sage ended their talk as usual with words of love.

"I love you, Sage, and I miss you."

"I love you, Darius, and I miss you."

When Sage attended classes with Kay Lee, she was introduced to the other teachers at the school and to the school principal.

"She's a very experienced teacher," Kay Lee told everyone.

"We could most definitely use you here in our high school," the principal said.

"My experience and my preference is in the elementary grades. I've never taught in a high school," Sage said.

"That won't make a lot of difference here. Since you have the education and some experience in teaching, we feel you're qualified to teach in all the grades."

"Thank you, I'll think about it," Sage said, trying to be as congenial as possible, yet knowing that she was not planning to stay in Proctor, and she knew that Kay Lee was thinking that this was a way to keep Sage here, and consequently, that would keep her from marrying Darius. It seemed to her that people who have prejudices never lose them, and although they may act differently toward those they don't like, very seldom do they seem able to erase the slate and wipe it clean of the hate.

Sage attended classes with her sister on Monday, Tuesday, and Wednesday, even leading some of the reading classes; but on

Thursday, she stayed at the house, telling Kay Lee that she was tired, which was the truth. She was more tired mentally than physically with everyone at the school obviously attempting to entice her to stay.

On Friday, Sage took the bus back to Tulsa. Mary Jane knew before Sage spoke that she was unhappy about her visit with Kay Lee.

"Oh, Mamma, it just seems like if people really love you, as they say they do, they would understand your feelings." She laid her head on her mother's lap.

"Baby, it's their problem and not yours. I love you, Sage," she said, stroking Sage's hair. "And I trust your judgment that you're not a young and foolish little girl who doesn't know her own mind, and just because Darius's skin is white and yours is not, has nothing to do with what's inside both of you. It's love, and God loves you, Darius loves you, and I love you. Don't forget that, and I just know somehow that God has joined you two together for a reason, and it might be that your being together will mean something, maybe to change some things for the better."

"I know, and it is so sad that Kay Lee, who is supposed to love me, and also my friend Iola can't see beyond some dumb skin color."

"Well, Kay Lee will always be your sister, and maybe one day, she'll change. But Iola, well, that's a different story. I know she was your roommate in college, but I have a feeling now after meeting her that she might be holding some hateful prejudice in her heart, but I really like that young man who's Darius's friend," Mary Jane said.

"You mean Charles?" Sage asked.

"Yes. He seems to be honest and true in his friendship with Darius. I like him."

"I like him too, and I think that Miss Iola has gaga eyes for him."

"I trust that he's got enough wisdom to figure it out for himself."

"I know," Sage said. "Maybe something will happen to cause her to change. I hope so. Whatever, I'm going to this party she's having. She says she's inviting some of our high school friends, so that ought to be nice. I don't imagine I can get in any trouble there," Sage said as she took her mother's hand, and they sat holding hands.

Darius called, and they ended their conversation as usual.

"I love you, my Sage," he said. "And I miss you."

"I love you, my Darius," she said. "And I miss you."

Darius, knowing her as he did, could hear the sadness in her voice, and he again wondered if he was the one causing her pain. Even doubts.

Iola's get-together was scheduled for Saturday afternoon.

Charles was thankful for Burnett, and he knew he preferred staying with him to staying at Iola's place. Burnett had also given Charles the use of his car for the afternoon, and at exactly five o'clock, Charles lifted and released the brass knocker on the front door of Mary Jane Copple's house.

Charles felt a sudden flash of pleasure at the aspect of seeing Sage again, and he knew from his conversations with Darius and from Darius's tender looks at Sage that he was truly in love her. Similarly, since meeting Sage and seeing her calm yet bright, sun-shiny demeanor, he felt sure that she was a perfect match for his dear friend.

When Sage's mother opened the door and welcomed him, Charles felt a renewed feeling of closeness to Mrs. Mary Jane Copple.

When they arrived at Iola's house, Sage was surprised to find that she and Charles and Fred Hunter were the only guests. Sage had gotten the impression that Iola was inviting a number of their classmates from high school. Was Iola hoping to hook Sage up with this Black man and thus luring her away from a marriage that she was opposed to?

Charles smiled. *Is Iola trying to match Sage up with Fred because he is Black, and am I the chosen one for her?*

Seeing the dazed expressions on their faces, Iola thought to try and clear herself from the truth that she had purposefully only invited Fred.

"Sorry," she apologized, hugging Sage and Charles, "but it's only going to be the four of us. There's that big concert at the auditorium downtown and seems everybody is going. I didn't want to cancel you all coming, so hopefully we can still have a pleasant time."

Fred had risen to greet them, and Sage (not wanting to act a fool, as she said to herself) smiled and greeted Fred as if she was pleased to see him, which she was, but she did not now and had never had any romantic feelings for him.

"Well, my word, you look great," Fred said, going to Sage and giving her a great big hug.

"Thank you, and so do you," Sage said, allowing the hug, which was only that: a friendly hug.

"This is my friend Charles Williams. Charles, this is our friend from school, Fred Hunter."

"Glad to meet you," Charles said.

"Yes, I'm glad to meet you too," Fred said. There was an awkward pause as these three felt uncomfortable, now aware of what was taking place.

"So, now," Iola said, hoping to remedy the awkwardness of her three guests, "let's sit down and have something cool to drink." And taking Charles's hand, she asked him to come and help her in the kitchen, but Sage could sense that as an obvious ploy to leave her alone with Fred in the living room while she and Charles went to the kitchen, and she spoke up immediately.

"Oh no, I'll help you. Sit down, Charles, and you men can get better acquainted."

In the kitchen, she confronted Iola. "What is this, Iola?" she asked. "I had the impression you were inviting a group of our old classmates."

"Like I said, I tried, but they were all going to that big concert, you know."

"All of them?" Sage asked.

"Well, all those I was able to contact, and after so many calls and negative answers..." She sighed.

"So Fred was the only one who wasn't going to the concert?"

"Now, Sage, don't go getting any ideas in your head that I planned it this way on purpose. I didn't." Then the truth came out, and she thought that since she had been confronted, she might as well tell Sage what she had on her mind. "But I still think you ought to leave your options open. Not that it would be Fred, but we all think you could wait a while. There's—"

"I know. There are a lot of eligible Black men out here. Oh, Iola, please stop trying to control my life," Sage said. Iola opened her mouth to say something, but Sage held up her hand and stopped her. "It's all right, Iola. I'm here, and Fred and Charles are here, so I'll play bid whist and whatever else you want me to do. But I'm not interested in Fred or in any other man except Darius. That's who I love, and, Iola, please get it through your head, that's who I'm going to marry." She turned and left the kitchen.

Sage stayed, and they played cards. They drank beer, they laughed, and after a while, Sage turned to Charles. "I guess we'd better be going. It's getting late."

"Well, Fred can take you home," Iola said. "I thought Charles might want to stay awhile." She had not given up on Fred and Sage, and she still had some longing for Charles to become a part of her life, and she was bold enough to keep trying.

"No," Charles said, also having analyzed the situation. "I brought Sage, and I'll deliver her safely home." He held out his hand to Fred. "It's nice meeting you, Fred, and maybe I'll see you again sometime." He shook Fred's outstretched hand and thanked Iola for a pleasant afternoon.

On the way home, Charles apologized for Iola. "I'm sorry, Sage, but I didn't have any part in this."

"I know that, and don't worry, I'm all right, and thanks for coming with me." She reached over and gave him a hug, and he hugged her right back.

After Sage and Charles left, Iola wasn't sure if Fred had come to any conclusions about the afternoon; but for some reason, she wanted to explain, perhaps hoping she could still impress on Fred the importance, as she categorized it, of Sage changing her mind about marrying Darius.

"You can stay a little while longer if you want," Iola said, smiling her broadest and most false smile. "You can have another drink with me. You know, one for the road."

"Sure, I will have another beer," he said as he too wanted to talk about the afternoon.

"So, Iola," he said when she returned with the beer, "you know it was real good seeing Sage again. She looks wonderful."

"Yes, she does." Iola was encouraged thinking that he really might be interested in Sage as more than just a casual friend.

"But I was a little confused about, you know, it seemed like a double date. You know, like it was planned that way."

"Yes," she said. "I'm guilty. You see, the truth is, Sage is engaged to a White guy."

"What?"

"Yes." His shock gave her encouragement that he disapproved. "Do you remember the night we went to that tent meeting at school?" she asked.

"Yep, and I only went because Sage begged us to go. It was like a joke to me because I always thought a tent meeting meant a church meeting."

"But it wasn't. They were talking about trying to get equality in education for Black students, and that ain't never going to happen."

"Maybe so, and maybe no. It might."

"Not in our lifetime, but anyway, do you remember the White guy who spoke?"

"Not really, because I honestly wasn't paying that much attention to any of it, but I do seem to remember that there was a Black guy who was involved with them."

"Well, the Black guy was Charles."

"Really? The same Charles who I met today?"

"Yep, the same Charles. Then you have to remember the White guy who was the main speaker."

"Hmm. Now that you mention it, I guess I do remember him. Yeah. Sage said her mother worked for his family."

"Believe it or not, that guy is who Sage intends to marry."

"You can't be serious. Sage is going to marry somebody White, and I assume he's rich. That's funny."

"It's not funny. It's pitiful."

"But I thought it was illegal for Black and White to marry. How are they going to work that out?"

"They're planning on moving to Washington where it is legal. He's already gone, to get things settled, you know, a place to stay and all that. Sage is planning on going later—unless, that is, we can stop her. Poor girl. She doesn't know what she's getting herself into."

It took a little while for Fred to digest all that had been said, and he paused and drank some more of his beer. Finally, he looked over at Iola's face.

"I see. Well, you know, I wish her luck."

"That's just the point. Luck won't help her. I think she's making a mistake, and so do a lot of other people, including some of her family, and of course, his family. And you're right that I had some ulterior motive in asking you. I thought maybe, you know, if she met some nice Black guy like you"—she patted him on the leg—"she might reconsider hooking herself up to a White guy."

"So I was the bait," he said, and seeming to find it funny, he laughed. "And what about Charles? How does he fit into this picture?"

"He and Darius went to law school together, and he came here for Sage and Darius's Mock Wedding Ceremony, and…well, I'm sorry, but I was just trying to save my friend from…"

"From what?" Fred asked, shrugging his shoulders.

"From the hell's fire. That's what. White people are not going to like her, and Black people won't like him."

"But knowing Sage," he said, smiling as he thought of her, "if anybody can make it work, she will. Seems like she was always a pretty strong girl."

He gave Iola a hug, and he left. His thoughts were with Sage, and he wanted to be her friend; and if things went well with this marriage, he wished her well. But if things turned bad, he wanted to be Sage's next choice.

Unknown to Sage, after Charles saw her safely home, promising to see her tomorrow at church, he returned to Iola's house to tell her what he thought of her attempt at matchmaking between Sage and Fred, which he recognized for what it was.

On first seeing him, Iola was pleased and thought it meant he was interested in her as a romantic partner.

"Hello again. Come in. Come in," she said, stepping aside as he came in and stood by the door.

"Would you like another beer?" she asked.

"No, thank you," he said, still standing. "I've come because I think you owe Sage an apology for trying to do some matchmaking for her. I'm Darius's friend, and I know that Darius loves Sage, which automatically makes me love Sage, and I know that Sage loves Darius."

"Okay, but loving Sage ought to make you see the light. Sage is Black, and you're Black, and you ought to know that trying to have any close relationship with a White person can only mean trouble for both of them. This world is not going to let it happen. It might seem like love now, but it's probably just infatuation, you know, a passing fancy. You mark my words."

"I do. I hear exactly what you're saying, and I know that we can't control the world, but we have our own minds, and I know that there are a lot of nice Black men out there, but Sage has chosen Darius, who's White, and that's her privilege. And if you really want to remain as her friend, you need to accept that." He kissed her hand and left.

Iola didn't want to lose him, and her eyes filled with tears. She was also beginning to realize that she really did like Sage, and then hoping she could rectify her actions, she sat down and cried.

Sunday after church, after more thought about Sage and thinking that he was definitely attracted to her as Iola had hoped, and hoping Sage could like him, Fred paid Sage a visit. He apologized for Saturday afternoon, and he assured her he wasn't in on the planned deception.

"I didn't think you were," Sage said.

"But I've been thinking about you, and I'd like for us to be closer friends. Say, why don't you come out and let me show you my new store?" Fred offered. "I'm planning on expanding and selling books and magazines. So, Sage, if you decide to stay, I'd like for you to head that department for me."

"That's very kind of you, Fred, but I can't accept that offer because I'm not staying here."

"It's not going to be easy, going to a whole new state and starting all over, and I guess nothing worthwhile is easy, but you're different, so you'll probably be all right."

"Thank you," she said.

"Well, if you change your mind, you just let me know."

Having listened to Fred, whose words echoed those of so many others, Sage thought, *There must be something wrong with me, for I've often heard others say, "You're different," "You're not like other people," "You really don't fit in." Then to add proof to their criticism of me, I had to go and fall in love with a person of a supposedly superior race. Then, of course, they accused me of thinking I was superior.*

"You don't know it, but you're colored," her sister Kay Lee said. "Why don't you come down out of the clouds and look at yourself? You're a Negro."

She thought about Fred. *Poor soul. What would make him think I'd want to work for him, and in a drugstore? Oh dear. There you go, thinking you're too high-class for that kind of work.*

The next day, Sage sat with her mother in her sewing room helping her cut blocks for the quilt she was making; and although Sage always felt at peace with her mother, today she was not at peace with anyone. Her mind was on Darius. *Will he always love me? We've never spent any real quality time together. Who is he? What is he? What are his likes and dislikes? And now that so many people have disagreed with my decision to marry him, do I know myself? Am I looking at myself closely enough to see that I could be wrong? Should I stay here and teach as Kay Lee suggested?* Those questions and those thoughts still filled her mind. They were still with her the next day and the next week. She couldn't shake them. She was depressed.

6

On Monday morning, Major Marvin Hawthorne rose early as had been his habit from having to observe the early morning rising requirement of his many years in the army. He dressed very carefully in his uniform, having already put the proper pins and name tags on his shirt. After shaving, he poured the pleasant aromatic after-shave lotion into his palm and gently massaged it onto his face. He went down stairs, and humming gaily to himself, he sat down at the table for his morning coffee. Mamie had already placed his coffee and breakfast sandwich and sweet roll at his place. She also placed the morning newspaper beside his plate. His wife only joined him for breakfast on the Saturdays when the rest of the family came, but they always ate the evening meal together.

"Good morning, Mamie," he said. "And how are you today?" He liked Mamie as a person, even though his wife never had a friendly conversation with her and accepted her in their house only as a servant.

"I'm blessed, sir." She always said this.

"And I feel blessed having you as a part of our household."

"Thank you, sir," she said.

After he finished his breakfast, he went into the den and opened up the newspaper. Major Hawthorne read every headline, and unless it held a special interest for him, he did not read the entire article. He was what one would call a neutral, having neither pronounced liberal nor conservative views. He always voted Democratic no matter who was on the ticket. He felt that politics was mostly a waste of time and that it was a common truth that the running of the states and the laws and rules of the entire country were out of his control. Do as you're told and don't ask too many questions. It was "yes, sir" or "no, sir" to his superiors, "hello" or "goodbye" to his acquaintances. He loved his wife and his daughter and his grandson, and he always treated them with love, respect, and attention. He was not frivolous in the world outside his home, although he had had a few one-nighters. Of course, opportunities always presented themselves as he was a very handsome man, but generally he would smile and go about his way.

Thus, the phone call which he received this particular morning, although causing him momentary alarm, did not cause him a total collapse.

In this small suburb outside the city of BeachSide, Washington, in the home of Major Marvin and Mrs. Alicia Hawthorne, the ringing of the phone got the attention of the husband and the wife, she upstairs in her bedroom and he downstairs in his den. They each, not aware of the whereabouts of the other, picked up the receiver at precisely the same moment. Before Alicia got the word *hello* out of her mouth, she heard her husband's voice.

"Marvin here," he said as that was his way of answering the phone. She had waited to see if the call was for her, and if not, she had every intention of hanging up, not wanting to be a nosy eavesdropper. But then she heard the voice on the other end of the line, a Southern-sounding voice but with a slight foreign accent.

"Yes, Mr. Hawthorne," the caller said. "I have some information that I'm sure you wouldn't want that pretty wife and daughter of yours to know."

"What?" Marvin said with surprise sounding in his voice. "What kind of damn information, damn it? What the hell are you talking about?"

"What I'm talking about, and I know you ain't wanting them to know, is that you are the father of a Black child."

Alicia put her hand to her mouth to silence the sound of her gasp, and in a state of utter shock, she softly laid the receiver on the cradle and sat down. Her heart seemed to beat against her chest like the beating of the sticks on a bass drum, and great beads of perspiration oozed out on her brow and rolled down on her eyes. She lay back on the bed, her body shaking as if in convulsion, and she turned on her side in a tense fetal position and cried soft, quiet tears. Thus, she did not hear the rest of the conversation.

"I beg your pardon," Marvin said, quite bewildered as if he hadn't heard what he was sure he had heard. "Who in the hell is this?" he asked.

"Sir," the strange voice said, "my name is not so much important as my information is, if you know what I mean."

"No, dammit, I don't know what you mean. What kind of freak are you anyway?"

"Sir, it won't help you to be calling me names, and I am informing you that you have a child, and she is Black."

Shocked and confused as to what this man was talking about, the major's tongue was stuck in his mouth, and his body became rigid, and he couldn't hang up the phone, as much as he wanted to.

"You son of a bitch, get real here."

"I'm real as the sky, man."

The awful pause in the conversation attested to Marvin's discomfiture. His brain was whirling with pain and questions, and he shook his head from side to side in pure confusion, wondering what this could mean.

"I know you don't want those two beautiful ladies of yours— you know, your beautiful wife and daughter—to know this, so I have a way to make sure they never find out."

"What is it you want?" Marvin asked, being sure that keeping this terrible, terrible information from his family would not be free. "Blackmail, I'm sure."

"I'm thinking in the amount of ten thousand dollars."

"What?"

"Oh, sir, that ought to be chump change to a rich White man like you."

Marvin shuddered as he heard the eerie laugh coming through the phone.

"So get it together, and I'll be in touch real soon with some directions. Yaw'll be good now."

Marvin heard the click, and the line was dead.

The wife waited. After she hung up, hearing only part of the conversation, the wife waited for her husband to come up and tell her about this child. Although she was still in utter engrossing shock, she knew they had to face each other and face this horrible situation. Her mind was racing. *A Black child? Oh, dear God. And how old is she? Or is it a boy child, and who is the mother? Does he still see her? How can I lie with him knowing his chest has been on her black chest, his private parts in her black private parts? And who was this on the phone? Surely, whoever it was wants some hush-hush money. Oh hell!*

Divorce just naturally entered her mind, but when she thought of the disgrace of why, she knew it would probably kill her, and her separation from Marvin would kill Miriam, for she loved her father and her mother. *Can I stay with him? And what if Miriam knew that she had a sibling who was Black?* Questions with no answers.

At the same time, the husband waited. He was trying to settle his mind with some decisions. Should he tell his wife about the phone call? *Can this really be true? Do I really have a Black child?* It could very well be that this phone caller was lying. *an a blood test prove that the child is mine?*

Oh damn, damn, damn. He sighed, thinking of the amount the caller was asking. *Number one, how could I secretly get that much money from our accounts without my wife knowing? And if she did know about the blackmail threat, could I tell her what the threat was about?* Of course, it was true that he had a few extramarital flings—*But oh shit.* He moaned. *For all these twenty-eight years, we have been a happy family. We have been good parents, although it is true that my wife has always lived a totally White life. Miriam never had an article of clothing that was colored until she was a year old. She wore only White, which might have occasionally been trimmed with a little pink. Miriam had attended all-White schools, an all-White church, and unfortunately, she is married to a very prejudiced White man who looks down on, feels superior to, and does not associate with Blacks.*

Unfortunately, also, Marvin Hawthorne is just the opposite; and since the government has desegregated the Armed Forces, he has been in daily association with many minorities as coworkers. *I have a Black barber, and my van driver is Black, and now—jumping holy shit—I have a Black daughter or son.* Instead of crying about it, somehow, from somewhere in his throat, there came a laugh, but he managed to pull himself together and resume his seriousness. *That can't be true, and that's not funny.* The laugh soon became a sigh. *Oh, dog shit and horse shit. Shit! Shit! Shit!*

He was already dressed. He had drunk his usual two cups of coffee. He had eaten his breakfast, and he was glad Alicia hadn't come down today as she would have known there was something sinister about the phone call. He didn't know that she had heard one little part of it and that she had labeled him a cheater with someone Black. Then looking at his watch, his presence of mind returned, and he realized it was time for him to keep his appointment with Darius and Reverend Deavers.

Major Marvin Hawthorne said "have a good day" to Mamie. He picked up his briefcase and his car keys, put on his coat and hat, and left the house.

Alicia Hawthorne waited for her husband to come up and talk about it, but after a number of minutes, she heard the opening and closing of the garage door and the sound of his car as he drove out of the driveway.

As he drove along, he thought about the threat. Knowing that Darius Deavers was a licensed attorney, it came into his mind to tell him about the threat and ask if there was some legal way the captain could help him, but he didn't know anything about Darius's feelings for Blacks. Rich White Darius. Ha! *Darius might harbor the same feelings as my family—my wife, my daughter, my son-in-law, none of whom thought of Blacks as their equal.* He wondered how Captain Darius would deal with the possibility of him being the father of a Black child.

Well, he said to himself, *I will present my problem to Attorney Darius Deavers, and then I'll have to respect his feelings, and whatever he says, I'll have to deal with it. I can't hide in a foxhole hoping the danger will pass. I'll have to stand up and fight.*

Soon after the major left his house, Miriam came. When Miriam entered her parents' house, she felt a chill in the air, and going upstairs, she found her mother sitting on the side of the bed, crying. Miriam could see that her mother was very upset because it was not a cry of sadness but more of anger and frustration.

Alicia hadn't convinced herself that she should talk with her daughter about what she'd heard. *After all, she loves her father*, Alicia thought, but she knew that sooner than later, she would tell her, for truthfully, Alicia Hawthorne didn't have anyone else that she could talk to in confidence. And with Miriam's usual calm in dealing with crises situations, Alicia Hawthorne trusted her daughter's judgment. She motioned for Miriam to sit.

"Calm down, Mom," Miriam said, sitting beside her and placing her hand on her mother's shoulder. "I don't like to see you crying. It can't be that bad."

"It's that bad. It's worse than bad."

"Do you want to tell me about it? You aren't sick, are you? Did you get some bad news?"

"It's your father," Alicia managed to say, wiping the tears which were running down her cheeks.

"Daddy? What about him? Is he sick?"

"He's sick all right, but not physically. Oh, it's hard for me to tell you."

"Well, just tell me. I'm strong, and I can take it, whatever it is. Is he playing around? Is that it? He's got a girlfriend? That's about the worst thing I can think about if he's not sick. Unless he's killed somebody."

Alicia wiped her eyes, blew her nose, and gave a sigh. "Very well. I'll tell you. When the phone rang this morning, we both picked up the receiver at the same time, and before I could say hello, I heard him answer. And I wasn't intending to be eavesdropping, but I thought the call might be for me." She again tried to suppress her crying.

"It's all right, Mom, just stop talking. You don't have to tell me. I really might not want to know anyway."

Taking another tissue and blowing her nose, Alicia Hawthorne continued, "Then I heard this person say—oh my word, whoever it was said..." She stopped and seemed to be having trouble breathing.

"I think I ought to call the doctor. What's his number?"

"No, don't do that. I'm all right. Just give me a minute." Alicia took some deep breaths, which seemed to bring on some calm. "The voice said, 'I know you don't want that pretty wife and daughter of yours to know"—Alicia paused, and Miriam waited for her to continue—"to know that you're the father of a Black child.'"

"What? A Black child?"

"That's exactly what the voice said."

"Is that all?"

"That's all I heard, and I was so shocked, but I managed to softly hang up the receiver, and then I sat down on the bed, and I was... I was devastated. I haven't been able to stop crying since."

"Well, what did Daddy say? Did you talk to him?"

"No. He left soon after the call, and I don't even know if I can talk to him, and I don't think he knew that I heard anything."

"Shucks, Mom, it's probably not true at all. Whoever was on the phone is most likely a phony. You know, most of the time, people just want some money, and they think of all kinds of things to threaten you with."

"I know that Marvin has worked with some Black people because since that damn war, Blacks have been allowed in a lot of places where they never were before, and he could easily have gotten involved with one of them. You know, men can be fickle."

"I don't think Daddy would do that, you know, have an affair with a Black person. To be really honest, I don't think he would ever play around at all. You should just ask him because you weren't eavesdropping. You just happened to pick up the phone, and it's probably good that you did. Poor Daddy."

"I thought that when the war was over, he wouldn't have to deal with those people anymore, and now this opens up a whole new can of buckshot."

"Stop worrying, Mom. I know Daddy better than that. He had to accept them being in the army, and he's had to work with them, but gee-whiz, no. No, he is not a frivolous person. No way. Let's just put it out of our minds and go for our swimming lessons. I'm sure Daddy can work it out, and I'm sure he can find out about this evil person who called."

"Yeah. And when Marvin finds him, he ought to have his Black ass arrested."

"How do you know that he's Black?"

"He sounded Black."

"I still don't think it's true," Miriam said. "But true or not, we most definitely cannot—I repeat, cannot—mention any of this to my husband because if it turns out to be true that Daddy has fathered a Black child, heaven forbid, she would be my sister. Oh my! Bertram would have a heart attack and die on the spot. You know how he feels about those people and them wanting to be equal, as he says."

Trying to digest all the traumatic information, Alicia and Miriam just sat there for a long while and looked off into space as they couldn't come to any logical conclusion; and Miriam, seeing her mother's tears and pain and knowing she had to be strong for her, took her mother's hand and stood up.

"Come on, Mom. As I said it, probably isn't true at all. Let's go on to our lesson. Come on. I'll drive."

"Oh, darling, I'm in no mood for swimming, so you go on."

"Are you sure? Are you going to be all right?"

"Yes, darling, I'll be all right."

"Okay, but calm down. I know that it isn't true." She paused and looked again at her mother. "I'll call you later, okay?"

"All right. I love you."

"Yes, Mom, and I love you too."

At ten o'clock that morning, Darius and his father took the elevator down to the first floor lobby of the hotel. Stepping out of the elevator, they saw Major Marvin Hawthorne sauntering through the door, wearing, as always, an impeccably pressed uniform with an ever-present smile on his face. The major nodded his head and did a partial salute, more like a wave of the hand, and he greeted the doorman as if he knew him personally, which he didn't, being friendly with everyone he met. He then greeted Darius and Reverend Deavers with a smile and a complete army salute. Darius responded with a smile and a salute. Reverend Deavers reached out and gave the major a handshake.

"Good morning," the reverend said. "So we meet again."

"My pleasure. This is a beautiful place," Major Hawthorne said, looking around.

"It's comfortable, and it'll suffice until we find something permanent," Darius said.

"I'm sure you will. We can drive through some of the residential neighborhoods and check them out. There are some beautiful houses in this city."

"That's good to know," Reverend Deavers said.

"Okay, our chariot awaits," Major Hawthorne said. He clapped his hands and smiled, displaying his jovial manner.

"Okay," Darius responded in a like manner, smiling. He enjoyed being with Major Hawthorne.

The tour went well. They passed the university where Bertram worked.

"If you decide you want to work there, I'm sure Bertram can help you, you know, put in a good word for you. Sometimes it's not what you know. It's who you know," Major Hawthorne said.

"I'm sure you're right, but I prefer to depend on what I know."

They stopped and picked up the schedules for traveling to the Peace Arch.

"We wouldn't have time today to go there and look around, but we can go another day before your lady gets here, if you like," Major Hawthorne said.

"Sure, we can think about that later, but right now I'll accept your word that it's as beautiful as you say it is," Darius said.

The major drove through a couple of residential areas, and Darius saw a house he liked. And although he didn't say anything about it, it stayed on his mind.

They toured the downtown business district, and the buildings reminded Darius of the elite buildings in Boston.

"If you decide to open your own law office, this is where most of the plush elite suites are located," Major Hawthorne said, and Darius thought of the fact that Charles might be his partner, and he was almost sure he didn't want to be in that kind of "elite" area. They passed a place called the Coon Chicken Inn. A massive grotesque coon's head with a black face, a big-lipped mouth painted red, was on the restaurant's front door.

"That's one of the favorite eating places for Whites, but Blacks are not allowed to eat there, despite that ugly Black thing on the door," Marvin said. He was just giving information, not yet knowing about Sage.

Darius's mind was asking, *Well, where can Blacks eat?*

"Speaking of eating, I am ready for some lunch. How about you, Reverend?" Marvin asked.

"I would like to go back to the hotel, and you two can enjoy each other together for a while," Reverend Deavers said. He was thinking that since Darius would be staying here, he could get to know the major more personally, just the two of them.

After dropping the reverend off, they rode for a while in silence, each man considering thoughtfully when and how to tell the other man what was uppermost in his mind. One man: *Do I have a Black child somewhere? How do I deal legally with the caller's threat? Do I share this information with this man?* The other man: *My wife-to-be is Black. How do I proceed here in this racially divided city, and do I share this information with this man?*

"I know where there's a lovely little restaurant downtown, and we can eat there," Major Hawthorne said.

As they entered the restaurant, one of the major's favorite, Darius's mood brightened somewhat because everyone seemed to know the major; and everyone, including the patrons and the employees, greeted him with a warm "Hi, Major" or "Good morning, Marvin, good to see you."

"Does this place suit you?" he asked. "They specialize in a brunch, you know, so you can order either breakfast or lunch at this hour."

"This is fine," Darius said, but as always, he looked around for any Black patrons, and not seeing any, he imagined that all of the employees were White too.

"We can go someplace else if you like. You seem hesitant."

"No. This is fine," he said, and realizing he was making the major uncomfortable, he changed his demeanor.

"This way, Major," the hostess said, coming forward. She was nicely dressed in a blue-and-white silky-looking uniform and wearing silver jewelry. "Your table is just sitting here waiting for you," she said, leading them to a corner table. It was covered with a white linen tablecloth, and a lighted candle sat in the center. She poured them coffee, and they ordered their food.

As they sipped their coffee, it was uncomfortable for Darius thinking about Sage with his newfound friends, Marvin's wife, Alicia, their daughter, Miriam, and Miriam's husband, Bertram—"all White as the driven snow." He was somewhat sad inside thinking about them.

Their food was served, and they ate for a while in silence, each feeling awkward to approach what they really wanted to talk about.

"What are you thinking?" Marvin asked. "You seem preoccupied."

"Well, yes, I am actually somewhat preoccupied because there's something I need to tell you. I've been hesitant, but, well, I don't want to spoil our meal, so we'll talk about it after we've eaten."

"Well, it just so happens that I'm a good listener," Marvin said.

They ate and seemingly did enjoy their food, which was well-prepared and cordially served.

"I know you'll be in much better spirits when your lady gets here."

"My Sage. Yes, I will."

"And I'm sure you'll make her very happy, you know, as you impress me as being quite even-tempered. You know, marriage really can be tough, but it can also be beautiful. You just have to be strong and patient. You two are just starting out, but I've been in it for a lot of years."

"Seems like good years. You have a beautiful wife and a very beautiful daughter, and I might say, a very beautiful grandson. It has to be good."

"Sometimes good and sometimes not so good, but right now, I guess we both have something on our minds that we want to talk about."

"With my training in the legal profession, I'm also a good listener," Darius said.

"It would most likely be better to go to my office, and we can talk there with some privacy."

When they arrived at the major's office, his secretary handed him a brown envelope. "This was brought by special messenger, and he said it was important."

"Thank you," Marvin said, receiving the envelope. He took Darius to his private lounge and indicated that Darius sit in one of the comfortable chairs. "All right, sit down and make yourself comfortable, and I'll see what this thing says. The government thinks everything is a priority."

"Take your time," Darius said, trying to relax.

After reading the note and still holding it in his hand, Major Marvin Hawthorne groaned without lifting his head.

"Bad news, I gather?" Darius asked, aware of the major's seeming frustration. "But probably I shouldn't ask."

"It's all right," Marvin said, pulling himself together, yet he wasn't sure he could talk about it now. "Why don't you relax and tell me what's on your mind."

"All right, your wife asked why I chose Washington to live," Darius said, calling on all his bravery. "Well, I guess it's time to tell you my Sage is Black."

"What?" Marvin asked.

"Yes, my Sage is Black, and you see, there is such a thing as a miscegenation law which exists in Massachusetts where I was employed, and in Oklahoma where we both lived." He stood and walked over to the window. "The state of Washington doesn't have such a law, so we thought we could live here in peace. At least, we can be legally married here." Darius was standing facing the window, his back to the major. "After hearing what your wife said about Blacks—you know, that they live their lives and we live ours—I was reluctant to tell your family about Sage. But my father kept reminding me that I had to tell you. You see, I not only love Sage, I adore her, and I need her in my life. I can't imagine living without her. She's very levelheaded, and she's very beautiful." He stopped talking and turned because Major Hawthorne was laughing.

"Why are you laughing?"

"I'm sorry, but you can't imagine what you've done for me by what you said. Man, oh man. Do sit down and let me tell you my problem." He told him about the phone call and the threat.

"Do you have a Black child?"

"I don't think so. I did have a few extras, but I tried to be cautious. Here, read this. It's the man's instructions about how to get the money to him." He gave the letter to Darius.

Darius sat down and read the letter. He read it a second time. "Oh dear, I guess you do have a problem."

"You know," Major Marvin Hawthorne said, "you go along in life doing and being the best you can be, making decisions which you hope will help to make your living smooth and comfortable, but then it seems that disaster is just sitting close by someplace, waiting for your happiest time. And things just pop up that you didn't plan, but you are still forced to deal with them."

Darius looked over at his friend, and even though they both seemed to be sitting among the ruins of a disaster, both men wanted to laugh, knowing now that each of them had almost the same problem.

"And to think, my dear friend, my problem may be the same as your problem. I may have a Black child out there somewhere, and your precious wife is Black. And here we sit, two White men, living in segregated, prejudiced BeachSide, Washington."

But they also wanted to cry, realizing what a great problem it could be, which could not be washed away by all the waters around this beautiful area.

"Yep, that is true. We won the war abroad. Now we have to fight the race war here at home," Darius said.

"I suppose the probability that I might have a Black offspring out there someplace is only part of the problem. My wife will definitely have a gigantic problem thinking that I cheated on her."

"Does your wife have to know?" Darius asked.

"Well, no, she doesn't, but there is no way I can get that much money out of our accounts without her knowing, and you read the letter. The caller threatened to tell my wife and my daughter if I didn't pay him ten thousand dollars," Marvin said.

"Ten thousand dollars is not so great an amount," Darius said. "What we have to do now is decide if you want to pay it or ignore the threat and deal with the consequences. The letter sounded a little amateurish."

"I don't know what to do. You'll have to help me decide."

They were quiet as each tried to think about the solution. Then putting the letter back in the envelope, Darius laid it on the desk.

"Here's what we'll do. We'll follow the instructions in the letter, make the drop, then follow whoever it is that picks it up and confront them. I'll let you have the money if you need that."

"Would you really be willing to do that?" Marvin asked, almost pleading. "I'd figure out how to pay you back."

"Sir, we won't concern ourselves with payback right now because right now, here in BeachSide, Washington, you're my only friend." Without hesitation, Major Marvin Hawthorne stepped forward and hugged Attorney Darius Deavers. They had each acquired a new friend.

The ransom note demanded urgency: "Do this Friday, or Saturday I call your family. Put the money in a bag and take it in the alley behind that Priceline Grocery Store on Main Street. Put it behind the big green trash bin and leave. Don't call the police."

On Friday, Marvin and Darius went together, and after placing the bag as instructed, they watched from well-hidden places, each at an opposite end of the alley. It was a female who emerged from the back door of the store and looked around before grabbing the bag. She began walking down the alley at a rapid pace. It was not difficult intercepting her, and Marvin recognized her as Anna Mapoli, one of the nurse's aides who worked at the hospital. Although Marvin was concerned about the money, he also wanted answers to his questions. "Do I have a child somewhere? Where? How can I find out the truth? Are you the mother?"

"No, I'm not," she began immediately apologizing and crying. "And I'm so sorry, sir, but me and my brother devised this scheme in order to get some money. We don't know anything about a Black child."

"I don't understand."

Then she proceeded to tell her story. "You see, my brother came here on a fellowship to study medicine, with the promise that he would come back to our country and practice there. Well, things started off good, and for two years, it looked like he'd make it. I came into some money from our grandparents, and since he gave such a bright picture of life in America, I came here, hoping for a better life too."

"So what happened?" Marvin asked.

"Sir, well, my brother was doing good at school. He was going to chapel services, and he was really doing good. But then it was like…it was like all of a sudden he discovered a different kind of life. He began whoring after women. I don't know if American women like foreign men or if foreign men like American women, but it was four or five different women who was calling him. He started staying out all night, coming in all drunk and hungover. And, sir, like—if you don't keep up a certain grade average, you lose your fellowship. He even got arrested."

"For what?" Marvin asked.

"For fighting over a woman, and now, sir, he's sick. He don't eat, and he can't go to school, and I've been trying to take care of him, and so now with trying to work and take care of him, it's hard, and my money's running out, and you see, sir, being Black and with no proper schooling, I haven't been able to get a decent-paying job."

"So why me?"

"I knew that you had money, you know, that you weren't poor by any means. And I know it was wrong for us to threaten you, but it looked like the only way we could get any money to go back home."

Marvin thought that she looked so pitiful. Her eyes were full of tears, and for some reason, he believed her story.

"Where is your brother now?"

"He's upstairs. I can take you to him, and you'll see. You'll see that he is bad off."

On seeing him, it was quite obvious that he was not a well person. He was thin, and when he tried to sit up, he had a sudden fit of coughing and heavy breathing. Marvin felt more sorrow for him than he did anger, and he imagined this pitiful person might have once had potential to be a doctor and to be a strong individual.

"He was good-looking, and he was smart, you know, very intelligent, and with the money, we can get back home, and maybe he can get well again," she said.

Darius was quiet, and he was thinking that these people really didn't have a case, but they were so pitiful, and he was thinking about the reason he saw of this poor man's dilemma. His sister's dilemma. He was thrown into a culture that he didn't understand and one he had never experienced. Money and freedom. His sister's dilemma was that she didn't have the skills necessary for a better-paying job, and her skin color categorized her potential. It was becoming more and more obvious to him that the plight of the Black race was dire in America, so he concluded that he wanted to help Major Hawthorne and also these poor people.

Darius drew up a paper for them to sign, saying the money was given to them as an act of kindness for their family. He and Marvin arranged for their trip back to their homeland, bought their tickets, and to be on the safe side, they came back and saw them safely to the airport and on the airplane.

Marvin was also pensive. "You know," he said, "people like you are few and hard to find. I felt sorry for them too, but something in you made you decide to help them, and that opened up a different way for me to look at life." He was able to smile a little. "And you know, here we are, you and me, almost strangers, only having known each other through working in the army together, and I don't know anyone else I could have talked to about this. I guess you have a lot of your father in you—his spirituality, his knowledge of the world, and his love of people—and if I can ever be of any help to you and your father, you just let me know."

Darius said, "We've gotten your problem solved, but not mine. Your wife sounded like she isn't too fond of Black people. What did she say? They have their lives, and we have ours, and never the twain should meet?"

"She did say that, didn't she?" Marvin asked.

"What do you think she will do when I bring Sage here, and she learns that Sage is Black?

"Well, I'll just have to find out, you know. I'll tell her, and then I'll hope for the best."

Back at the hotel, Darius told his father about the incident and the payoff.

"I hope that you agree with my actions," Darius said.

"I imagine it was a tough decision, but you made it, and I'm proud of you, for I'm confident that you decided it was the right thing to do."

7

The next Sunday after church, they sat around the dinner table at Mary Jane Copple's house. There was Burnett, Charles, Kay Lee, and their family friend Sophronia. While they were eating, Mary Jane spoke to them about Sage, being concerned when Sage didn't attend church.

"Something is not right with my youngest child, and I'm sure I know what it is. She is depressed from all the negative things being said to her about Darius."

"Are you sure that's why she's depressed?" Kay Lee asked. "Or has Darius deserted her? Is she pregnant and doesn't want anyone to know? And as time is passing, how would she handle it when she begins to show? Is she unsure about going off to a strange place, so far from home?"

"My goodness, Kay Lee, don't be so negative. We ought to be trying to think of how we can help her," her mother said.

"She's already spent some time with me, and I'm sure she hasn't changed her mind at all about staying and taking a teaching job here."

Sophronia worked as a nurse in an old folks' home, and she suggested that she could invite Sage to come and spend some time helping her.

"She could read to those old folks and help them get dressed. You know, cheer them up. She'd be good at that, and that might help her get her mind off her problems."

"I could use some secretarial help, and so could you, Charles. You're learning some things about a lawyer's work, and if you decide to stay here, it might encourage Sage to stay too."

"Right now," Charles said, "I'm thinking more about Sage's future than my own. I know that the attitudes of all those people who were opposed to her marrying Darius have really affected her mental and physical wellness, and I'm really worried about her."

"So am I, and I know that something has to be done," Sage's mother said.

"But what?" Burnett said.

"We don't want to alarm Darius," Mary Jane said, "but I'm going to talk to Reverend Deavers. I'll ask him how much longer Sage will have to stay here, away from Darius and around all these negative people."

"It's not the right time just yet for Sage to come here," Reverend Deavers said, and after some thought, he offered a suggestion, which seemed to be the perfect solution. "Darius went to Colorado when Sage graduated from the university in Denver, and I asked him to visit my friends Beth and Paul Porter in their beautiful home in the Colorado mountains. He took Sage with him, and I know that they are on the positive side of Sage and Darius being married. You met them at the ceremony, remember?"

"I do, and they seem to be good people."

"They really are good people, and I'm thinking it would afford a wonderful respite for Sage to spend some time with them, bless her heart. She could rest, and getting away from, well, so many different opinions, might be just what she needs. I can imagine how she feels, and I know that the Porters would welcome her and help her clear her mind. What do you think?"

"That sounds like just the right thing for her," Mary Jane said. She had always trusted Reverend Deavers in things concerning Sage and Darius. He contacted his friends.

"She is welcome to come here and spend her waiting time with us. We love Sage and Darius," Beth said.

When Mary Jane talked to Sage, she readily agreed. She thought about the beautiful water in the creek across the road from the Porters' residence and about the beautiful Colorado mountains, and she felt she could find some peace there. Burnett drove Sage to the train station in Proctor, and she boarded the train.

"If you're not happy there, you just call me, and I'll drive out there and get you," Burnett said.

Sage boarded the train and waved goodbye from the window. She was at peace.

When she arrived in Colorado, her comfort level was strengthened by the hugs and kisses, the smiles, and seeming joy coming from Beth and Paul Porter at seeing her again. She was thinking, *They're still such a genuinely pleasant couple, and since I must spend time away from my family and quasi-friends and from Darius, I feel this is a good place to spend it.*

The Porters' residence was a spacious two-story house. On the first floor, there was a large lounge, the main dining area, the kitchen, a powder room, and an atrium with flowers and several birdcages. Four bedrooms and four bathrooms were upstairs on the second floor. They owned a bed-and-breakfast called the Dew Drop Inn. It included seven individual log cabins along a walking trail across the highway from the creek.

The clientele in the cabins, of course, was White. The Porters, in the interest of business, had maintained Colorado's character of White only, so Sage was allowed to stay in one of the bedrooms in the main residence. With her being Black, some of the occupants might see her as a maid; and of course, Sage didn't want to be that, so Beth allowed her to take care of the three birdcages, which were in the atrium, and the six yellow birds that lived in them.

One hour each morning, Sage joined Beth and Paul in meditation and prayer in cabin number 1 which was set aside for that purpose, and the renters could also schedule its use by the hour. As instructed, Sage let her mind and body relax, and she concentrated on cleansing them of all negative thoughts.

The cabins were mostly rented by couples, but there was one cabin which was occupied by a mother, her daughter, and the teenage granddaughter. After the first day or two, the young girl became bored with the adult company; and the next day, as Sage was tending the birds, the young girl, passing through the lounge, stopped, and after watching Sage cleaning the cages, filling the food and water bowls, petting the birds, and talking to them, she asked if she could help.

Sage turned and, welcoming the companionship with a younger person, said yes. "Do you like birds?" Sage asked.

"I guess," she said, coming closer. "I've never had a bird."

"They're very lovable," Sage said. "Would you like to hold one?"

"Sure," she said, brightening up and coming closer. "I don't know though," she hesitated. "I might let it loose."

"Don't worry," Sage said. "It can't go anywhere. It'll just fly around a minute or two, and then it'll come back on its own."

She reached out, and Sage placed a little canary in her open palm.

"Now close your palms so only its head is out. Don't be afraid. You can't hurt it."

"Oh, it's so little," she said, and then looking up at Sage, she smiled brightly. "Thank you."

"You're welcome. My name is Sage. The Porters are friends of my family, and I'm visiting with them for a while," she said that to hopefully distinguish her presence from that of the hired help.

"Hello, Sage, and thanks for letting me pet your bird. My name is Clara, and I'm here with my mom and my grandmom. We're from Kansas, and I've never seen any mountains before."

"Hello Clara, it will be a lovely experience seeing the mountains. Where is your mom?"

"She and Grandma are down in the city shopping. My mom loves to shop, and my dad just shakes his head when she comes home with her bags, he calls them."

Sage let Clara hold another little bird while she worked on its cage.

"So what's your favorite subject in school?" Sage asked.

"It's art. Mostly drawing and painting. It started as a hobby of designing and making greeting cards. I draw scenes, and I paint pictures, and believe it or not, I compose the verses or whatever sayings that go inside, and each one has a Bible verse on the left-hand side, mostly at the bottom."

"How interesting," Sage said, taking the bird and putting it back in the clean cage. "My mother designs and makes quilts. I guess you could also call that a form of art." Sage closed that cage and opened up the second one.

"I'd like to see some of your creations. That is, whenever you have the time."

Clara came every day around noon. She said that besides shopping, her mother and her grandmother had also enrolled in a yoga class. And they went there a couple of hours each day. One day, Clara asked Beth if she could take pictures of the rippling waters in the creek, but she and Sage weren't allowed to go across the highway alone, so Beth held each girl's hand, and they walked across the busy highway when there was a lull in the traffic. While Clara took pictures, Beth and Sage took turns reading aloud to each other, there along the mountains that rose up around them. After a while, the three sat on the edge of the creek enjoying one another's company and the beautiful flowing and bubbling water. They sang, and an aura of peace surrounded them.

Another day, Beth took the girls down into the city, and they visited an art store, a card shop, and a fabric shop. Sage bought cloth scraps. Clara bought paint, card stock, and pens; and when they returned, Sage showed them how to cut quilt squares and sew them together. Clara gave Sage and Beth each a blank piece of card stock and asked them to write a poem.

"I'll put one of my pictures on the cover and a Bible verse on the inside of each, and you can put your poem inside," Clara said, smiling a happy smile.

On another day, Paul Porter, seeing how they were enjoying their activities, offered them another one. He took them across the highway to the creek and showed them how to fish. They laughed when they each caught a small fish, which they threw back into the water. They sat quietly in meditation for a while, and then Paul took them back across the road and into the house. Beth shared warm tea and cookies with them. It was a beautiful day.

Clara only came to visit with Sage on days when her mother and grandmother attended their class in the city, but alas, one day the mother and grandmother returned early from their adventures; and when they came looking for Clara, they found her sitting with Sage, obviously enjoying her company. These two adults were not only very surprised, but they were also very angry, for they had led a very segregated life.

Clara was gravely reprimanded by her mother, and for the remaining few days of their vacation, Clara never came to visit. But before she left, she gave Beth one of her cards and asked if she would give it to Sage. Inside was a letter.

Dear Sage,

I apologize for my mom and my grandmom, but I want you to know that although I was lonely and alone here, that wasn't what led me to seek your friendship. I saw something wonderful in you that attracted me to you, and I wanted it for myself. I could feel your goodness even before I spoke to you. You became my angel, my spiritual side, and when we meditated, I knew your life included prayer. I fell in love with you the minute you turned to face me with the little yellow bird in your hand, and you smiled at me. Sage, I never had a Black friend, not even a Black acquaintance, except for our maid who was Black. But she wasn't a person to me; she was just there in our lives.

Sage, I know about prejudice, but try to stay strong. I took a lot of love from you because I know you're filled with it, and you were so willing to share it with me. I've learned to live with my mom and her hate, but I've learned that I can also love her. It's like your love has delivered me from my world of hate and prejudice on the wings of a yellow bird.

From your friend,
Clara

On the outside of the card was a drawing of a yellow bird. On the inside was a Bible verse: "There shall no evil befall thee."

Sage shared her letter and card with Beth and Paul, and they agreed that Sage had received what she came to Colorado for. The Porters felt a comfort, knowing in their hearts that Sage was at peace and that she had expelled all the negativity and that she could now look forward to a steadfast, blessed life with Darius Paul Deavers, the man she loves.

8

Darius and Reverend Deavers began looking at houses in BeachSide, but Darius kept thinking about the house he had seen, and he couldn't get it out of his mind, so he mentioned it to his father.

"When I was on the tour with Major Hawthorne, I saw a house that I really liked, and it had a 'For Sale' sign in the yard. I didn't mention it at the time, but I would love to go back and take a better look at it to see if I still like it."

And they did. They peeked through the windows and determined that the house was empty. They walked around the back and observed the landscaping and the trees. Seeing it again, Darius liked it all the more. When he talked with Sage that night, he described it to her.

"If you like it, my dear, so will I," she said. He was sure of what she would say before he called, and each time he talked with her and when she trusted his judgment, he loved her more. And more.

"I love you, my Sage, and I trust that we'll be happy there."

"I love you too, my Darius, and anywhere you are is where I'll be happy."

After, Darius consulted with his father, whose words almost echoed those of Sage's: "If you like it, so do I."

Reverend Deavers called the real estate agent and made an appointment to see the house.

Keeping their appointment with the real estate agent, Darius's whole countenance brightened the moment they approached the house, and he began thinking of how nice it would be to live there with Sage—living and loving, raising their children, *here*.

The real estate agent greeted them with a handshake and a smile. "Good morning. You're Mr. Deavers, I presume."

"Yes, I'm Paul Deavers, and this is my son, Darius Deavers."

"Glad to meet you both," he said. "So let's go inside. I take it that you've already explored the outside."

"Yes, we have," Darius said. "And I liked everything I saw, including the neighborhood."

"It's a beautiful neighborhood. Families, couples with and without children, and it's quiet, and I understand that every month they have a neighborhood meeting. That'll give you a chance to meet your neighbors and listen to their conversations about the neighborhood."

The house was empty of furniture, but there were draperies and lace curtains at the windows. It was obvious that it had been a well-kept house.

This was a new experience for Darius, and even though he loved the house, he depended largely on his father's opinion, and when his father turned to him and nodded his head in approval, Darius felt quite at ease.

"So you'll be living here with your father?" the agent asked.

"No," Reverend Deavers said. "My son will be living here with his new wife. You see, the house is a wedding present."

"So whose name will be on the mortgage?"

"Their names will on the deed," Reverend Deavers said.

"I mean, who'll be making the payments?" he asked.

"Thankfully, I'll be able to pay cash, so they'll start out with a little security," Reverend Deavers said, noticing the surprised expression on the agent's face.

"Well, congratulations. You're very fortunate," he said, looking at Darius. "Where is your wife?" he asked.

"She'll be arriving soon."

"So do you have a job here?"

"My son is a lawyer, and we'll also be interested in either renting or buying some office space. As we were driving around, I saw a little building that's for sale, and we would like to look at it also,"

Reverend Deavers said, noticing that Darius was having trouble trying to answer all the agent's questions. He handed the agent a note with the address of the building.

"Oh yes. I know of that little building, but I don't think you'd want to locate there. In case you didn't know, it's in the Black business area."

"I see. We'd still like to look at it, and then we'll decide."

The real estate agent showed them the building, and they liked it, and the agent couldn't protest as he was very impressed with the reverend's ability to pay cash, so whatever other request these men made would be fine with him because, for him, it was all about money. They sat down and drew up a contract, and later that week, the real estate agent called.

"Mr. Deavers," he said, the pleasure at getting such a prosperous deal was obvious in his voice, "your check has been approved, and at your convenience, we can get together and complete the deal. Congratulations, you will be the owner of both properties."

Although Darius was on cloud nine, things and decisions were happening so fast his mind was in turmoil.

Later that day, following the suggestions made by Major Hawthorne and Bertram Withers to apply for a position as law professor at the university where Bertram worked, Darius stopped at the university and picked up an application. With a recommendation from Attorney Withers, Darius felt encouraged that he could secure employment there, if he chose, and he could earn a sizeable salary.

After filling out the lengthy application, he drove back to the university and turned it in at the personnel office. The university representative scheduled an interview for Darius on January 20.

Honoring their schedule, Darius Paul Deavers was now on his way to the university for that interview. *Well*, he thought, *I have the educational qualifications, and perhaps I could mentor some young minority students who have the ambition to pursue the legal profession. It might be wise to start here, learn more about the city, and then open my own law firm, as Burnett Copple did.*

After arriving at the university, Darius was escorted to the conference room, and the chancellor, Attorney Bradley Clark, greeted him as he entered. After the proper introductions were made, to Darius, it turned out to be more of an orientation meeting than an interview with the chancellor and the two professors he would be working with.

"We heard you were coming, and it appears very positive that you will be accepted. Your academics are above par, and it'll be good to have another professor to relieve us from some of the pressure. Some departments seem to have become a little understaffed."

"Thank you. I'm looking forward to working with you," Darius said, but after taking a seat, he felt that he wasn't really expected to participate and that whatever decisions they had arrived at would be the accepted way. Besides that, as the discussion continued, Darius felt that they were more interested in the caliber of the students than in either the curriculum, the syllabus, or the testing methods.

Attorney Cambus Delaware joined the conversation. "I'm fortunate to be included in the screening process for potential law students, for I have some good friends, men in very high positions in the business world, with sons who want to study here, and I think it would be fitting and to my advantage, needless to say, to admit them."

"Does the university consider the grade averages of students who apply?" Darius asked as this was on his mind.

"Oh, we most definitely prefer the grade averages to be the highest, but for those purposefully picked, you understand, we could always adjust their averages to fit our qualifications," Attorney Delaware said.

Then calling up his bravery, he asked about their recruitment policies regarding Black applicants. "Therefore, there would be an interest given to remedial studies for those students who might require some extra attention, which would include, perhaps, some Black students."

The atmosphere in the room changed like a sudden burst of wind that came out of seemingly nowhere and blew away everything in the room that had been accomplished and discussed. These four lawyers looked at Darius and then at each other, as if to ask, *Do we have to deal with this threatening question? And why is this White person asking about minority students?*

Then the chancellor, the highest authority over this department, smiled. "Of course, that is something to look into," he said as if that would end the discussion, but then his eyes and his manner of speaking belied the next words he spoke to Darius. "We're very pleased that you've applied, and we'll keep in touch."

"Thank you," Darius said, all the while thinking, *It doesn't change, does it? I may not be happy teaching here unless, of course, I am able to overlook some things. Darius Paul Deavers, who is doing your thinking for you? You are allowing your thoughts, your ambitions, your life goals to become influenced by things outside yourself, especially by people who think they might know what's best for you. As the traffic rule has told us from a child on through life: stop, look, listen. Why? You stop, mainly for your safety, and your awareness of the pitfalls you may encounter in order to get wherever you're going. You're going across the street and on to your planned destination, so look at yourself and listen to yourself. You have a building, and you've planned to establish your own law firm. Why are you interviewing for a position as a law professor?*

The discouraging interview was compounded by the depressing experience concerning the threat to the major, for after he and Major Hawthorne saw the pitiful couple off, Darius was also torn in several directions. He could smile thinking that there was a bright side to his situation, and it was in helping people. *I've helped Major Hawthorne and surely those pitiful people. But there is another side of this same situation: a dark side. Aphotic. Lightless. Like at the bottom of the sea. It seems to be a terrible onus to have a Black child, and it is most definitely a worse one to be a Black person.*

Darius wondered if the threat was more of a problem for Major Hawthorne because it involved a Black child. And if the major had been confronted with having a White child out of wedlock, would it have been as dire? *I think not. Being in love with and planning to marry a Black person, will I find myself in the same situation? Struggling to cope. Not only having a Black wife but the possibility of having a Black child and being confronted with problem upon problem because of that.*

Back at the hotel, Darius was sad and out of sorts. He didn't even want any dinner, which gave his father reason to believe his son was unhappy. Knowing that Darius would confide in him whenever he felt like doing it, he didn't ask any questions.

Darius wasn't able to sleep, and he didn't have the strength to tell his father about his feelings. *Whatever it is, it's because of my love.* He thought of the French proverb, "Try to reason about love and you will lose your reason." *Can I trust my reason, or should I listen to my father and put my faith in God? The Bible says, "Faith is the substance of things hoped for, the evidence of things not seen."*

I hope for a peaceful future which I cannot see. I am an educated man, so I should trust my intelligence enough to figure out the answers to these questions. I am a Christian man, which should equip me with faith enough in God to believe that where I am is where I ought to be, and what I've done is what I should have done. But my reason has disappointed me, and so has my faith. I am lost. I am lost.

When he was sure his father was asleep, he wrote to Charles, and he went downstairs and asked the desk clerk to send the letter. First class.

Dear Charles,

I am in a state of pure perplexity. I'm not sure what it is I want to say to you about how I decide to proceed with my life and how my decision will affect those whom I love. Of course, you know that Sage and I chose Washington because it is legal for Black and White to be married here and to live here. That was as far as we got in our thinking as our love for each other and our overwhelming desire to live together as man and wife overshadowed everything else.

Well, I'm not sure that I want Sage to come here because Washington is just as prejudiced against Blacks as any of the other places we've been in and have run away from. The only difference is that the miscegenation laws were abolished here. Other than that, everything here is either Black or White. The restaurants are segregated, schools and movie theaters are segregated, and yes, the churches are segregated. Hospitals and hotels are either Black or White. Sage and I could not go together to any of those places. So you see, there are very few places where we could go together. Charles, I love Sage too much to subject her to all of this hate and prejudice and segregation at this time. Here, we're a mixed-race couple, a despised Black woman and a White man stupid enough to marry her.

I also thought about what effect my decision would have on you and how you proceed with your life. I know that we talked about you coming here. And I wonder how much success we would have, you and me, Black and White, opening a law office together? So what can I do? Am I wrong in wanting Sage to come here? I know that if I ask Sage to make the decision, she will come, as long as we can be together. Bless her heart. I love her so, and now that you've met her, I know you love her too. I was thinking and hoping that maybe as a lawyer, I could help elevate the minds of Black people so that they could cope with some of the animosity that faces them, and we could fight the unequal laws. And as a teacher, Sage could help broaden their lives with education.

This is mainly for your knowledge as I'm not sure that I want Sage's mother to know how I'm feeling, although she and my father think so much alike, and if I ask them, I know they will say, "It's up to Sage." I didn't want to burden you in such a decisive matter, but you're truly my only Black friend, and you know about what Blacks have to go through, and you're the only one I can trust to help me with this seemingly bleak decision. Would it be right or selfish for me to subject you and Sage to this problematic conglomeration? I thank you for being my friend. Let me hear from you.

Darius Deavers

Charles felt he had spent as much time in Proctor as he needed in order to know if this was the place where he could further his career and fulfill his purpose in life. He remembered his mother saying to him, "Son, stay on whatever path that you choose, but choose wisely. Try to always be helper to those who are less fortunate than you."

I began to think of it that way, and I remember, when the playground bully took a smaller boy's lunch, I gave the little boy my own nickel so he could buy a lunch. It was very likely my focus on being a helper that caused me to choose law as my major course of study. The job of a Black lawyer, to me, is to give legal advice and help to those who have been trampled on unfairly because of their skin color. At the university, Darius and I were members of a group called Students for Equality in Education. The slogan was, "Freedom and Justice for all includes Freedom of Education for all." Darius's place and calling, whether he is totally aware of it or not, is as a helper for those who are Black. Darius is now trying to make peace with himself as a White person because after meeting Sage and her entire family, he knows he has to be at peace with the Black race in order to keep the world's wolf of hate from the door of his heart, which is housed in his deep love for Sage.

Now reading and rereading his letter, I know where I am most needed and where I can help the most. Sage and Darius have not only become my friends, they have become my family, for I feel that I am a part of both their families, and Sage's mother has helped fill the void left by the loss of my mother.

Not wanting to betray Darius's confidence but at the same time concerned about what Darius had written, Charles shared the letter with Mrs. Mary Jane Copple.

"May I call you *mom*?" he asked. "Mrs. Copple seems so formal and impersonal."

After reading Darius's letter and thinking and praying about its contents, Mrs. Mary Jane Copple told Mrs. Lucy Deavers about the letter and, not wanting to read it to her on the phone, suggested that Lucy Deavers come over, and she'd share Darius's letter with her in person.

There had been one of those spring snowstorms, and everything was frozen, and Lucy Deavers, not trusting herself to drive to the other side of town on the streets that were covered over with ice, called a "White" cab company. It was true that White drivers didn't like so much to drive into the Black part of town, the same as Black cab drivers didn't like so much driving in the White part of town. But necessity prevailed.

Arriving at Mary Jane Copple's house, Lucy felt as if something cheerful had happened. She was always cheered by Mary Jane's smile and her calm, peaceful manner, for it was like she never had a care in the world. And these two mothers, aware of the loving relationship that existed between their children, loved them both. Lucy Deavers had come to love Sage more as a person than as a Black person, which had defined her for so long a time. And similarly, Mary Jane was able to see beyond Darius's whiteness, although that was a part of him.

"Well," Lucy said, smiling as the two ladies greeted each other with a hug, "so what are your thoughts, you know, about Darius's letter?"

"Here's the letter. Read it yourself and see what you think," Mary Jane said, giving her the letter and sitting quietly while Lucy read it.

Lucy Deavers could feel her son's pain as she read his words, and she began to cry. "My poor baby," she said. "How could I have lived all my life as this White person who never even considered that there were Black people in the world? Then I let the hate I'd been taught consume me. When you were our maid, I had not looked at you as a person at all. Oh dear, until our son forced us to look at that beautiful little girl of yours—and at you." She looked up at her friend and tried to smile.

"So here we sit, loving our children and thinking we know what's best for them and thinking we can advise them on what they should do. But I think what we should be doing is asking ourselves how we can help them in whatever it is they decide," Lucy said, wiping her tears.

"You're right because we ought to know that, after all the struggles those two children have gone through, they aren't going to turn back now."

"I'm sure that Darius wrote to Charles because he didn't want to worry his father with his negative thoughts, but I think I should share this letter with my husband."

"And so do I. Come," Mary Jane said.

And she did.

"It is a little more complicated out here than we could have imagined," Reverend Deavers said. "But it's something these two children will have to wade through, and they'll either sink or swim, or they may decide to abandon the water altogether, which would mean abandoning each other. Then they could settle on dry land where it's safe and comfortable."

"And where in the world could that be?" Lucy asked. "You know as well as I do that they've already tried that."

"My dear," he said, "we're as much to blame as anyone or anything. We encouraged them to defy the law. Now we need to see what we can do to help them."

"Oh, my dear," she said, laughing and chiding him. "You're the one who started it all. If you hadn't taken Darius to that farm with you..."

"I know. Then they'd never have met. But they have met, and there's no use in worrying over something we can't change."

"Yes, and I think what we'd better do is call on your Lord."

"Seriously, my dear, I have done just that, and the answer I get is, 'Trust in the Lord with all your heart and lean not unto your own understanding. In all your ways acknowledge Him, and He will direct your path.'"

"Of course, I know that you and Sage's mother are right in looking to your faith."

He smiled thinking that she'd come a long way on this path. "But you know that in the end, Sage is going to make her own decision. I'm rather sure about that. But our son is in unfamiliar territory, and he's scared. That's only natural, but it's really too late for any plans to be changed. I've already purchased a home for them, and I've purchased a building for his office, however he chooses to use it."

"I guess he'll have to work it all out, huh?" Lucy said.

"Yes, dear, he will." She hung up the receiver and looked over at her friend. "We should have known he'd say that Sage has a mind of her own, and Darius will have to rely on that."

"And that's the truth."

"Has Sage seen the letter?" Lucy asked.

"No. Not yet."

"Then we're all just wasting our time trying to decide what she should do before she reads it."

Mary Jane Copple thought for a moment, and then she made her decision. "I'll show it to her, and then I'll call a family meeting, let's say for tomorrow, and we'll all try and help Sage with her decision. You're welcome to come," she said, taking Lucy's hand. "Really, I encourage it. Ha-ha. You're family now, you know."

"Thank you," Lucy said, squeezing Mary Jane's hand. "I feel honored."

When Sage read the letter, she smiled and laid it on the table. When Darius called that night, she could hear the anxiety in his voice as soon as he said hello. So before he could say more, she spoke.

"My darling, Charles shared your letter with my mom, and she shared it with me."

"Oh no. He shouldn't have done that."

"Oh yes, he should have. If anyone should know what you're thinking, I should. Don't you know that you're all there is in the world for me, and I have no other desire except to be wherever you are? You and I are one, and there's no one and nothing in this world that can separate us. I don't care a hoot about what's happening there in the city of BeachSide, but I know that, together, we can work it out. So don't give up hope because besides our love, my dear, all we have is hope, and I know that hope in God doesn't disappoint."

"My dear Sage, I love you so much," he said amid his tears.

"I love you too, so much. But don't cry, Darius. My mom has planned a family meeting for tomorrow, and by the way, your mom is coming. Isn't that something? But no matter what any of them might have to say, I'm coming to Washington." And that was that.

Mrs. Mary Jane Copple opened the meeting with a short prayer. Everyone was there: Sage, Kay Lee, Burnett, Charles, Sophronia, and Lucy Deavers. Since Burnett had always been the one to take charge, he read the letter aloud.

"Well, Sage, this is what the meeting is about," Burnett said. "We think it might help if we just think about what Darius has written, and then we can discuss it. But I think it's up to you to make your decision as to how you'll proceed."

"You're right, Burnett. It's up to me," Sage said. "When I decided to marry Darius, you all felt the need to have a family meeting, and you almost convinced me that I should not marry him. But now that's what I'm going to do. I made the decision to go to Washington and to marry Darius Paul Deavers, and as Mamma says, 'Come hell or high water,' I'm going as soon as Darius says he's ready for me to come. I know you all love me and you want the best for me, but you can't live my life. The time I spent in the Colorado mountains, looking at God's beautiful world, meditating by the rippling water of the creek with three very spirit-filled unbiased people, I was able to clear all the negative things from my mind. So I'm going to Washington."

The meeting produced each person's feelings, thoughts, and decisions.

Kay Lee said, "I still think you should wait. These are awful times, and you're trying to defy the law, and my word, you ought to know that you can't go against the law. Segregation and prejudice are real. Look at what's happening in some of the other states. There's rioting and boycotting of schools and all kinds of mean and evil things going on just because of us being Black. I say you ought to wait until things get better."

Charles remarked, "What is the old saying, 'Weight is what broke the wagon down'? I put the word *wait* in the place of the word *weight*. We can't carry the weight of the world on our shoulders, and we can't wait for things and laws and prejudiced people to change. And, Sage, I'm really glad that you're going as planned. But you're not going alone. I'm going with you. We're both in Darius's corner, and we're going to be with him to help him with whatever his program is. You're both going to need a friend, and I'm it." He smiled. "As a matter of fact, you're both definitely going to need a Black friend."

Mary Jane said, "Thank the Lord for you, Charles. Darius and Sage will most definitely need the kind of friend you are."

"So," Burnett said. "So…"

Everyone turned to him, waiting for what he was going to say. "So since the death of our father, Isaac Columbus Copple by name, I've been considered as the head of this family, and also, since I've been in the legal business longer than both Charles and Darius, and I know a little more about legal *strategy*—"

"Oh Lord," Kay Lee interrupted, shaking her head. "Mr. Know-It-All."

"As I was saying, since I have more experience in law than Darius and Charles, I think I'd better go too, you know, to be their advisor in trying to get a law firm started."

"What?" Kay Lee continued shaking her head.

"Boy, history sure repeats itself," Sophronia spoke up. "Seems like I've heard this same argument before, but I know that Darius ain't nobody's idiot. He's not only smart, and now he's blessed to have some sensible support. Thank you, Charles. He and Sage will need a young friend. And thank you, Burnett. He'll need somebody who's older."

"Yes, thank you, sir," Charles said, wiping a tear from his eye. "We'll all feel better with you being there."

Lucy Deavers not only spoke, she stood up. "Okay. I love my son too, and it's good of you young men to be thinking about him. But I'm thinking about Sage, and I guess you all forgetting about her since she's a woman. Sage can't be in this all by herself while all the men do the planning. That includes my husband too, bless his heart. So there, I'm going with you, Sage."

"Well, that's good," Kay Lee said. "You all go, but have you thought about how you're going? On the train? Mrs. Deavers, are you going to sit in the colored coach? They sure can't sit in the White coach."

"Okay," Lucy Deavers said. "That's no problem. We'll fly. That's what we'll do. We'll fly."

"Well, Mr. Burnett, do you know how much it costs to fly?" Kay Lee asked. "I don't think you have that much money."

"I have that much money, and I'll get tickets for everyone tomorrow, and we'll all fly together," Lucy Deavers said this.

Sometimes when you don't know what to say, you say nothing. Except Mary Jane. She said, "Thank you, Jesus."

That night, when Reverend Deavers talked with his wife, she told him about the meeting.

"I'm considered family now, and we discussed Darius's letter. So, my dear, you know that Sage said, 'Come hell or high water, I'm going.' I know she got that from her mother. They have so many little sayings. Burnett and Charles are coming too. They think they can help Darius get his law firm set up, and I know you're going to be right there to help them. So you men can do whatever it is you have to do. But I'm coming to be with Sage, and we'll weather whatever we need to weather. My goodness, I'm really getting excited about this. I can help my girl furnish the house, select colors, *shop*. You know how I love shopping."

"Bless you, my dear," Reverend Deavers said.

"I'll get the tickets tomorrow, and I'll let you know when and what time we'll arrive so and you and Darius can pick us up, okay?"

"Yes, we'll do that, and I love you."

"I love you too."

9

Darius, although happy about their coming, was still somewhat nervous about it all. He told his father, "I think I'll go for a walk." His father, understanding him very well and quite aware what his son was thinking, decided not to discourage him.

Putting on his coat and hat, Darius left the confines of the room and the hotel and walked outside. He had no particular destination in mind, so he walked up and down the unfamiliar streets of the city. He felt both happy and scared. He was elated beyond measure that Sage was coming, but he was apprehensive thinking about how their life was going to be. Would it be easy, or would it be hard? How would it be for Sage?

His wandering carried him up to the top of one of the city's hills where he sat on a bench to rest and hopefully to clear his troubled mind. As he looked out, he had a clear view of the scenic wonderland of evergreen forests, clear lakes, and the snowcapped peaks of the Olympic Mountains and of Mount Rainier, one of the highest peaks in the United States. But his troubled mind had clouded his ability to enjoy all the beauty of God's creation, and he hung his head and watched the tears fall on his folded arms.

He thought of all the people who were making changes and sacrifices in their lives in order to help him keep his head above water, hoping he wouldn't drown in the responsibility of being a husband and head of his household. Yet he was drowning in self-doubt. *Why, oh why, did I defy every law and every tradition and make a decision to marry someone of another race, the Black and despised race?*

He thought of his mother and how she had changed her life because of his love for Sage. Charles and Burnett were interrupting their lives to come to his aid, all because of his decision to marry Sage. But, Lord Almighty, he couldn't imagine any future life without her. And what if he decided not to marry her because she was Black? He couldn't imagine any White woman being able to fill Sage's place and to share his life. His whole happiness, he knew, depended on being with her. *But what kind of deep dark water am I getting her into? Oh, Sage!*

Then thoughts of suicide entered his mind as a solution for everyone. Remove the cause, and everyone's problems will be removed. They could get on with their lives. Happy. Unburdened. *Will my absence make them happy? What about Sage? Can I abandon her after all the sacrifices she's made because she loves me? Didn't she say, "Don't you know that you are all the world to me"?*

He tried to pray, "Our Father who art in heaven…," and suddenly a cool breeze caused him to shiver, and his body began to shake. Conversely, a fire seemed to be burning within his chest. When he looked up, stopping his prayer, he saw the trees and forests, and his focus shifted to them. He recognized the hemlock and the willow. The hemlock is the state tree of Washington. He knew that there is a herb called poison hemlock, which is associated with wormwood and gall. But the hemlock tree that he saw is a stately evergreen tree belonging to the pine family. So one is poison while another is good. His confusion was increasing, and his energy was waning.

When the breeze and the fire had subsided, Darius Paul Deavers heard a voice coming through the trees, saying, *What are you doing here?* And in his mind, he answered, *I'm here because I'm lost. The world and the segregation laws have destroyed my confidence in myself.*

Then the voice said, *Those are man's laws, but God's laws are different. Get up and go back to your father. Go and take your life back. You can't be weak. Think about using your strength and determination to help Sage and her people regardless of the debilitating laws.* These words seemed to help him clear away his confusion.

"All right, all right. I know that I can't abandon Sage. I can't abandon any of them, and especially not myself," he said aloud, and looking up at the willow tree, he knew that it was known for its tough yet pliable branches. The willow trees also add beauty and charm to their environment, and they have strong roots. With hopes for a beautiful and happy life, he got up, and his feet led him back to the hotel. All the while he was walking back, the words *strength and determination and tough and pliable* echoed in his ear. He became all joy thinking of Sage's coming and all the other people who were coming to help him. He was forced to say, "Lord, have mercy."

When Darius informed Major Hawthorne that his whole family was coming, the major smiled.

"I can't get them all in my car, unless I sit one on top of the other," he said and laughed. "But don't worry, I've got you covered. I'll get one of our army passenger vans, and I'll pick you and the reverend up, and we'll go to the airport and pick them up, and that'll take care of that."

"I hate to put you to all that trouble," Darius said.

"No trouble at all. My word, after what you've done for me, I'm happy to be able to do something for you. When are they coming?"

"The plane arrives at three thirty on Monday afternoon."

"So let's say that I pick you and the reverend up about two o'clock. Yep. That'll give us plenty of time to get to the airport."

So it was decided, and Major Hawthorne wondered how his family would react to the news that Sage was Black. But after some thought, he decided it would be better and would possibly prevent a scene if he told his wife and his daughter beforehand.

Knowing his schedule, Miriam was waiting for her father when he came home. He knew by the unpleasantness on her face that something was wrong.

"Hi, baby," he said, kissing her. "What's the matter?"

"Oh, Daddy, Mom told me," she said.

"Told you what?"

"About the phone call."

Marvin looked askance, not knowing that his wife had overheard, and he was thinking, *So she must have been listening, and she knows what the caller said.*

"Oh, Daddy, how could you do it?" Miriam asked, and he was still at such a loss, not only what to say but how to act.

"But I don't believe it," she said. "I know you don't fool around with women, and I can't even begin to believe that you'd mess around with someone Black."

He began to realize that his wife had been listening, and he was sorry that she had told Miriam.

"What exactly did she tell you?"

"Mom said she only listened a moment, and after she heard the man say—what was it?—'I know you don't want that beautiful wife and daughter to know that you're the father of a Black child.' Then she said she was so shocked that she hung up the phone, and she didn't listen to any more of the conversation."

"Oh, damn," was all he could say. He thought he and Darius had taken care of the situation. *Will it ever go away?* was what he was thinking.

"So where is this child? And how old is it? Is it a boy or a girl? How could you do this?" Then looking at him and trying to read his expression, she knew at once that it wasn't true. "Daddy, say something?"

He gave a sigh and looked at her, and what he said was the truth.

"Baby, I have only one child, and her name is Miriam. You know, people can threaten anybody they choose, hoping to get some money. Of course, it isn't true. I know some Black people on the staff at the hospital, but none of them personally. Rest assured, it isn't true."

"I didn't think it was, because I know what a good person you are. And if you did have another child, I believe you'd claim it, regardless of its race."

"Thank you, baby. I most surely would. I love you."

"I love you too, Daddy. Now go and tell Mom and try to convince her that it isn't true."

Going upstairs to his wife's bedroom, he was able to calm her down enough to talk to her, but her calm didn't last long.

"You misunderstood the conversation. Somehow a nurse at the hospital and her brother were trying to threaten me with that stupid story. But it was all a hoax, and it's been taken care of."

"How?"

"I have to thank Darius for his legal action in making them sign a document saying it was all a bad lie, but to settle any further threats, he paid them some money. I have not (he emphasized the words 'have not') fathered a Black child, okay?"

"So we're in debt to him for paying them off. How much?"

"We won't worry about that right now. I'll settle with him later." He was thinking that one hurdle had been crossed, and right now, that was enough.

"But I do have to tell you that I'm going to the airport to pick up Darius's family. His fiancé, her brother, a friend, and Darius's mother are coming. But you ought to know before they get here that the girl Darius is going to marry is a Negro. She's Black."

It took Alicia a moment to digest his words. "Hell and damnation," she said after a moment. "I get it now. She's your Black child. So that's why you're so friendly with Darius. Uh-huh. I thought it was funny that he came here, and it was because he couldn't marry anybody Black in Oklahoma. So you planned it all, you…you bastard."

She threw a jar of face cream at him, but it missed him and hit the wall, and the noise brought Miriam back upstairs. Marvin didn't know whether to laugh or cry—or die. Then leaving his wife in her bedroom, he took Miriam downstairs. He tried to explain it all to her.

"The phone call was an attempt for those people to get some money from us, but it wasn't true what that man said, and it's been settled. Darius used his legal brain, and it was over."

"So what's Mom so rattled about?"

"You might as well know too. The young lady Darius is going to marry is a Negro."

"You're not serious," she said, but looking at him, she realized that he was very serious.

"I'm serious, and you have to know that your mother has the mistaken idea that the threat was real, and…well, that the reason I'm so friendly with Darius is that the man on the phone was telling the truth and that I have fathered a Black child and she is Darius's lady."

"What? Oh my word," she said. "Now I am confused. So is this really why you're his friend?"

"No, sweetheart, it isn't. Darius is not a bad person. He just happened to fall in love with someone Black, and I am not her father, and I'm just about the only friend Darius has out here, and I can't abandon him. Your mother will just have to understand, and I hope you will too. I'm going to the airport to pick her up and her brother, who of course is Black, and a Black friend. Darius's mother is also coming." He smiled. "But she's White."

"Thank the Lord for that."

"Miriam, I was hoping you and your mother could be nice to them. It's about time this damn world made some changes."

Miriam saw his frustration, and loving her father as she did, she felt she had to support him, and she'd try to make her mother understand. "I do understand your feelings, and I'm in your corner. I guess the poor girl is going to need a friend, so I'm going to the airport with you."

And she did.

On the way to the airport, these four people—Major Hawthorne, Miriam Withers, Darius Deavers, and Reverend Paul Deavers—joined in a conversation; and although speaking of pleasant things, they had pockets of negative thoughts taking up space in their mind.

"I checked," Major Hawthorne said, "and the plane is arriving right on schedule. Flying is such a good way to travel. It's fast, and it's comfortable." But he was thinking of how segregated public transportation is and how cruel the people had been treated who were trying to change the laws. He had read about a civil rights activist named Bayard Rustin who was arrested for sitting with a White man on a public bus in North Carolina and had to spend twenty-two days on a prison chain gang. Thinking about how Sage would be treated made him sad.

"That's a blessing," Reverend Deavers said. "I don't relish waiting in lines." But in his thoughts, he was remembering how Sage's mother was forced to stand in the back of the line behind the White people who were waiting to ride the White city buses. Such unfair laws. He was sad.

"I wish my son could have come with us," Miriam said. "I don't think he's ever been on an airplane, nor even been to the airport, but I didn't want to take him out of school," Miriam said this, knowing that wasn't the real reason. If she brought him, he'd tell his father, and the whole subject of Sage being Black would have been the cause of another world war. She was sad.

"Just think, this time next month, I'll be a married man, and I'm on cloud nine just thinking about my dear Sage," Darius said. But he was suddenly overcome by fear that his happy life with Sage could be hampered by prejudice, and he wondered if he could use his legal knowledge to help change the Black condition. These thoughts caused him to become sad.

Then, without warning, like out of the blue, a bird hit the windshield, and Major Hawthorne had to very quickly and strongly apply his brakes. They were traveling north, and just as suddenly, a car, traveling in the east direction, ran the red light and barely missed hitting them. It took a while for them to recover.

"Thank God for the bird," Reverend Deavers said. "God must have been guiding that little sparrow." And without realizing it, that sudden change of pace jolted all the negative thoughts from their minds, and they rode on with peace in their hearts.

Sitting there on the airplane (which was a new experience for Sage, not having flown before), she began to wonder. *Am I off in a magic garden of anywhere? Or nowhere? And if nowhere, how do I find my way out of this garden? I'm going to a new place with new people, a new house, and a new person. Darius really is a new person, and I should know him, but do I? How much time have we spent together, just the two of us? How long were we engaged to be married? And even though I do love him, does love conquer all? Does it move all discomfort out of the way and leave only comfort? Well, what does any of that matter? I've known him and loved him from the very first time I saw him.*

Looking out the window as we are approaching land, I can see houses, lakes, rivers, and trees, and I know this is the real world. I have to transfer myself, my body and my mind, out of the magic garden and get acquainted with the real world and with Ariel Sage Copple, soon-to-be Deavers. What kind of name is that anyway? Deavers. It's a White name. Ha-ha. As I look at those ones who are accompanying me, I know they are not only happy to be with me, but they are happy about me. And now I'm going to have my own home, which will also be a new experience, as I've always lived with other people. It was always someone else's house.

Now the airplane is landing...taxiing, stopping. Oh dear. Now I'm here, watching Darius and his beautiful smile, feeling his soft lips, and feeling my heart beating. His wonderful father is here, smiling a happy smile, and I feel myself surrounded by love. I must let that love, and that love alone, stand as a shield that can protect me from the spears and arrows that are sure to come. But my peace doesn't come from them, and no matter how kind or supportive they may be, my peace must come from inside of me. Remember, you're Black, and Darius is White, and you're entering the real world of different opinions and different people. You're in America, and America is not a world of sameness. Nowhere is, and most especially not BeachSide, Washington.

When they arrived at the airport and they saw the travelers as they walked through the door leading from the plane, their whole world became brighter. The sun smiled.

Such a sweet reunion: Darius and Sage, Darius and his mother, Darius and Charles, Darius and Burnett, Lucy with her husband, Sage with her brother, Reverend Deavers with everyone, Charles with the feeling that he had a family.

Miriam was momentarily numb. *How am I to receive them? Everybody is hugging everybody else. I've never hugged a Black man, nor a Black lady either. Not even my mother's maid Mamie.* But Lucy immediately understood Miriam's fears, and she reached out and took Miriam's hand and hugged her. This calmed the waters for everyone, who had seemingly forgotten Miriam and her father.

Reverend Deavers was the one who, also standing beside his wife, made the introductions. "Major Hawthorne," the reverend said, "this is the family. My wife, Lucy, and a family friend, Attorney Charles Williams. And my brother-in-law-to-be, Burnett Copeland, also a lawyer. Seems you're surrounded by legalese."

"So if you're ever in trouble, call us," Burnett said, smiling and shaking the major's hand.

"This is my daughter, Miriam. She's basically my family. My wife was rather indisposed," the major said.

Reverend Deavers also noticed that Miriam's husband hadn't come with her. "And meet Sage, that is, if Darius will release her."

It was such a joyous gathering, with everyone hugging and seeming to love everyone else, and Miriam wished for a family like this. She was an only child, and she had one child. When she looked at Burnett (who managed to hug Sage despite Darius's continued closeness to her, having never taken his arm from around her waist), a little spark of something weird floated through her vision and into her brain. *He could be my brother if he were White or if I were Black. I wish he was my brother and Sage was my sister.*

Then as she was being introduced to Charles, her vision, which she thought was idiotic, caused her to like him. Then shaking her head in an attempt to get rid of it, her face smiled at him without her ordering it. She was thinking, *What is the matter with you, Miriam Withers? Come out of that horrible dream world. You're White, and they're Black, and my mom says that they're different. Different in a negative way. But regardless of what my mother said, I feel quite comfortable, more than comfortable, with this family. Like it was my family. Oh dear, how funny you are today.*

On the way out of the airport, sitting in the van next to her father, Miriam could see Sage's face in the mirror. *She is so beautiful, but poor Darius. He's going to have a difficult time living in this city with his beautiful wife, so I really do want to be her friend.*

Charles was in seventh heaven (wherever that old saying takes you) looking at all the water. *Water, water everywhere, and I'm thinking that swimming and boating and fishing will be my main pastime. My focus, of course, will be as a legal partner with Darius. Burnett, with his experience, can get us started on the right foot, and I feel so honored and privileged to be associated with Darius and his whole family, and Sage and her family.* Looking at Miriam and her father, somehow it was like they fit in as the last piece of the big jigsaw puzzle. He wondered where the word *jigsaw* came from.

Lucy Deavers was filled with pleasant thoughts. She patted her husband's hand; then she reached over and kissed him on the cheek. *He's such a wonderful man. Had it not been for his clear vision into the character of Sage and her mother and then, later, the whole Black race, I would never have seen anything except hate and prejudice for Sage. My son, bless his sweet soul, has found love, and that also has helped me overcome the hate and has allowed me to find another whole world of love. So now I can do one of the things I enjoy so much. I love shopping, and if Sage will let me, or if the laws will let me, I can go shopping with her, and we can purchase the furnishing for their house, or we can buy all those magazines that have décor in them, and she can pick out what she wants, and then I can go and buy them. I wonder if she has a particular color scheme in mind. Hmm. Don't be pushy, but, oh, when she marries my son, she really will be my daughter. I never had a daughter.* And then looking at Miriam, Lucy wondered, *Where is her mother? Well, Miriam seems to be about the same age as Sage, so I can be like a mother to her too. I wonder if she likes to shop. I'll ask her.*

Sitting there in Major Hawthorne's van, holding hands with Darius, Sage was thinking, *I'm here, and I'm not alone. I'm surrounded by love. I think of my future as being beautiful and highly productive of good. All things are working together for good in our lives, and for this, I give thanks.*

Major Hawthorne had obtained housing for everyone on the base. He knew Sage and Charles and Burnett would not be allowed accommodations at the hotel where Darius and the reverend were staying, and he had employed the services of a caterer. After everyone was settled in their living quarters, they enjoyed a very well-prepared evening meal, which was served in a private dining room.

The wedding was planned for three weeks hence at the Peace Arch. This would give them some time to get the house and other necessary things in place.

Part Two

10

When the meal was over, they sat in the lounge of the officers' quarters enjoying an after-dinner drink for those who wanted it and after-dinner mints for those with that preference.

"I'd like to meet your wife," Mrs. Deavers said to Major Hawthorne. "You've been so kind to us, and I'd like to thank her for letting us take you away for so many hours. I hope she's not ill."

"No," he said, trying to go through in his mind the best way to handle this. He didn't want his wife to hurt Sage's feelings, and he couldn't just take Mrs. Deavers to meet her since she's White and not take Sage, Charles, and Burnett. *What must I do? Well,* he thought, *there's only one answer to life's complex questions, and that answer is, do what you think is right and deal with the consequences as they come.*

"No, she's not sick," he said. "I think she was just tired this afternoon. But sure, I can take all of you over whenever you have time as I know there are a lot of things you have to do before the grand day."

"Yes," Lucy said. "There's shopping for the house and for Darius's office, you know, and I'd love to help Sage with planning the decor of her house, that is if she'll let me."

"Let you? I don't think I'd want to do it without you. We can meet Mrs. Hawthorne later," Sage said, turning to Major Hawthorne.

"I was thinking," Miriam spoke up, knowing her mother's mind-set right now, "that I'd love to help you all with that house planning and the shopping. I have some home-decor magazines and some home journals that I can bring over. Then we can do some planning before we do the actual shopping." She stopped as everyone was looking askance at her. "I know, I'm just going on like I've been asked."

"Well, I'm asking you," Sage said, smiling her beautiful smile. "I'd love for you to go with us. You already have a house, and you know the city better than we do, and I imagine you know the best places to shop." She didn't want to say, *the places where I would be welcome.*

"That sounds just majestic," Lucy said, accenting the word *majestic.* "You young ladies might have some younger ideas that this old lady has."

"Now, Mom," Darius said, laughing, "if somebody called you old, you'd be angry."

"And don't you forget it."

Everyone laughed. "But you know what I mean. Times have changed and styles are different, but that's all right, because we three, we'll be fine."

"So I can bring the magazines over whenever you say, and we'll go from there. Just name your day and time," Miriam said. "And I'm sure my dad is available if you men need him."

"Right. I'm at your service," Marvin said, clapping his heels together and giving a salute. "And now I think it's time to bid you good people good-night."

"Thanks. We'll be in touch," Reverend Deavers said.

"Wait just a minute," Sage said, holding up her hand. "First, I'd like to see my house. Do you all realize that I haven't seen it?"

"Oh, sweetheart, you haven't," Darius said. "And I'm sorry. Let's go now, all of us, and have a look. It's not too late, then Mom and Dad can go to their hotel."

"My dear," Mrs. Deavers said to her husband, "you and Darius keep the hotel, and you two stay there, but I'm staying with Sage until the ceremony, and Charles and Burnett can stay right here too, if that's okay, Major."

"That is definitely okay," Major Hawthorne said. So that was the arrangement.

When they got to the house, Major Hawthorne knew right away that it was located in a White-restricted area. Negroes were not allowed to live there, but he didn't say anything about it because they'd already purchased the house. *Maybe times have changed. I hope so*—these were his thoughts.

It was a lovely house, and the tour went well. After taking them to their lodgings, Marvin drove Miriam to his home, where she'd left her car.

"Dad, I've been thinking about what Mrs. Deavers said."

"Yes, she wants to meet Alicia."

"I don't want to take them to meet Mom just yet. Seeing how upset she was this morning, I don't know if she's calmed down enough to meet Sage and her Black family."

"She's going to have to meet them sometime. Sooner or later."

"I'd prefer later," Miriam said, shrugging her shoulders and smiling.

"You're probably right. This may not be the right time. I'll talk to her and try to calm the waters with her, but I'm really, really glad that you've accepted them."

"It's that this is all so new to me," Miriam said. "I've never associated with any Black people before. Actually, I never had to come in close contact with them, except Mamie, and she was never a person before. You know, like never, but today, it was like the curtains on a stage had opened up, and there they were. At first, I was a bewildered observer, but something inside of me—I don't know what— just seemed to open up with the curtains, and for the first time ever, I saw them as people. I saw them as people just like us, only the color of their skin is different. I was like a puppet on a string, with my words and movements being directed by the puppeteer, and I wasn't in control of myself. Maybe God was the puppeteer, and He was directing me. And gosh, how can I call myself a Christian if I'm going to hate Black people, like my mother does, when the Scripture tells us to love everybody?"

"I can't answer that for you. I'm not a Christian like you are, but somehow I feel the same way."

"Oh, Daddy, I want to be their friend. Especially Sage. She is so pretty and so humble, and for the briefest minute, I saw her as a White girl, and we were twins."

"Hmm. Maybe you would like that." Major Hawthorne thought about the negative things his wife said about Black people and that she knew Sage was his daughter. "But, well, if I did father a Black child, which I didn't, but if I did, I'd want her to be just like Sage. And now I'm wondering how Bertram will react to Sage and Charles and Burnett, and when you're going to tell him that they're Black," he said, looking at Miriam.

"Ha. I don't know, Daddy, but you know life gets hard sometimes, doesn't it?"

"Yep, it sure does, and then you die."

"Oh, Daddy, that's mean."

"I'm sorry, it's just a saying."

When Miriam arrived at her home, she told her husband about meeting all the new arrivals, and she told him of her plans to go shopping with Darius's fiancée and his mother.

"I can show them around the downtown district and tell them the best places to shop."

"Darling, I think that's mighty nice of you to do that," he said.

Hmm, Miriam thought, *this might not be the right time to tell him that Sage is Black. Later.*

The morning of the planned shopping trip, after eating breakfast, Bertram kissed his wife briefly on the mouth, and then he left for his office. At eight thirty, Miriam took Timothy to school, signed him in, and drove to the officers' quarters. She sat with Sage and Mrs. Deavers, and they looked through the magazines with Sage, choosing her colors, style, kind of wood, towels, and most things for the bedroom, bath, and kitchen. Sage didn't feel the least bit intimidated by Miriam, for she didn't think that Miriam showed any of the high-minded airs she expected of White ladies in her circle. She felt that Miriam was genuinely honest, although there seemed to be something unhappy that she bore underneath her friendliness.

When they were ready to go shopping, not wanting to have the same problem she and Mrs. Deavers had, Sage decided to clear the air.

"Miriam, I'm hoping you know that there are some places where I'm not allowed to shop."

"I do know that, and where we're going, we'll be all right."

Mrs. Deavers felt a great moving forward, which had been started by this love between her son and Sage. She also felt that something had sprung up in Miriam that was new to her. She smiled and imagined that they were both her daughters, Sage by marriage and Miriam by, perhaps, adoption. *I should write a book about this. I'd call it* The Great Conversion, *and we'd all be the same color. Maybe ecru as that's a nice neutral color.*

The ladies went every day shopping, arranging, furnishing, and enjoying all of it. Darius and Reverend Deavers took Burnett, Charles, and Major Hawthorne to see the building they'd purchased. It had two floors. The first floor was large enough to accommodate two offices, one for Darius and one for Charles, and a reception area. There was a kitchen with a counter, shelves, and cabinet space. There was a bathroom. The upstairs had the same amount of space and the same number of rooms, and they decided the upstairs would provide living space for Charles until and if he purchased a house. Reverend Deavers's idea was that whatever avenue Darius chose, he would always have office space to accommodate it. With Burnett's experience and know-how in having his own law office, he helped them get the office furnished with everything he knew they would need. They purchased bedroom and kitchen furniture for Charles. Darius had not noticed before that only one other building in the block was occupied.

That evening at dinner, a discussion took place about the future of the three young people—Darius, Sage, and Charles—here in BeachSide. Should Darius open his own law firm immediately, with Charles as a partner? Or would it be more advantageous for Darius and Charles to work with an established law firm first, perhaps as interns, and thus learn the business of being a lawyer before launching out on their own? Burnett was in favor of the latter option for the reason given that it was what he had done.

"My first job was as district attorney in my court jurisdiction, and after I gained some experience and some knowledge of legal and court procedures, then I opened my own law office in the Black community where I grew up. I felt I was ready to fulfill the needs of the community and my need to help my own people."

"That was good for you, I'm sure, but I want to test the waters in my own firm. I worked at a law firm in Boston, and I have a pretty good idea about how to proceed," Darius said. "And I have felt that I wanted to be more than just a lawyer. Like my dad, he's a minister, but he also organized a plan to help minority students go to college."

Reverend Deavers said, "No one can decide for you. First, become a little more familiar with the needs for legal assistance here before making any definite decisions for your future. Not only for your future but your contentment and how you can be of help to those people you feel need it most."

"Yes, Darius, take some time," Lucy Deavers said. "We're here for you and Charles, in whatever you decide. And, Sage, as I think about you, I think about myself. I never worked full-time, and you don't have to even think about full-time work right now. I've always had my own personal bank account, thanks to my husband, and I made sure you'd have your own bank account to do with what you want, okay? You have experience in teaching, so you might want to do some volunteering first. Relax. You know, take some time and enjoy your home and your surroundings. You have a good supportive partner here," she said as she kissed Darius on the cheek.

"Right, Mom, I agree," Darius said, smiling at Sage.

"Enjoy being married for a while," Lucy Deavers said. "And have us some grandchildren, four or five."

Everyone looked at Sage and smiled, and Sage listened and relaxed through it all. She was happy.

11

It was the day before the ceremony, and Miriam was excited about seeing the Peace Arch again, remembering that she and Bertram had gone there after Timothy was born to renew their wedding vows. She didn't want to speak with her mother again, but she and her father had decided to attend the wedding, so she called him.

"Since Mom knows Sage is Black," she told him, "maybe if you act real nice and talk real sweet, she might be able to put aside her problems with Black people. You know, tell her that they're actually nice people, and they're not at all like she thinks they are. And I'll talk to Bertram, and I'll have to tell him that Sage is Black. He doesn't know."

"Ha. Do you think you can talk sweet enough to your husband so that he'll be able to put aside his hate? I wonder."

"We can try. I'll talk to Bertram, and you talk to Mom."

"And what if they won't go?"

"I don't know about you, but if Bertram says no, then I won't go either. I couldn't defy him, not and still be his wife. Not Bertram Withers. No. No way."

"You know, it would be kind of hard for me to desert Darius, but it's like being between a rock and a hard place, if you know what I mean. You're damned if you do and damned if you don't, because if my wife refuses to go and I go anyway, I think it would be the end of this marriage too. But as you said, all we can do is try."

"The ceremony and a reception are planned for tomorrow," Miriam said to her husband, calling up all her nerve. "They're going to the Peace Arch. Would you like to go?" she asked, rather afraid of his reply. Sooner or later, Daddy had said. So true. So true.

"Sure, we'll go. I'd like to see that park again. It's so special."

"It is."

"And I trust that you bought them a nice present, from us."

"I did, but there's something I have to tell you." She paused and took a deep breath. "I think you should know that Darius's wife-to-be is Black."

It took Bertram a few seconds to digest what she said. He looked up at Miriam, and his body was becoming rigid. Miriam thought he might faint, or worse.

"You can't be serious. A Negro. He's going to marry a Black Negro?"

"Yes." She sighed. Sooner.

"White Darius Deavers is going to marry someone Black."

"Yes." She didn't look at him.

"And didn't you say that you went shopping with her?"

"Yes."

"How could you do that?" he asked, turning red so that she knew he was getting riled, but he didn't faint. "It's as if you accept this, this whatever it is!"

"If she's his choice, who am I to oppose it?"

"You're my wife, that's who you are, and we're an important part of a certain society in this city, one that they can never be a part of, not if I have anything to do with it. I knew there was something wrong with him when we met him at your parents' home. He acted so devious. And his father, calling himself a reverend and accepting this…this atrocity! That's funny. No, it's not funny, it's ridiculous. Well, this changes a lot of things. I will not attend the ceremony or the reception, and you won't either. I forbid it, and let that be the last time you go anyplace with her." He stopped for a moment and shook his head from side to side as if clearing it of what she said.

"I can't imagine any White man in his right mind marrying someone Black. I won't even call her a Black lady." His negative thoughts carried him on to speak further. "And you know that means it's impossible for him to teach at the university. I'll tell them that."

"Them who?" she asked.

"The president and the committee."

"But it's so unfair that you've made this decision because she's Black, and I don't see what her color has to do with where he works, and besides, she's a very nice person. At least meet her. Please."

"Miriam, this discussion is over. Do you understand?"

"Yes." She looked at him, and she saw something she hadn't noticed before: he had hair on his fingers.

The news from her father was equally disappointing. "Your mother informed me that if I go to 'that charade,' and also if I continue being friends with that 'damn ignorant Darius Deavers,' she called him, well, she says she will divorce me."

"Oh, Daddy, I had a very negative response too. So I guess we won't be going."

"Well, it won't be the end of the world if we don't go, and anyway, it might be nicer if it's just Darius and Sage with their family and friend."

"We'll have to trust that things will work out good for them."

"Yep, and I'll be the brave one. I'll call Darius and tell him. I think he'll understand. All right, baby?"

"All right, Daddy. I love you."

"I love you more."

When Major Marvin Hawthorne called the hotel, it was Reverend Deavers who answered the phone.

"Hello."

"Yes, sir, this is Marvin Hawthorne. How are you doing today?" he asked, trying to calm himself.

"Good morning, Major. I'm blessed," Reverend Deavers said.

"I'm sorry, but I won't be able to…uh, attend the ceremony. There's been some"—pause—"problems with our schedules, and I know you all had planned riding with me in my van, you know. But as I said, I'm sorry, but I won't be able to go." He hurried on while he could without tearing up. "You have the schedule of the public transportation, and I understand it's a very scenic ride." There was a pause in his speech and in Reverend Deavers's reply. "I'm sorry," the major said again, breathing a sigh.

"Sir, I do understand," Reverend Deavers said. "You've done enough for us already, and we'll be fine. Don't you worry. We'll be quite all right." He imagined that this was going to be a normal occurrence here as Darius and Sage dealt with the racial climate, and he thought that the major's wife had very likely played a role in his refusal.

Major Hawthorne continued, "Miriam also sends her apologies. She and Bertram had some scheduling problems too."

The reverend and Darius received the news with sadness but also with understanding.

The next morning, they were all dressed for the wedding. Sage and Darius had again chosen to wear white.

"I'm not going to let them spoil my day," Sage said, standing and taking a deep breath. "You all are here, and you're the most important people in my life. It's too bad that Major Hawthorne won't be taking us in his van, but we'll be all right. So let's decide. Darius, sweetheart, do you think we can all fit in your car, or should we take public transportation?"

"You know that public transportation is segregated, don't you?" Burnett asked.

"Well, I think it's time somebody defied that, and I'd be willing to try it," Charles said.

"Wait just a minute," Sage said. "This is a very special day for me, and I'm not going to have it spoiled by any protest or any defiance of the law. We knew before we came that this city was full of prejudice, just like all the other cities in this country, and we came here because we can get legally married here. That's my goal, so whatever we have to do to get to the Peace Arch Park, which by the way is not segregated, let's do it."

"Bless your heart, Sage. You're so sensible," Reverend Deavers said.

"Yes, you are," Darius said, kissing her hand. "And I love you so much."

"So we'll take the scenic route on that public transportation," Sage said. "We'll all sit in the back, and we'll all be Black today."

And they did.

12

The train took the wedding party up through several cities, by ponds and works of art. It was truly a beautiful route and a beautiful experience.

The Peace Arch stands on the international boundary between Blaine, Washington, and Douglas, British Columbia. Its location is at the intersection of an international border of Canada and the United States. The American side of the arch is inscribed with the words, "Children of a Common Mother," the Canadian side with the words, "Brethren Dwelling Together in Unity." Within the portal of the arch on the west side are the words "1814 Open One Hundred Years 1914," and on the east side, "May These Gates Never Be Closed."

The park hosts ethnic and family gatherings, picnics, weddings, civic events, and annual events of international significance. The park gardens are the home of over two hundred perennials and fifty-five thousand annuals that are planted each year. It is a place of binational mingling. Since 1937, an annual celebration of "Hands Across the Border" has been held in the park, sponsored by the International Peace Arch Association. The history of the Peace Arch reflects more than our past; its existence gives meaning to our present and is a beacon of hope for our future.

The Ceremony

Reverend Paul Deavers, presiding.

REVEREND DEAVERS. Dearly beloved, we are gathered here in the sight of God and in the face of family and friends to join together Darius Paul Deavers and Ariel Sage Copple in holy matrimony. It is before this honorable estate, instituted by God signifying unto the union that is between Christ and His holy estate, that Darius and Sage come to be joined.

MRS. LUCY DEAVERS. From the Old Testament scripture, I'll be reading from the book of Ruth, where it is written, "Do not urge me to leave you or turn back from following you; for where you go, I will go, and where you lodge, I will lodge, your people shall be my people, and your God, my God."

ATTORNEY BURNETT COPPLE. From the New Testament scripture I'll be reading from First Corinthians, where it is written, "Though I speak with the tongues of men and of angels, but have not love, I am a noisy gong or a clanging cymbal. If I have the gift of prophecy and can understand all mysteries and all knowledge, and though I have all faith, so that I could remove mountains, and if I have not love, I am nothing... And now abideth faith, hope, and love, these three, but the greatest of these is love."

REVEREND DEAVERS. Let us pray. We thank you, God, that you have brought Darius Deavers and Sage Copple together, who on this day, April 3, 1947, are pledging their love to each other in holy matrimony. Keep them forever surrounded by your love and in your peace and grace. God, may you always be the center of their joy. May they always be ready to forgive each other, even as Christ forgives us. Bless them now that they will continue to find new ways and reasons to fall in love with each other over and over again. In Jesus's name, we pray. Amen.

Charles stepped forward with the rings.
Sage and Darius exchanged rings and said their wedding vows:

> SAGE. I take you, Darius Paul Deavers, to be my lawful wedded husband.
> DARIUS. I take you, Ariel Sage Copple, to be my lawful wedded wife.
> SAGE AND DARIUS (in unison). I love you now, and I will love you as you grow and become all that God intends for you. I will love you when we are together and when we are apart, when our lives are at peace and when trouble comes. I will be supportive of your goals and dreams, and I will do all that is in my power to help you fulfill them. We will rest together, work together, pray together, love our families, love our children, and love and honor God. We say this before God and man, knowing that they hear us.

Reverend Deavers lit the unity candle.

> REVEREND DEAVERS. The unity candle represents their endless love. Their two flames have

become one—to shine bright, to provide direction on their path, to provide heat to warm their hearts on days it may get cold, to be shown to all and not hid, for God has ordained this marriage.

Darius Paul Deavers and Ariel Sage Copple, by the authority invested in me by the Almighty God, as an ordained minister of the Gospel by the State of Washington, I do now, in the presence of this body, pronounce you husband and wife. Darius, you may kiss your wife. Sage, you may kiss your husband. Now go in faith, go in hope, go in love."

* * * * *

Going over to the Canadian side of the park, they enjoyed a beautiful reception there among the flowers and lakes and also the sunshine in their hearts. They ate fruit, green and yellow squash, cold ham, chicken, beef, buttered bread, ice cream, and cake. They drank fruit punch.

It was early evening when they arrived back at the hotel, and Reverend Deavers, the clearest in his thinking, had decided that he and his wife had done enough to prepare the couple for married life, and it was time to "give them their head" as was always said about anyone beginning a race, and they'd either win or lose but would run a good race.

"We'd like to give you our blessing, and then we'll be on our way. We think you can make it now on your own with love and God to guide you."

They made a circle, holding hands: Reverend Deavers and Mrs. Deavers, Charles and Burnett, Darius and Sage. Darius looked into Sage's eyes, and what he saw assured him of her love. She smiled her smile of acceptance and love.

Reverend Deavers prayed, "Dear God, who has brought these two into unity as one and has blessed them with a strong bond of love, lead them and guide them now on a smooth path as they share their lives together. We know you are a merciful God, and to you we pledge our honor in the name of the Father and the Son and the Holy Spirit now and forever more. Amen."

Mrs. Lucy Deavers said, "We'd like to give you a honeymoon to anywhere you want to go. The purpose of a honeymoon is to get away from family and familiar surroundings and to get to know each other."

"No," Sage said. "We'll have our honeymoon right here in our own lovely home. This is all new to us, the house and the city, even each other. I'd like for us to take some time, maybe a week, just the two of us to get to know each other better, you know, and decide what we want to accomplish now and in the future and how we'll go about it."

Darius listened, and he was still in a state of awe. He could only feel joy just being close to her, and finally being married to her was pure happiness for him.

"Yes," he said. "Of course, we will most definitely enjoy some time here alone, together, getting to know each other and getting to know ourselves in our new life and in our beautiful home." That was the plan.

Reverend and Mrs. Lucy Deavers and Burnett Copple bade goodbye to the newlyweds. They spent the night at the officers' quarters, and they left the next morning on an early flight.

13

After Reverend Deavers, his wife, and Burnett left, Charles thought about his purpose in life and why he had come to Washington. He had planned, basically, to use his education in law to become partners with Darius in their law firm, and the reason he had majored in law was the hope that he could practice in his hometown. He knew that there was only one Black lawyer who had an office there, and he was an old man. Seventy years old. *Now, however, I'm here in a different place from my original plans, but perhaps with the same needs. Given time and hard work, we might succeed, Darius and I.*

Besides his law degree, Charles was a trained and experienced lifeguard, so when he thought about his purpose in life, he couldn't ignore his strong talent and his avid love of swimming, so while waiting until they opened their office, he spent his days in doing some research into the water activities of the Black people of BeachSide, and he discovered some startling facts. However, not so startling because Black children in most segregated cities (and most cities were segregated) were below par in many things including swimming. Statistics showed that nearly 60 percent of Black children between the ages of six and sixteen cannot swim. Swimming pools—the same as hospitals, schools, housing, even cemeteries—were divided between "White only" and "Black only." There was one pool in the whole city where Black children were allowed to swim only on Thursday, and then the pool was drained and the water changed. Most beaches where swimming was allowed were for Whites, and the ones where Blacks were allowed, if they were brave enough to try and go there, they either got taunted with "Nigger, go home," or they got beat up, or White parents, on seeing them, would take their children and leave.

One day Charles visited the City Recreation Center for Blacks, and he learned that there was a gym with markings for basketball and rather ragged nets under each hoop. There was a ping-pong table but no balls or paddles, and when he asked the attendant, he was informed that they'd gotten broken, and there was no money in this month's budget for new ones. There was no swimming pool in operation inside or out. The question in his mind and on his heart was, *How does this compare with the city recreation centers in the White neighborhoods, which were off-limits to Blacks? And how can I find an answer if I'm not allowed entrance? I could ask Darius to visit those centers for Whites, and then Darius could inform me, but knowing and seeing the situation firsthand is better than secondhand information from another person's observance. Hmm.* This was his dilemma.

14

Standing at the threshold of his new life, his new house, and his new wife, Darius Paul Deavers was filled with a feeling of elation and delight and renewed love as he looked at Sage. The memory of all the frustrations and warnings that had led up to this moment were erased by his present joy and happiness. All the hateful feelings that so many people had toward his relationship with her were like a bad dream from which he had awakened. He wanted his life with her to evoke only pleasant dreams and pleasant awakenings. He had sacrificed a good job, familiar surroundings, and yes, marrying someone of his own race for the blessed enchantment of being here at their own home, alone with Sage Copple, now Sage Deavers—and, oh, the joy that filled his soul. He remembered Kahlil Gibran's words on love: "When love beckons to you, follow him though his ways are hard and steep."

Standing outside in front of the locked door, Sage thought about some of the traditions and beliefs that were prevalent about a couple on first entering their new home. The idea for carrying the bride over the threshold originated generations ago with the belief that a newlywed couple was very susceptible to evil spirits that lurked on the lower levels, and by carrying the bride over the threshold, the groom was putting a protective space between her and the floor. In one country, a large piece of satin cloth was laid on the floor, and the first one to step on it, after being blindfolded and spun around, would be the boss of the household.

But Sage was not concerned about any of those traditions. Her soul, mind, and spirit were filled with joy, peace, and love. She wanted to leave behind all the doubts and fears and look only forward and to think of being happy. This was a new life and a new beginning, and as a newborn child, it needs nurturing, caring for, in order to grow and stay alive. "Till death do us part" meant that for all of her life, she would revel in the joy of his presence, of his love, of his strength, and of their being equal.

She remembered Kahlil Gibran's words on marriage: "Let there be spaces in your togetherness, and stand together, yet not too near together, for the pillars of the temple stand apart, and the oak tree and the cypress grow not in each other's shadow."

Darius put his hand on top of hers, so they both turned the key and opened the door at the same time. He took her hand, and she took his, and they stepped across the proverbial threshold together, at the same time.

They spent the first entire week of being married just getting to know each other better. Sleeping together. Bathing together. Laughing together. Sharing back rubs and shoulder massages. Sitting on the couch at night listening to Chopin. Sipping wine. Holding hands. Walking through their new home together. Naked. Making love. They knelt down together each night, holding hands and saying the Lord's Prayer together. Then they prayed for each other, their parents, and they gave thanks for their life and their love. It was a marvelous way to end the day. Peace. Love. Joy. Happiness.

Darius's heart still skipped a beat each time he realized that he and Sage were really and truly married, and every time he kissed her, which was often and delightfully enchanting, he thought to himself, *I never want to be parted from her one second, and I wouldn't be, for when I am not beside her physically, I am filled with her presence mentally.*

Sage was back on the farm remembering when she first saw Darius, a little blond-haired, blue-eyed White boy. *It really must have been love at first sight because somehow I never forgot about him, and as way leads onto way, our paths were constantly crossing. I don't think we actually knew when love began, but we felt its presence long before we were actually sure of what it was. When he first kissed me, I was sure, and now I know that I want to be near him for the rest of my life.*

The morning of the second week, Darius lingered in bed for a few minutes just thinking about her. Sage. Dear Sage. He always called her by her given name even though he often added a word of endearment. He was happy when he went down to the kitchen, kissed her on the mouth, and she took his hand in hers.

"I want to help," he said, and Sage smiled, knowing that this was new to him.

Following her instructions, he placed the dishes at their places, she filled the plates, and he poured the orange juice. She made the toast, and he poured the milk and the coffee. They shared the blessing of the food. Some of the chores they shared were necessary to be done now, but he sat her down, took her hand, as she had done his.

"This is fine for now while we're alone, but I want us to have some domestic help. You decide what you want, and I'll get it for you. I know you want to do some tutoring, so I don't want you to be burdened down with housework," he said.

She smiled. She agreed, and even though she wondered about having a maid—domestic help, as he had said—they each felt the soft entrance, like a cool summer breeze on a hot day, of a new beginning, a new togetherness, a new kind of sharing.

Having been raised rich with everything done for him, all the household chores done for the family, he hadn't thought about who made the beds, cooked their meals, and did the laundry. He never had to think about those things. Even when he was a student at the university, he was provided with a housekeeper who cleaned his living quarters and did his laundry. He had no idea how to make a bed.

A new feeling of joy filled his being, and that feeling, he knew, came from the knowledge that a new life was starting for him. Before they were married, he could only think of the time they would be together in each other's arms in their own home, loving and being loved, far from the madding crowd. That's what he thought about. Only that.

Now Darius Deavers had to look at his wife and at his marriage in a different way. *Sage is more than just the joy of your life. She is your wife and entitled, as your wife, to live a life different from how her mother's life had been. She is entitled to all the benefits and privileges of your money, and yes, loving her as you do, you can reprogram your mind to understand some of her culture, and you can share some of yours with her.*

Sage shared some information about corn, stemming from his questions about cornbread. "The ear of corn is covered with corn silk, so my sister showed me how to make a corn-silk doll. Hominy is hulled and dried kernels of corn, prepared as food by boiling. Corn meal is ground from corn. Popcorn is made from dried kernels of corn."

During the next week, Darius made corn bread. He learned how to change the bedsheets and put on clean ones, tucking under the ends and folding the corners of the sheets, and how to mop the kitchen floor and vacuum the carpets. Sage shampooed his hair and was introduced to Brylcreem. Darius shampooed her hair and was introduced to hair oil. Darius learned to cook collard and turnip and mustard greens. She washed the dishes, and he dried. He washed the dishes, and she dried. They laughed and laughed. And they laughed.

On the morning of their third week of marriage, Sage and Darius stood on the back porch of their new home and breathed in the warm morning air. It was such a lovely time of the year with tiny buds beginning to burst forth into leaves and making the trees, asleep and bare in winter, come alive to provide shade or fruit or just beauty for the beholder.

As she thought about her future, she knew that she wanted a large portion of her dedication to be to her marriage, and her beautiful home and her loving husband, and to the delightful anticipation of her own children. However, she also wanted to use her education and to channel her other energies into helping Black children learn to read; and knowing how to read, she thought to herself, is so fundamental in life. It opens doors for much-needed qualification and direction.

In thinking about how he could share some of his culture with her, he knew that she did not know how to drive a car.

"You will need your own transportation," Darius said, "for not knowing where this chosen quest will lead you, getting around in the city is a necessity."

Sage gathered up her nerve and finally agreed when Darius insisted she learn to drive. He bought a car for her, and they went each morning for her lesson. He laughed at her the first day as she tried to master the clutch. The city was so hilly, and driving was so thought-provoking, and she had to think about what she was doing with her feet, each one differently, first the clutch, the gas pedal, and the brake. She had to think about what she was doing with her hands, shifting gears, and at the same time keeping her eyes on the road. "Oh my," she said.

Darius was extremely patient with her, although he had a couple of frightening moments. Once when she couldn't get her coordination right, the car started to roll backward down one of those steep hills. Another time, she was trying to shift into second and went through a red light. Luckily, he had chosen sparsely traveled streets and early mornings when traffic was light. It was a calming feeling for her when she looked at him and instead of looking annoyed at her mistakes, he was smiling, and he reached over and patted her hand.

"It's all right, Sage darling. It gets easier as time goes by."

And he was right. After a while, she lost her nervousness, asking for peace and absence of fear. She took her guardian angel with her, and when she finally got her license and went out on her own, she felt at ease.

On Saturday of that third week, Sage and Darius began thinking of church. Their Sunday agenda, for both their lives, had been to attend church. Both were raised in a Baptist church, but they knew that churches in BeachSide were not integrated.

"Then how do we choose? I go to a White church and you go to a Black church?" He looked at her, and he knew it was important that this kind of situation be settled now. He could see the sadness on Sage's beautiful face, and he knew he was the one to decide.

"Whatever we do, babe, I want us to do it together," Darius said. "So we'll go to a Black Baptist church. They'll accept me, whereas a White Baptist church won't accept you."

Sage agreed, but she knew that besides church, it would be necessary for her to enjoy some Black activities without him; and vice versa, he would find enjoyment in some White activities without her.

Hopefully, neither situation would cause a rift in their marriage or a lessening of their love for each other.

The Wise Counselor said, "You have been joined together in love and marriage, and you must find a way to live this life together."

So on Sunday morning, dressed in their Sunday's best, they went to the Black Baptist church of their choice. Charles went with them. When the minister said, "The doors of the church are open. Give me your hand and God your heart," they stood and walked down the aisle together—Sage and Darius and Charles.

A few eyebrows were raised but were, as quickly, put down. Darius received the same warm handshakes and hugs as did Sage and Charles. Darius fought back the tears of happiness as he felt he had not only become a part of her Black life, but he had become a part of his own life, not being defined only by his color but also by his belief. His bravery was a testimony to his love of God, his love for Sage, and his strong friendship with Charles. However, included in the word *testimony* is the word *test*, which might also include a test of his love of God, his closeness with Sage, and his strong friendship with Charles.

"Where did I find you?" Sage asked, putting her arms around him and kissing him on the cheek. "You're absolutely too wonderful to be human." Her feeling at that time was also a testimony but would also be a test for her later.

"Those whom God has joined, let no man put asunder."

"What does *asunder* mean?" Charles asked.

"It means ain't nobody gonna take this jewel away from me."

"Okay," Charles said. "I'm hungry. Let's go somewhere and eat." And they did, and after enjoying a friendly meal, Charles went home.

When Sage and Darius returned home from eating, they found an envelope stuck in the door, and there were rocks in the yard, and there were two signs. One read, "Nigger, read and run. If you can't read, run anyhow." Inside the envelope was this message: "This is a restricted area. No race or nationality other than of the White or Caucasian race is allowed to occupy this property. Under no circumstance will it be owned, leased, or rented to Negroes or any person of Negro blood. There is a legal covenant preventing it."

A lump of sadness formed in Sage's heart, but she was determined not let it overcome her. She remembered feeling the same kind of pain when her mother told her that they had to sit in the back of the bus. *Why, Mamma? Because we're Black.*

But, she thought, *I remember that as I grew up, finished high school at my all-Black school, finished college at my all-Black college, I was proud of myself, and my family was proud of me. And I thought that everything in my life would be all right. But now, married to the only man I ever loved and the only man I ever wanted to marry and moving to Washington and thinking it would work out smoothly, I'm back on the bus. I was able to remove myself and my mind from all of it then, and by the grace of God, I will do the same now.*

The other sign was worse. It read, "Go fuck it somewhere else." Sage looked at the beautiful white clouds, and she smiled as she saw in her mind's eye her angels sitting up there on one of them, smiling down at them. And she remembered her mother's words: "Don't let them steal your joy."

Darius, however, felt a tear drop. He had grown up in a family setting, with a mother and father who loved each other and loved him. He knew he wanted to be married too and to raise a family, and now he was married to the only woman he ever loved, and he knew he had to call up all his strength to either live with the restrictive laws or find a way to fight them. He thought of the song with the lyrics, "Like a tree that's planted by the water, I shall not be moved," which was really hopeful thinking. He put his arms around his wife, and they went into the house.

15

On Monday morning of the fourth week, sitting alone at his desk in their office, Darius had to consciously strive to move Sage from his presence in order to get his mind focused on his work. His wanting to be with her, to hold her, was a strong and ever-present sensation.

After Darius and Charles had become partners in their own law firm, in order to avoid conflict, they decided Charles would handle domestic cases like divorce, child support, restraining orders, and domestic violence. Darius would focus his attention on cases involving racial segregation in housing, education, and jobs. They would spend the morning hours at the office, and in the afternoon, they would be free to pursue any other plans they might have in pursuit of their goals.

They would start each day with this prayer: "Lord, let this day be one that is profitable and highly productive of good. This is a new day. Help us to live this day with enthusiasm and joy. With your help, we know that all things will work together for good in our personal lives and in our business ventures. You are our refuge and our fortress. It is in you that we place our trust. We thank you for your blessing. Amen."

Now, hearing footsteps coming down the stairs, Darius stood and greeted Charles as he entered the room. Charles was dressed in a business suit, matching shirt and tie, and he carried his new leather briefcase. Darius noticed that there seemed to be a pleasant air about Charles. He was smiling, so Darius smiled.

"We really have to advertise. Let the people know that we are here, one Black and one White. Sometimes Blacks think that White professionals know more, and they trust them more than they do Blacks. But sometimes they trust Black professionals more than they do White. Then there is a great number of Blacks who don't trust anyone," Charles said.

"We'll try to find a way to make all of them trust us. Both of us. We won't discourage White clients, but we won't assist them with any complaints they might have against Blacks as their complaints would, of a certainty, stem from hate and prejudice," Darius said. Charles agreed.

They put their artistic hats on and began to create flyers and business cards. They wrote letters and sent ads to the newspapers. They posted their professionally made sign "DEAVERS & WILLIAMS, Attorneys."

As soon as their sign went up, they had a visitor. The White man introduced himself as representative of a newly formed group whose first direct action was to challenge segregation on interstate buses.

"So far," the visitor said, "we have twelve men who signed up to participate, five Black and seven White. We plan to take a trip in the northern states where buses are still segregated, you understand. We'll board a bus and sit together in the seats designated for White only. I'd like to have your participation, either as our lawyer or as one of the riders. Since we're newly formed, we don't have much of a treasure built up, so each man would be responsible for his own expenses. I didn't know, when I saw the sign that you were White, and you're mighty brave to set up business in the Black neighborhood. But don't misunderstand me, we welcome you."

Darius wasn't surprised at this reaction, and his feeling evoked a smile from him.

"I'd certainly like to join you," Darius said. "But my consideration for a protest would be segregation in housing. We've purchased a house on Beach Street, and already we've had rocks and some mean signs in the yard."

"Why would they throw rocks in your yard? You're White, aren't you?" he said, smiling.

"Yes, I am." Darius chuckled. It was at this moment that Charles entered from his upstairs living quarters. Darius made the introductions. "This is my partner, Attorney Charles Williams." And Darius saw that confusion reigned. He knew the visitor was asking if Charles was his wife and if they were a gay couple.

"Does he live with you?" the visitor asked.

"Attorney Williams doesn't live with me. My wife is Black."

Darius smiled and looked out the window to allow his visitor to catch his breath and to overcome his shock and wonder. Outside the window, across the street, Darius could see that spring was unfolding. The daytime temperatures were warm and sunny. New grass was sprouting. A robin flew and lighted on a bare limb as the trees didn't have many new leaves. *Wait*, he said in his mind to the robin, *the leaves will come.*

This man's reaction was not new to Charles Williams. Not one person had said, "How nice" or "Congratulations." And Darius knew what most people, including this visitor, were thinking: *Why? Why, when you have all the privileges life can offer, would you burden yourself thusly? In a Black neighborhood with a Black partner and a Black wife.*

"Sir," Darius said, "it's good to meet you, and at a later time, I might seriously consider becoming a member of your group. But I'm sorry, right now I can't take the time off from my own agenda to participate in the ride."

"How about you?" the visitor asked, directing his attention to Charles.

"I'm sorry, sir. You see, we've only been here a short while, and I'm also in the planning stage of my agenda here. Maybe I can help in some way later on down the road, but not now."

"I understand, but for your information, we're planning to follow an example which was set by the group who call themselves CORE: the Congress of Racial Equality. They planned and carried out a 'journey of reconciliation.' It was a form of nonviolent, direct action to challenge segregation laws on interstate buses in the

Southern United States. Here is copy of the report we received. You can read it at your leisure."

The article was titled "Journey Of Reconciliation." It read,

The Journey of Reconciliation was a form of nonviolent direct action to challenge segregation laws on interstate buses in the southern United States. Sixteen men from the Congress of Racial Equality took part, eight White and eight Black. Also taking part were the organizers, some ministers, students, and professional people. They planned to ride public transportation in Virginia, North Carolina, Tennessee, and Kentucky—all with segregated systems.

During the two-week bus trip, Blacks sat in the front seats, and Whites sat in the back. Sometimes Blacks and Whites sat side by side. Although they were supported by a recent US Supreme Court ruling which prohibited segregation in interstate travel as being unconstitutional, the Southern states were refusing to enforce the court's decision.

The riders received death threats. Some were knocked unconscious. They were arrested. When they went before the Southern court, there were Bibles for swearing in Whites and Bibles for swearing in Blacks. The White clerk would not hold the Bible for the Blacks, so they had to call a Black person to do that. One judge who expressed his distaste for the White men involved said, "It's about time you Jews [referring to the White men' from New York learned you can't come down here bringing your niggers with you and try and upset the customs of the South. Just to teach you a lesson, I'm giving you Black boys thirty days on a chain gang, but I'm giving you White boys ninety."

When the riders were asked if it was worth it, they replied, "Yes. Although no laws were changed in the South, we did have a success with the first Black player in the big leagues. [The reference was to Jackie Robinson.]"

Every night, Darius and Sage saw that more rocks were thrown into the yard, and some days there were trash and bottles, some empty and some filled with urine.

Should we stay here and fight? Or should we just move into an all-Black neighborhood now, and we could avoid all this meanness? These were Darius's thoughts.

16

Almost two months had gone by since the young couple's marriage, and during that time, Major Marvin Hawthorne's thoughts hardly strayed from them, and he wondered how they were doing and if he could be of any help to them.

Once a month, the major and his wife had Miriam and her family over for breakfast and once a month for dinner. The breakfasts were on Saturday when most of their schedules weren't so full. Now, however, there remained the estrangement between the major and his wife, Alicia, which was caused by the phone call, so there was not the possibility of either family breakfasts or dinners at their house.

When Bertram questioned his wife about Alicia's reasons for not honoring the tradition, Miriam couldn't tell him about the phone call; therefore, she couldn't tell him the reason for her mother's anger.

"Mom wasn't feeling well, so she decided to just rest today." This was basically the truth, but not the whole truth. "We could go out and eat, if you like," Miriam said.

"You know, I am required to go to so many lunches and dinners at my job, so I'm rather tired of eating out," Bertram said.

"Is it okay if I call my dad?" she asked. "He and I can perhaps go someplace and eat. He might be feeling the need for company, and I'm sure Mom will be all right by herself for a while."

He hesitated for a moment. "Sure. Sure. I don't mind you doing that." He required that she get his permission for everything she did.

When she called her father, the major asked, "What about Bertram? Did you tell him the reason Alicia canceled?"

"No, I didn't want to get into any discussions with him about that. Then I'd have to listen to all the rhetoric about his prejudices. You know he'd agree with Mom, so I just told him that Mom wasn't feeling well."

"And will Timothy be coming with you?"

"No, he wanted to stay and play with his new toy."

Major Hawthorne was pleased with his daughter's invitation, and he really wanted to get out of the atmosphere that was permeating his home.

"Let's invite Darius and Sage to come and have breakfast with us. We can go to the Pancake House. They serve everybody," Miriam said after her father had picked her up. He recognized that Miriam felt drawn to Darius and Sage, and she wanted to be Sage's friend. She never really had any close girl friends, and since being married, she was kept isolated. She never had a sister, and she often felt the need to have the kind of talks that sisters near the same age could share, especially those who were married.

Stopping at a phone booth, Marvin Hawthorne called, and when Sage answered the phone, he invited her and Darius to come out and have breakfast with them.

"That's very kind of you," Sage said, "but we've already started making our breakfast. Maybe some other time."

"Who is it, dear?" Darius asked.

"Just a moment, Major," Sage said. "It's Major Hawthorne, and he and Miriam want us to come and have breakfast with them."

"At their house?" Darius asked, thinking that he had not been there since Sage arrived, and the major's wife had not met Sage.

"No, at a restaurant," Sage said.

"Here, let me talk to him," Darius said, going to the phone. "Sir, we've already started preparing our breakfast, and Charles is here, so why don't you and Miriam come and eat with us. It wouldn't be a problem, and it would afford us a very great pleasure."

"We wouldn't want to impose. Maybe some other time."

"No imposition. None at all, and we won't take no for an answer. Besides we haven't seen you since our marriage. Come. Please come."

And they did.

After Miriam left her house, Bertram Withers and his son, Timothy, sat at their breakfast table eating cereal. Bertram looked at his son and smiled. He noticed, however that Timothy seemed to be playing with his cereal, rather than eating. Timothy was a beautiful child with his light brown curls, which matched his light brown eyes.

Bertram Ambrose Withers's life was devoted to his employment. His position as head of the law department at the University was his first thought for every minute of his day and night, for he regularly had meetings and business dinners at night. He had worked hard and tirelessly from his beginning as a law professor, and he had worked himself up to being head of the entire law department. His duties were to oversee the complex academic and research needs of the department. Although this was a lofty position, Bertram Withers's ambition looked higher. He had hopes and aspirations of becoming president of the university. His ambition overshadowed every other aspect of his life, including his family. Bertram was proud of his family, especially his well-bred, sophisticated, and well-mannered wife, not because he loved her so much but because she and their son were necessary only as personal assets to depict him as an upstanding and respected family man. He attended church regularly with his family, which portrayed him as a Christian (which was also a necessary part of his act) and a very responsible person.

After he finished eating, and Timothy was busy with his toys, Bertram went into his study, read some papers, signed some correspondence, and made some necessary phone calls. His time was held to a very strict schedule. His son was quite fond of his grandparents, and he loved going to their house to eat. Alicia always made him feel special. For breakfast, she made happy-face pancakes for him, and she always had a present, some knick-knack or a toy car, beside his plate or under his chair. Now, sitting on the floor trying to think about his playthings, his mind was occupied with his grandmother.

"Daddy," he called.

"Yes. What is it?" Bertram asked, coming out of his study.

"Can we go and see how Grandma is feeling?" he asked. "She might need something."

"I guess we could go over for a few minutes, but she might not feel like making you any smiley-face pancakes."

"I know, and that's all right." Timothy was quite astute in his thinking capacity.

Bertram wondered why his father-in-law would leave his sick wife to have breakfast with his daughter, but he didn't linger on the thought. He dropped his correspondence off at the post office, and he and his son went to check on his mother-in-law.

Alicia Yvonne Hawthorne was born and raised in the state of Washington in a life of plenty. Although her parents weren't considered to be rich, they were in the category of "those with money." They lived in an upper-class district, strictly White and strictly privileged. Her father spent his early years working as a merchant seaman. Later he moved into a more profitable venture in the shipping business, and when he became involved in the shipment of pianos, he gave his daughter a beautiful grand piano as a birthday gift. It was only natural that she took an interest in music, and as time passed, she became a member of the board of the City Symphony Orchestra.

Alicia had met Marvin Hawthorne at one of the symphony concerts given at the army base to which Marvin was assigned. They had a brief courtship and were married while he was stationed as a commissioned officer in Washington. They bought the house they now live in, and he was often required to travel to other military bases on business. Alicia only chose to travel with her husband during the summer months. After her parents passed and she married Marvin Hawthorne, Alicia kept up an interest in cultural things, especially the symphony concerts, and she took Miriam with her. Miriam was raised in that cultural environment.

Marvin, however, was not a lover of classical music, and he only went to the concerts because she insisted, but he kept up his habits of Friday-night ball games and beer with his friends. Alicia always resented that part of him as she was not a sports enthusiast, nor was she a very social person. She had no close lady friends and no one she talked with often or personally. She participated in swimming lessons at the YMCA once a week with Miriam as her life was dedicated to her daughter and her grandson. She never worked outside the home, and she took care of Timothy until he was two years old and potty-trained. Then Miriam took him to day care, and when he was five, he entered kindergarten.

This bright spring morning, Alicia Hawthorne was sitting in her lounge chair staring at nothing in particular, and in spite of the brightness of the morning, both her thoughts and her mood were in a dark corner of the room.

Of course, it's true, she was thinking. *He has worked around those people during his army adult life, and his travels have kept him away from home for long periods, and I know that men have needs. He is so handsome and friendly, and he is a social animal, so of course, it's true. Otherwise, why would someone fabricate such a story if there weren't the possibility of it being true? Oh hell. That Sage girl is Marvin's daughter. I'd bet money on that. Oh, I hate him so much, and I don't think I can live with him anymore. Of course, it's true,* she kept telling herself. *He is the father of that Black girl. And what about Miriam? Her life would be ruined if she found out that she has a Black sibling. And that means he has had sexual relations with one of them, and damn it, he has a child who is half Black and half White, half Hawthorne and half monkey. And what kind of name is Sage? It's a bush. It's also a herb that you can cook with. Yes. Put her in a pot like the Africans do and boil her. Get rid of the little monster.*

Alicia asked herself, *What can I do? What should I do? Can I go on living with him as though nothing has happened? A divorce would be as catastrophic as the reasons for it. I need help.* She was thinking these thoughts when the doorbell rang. She was not expecting anyone, and Marvin would not ring the bell, so she wasn't going to answer, but she heard Timothy's voice from outside the door.

"Grandma, Grandma, it's me, Timothy. Open the door."

Alicia didn't want Timothy to see or feel her anger and frustration, and she was able to hold back the tears that were so close to making an appearance. But as soon as she had him settled with the new toy she had bought for him, she took Bertram into the other room, out of the child's hearing, and she couldn't prevent the pouring out of her tears. All those who were close to Bertram and who had personal contact with hi——students, secretaries, even his son—knew that he felt tears were a sign of fear and weakness. Both Timothy and Miriam were very aware of his inability to see a reason for tears and his anger on seeing them. "Men don't cry," he'd tell Timothy, and "Enough with the tears," he'd tell his wife.

Now, although Alicia's tears made him cringe, he reasoned that maybe she had some very serious health problems, and she had gotten a bad doctor's report, so he swallowed his feeling about tears and crying.

"Do you want to tell me why you're crying? Is there something I can do to help?" he asked, knowing he couldn't bid her to stop crying, although he wanted to do just that.

Alicia told him about the phone call and the threat. She told him about her husband's denial, about her anger with him, and about Miriam's words of consolation. Bertram Withers was stunned by her words, and it took a moment for him to think about the whole of it, including her saying that Miriam knew, for his wife had not mentioned it to him.

"Do you think you could do some research for me and find out about that girl?" she asked, knowing that Bertram was a professional in the field of research.

"Yes," he said, speaking slowly, "that's possible. I guess I could do that for you. But have you met the girl? Do you know what she looks like?"

"No, I haven't met her, and I'm not anxious to meet her."

"I haven't met her either, but maybe you could pretend you've reconciled with your husband, and you could have them over for our monthly family dinner, and we could get a good look at her. And you can also see how your husband looks at her. Do you think you could do that?"

"I suppose I could, if you think it will help to solve this damn mystery."

"It couldn't hurt, and in the meantime, I'll see what I can find out. I'll put my research team on it right away," he promised.

"Her name is Ariel Sage Copple, now Deavers, and she's from Oklahoma, and she's Black."

When Major Hawthorne and Miriam arrived at Darius and Sage's house, they were saddened to see a large number of rocks in the yard and a mean and hateful sign which was nailed to a stick and planted in the yard. The sign displayed the words "ANNA—AIN'T NO NIGGERS ALLOWED."

Miriam picked up the rocks, and the major pulled the awful sign out of the ground; and when Darius answered the doorbell and opened the door for them, the major saluted.

"Did you know they were out there?" Miriam asked, breathing a sigh and shaking her head from side to side in sadness.

"Oh yes, we knew," Darius said. "They're an every-night occurrence, but I decided to leave them there and let them accumulate for a while."

"Why are they doing this?" Miriam asked.

"They're trying to make us move," Darius said, inviting them in.

"Will you?" Marvin asked.

"Well, of course, we can't move today. First, we have to find someplace to move." Darius showed them the covenant letter, but Major Hawthorne already knew that this was a restricted neighborhood.

Miriam bowed her head, and looking up at Sage, she tried to think about the whole scenario. *All this hate because this beautiful young lady is Black? Oh my.*

"I just hope they won't do anything worse, like setting fire to the house or shooting us," Sage said.

"Do you know who's doing all this?" Marvin asked.

"No, but there're only eight houses in this block, so it has to be one of them, or all of them," Darius said.

It took a moment for them to digest the situation, but then they all decided to have a peaceful meal and think about positive things. At least for now.

"We brought you some presents," Miriam said, breaking the silence.

"Thank you," Darius said.

"Welcome to our home," Sage said, walking from the kitchen and accepting the beautifully wrapped boxes.

"Are you sure this isn't an imposition?" Marvin asked.

"Not at all, and thank you for the gifts," Sage said, taking Darius's hand and giving him one of her loving smiles, her green eyes looking at him with admiration.

"We're very glad you've come," Darius said, emphasizing the word *very* and returning a loving look to Sage and giving her the semblance of a kiss. "Sit down here," he said, indicating a couple of empty chairs at the table.

"You're our first guests, except Charles, but of course, he's like family."

Charles was already seated at the table, and he stood and greeted them, standing until they were seated. "Good morning. So good to see you again," he said.

"And you as well," Miriam said as she and her father reached out and shook his hand.

"And your husband?" Darius asked, addressing Miriam.

"Oh, he always has some kind of work that needs to be taken care of, and Timothy was happy to stay home and play with his trains."

"We usually have breakfast at least once a month on Saturday at our house, but Alicia wasn't feeling well today, so we're glad we could spend this time with you all," Marvin said.

The situation seemed a little odd to Darius, but he didn't ask any more questions. He remembered that Mrs. Hawthorne had not felt well when his family arrived, and neither the Hawthorne nor Withers family had been able, for whatever reasons, to go with them to the Peace Arch for their marriage ceremony. He looked at Sage, and she could read his thoughts, for she was asking the same questions in her mind.

"Well, make yourselves comfortable. I'm so happy to see you. I'll just throw some more pancakes on the grill and fry up some more bacon," Sage said. And she wasn't being false as it was a part of her culture, for her mother always welcomed guests into her home, and she always offered them some kind of food and drinks.

Miriam began to feel surrounded by a comfortable aura that she was among friends. It was a different atmosphere than at her home, where guests were always there by invitation only with the expectation to RSVP, acceptance, or apologies—yes or no. And the guests were always business associates of her husband, and the wives who came were there by requirement, trying to give the impression that this was a family affair. At such times, Miriam felt like her husband was king in this chess game, and she was a pawn, the one of the lowest value. She always felt as if she was just someone who was used for Bertram's business purposes. She knew how to act the part of a gracious hostess and to have a tasty meal prepared and served by hired help.

"I can certainly help," Miriam said, standing and going into the kitchen with Sage. She felt that she and Sage were queens, the most powerful chess pieces.

"Thank you," Sage said, giving Miriam an apron and experiencing a warmth of friendliness yet a shade of uneasiness because Miriam was White.

The three men, all having served time in the military, did not feel at all like strangers to one another. Their everyday meals had been shared by persons from different sections of the country and different levels of culture. Charles became aware that he was a minority in this company of Whites, yet he didn't feel like the "fly in the buttermilk," as his uncle said when in the company of Whites, and it was probably because he felt the warm presence of Sage as she patted him on the shoulder. Darius was feeling that he'd just won the office jackpot, and he was sharing it with his friends by treating them to breakfast as they were his only friends in this city. And Major Hawthorne was feeling like the father of them all, and they'd just become of age, and he was here to help them in their new life pursuits.

Sage indicated a holding of hands for the blessing. It was like a needle had been threaded with a thread of peace, love, and joy and sewn through this group of friends.

"Dear Lord," Sage said, "thank you for the food we are about to receive and thank you for our guests who are here as friends, and thank you for the blessing of our little corner of peace. We look to you to take care of all the hate from outside. Amen."

"Oh, what a lucky man you are, Darius," Marvin said. "You've found that illusive jewel in the haystack."

"Daddy, I think what they found in the haystack was a needle." She chuckled. "But since you're talking about Sage, it was surely a gold or diamond needle."

"They might have found a needle, but Darius found Sage, and she is a precious jewel, and she outshines them all." The Major was thinking how calm and unbothered Sage seemed to be despite all the prejudice and hate which was right outside in the front yard.

They enjoyed the tasteful meal and the pleasant company, but each had in the back of their mind that this would not last.

"We want you to know that we're here to offer our help. Just name it, and we'll see what we can do to help," Marvin said.

"Sage, I see you haven't hired any help yet. I can ask my mom's maid Mamie to recommend someone to work for you, if you like," Miriam said.

Sage breathed a sigh and looked at Darius, and he responded for her.

"We've talked about that, and my darling wife has some definite ideas about it, and I'm not sure that she's ready to share them with anyone."

"Oh, I don't mind since I feel we're among friends. You see, my mother was a cook and laundress for White people."

"For my parents," Darius said.

"And although she was treated well, she was still the colored help, and we were always classified as lesser. So I don't know how I would look upon a Black servant in my house or how she would feel about me. I've never had a house of my own, so all this is new to me. Thanks for offering your help with the maid situation, but I'll wait a while."

"Oh, dear, it's different, isn't it?" Miriam asked, almost in tears. "I try to imagine how I'd feel if I were Black, and I can't. You and Charles are the only Black people I've ever had any social contact with, and for some reason, I don't feel that I'm White and you're Black. Why is that? I haven't been able to figure it out."

"It's because of the heart and not the eyes," Sage said. "Your heart has taken over, and you can't stop it. We are defined as Black and White because our skin color is different, but our hearts are the same color."

"Hey. That's enough of this pity party," Marvin said. "Now what can I do for the three of you? How about you, Charles? Is there some way we can help you?" he asked.

"Well, other than law, my interest is in finding places where Black children can swim," Charles said. "I was a lifeguard during the summer months in my hometown, so I have a lot of experience in that area. I visited the Black recreation center here, and it is woefully ill-equipped. But there must be some good folk around here someplace who can help me. I'd like to talk to the director at the White center and ask his help, but I'm sure they won't allow me to go in any of them."

"Perhaps I can speak to the director at the center where mom and I swim and see if he would help you," Miriam said. "I know you're not allowed to swim there or even to belong as a member, but I'm sure he can tell you where to go for help. It is city-owned, you know."

"So is the Black center," Charles said.

"Why don't you come by Wednesday morning, that's when my mom and I have our swim class. I take her home around ten, and then I can come back, say around eleven, and maybe if I ask him, he'll at least let you look around and tell you where to go for help."

"That sounds like a right good idea. Thank you, I'll do just that," Charles said.

"How about you, Sage? Can we help you with anything?" Major Hawthorne asked.

"My plan," Sage said, "is to get a list of the Black elementary schools and go to each one and ask if I can start a reading program for the children who need help. Thanks for your offer to help," she said to Major Hawthorne. "But you see, now that I have my own my transportation, I'm sure I can do this."

"You have your own transportation?" he asked.

"Yes, and my darling husband put his nerves in a paper sack and taught me to drive."

"Bully for him, but If you need any help, my dear, just let me know, and I'll do what I can," Major Hawthorne said.

"Thank you," Sage said.

Darius poured coffee and they were all silent for a while, and then he spoke.

"As you know, Charles and I have opened our own law office, and we'll have to wait and see what kind of cases we get, but now, since moving into this house, this neighborhood, where I would be welcome if it weren't for my beautiful wife, who, in the eyes of me and God has every right to live here, I'd like to see if I can use some of my legal knowledge to fight this restrictive covenant in housing."

"You know, that might be an uphill battle, especially by yourself," Major Hawthorne said. "Think about this. We can canvass some of the White neighborhoods, you know, knock on doors where there's a 'For Sale' sign and ask if they would consider selling to a Black family."

"I guess I'd be willing to try that," Darius said. "It could be a start."

So their plans were developed. Charles would go to the White recreation center, and Miriam would speak to the director to see if there was any way to get help for the Black community. Sage would research the Black elementary schools to ask if any of them would allow her to tutor the students who needed help with their reading. Darius and Major Hawthorne would go into the restricted neighborhoods and knock on doors where there was a "For Sale" sign in the yard and ask if they'd be willing to sell to Negroes.

They ate. They shared peaceful conversation. They said their goodbyes with hugs and handshakes, and as Miriam and Marvin were getting into their car to leave, Sage looked at them and smiled. Despite never having been so close to anyone White as a friend, she felt they had come and left as friends.

17

Evidently, Charles hadn't listened when Miriam told him what time to come—at eleven, she said, after she took her mother home—for she didn't want him to come while her mother was still there. Unfortunately, he went at ten, parked his car, and asked his inner self for courage. He walked boldly through the front door as if he had a right to be there. Even though he could feel his heartbeat knocking against his chest and perspiration forming on his brow, he looked straight ahead for signs that would lead him to the director's office, where he thought Miriam would be.

So far, so good. No one had confronted him. At the entrance to the swimming area, he stopped outside the glass enclosure and looked around, and he recognized Miriam even with her swimming cap on. She was sitting on the edge of the pool, talking to a lady.

What? Charles thought. *That must be her mother, and goodness gracious, she hasn't taken her home yet.*

Miriam looked up, and as she recognized him, she smiled but quickly turned her head. And although Charles couldn't hear the conversation that she was having with the lady beside her, he imagined, rightfully, that she was Alicia Hawthorne, Miriam's mother. Alicia saw Miriam smile and followed the direction of her eyes.

"What's he doing here?" she asked, talking to no one in particular.

"Who?" Miriam asked.

"That Black guy over there."

"Oh, him? He's probably just a janitor," Miriam said, looking around as if searching for that person.

"Well, if he is, he's not doing his job. He's standing there as if he belonged. Surely, they're not going to let him swim here."

Miriam was trying to listen, but her attention was on Charles, and she tried not to look at him, but her brain betrayed her, and she looked directly at him and smiled.

"You know, if you let one of them in, then they all come," Alicia said, beckoning to an attendant. "What's he doing here?" she asked the attendant, pointing to Charles.

Charles, becoming aware of what she was doing, quickly turned and left the building. He had seen a part of what he came to see—the great disparity between the two recreation centers—and his data bank told him that she had said eleven o'clock, but his common sense told him not to come back at eleven.

"Oh dear, oh dear," he said aloud.

Miriam went back to the center at eleven, and she spoke to the director concerning Charles, but her effort to gain his support proved to be unsuccessful.

"Seems they have a building, you know," the director told her. "And they were funded by the city, but of course, they didn't handle the money right, and it seems like the staff that was hired to take care of the place wasn't there half the time."

"I know of a colored man who is quite capable. He has a college degree, and he's very intelligent, and with some help, I'm sure he could improve the situation over there," she said. "Is there someone he can talk to who could help him get it operating smoothly?"

"You say this man is colored?"

"Well, yes, he is."

"Then there's your answer. They're just not capable of handling a high-class job like being the director and having to make decisions. No, I can't help you. I've never seen one yet that could be trusted."

And that was the end of that.

Alicia Hawthorne sat in the large upholstered armchair in her bedroom, her left leg crossed over the right knee, her left elbow bent and resting on the arm of the chair, her chin in her hand. She relaxed and began making a list of the articles of clothing she would take with her, which did not include her entire wardrobe. Although in these last few days, she had decided to leave him, she had not been able to go. *What if it isn't true?* she asked herself. She had every intention of leaving him if the statement of the caller was true. *But what if Bertram discovered in his research that it wasn't true? And what was so contemptible about a man, any husband, having a sexual fling once in a while? I could ignore it, which would mean keeping my marriage, my home, and staying with him for the sake of Miriam and Timothy. Oh hell.*

That evening, when she and her husband were having dinner, Alicia Hawthorne took some deep breaths, told herself to calm down, and to do as Bertram suggested—act as if she was no longer angry and invite the young captain and his wife to join them for their monthly family dinner with Bertram, Miriam, and Timothy. And then she could see what Sage looked like.

"I was thinking," she said, "that I would like to meet your friend's wife and to let bygones be bygones, especially since he's your friend. Maybe you could ask them to join us for dinner this month with Miriam and Bertram, and of course, Timothy. What do you think?"

It took a few seconds for him to digest what she said, considering that she had previously expressed such ill feelings about Black people, especially Sage.

"Hmm. Well, that sounds like a good idea," he said.

"I think it might be better if you called and invited them instead of me," Alicia said.

"All right, I'll do that," he said, still harboring some doubts, but if she was really sincere, he thought, *I won't refuse.* And in considering the invitation, he wondered if he should invite Charles. *Well,* he thought, *no need to further muddy the already cloudy waters by not inviting him.* He called and talked to Darius, and Darius accepted for the three of them. Major Hawthorne was not aware that his wife had ulterior motives and her request to invite them was not an honest, friendly gesture.

The Wise Counselor said, "Evil deeds produce evil results."

When Darius, Sage, and Charles entered the Hawthornes' home, Major Hawthorne made the introductions.

"Alicia, you remember Darius Deavers," he said.

"Yes, I do, and it's good to see you again," she said.

"Thank you for inviting us. It's a pleasure," Darius said. He didn't offer his hand for a handshake, and neither did Alicia.

"And this is his wife, Sage," the major said.

"It's good to meet you, and welcome to our home," Alicia said. She was thinking, *So this is Sage. I won't stare, but I'll look at her more closely after a while.*

"Thank you," Sage said, nodding her head and smiling, but she didn't get a good feeling coming from this lady.

"This is their friend Charles Williams. He and Darius are planning to share a law office here," Marvin said, continuing the introductions. At once, a horrible expression took over Alicia's face at seeing Charles.

"Didn't I see you at the swimming pool the other day?" she asked, and even though Charles knew she had seen him there, he denied it.

"Me?" Charles said, putting his hand on his chest. "No, ma'am, it wasn't me. I wasn't there. You know they say that all of us look alike. Funny, huh?" He laughed, but no one else did.

"Miriam, don't you remember?" Alicia asked. "I pointed him out to you."

"I remember you mentioning somebody, but I wasn't really paying much attention," Miriam said, also in denial, and immediately she turned away and introduced her husband. "Sage, this is my husband, Bertram."

"Hello, Sage. I finally get to meet you. I met your husband and his father, and they mentioned that you were coming. And this is our son, Timothy," Bertram said.

"It's nice to meet you both," Sage said. Sage smiled, but inwardly she suppressed a laugh, remembering that Miriam had invited Charles to go there, and evidently, he'd been seen. Funny, huh?

Then dinner was served, and they all sat down at a beautifully decorated table. Linen tablecloth and napkins, china plates, crystal glasses, and name cards.

Bertram Withers had never sat and shared a dinner table with a Negro, and his mind was racing. *And she's sitting here acting like she belongs. She doesn't belong here. If she belongs anyplace, it's in the kitchen cooking or washing the dishes, and she should be in the kitchen eating with the Mamie. I know the stupid politicians or whoever was in charge passed the law that allowed them to marry someone of another race, but for a White man to stoop down and make her his wife—well, there's something very, very wrong with him. My mother-in-law is concerned about some ignoramus saying some ignorant thing on the phone, and I'm sure none of it is true. I can't see the major stooping so low as to have sex with one of them. They say it's different from any other, but for me, personally, ugh! It's unconscionable, and it's beyond prudence or reason to imagine participating in such an act of lowliness. I wonder what this world is coming to. I would rather die.*

Well, it was because my mother-in-law asked me, but this is the last time I'll allow myself and my wife and child to be lowered into associating with Mr. and Mrs. Darius Deavers. Marriage between a rich educated White man and a Negro has never presented itself as a remote possibility to me, and it's forbidden in the Bible, for the Lord told his people not to marry any foreign wives. Well, at least she's not real Black and ugly. If you take a good look at her, you could say she's kinda cute, but Darius Deavers had to be crazy to marry her, and even crazier to think he could be successful with a Black law partner, and I won't even waste my thoughts on Charles Williams. He's probably crazy too.

Sage tried to be at peace, but there seemed to be an evil spirit in the house, and even though there was man and wife, mother and father, daughter and son—all the components of a happy family—she saw each as disconnected from the others, in their own little world with their own personal agenda. Where was the love? She kept looking for even an inkling of it. To Sage, Major Hawthorne, Miriam, and Timothy, with whom she felt a warm stream of love and goodness flowing among them, did not seem to belong here, either.

I don't belong here either, Sage thought. *I feel like I've been thrown into some quicksand, and I can't get out under my own power. Struggling to get out would only coat me with more of the liquid, and I'd sink deeper and drown. At one time, I felt the same way with Darius's mother, but she has come to love and admire me and my courage, and she's been able to see me in a different way from her lifetime disparity and evil thoughts about Black people. Likewise, Darius's father came to love and respect me. And now, since meeting and falling in love with Darius and being certain of his love for me, I know that I can easily rescue myself from any quicksand of hate. Our love, about which I see no falseness, no doubts, yet Black and White, is on solid ground.*

Suddenly, sitting at that table, she had the wings of an angel; and when Darius looked at her and smiled, she flew out of the mire.

After dinner, as they sat around enjoying an after-dinner drink, Bertram turned to Charles, hoping to somehow denigrate him.

"So your name is Charles Williams?" he asked.

"Yes," Charles answered.

"Where are you from?"

"I was born and raised in Georgia."

"How do you happen to know Sage and Darius?"

"I met Darius when we were students at law school, and we got to be pretty good friends there, and it was Darius who introduced me to Sage and her lovely family. And now I'm looking forward to sharing a law office with my friend." He looked over and gave a nod to Darius.

"How interesting," Bertram said. "I wish you luck." Of course, he was thinking, *You're going to need a lot of luck to make that work here. Black and White as law partners. A Black wife and a Black law partner. That fellow Darius is crazier than I imagined. Jee-sus!*

"And, Sage," Alicia said, intent on including her in the belittlement, "I understand you're also from the South."

"I'm from Oklahoma, and Oklahoma is not considered primarily as a Southern state. It's really Midwestern, so if you want to classify it as South, you say it's Southwestern."

There was a pause in the conversation.

"I see, but most people still think of it as being in the South," Alicia said.

Sage let that pass as she really didn't much care what Alicia Hawthorne thought. After another pause in the conversation, Bertram spoke again.

"They say that all Negro people, especially those from the South, can dance. Charles, do you and Sage dance?" he said with an obvious sneer on his face.

"Oh yes," Charles said, knowing that Bertram was trying to place them in a category. "Let me see what I can show you." He stood up and started singing and moving.

> You put your right foot in, you take your
> right foot out
> You put your right foot in, and you shake
> it all about
> You do the hokeypokey, and you turn your-
> self around
> That's what it's all about

To everyone's surprise, Timothy stood up and walked over beside Charles. "I like that," he said. "Teach me how to do it, and then I can teach it to the children at my school. Come on, Grandpa, dance with us."

It wasn't what Bertram expected, and when Timothy and Marvin joined in, his face turned red as they all sang and danced.

> You put your left foot in, you take your left
> foot out
> You put your left foot in, and you shake it
> all about
> You do the hokeypokey, and you turn your-
> self around
> That's what it's all about

And you couldn't tell if Bertram was angry or if he had a feeling of being made a fool of. It was surely a combination of both.

When they were ready to leave, Marvin, out of love for them, gave Sage, Darius, and Charles a hug and a warm handshake. Miriam wanted to do the same, but she knew her husband would disapprove.

In the car on the way home, Sage, Darius, and Charles were quiet for as long as they could manage; then the three of them burst out in laughter.

"And where did you learn the hokeypokey?" Darius asked.

Bertram Withers learned that the babies of poor Black people who lived in rural districts were born at home with a midwife, who was usually a family friend, in attendance. Doctors were rarely called, mostly because of the lack of money and lack of available doctors in the district who were willing to serve Negroes. Therefore, there were no hospital records, and the birth information was written in the family Bible. When Sage entered college, it was necessary to have a birth certificate, and not having any knowledge of the birth in their records, the birth certificate was based on what had been written in the Bible. The facts of her birth were given by her mother and a family friend who had attended the birth, and its authenticity was not questioned.

This was the information Bertram's research showed:

> Ariel Sage Copple was born on February 5, 1921, in Reggs, Oklahoma, the youngest of five children born to Isaac Columbus and Martha Jane Copple. Her other siblings are brother, Robert Burnett; sisters, Kay Lee, Anna Mae, and June. She graduated from Washington High School in Proctor, Oklahoma. She graduated from college with a bachelor's in English. She received a master's degree in Colorado. She and her family are Baptists. Her father owned a farm in Reggs, Oklahoma; her mother was a maid. Two in her family have passed: her father, Isaac Columbus Copple, and her mentally handicapped sister, June Copple.

Alicia noted the date listed as Sage's date of birth, and she figured that the time of conception was a time when her husband had been stationed in Oklahoma. *Of course, it's true*, she thought. *He is the father of a Black child, and that child is married and living in this city. And what kind of name is Isaac Columbus? It's very stupid. Isaac is biblical, but why Columbus, for Pete's sake?*

The Wise Counselor said, "It's easy for people to believe something is true, whether it is or not, if they want it to be true. Alicia had added up two and two and come up with not four as the answer but an off-the-wall, out-of-the-blue number like four thousand, which made her sure that Sage was her husband's child."

After all the guests were gone, Marvin Hawthorne, confused and perplexed at how Sage and Charles had been treated, spoke to his wife.

"Can you please tell me what just happened here?" he asked.

"What do you mean?" she asked sarcastically.

"I thought you invited them because you had resolved the questions you had about the whole outlandish idea that Sage is my daughter, and I truly thought that you wanted to be friends."

"Humph. If she isn't yours, then you probably have a Black child floating around out there someplace. And whether it's true or not, I do not—I repeat, I do not—want to be their friend."

"Humph back at you. Damn, and I'm really hurt by the way Bertram treated them. He must have been talking to you. And poor Darius, bless his soul, he just had to sit there and take it, out of respect for me, most likely."

"Respect, my butt. What kind of man is he anyway to marry somebody Black?"

"What kind of man is he? Well, for your information, he's a very nice, Christian man, and he loves his wife. I wish I could see that kind of love in Bertram for our daughter, but I don't. And what if the man was right, and you're the one who's all confused? What if it's Miriam he's talking about?" He said that before he really thought about what he was saying, but after he had said it, he wasn't sorry. What if? he asked himself.

"Oh shit. Now you've gone completely out of your stupid-ass mind. And for your information, yes, I asked Bertram to do some research into her background and find out where she came from because I don't trust you. And she could be yours. She was born in Oklahoma, and you were stationed there at the time her mother would have gotten pregnant, and it could very well be true. Maybe you are some kind of weirdo Nigger lover, and to include my daughter in this Black thing is stupid. It's idiotic and crazy. Here, read this, you idiot."

Major Hawthorne read the report, bowed his head, and gathering his calm and his "rightful place to be" in his mind, he could only look at her.

"And don't you ever invite that Charles into my home again," she continued her tirade.

"Your home?" He smirked.

"Whatever, I don't like the way he looked at Miriam." She sucked in her breath and blew it out. "I should have shot him."

"Your home," he repeated, standing. To him, the blowing out of her breath had deflated him too, and the breath had been sucked out of him, and he leaned against the wall to try and breathe and steady himself. "It's totally ridiculous what you're doing and what you're thinking. And Bertram is just as conflicted as you are." He waved his arms in despair as he whispered, almost as if talking to himself, "I can't stay here right now." But she heard him, loud and clear. "I've got to get away from you and *your* home, as you say. I'll stay on the base tonight, and I'll decide—" He fought back the urge to hit her. "I'll decide something, maybe tomorrow. Good night, Alicia, and to hell with you and Mr. Bertram Withers." He gathered up a few of his things and walked out the door.

Bertram Withers and Darius Deavers were only one year apart in age, Bertram being one year older than Darius. Their lives were alike in some ways. Both graduated from law school with an emphasis in education, so both were qualified as lawyers and teachers. Both spent one year in the United States Army, and neither was assigned to combat duty overseas. Both were White, and both were married. Bertram's mother and father were killed in an automobile accident when he was only seven years old, and he was raised by an uncle and aunt who only housed him. They didn't give him any love and no motherly or fatherly devotion. Fortunately, when he reached the age of eighteen, he could claim a sizeable inheritance left to him by his deceased parents. He and Miriam were high school classmates, and they had always been friendly with each other. Their friendship strengthened, and they attended the senior prom together. Although they went to different colleges, she in Montana while he studied in Seattle, they kept in touch; and when she came home one year for Christmas, she invited him to her home as he was alone with no family. He was impressed by the closeness of her parents, and he thought it might be to his advantage to become a part of this family. So when he decided it was time to marry, he chose Miriam, but now his limp dispassion had shown up in his family life, and he hadn't given any at-home appreciation to Miriam. He placed her in the role of a helpful companion to his career, a good mother, and a dutiful, pretty wife. His fatherly interaction with their son, Timothy, was the same. Bertram Withers only focused his mind and attention on his need to use people for his purposes and outward public notice, which was definitely the reason Miriam searched for friendship and love outside her home.

Darius was born in Ralstson, Massachusetts, and he was raised in a close-knit, loving family. His mother and father showed him love and compassion, empathy and consideration, for others. He and Sage were childhood sweethearts, and he was still truly and deeply in love with Sage, and she was not an ornament to embellish his life. She was definitely a part of him. Darius came away from the dinner that day with the impression that Bertram was a person with no pleasant personality and with little or no real compassion for people. Darius noticed Bertram's weak handshake and that he seldom made eye contact when conversing with people. Darius Deavers got the impression that everything Bertram Withers did was false, whereas Darius Deavers was honest and sincere in his family life and in his life altogether. His ambition was toward being a successful White lawyer who would help Black people who had been denied their rights because of the color of their skin.

18

Sage had made a list of all the elementary schools in the Black community, hoping that she could help one or two of them with a reading program. After visiting a couple of the schools on her list, she noted that the buildings were old, and the classrooms were overcrowded. Although Sage was a qualified teacher, she was met with obstacles.

"Do you have a child enrolled here?" one principal asked.

"No, but I'm a licensed teacher, and I have the proper education to help you with the students who are delinquent in reading," Sage replied.

"We're not authorized to allow people who don't have children here to come in and teach," he said. "If you would like to apply for regular part-time work or substitute teaching, then we could let you come as directed by the school board."

These rules seemed strange to Sage, but as she thought about all the unrest in the area of education throughout the state, it made sense that they were careful about the people they allowed to come in and volunteer, and she had no alternative except to abide by the system's rules. There were some organizations whose members were permitted to volunteer, but Sage was not affiliated with any of them. And after spending a week going to the different schools and experiencing the same negative reactions, she thought that she probably should start her own tutoring program, like Iola and her sister did in Oklahoma.

"Oh dear, oh dear, this is discouraging, but I can't give up," Sage Deavers said with a sigh.

This day, as she left a Black school on her way to where she had parked her car, she was met with a frightening and hostile situation. The street ahead of her was rife with at least one hundred Blacks. They were shouting, throwing rocks, breaking store windows, and cursing, and she heard the words, "Fucking honkie cops. Kill the motherfuckers."

She stood paralyzed with fear, realizing that she couldn't get to her car, which was down the street on the other side of the melee, and she became too scared to move. *I know I'm going to die*, she said to herself, standing there in fear for her life, thinking of her family, of Darius, of all the struggles she had overcome in her life, just to die in the street like this. She couldn't see a way out. But then, in the twinkling of an eye, God sent an angel, for someone walked up beside her.

"Terrible, isn't it?"

"Oh, I'm so scared. What's happening?" Sage asked.

"There's a riot going on down there because they say that a White cop killed a seventeen-year-old Black boy last week, and of course, they said it was the boy who caused the shooting and not the White cop. Now all this violence has come against the city police."

Sage turned now and looked at the speaker, and standing beside her was a Black lady, probably middle-aged; and like the sunshine after a pouring rainstorm, this stranger was a welcome presence to Sage.

"Where were you trying to go?" the lady asked, looking at the obviously frightened young lady beside her.

"To my car," Sage managed to say, her breath coming in short gasps. "It's parked down there."

"Do you live around here?"

"No, I don't. I... I ..."

Sage didn't want to tell this lady where she lived, for she had become afraid of everything and everybody; and hearing gunfire, she again became afraid for her life. She began to cry, and she knew she was at the end of her endurance, for she seldom cried. Then the lady, feeling Sage's fear, took her by the arm.

"Come on, let's go in this store. We can't stay out here. I pray they won't come down this far," she said.

165

As they were entering the store, the store owner was walking toward the front door; and a lady, who was standing behind the counter, was busy taking money out of the cash register. Evidently, they were both acquainted with Sage's angel.

"Yes," the man said. "Come on in, Mrs. Johnson. I'm going to lock this door and close the blinds, and maybe they won't get down this far," he repeated her words. "But, dammit, it's happening more and more down here. Me and my wife, we're thinking about closing up the store and moving away from here."

"But where can we go?" the lady behind the counter, who was evidently his wife, asked. "It's the same all over."

"This one of your children, Miz Johnson?" the lady asked.

"No, poor little thing. I found her on the corner trying to get to her car, but it's down there on the other side of where the awful hoodlums are at."

"Don't cry, honey," Mrs. Johnson said, putting her arms around Sage, who was still crying and shivering with fear. "We're safer in here than out there."

"I hope you're right," the man said.

"Well, Lord have mercy, it's probably going to get worse because another one of them Black boys was killed down there last night," the lady behind the counter said.

"Shot by the police?"

"Yep. Another White cop."

"Ain't hardly but one or two police that's Black."

"Well, our car's out back," the man said. "We'll just lie low in here till it calms down, and then I'll see if we can't get out of here through the back door."

The lady emerged from behind the counter, and she led Sage and Mrs. Johnson to a table in back of the room in a corner. She brought soft drinks.

"Thank you," Mrs. Johnson said. "The Lord's gonna bless you all, I'm sure."

They sat and waited, and Mrs. Johnson prayed silently. They drank the soda. When it finally quieted down and no more shots were heard, the owner cracked the door slowly and looked out. The streets seemed to have been cleared, and seeing no one, he thought it was safe to leave, so they bravely went out of the back door, got into the owner's car, and he drove down the street to Sage's car. They thanked the store owner, and Mrs. Johnson got out of the car with Sage, who had managed to stop crying.

"You gonna be all right, honey?" Mrs. Johnson asked. "I just live around the corner. I can walk home."

"I'll be all right, and you've been so kind. Get in, and I'll take you home where you'll be off these streets." When they got to Mrs. Johnson's house, before the kind lady got out of the car, Sage began to pour her heart out to her. She was Black, and Sage felt a peace with her.

"We came here because it was legal for Black and White to marry here. My husband is White, and we don't have any relatives here, and I feel so lost sometimes, and I was down here at one of the schools, and I was hoping to find some Black children to tutor in reading. I'm a schoolteacher, but I don't have to work full-time because my husband's family is rich. I'd like to have some help with my housework, but I don't think a White woman would work for me, and maybe a Black woman wouldn't either. Just only two days a week, you know, to clean the house and do the laundry. I can cook, and I don't know how I'd feel with a Black maid. You see, my mother was a maid, and I know how she felt."

Being spent and out of breath, Sage paused. "I'm rambling, huh? I'm sorry, but you remind me so much of my mother. Oh, I wish she was here," she said, trying hard to stop the tears that ran down again, as if they had a mind of their own.

And as way leads on to way, the Lord stepped in, and Mrs. Johnson told Sage that she did daywork; and before Sage left her to go home, this kind lady offered to come and work for her.

When Darius arrived home from work, Sage was trying as hard as she could to go about her usual habit of sitting with him and relaxing with a cool drink without allowing the tears to start again.

"It's so delightful for me that we are here together in our own home. I love you so much," he said, and as usual, he gave her a warm hug and a warm kiss.

"Yes, it is," she said, returning the hug and kiss and hoping he wouldn't sense the lingering feelings of terror and fright she had experienced. She was also hoping he wouldn't notice the redness of her eyes from the crying. Instinctively, however, he sensed that she was not at ease.

"Are you all right, Sage, my dear?" he asked. "You seem sad."

"I'm all right," she said, but as soon as she opened her mouth, the tears came, and the experiences of her afternoon burst from her mouth. She told him of the riot, of the lady who came along, the sanctuary in the store, and taking the lady home, and she was experiencing her pain all over again. At the same time, he was experiencing her pain, for in that moment, they were one. He shared her happy and sad sensations, her fears and frustrations, the same as she shared his.

"Thank the Lord for the lady," Darius said, hugging her closer to him. "We'll have to do something to show our appreciation. Maybe we could buy her something. What do you think, Sage dear?" he asked.

"Her name is Mrs. Johnson, and she lives in a real poor Black neighborhood. Reminds me of where I grew up."

"So how can we help her?"

"Believe it or not, she does daywork, and she said that she'd be willing to come and work for us. I liked her, and I'm sure we'd get along together."

"Hmm. Tomorrow we'll go and thank that lady. That was very kind of her to help you, and we'll see if it works out that she can work for us."

Darius looked at his wife and smiled as it seemed things were working out for the good. But something in her eyes told him she hadn't told him everything. He sensed that there was something she hadn't told him. They had gotten over the pain of the riot. They had been thankful for the help of the lady, but he knew there was something else. Didn't she trust him enough to tell him everything? Was she happy? Unhappy? Sick? Discouraged?

"Are you happy, my Sage? Is there something else that's bothering you?"

She squeezed his hand tighter, and with more tears, now of joy, she looked at his blue eyes and his blond hair, and she wondered what their children would look like. "I'm pregnant," she said. And, oh, what joy now filled his soul. His face was shining, and he put his hand on hers as in their usual expression of love.

The next day, following Sage's direction, Darius drove through the downtown district to the east side of the city and into the Black neighborhood where Mrs. Johnson lived. Suddenly he recalled what had happened to Sage here, and a fear rose up in his mind. He didn't want to be here, and he was certain he didn't want Sage to tutor at a school in this area. *And what about this lady? Does Sage know enough about her to go into her home and for her to come into ours?* Questions. Well, he knew that Sage would want him to meet the lady. All this was going through his mind as he drove.

This also reminded him of the time his father took him to pay a visit to Sage's mother in Oklahoma. *It was Christmastime, and I was out of school. My father had some presents for Mrs. Copple, but he also came because Sage's aunt Sophronia told him that Sage was having financial trouble staying in school, and my father decided to offer financial help for Sage from his FABCS organization, which would allow her to stay and finish college. But unknown to Sage and Mrs. Copple, he added some of his own money to her account.* It was a whole new experience for Darius to go from his White neighborhood, with the large houses and beautiful lawns, into the much different Black neighborhood where Mrs. Copple lived.

Black and White had been separate worlds to Darius until he met Sage and Charles, and now driving into the Black part of BeachSide, Washington, he was again entering their world while at the same time trying to remain in his, and he was soon to become deeper into another part of the Black world. He was coming, he thought, just to thank a kind lady who had helped his precious Sage, not knowing at this time how much this visit would change a large part of his life.

As he drove, he saw that there were young and old Black men hanging out on the streets. There were young Black children playing on the sidewalks and in the street. There was an old man pushing a cart, which seemed to contain all of his worldly goods, and he was accompanied by a little dirty White dog, probably his only friend.

When they arrived, Mrs. Johnson invited the young couple in and offered them something to drink. They said, "No, thank you." They met those who were living in the house with Mrs. Johnson: her twenty-four-year-old daughter, Karen, and Karen's two children, Jasper and Jasmine, ages six, and seven; and Mrs. Johnson's ill husband, who was confined to a wheelchair. Karen worked at a White-owned and operated hair salon as "the cleaning girl." That's what they called her. Karen and Randy Davis, the children's father, were not married, and they now lived separate lives. Mr. Johnson had injured his back lifting heavy boxes on the loading dock where he once worked, and now he was unable to work anymore. Every month, he received a small pension check and some warehouse food, including canned meat and vegetables, flour, cornmeal, and beans. Mrs. Johnson worked two days each week for a White family doing laundry and housecleaning.

"I came to thank you for helping my wife out of her dilemma," Darius said.

"You're sure enough welcome," Mrs. Johnson said. "I was mighty happy to help her. She was so lost, and bless her heart, she seems like such a sweet child."

"Yes," Mr. Johnson said as he extended a hand to them, and Darius and Sage walked over and took Mr. Johnson's hand. "That's a real pretty and sweet-looking little wife you got, sir, and I'm so happy to meet you and her. My wife told me about her being married and that you was White, and yes, you all might have it kinda hard in this old mean town being mixed, but you just hang on in there, and you pray 'cause I know that God is sho 'nuff good to good people."

Sage listened, and she had heard words like this time and time again, and she had to continue establishing who and what she was to herself. Not how other people saw her and how they labeled her, how they classified her, since she was married to a White man. She silently assured herself again, *I am Ariel Sage Copple Deavers, and I am Black. And I'm comfortable with that.*

"I feel so much goodness coming from your wife," Sage said, looking at Mr. Johnson, "I was telling my husband that she has offered to come and help us with our housework."

"No, ma'am. Not to help you," Mrs. Johnson said, knowing this was all new to Sage, and she didn't want Sage to feel uncomfortable having a maid. "I'd be coming to work for you."

Sage liked Mrs. Johnson, and she knew that she was in a position to help this lady and her family. She could also be comfortable in the role (ha!) of the wife of a rich White man with a Black maid. Being married to Darius had not resulted in her becoming color blind, but it had developed into an appreciation and love of color, her black and his white. She looked at the two children who were sitting quietly on the floor, and her angel's voice told her she could help by tutoring them in her home while Mrs. Johnson was also being helped by earning a salary. Sage smiled, her green eyes looking into Darius's blue eyes.

Darius was back on the road, traveling with a new set of thoughts. The people he saw on the way here seemed to spend the greater portion of their lives on the street, anywhere but in a home. This lady sitting here was trying to have a home. She was aware of the environment on the streets around her house, and she knew about the prejudice and ways her race was held down, pushed back, kept poor and always needy. But Darius sensed in her the same feeling of self-worth and contentment he had observed in Sage's mother. He liked her.

At the same time, however, he felt as if he was split in two. One part of him was Darius Paul Deavers: rich, educated, privileged, and White. The other part of him was becoming someone totally different, unintelligible, seemingly surrounded by Black people, in a Black church, his office in a Black part of town, with a Black law partner, a Black wife, and now these poor Black people, and it was hard to understand this part of his life and to place it in a category. *Where are the White people? Would attending a White church and working for a White law firm be the answer? Is trying to fight the covenant by staying in the White neighborhood a good thing?* Darius Paul Deavers knew he had to resolve this intimidating struggle that was raging within him.

He was certain, however, that a part of the answer was sitting beside him; and the other part of the answer, the denouement, would come from above. *So look up, Darius. Look up through the trees. They're God's creation, and so are you, and so is Sage. Talk to them. Talk to Sage. Talk to your father. Talk to God. You'll find the answer.*

Lying in bed that night, after their prayers, Darius Paul Deavers was still in the wilderness. *Can I trust God? And is there really, truly some supreme and unprejudiced being? Where is the answer? Well, my father is such a believer, and he preaches the Word of the Lord. Perhaps he can help me to understand the meaning and the reason for me even being here—in BeachSide, Washington, in a mixed-race marriage, in the world.*

Sage hadn't experienced the awful morning sickness with vomiting and extreme nausea that she'd heard so much about. She had begun to experience a blossoming of love for the seed that had been planted inside her. Every morning, she spoke to this new life and promised herself to take especially good care of the two of them, herself and itself. She was feeling a pleasant new joy.

All those who loved her, members of her family and those of Darius's family, had been notified, and they were overjoyed. Both mothers, Mary Jane Copple and Lucy Deavers, began planning to travel to Washington to be there with Sage a week or two before the birth and a week or two after. This new little person would be the Deavers' first grandchild and a product of this interracial marriage that had been the subject of so much controversy. Mary Jane Copple thought of Sage being her baby, and now her baby was grown and married and expecting a baby of her own. Although there were feelings of anxiety and concern for Sage, there was also peace, love, joy, and happiness.

Since Sage was pregnant, despite the uneasiness and concern for her safety coming through to her from her husband, she put on her brave hat and drove to Mrs. Johnson's house and picked her up with her two grandchildren, Jasper and Jasmine.

Darius helped Sage make a combination classroom and playroom, equipped with a table and chairs for writing, a blackboard, books, pencils, crayons, notebooks, paper, scissors—all the things needed for work and play. Each child was given the makings of a pallet for resting and quiet time.

After Mrs. Johnson fed them breakfast, Sage spent two hours with them on their lessons. She watched them as they enjoyed the books, none of which they'd ever had at home, much to her amazement. Sage asked Mrs. Johnson to encourage Karen to read to them every night, and she sent a bag of books home with them.

Despite their poverty and lack of so many things, they were happy children, and they loved their grandmother. As time went by, they began to love Sage. They looked at Darius for the few minutes they saw him in the morning, hugged him before he left for work, then they turned their attention away from him. They were instructed by Mrs. Johnson to call him Mr. Deavers, and by Sage's instructions, they called her Miss Sage, which they ran all together as one word: *Missage*.

At eleven thirty, Mrs. Johnson made lunch, and they all sat down together and ate. Although they were all Black, Sage was "Miss Ann," what the lady of the house was called, and she wanted their respect, but not their feelings of separation, higher and lower, less and more.

After lunch, the children lay on their pallets until one thirty to rest or sleep. They then had snacks and free time until three o'clock which they used for their jigsaw puzzles, singing to the music on the radio, or whatever they chose. At three thirty, Sage took Mrs. Johnson and the children to the corner by the drugstore near their home, and they walked to the house. Mrs. Johnson thought Sage would be safer doing it that way instead of driving into the neighborhood and driving out alone at that time of day when there was much more outside activity and more people hanging around on the streets than in the morning.

19

On the day they scheduled for knocking on doors, when Darius arrived at his office, he found Major Marvin Hawthorne outside leaning against his van and smoking a cigarette.

"Well, good morning, Major," Darius said, looking at his watch. "Have you been here long? Am I late?"

"No, it's such a beautiful day I thought it would be nice to get out early," he said, shrugging his shoulders. He didn't tell Darius that he had left home.

"Well, let's get started," Darius said.

The plan was to knock on doors in White-restricted neighborhoods, those houses that had a "For Sale" sign in the yard, and ask the owners if they would be willing to sell to a Negro.

All the while, before their appointed time to meet, Darius kept asking himself, *Why am I doing this? Is this effort just for Sage and me, or am I trying to change the law for everyone?* Suddenly, as he thought of begging some biased and prejudiced White people to let his wife live in their vicinity, it bothered him, and the whole idea became offensive to him.

As they were riding, Marvin began to have some thoughts of his own. He didn't want to go in his own neighborhood, and realizing this, he had to ask himself some questions.

Would I want a Black person living next door to me? Would I be brave enough to sell to a Black person? Will my wife ever change her mind about Black people? Those were questions he hadn't thought of before. It's not an easy thing to examine one's own feelings, and it's harder to cope with the honest answers. It's easier to make excuses.

Marvin thought of his own attitude toward the Negro-enlisted men who had come under his command, and he had often looked on some of them as being "ignorant," which now seemed like a harsh word. From now on, he'd say *uneducated* or *thoughtless*. There were times when he had become irritated with them for their drinking and making excuses for their behavior and often attributing being chastised to prejudice against them. Still in his heart of hearts, Major Hawthorne could see a problem with them living next door to him and his family. With these thoughts filling his mind, he chose an area in a different section of the city from where he lived, not knowing that one day he might be compelled to deal with this situation.

At the first house they chose, the man didn't even answer their question; he slammed the door in their faces. It was the same at the second house, except the lady called them "nigger lovers," and then she slammed the door.

"Wait," Darius said when they were back in the van. "I don't want to do this. Who are we? Suppose someone should ask. Are we real estate agents? No, we're not. Do we represent any organization, you know, CORE, or any church group? No. Here we are, two White men asking about Black people. What, for heaven's sake, is our interest? Oh, of course, I should say, 'Sir or Madam,' whichever one answers the door, 'my wife is a Negro, and we would like very much to live in this neighborhood. Would you be willing to let us buy your house? Ha!" (It was not a laugh. It meant, *This is a cruel joke.*) "We'd get the same response that we've gotten so far, or maybe worse."

"What could be worse?" Marvin asked.

"Well, spitting on us or turning the hose on us, maybe even shooting at us and telling the police we were robbers. And what if someone said yes, and I brought my precious Sage here? It wouldn't be any different than where we are now. No. I can't continue to do this. The entire system needs to be changed."

Major Hawthorne was at a loss what to say, for he knew that what Darius said was true.

"Right now, however, I want to live somewhere in peace with my dear wife. Maybe I'll just canvas my own block and ask them if they'll let us live there in peace, at least until our child is born."

"What did you say? Until your child is born?"

"Yes, Sage is pregnant. We're expecting in April."

"Congratulations. I think maybe that'll put a different spin on things. You probably won't have much success in your block, so I'm thinking that you should just move, you know, to a nonrestricted area."

"Yes, but that will take some time., so right now I'll have to think about how to deal with this."

On the way back to his office, they passed a sign that read SUN-DOWN ZONE.

"What does that mean?" Darius asked.

"Well, first it means that no people of color can live there. It also means that they are expected to be out of the area by sundown. Any Black man is likely to be stopped by the damn police—White, of course—and told that unless he worked there and could prove he worked there, he was told to get the hell out and that he better not be seen after sundown in this neighborhood again."

They arrived back at Darius's office, and before Darius got out of the car, Marvin touched his arm.

"One more thing," the major said. "I know Miriam invited Charles to come to the recreation center, you know, but, I'm...uh, I'm afraid if Bertram finds out she tried to help him, well, it won't be pleasant."

"I'll talk to Charles."

After they parted, both men were thinking along the same lines. Marvin was thinking, *I enjoy being with him, going out to eat and talking, but our lives can't intertwine because of my wife and her prejudice, of Bertram and his hate.* Darius was thinking of his wife and of the hate he had sensed emanating from both Bertram and Mrs. Hawthorne for Sage, and he concluded, *Our families don't fit. I wonder if they ever will.*

Darius got in his car and drove, not going anyplace in particular but just hoping to get rid of some of the tension as his mind was again filled with questions.

Well, Darius Paul Deavers, are you a man or a mouse?

Hmm. First, I am a human being, and I know that regardless of the definition and categories of race, there is only one race upon the earth, and that is the human race. Strip us of our outward covering, and we're all the same. My beautiful wife is a human being, and she deserves as much equality as I have. I cannot become discouraged because with her, wherever I am, in whatsoever state or community I am, I must make myself content. I can't govern my life by what-if. I have to live with what is. I can't make things like I want them to be, always orderly and peaceful.

Yet I would like to know how God, who is supposed to be the creator all things, could create such unfairness, such prejudice and hate? It's as if he sent the White giant to stomp on Black people with his big feet and to give, with outstretched arms, to the White people whatever they wanted. Loving Sage, I guess I wanted to make things better for us, and I thought I could do that by coming to Washington, but there is just as much hate here. I've prayed and prayed, but I don't think God hears me. I'm losing my faith in God.

His other voice said, *So what are you going to do about it? You poor man. You poor, pitiful thing. You poor little dribble. How long are you going to have this pity party? You must be a mouse, sitting in a dark hole hoping the big cat doesn't come and eat you up. Hmm.* He was sad.

Then from outside, over and above him, came another voice: *You can canvas your own block. Do it with your most reliable ally, which is that infinite wisdom inside of you.*

Darius went back to his office and wrote a letter to his neighbors, intending make copies, to get each name and address and mail it. He wrote:

Dear sir and madam:

I am Darius Paul Deavers, and I live at 121
Layton Street. My father purchased the house as
a home for me and my wife and for our future
children, not knowing of the restrictive cove-

nant. We are newlyweds. I am a college graduate, and so is my wife, and we are peace-loving and law-abiding citizens. I love my wife, but there are those who hate her, sight unseen, because of the color of her skin. My wife is Black, and I am White. You cannot imagine what the world's hate means to us. I am writing this letter to appeal to the goodness that I hope is in your heart as a part of the human race. I don't ask for your pity but for your compassion, if not for us, for our unborn child. We are expecting in April, so it would mean the world to us if we could at least live in our house until then in peace, which means no more rocks, no more signs, no broken windows.

We will begin today seeking another home immediately. Thank you very much, and may God bless you.

Signed:
Attorney Darius Paul Deavers

And as God works in mysterious ways, as Darius pulled into his driveway, the couple who lived across the street were just pulling into theirs. With some hesitation and with some fear, Darius asked himself, *Why not speak to them personally? They're here, and you're here. But of course, you could receive the same negative reception you got from those others.* Yet his body was not fully in sync with his mind, for he found himself walking across the street and calmly greeting them with a smile and an outstretched hand. Much to his surprise, they were cordial and shook his hand as if they were expecting him.

"I'm Darius Deavers," he said. "My wife and I live across the street from you, and my wife is Black. I have written letters to you and our neighbors, and I was intending to mail them, but I don't know their names. Would you read it and tell me what you think?"

The wife reached out and took the letter, and after reading it, she looked up at him and shook her head. "You are a very brave person, and evidently, so is your wife. I've seen her from time to time coming and going, and it dawned on me that, well, she's a person, and I'm sure you love her very much."

"Yes," the husband said softly and compassionately. "But, sir, you and your wife are defying the law. Being allowed to live here is not so much about us as it is about the law."

"Listen," the wife said, "we're not against you living here. You aren't creating any problems, so I'll be the brave one. Our monthly block meeting is coming up next week, and I'll pass your letter out to them." Shrugging her shoulder and looking askance at her husband, she added, "And we'll see what happens."

"My wife and I live in this block, so can we attend the meeting?" Darius asked.

"I wouldn't advise you to do that, but to be on the safe side, I would advise you to start looking for another place to live, you know, where there are no restrictions."

"Thank you very much," Darius said, trying hard to hold back the tears as he was so much appreciating the reception he received from them, which was different from the ones he had received when knocking on doors.

"You're welcome, Mr. Deavers. We're Colin and Gertrude Kingsley."

Darius was actually crying when he told Sage about the events of the day. "I should not have gone knocking on those doors. It was embarrassing."

"No, no, don't chastise yourself. How it happened is how it was supposed to happen, okay? Now, don't cry. It's going to be all right."

Her peace and calm were just a part of her nature, and after a while, he too became calm.

The Block Meeting

As is true in most upscale White neighborhoods, in the city block where Sage and Darius lived, the inhabitants who lived there held a block meeting every month. And as each month of the year is identified with the season in which it is placed—winter, summer, spring, or fall—so each residence in the one hundred blocks of Layton Street in BeachSide, Washington, is identified by the people who occupy it: their names, ages, occupations, church, and political affiliations.

The agenda at the monthly meetings included introductions, reports from the persons who are responsible for the needs of the block, things like animal control, upkeep of the alleys, trash removal, etc. It was the responsibility of one housewife who was not employed outside the home (as most of them were not) to watch for any strange cars, people, or activities seen at unusual times. The agenda also included new business concerns and old matters that had been taken care of. For instance, if it was reported that the barking of a dog across the alley on another street was constant and annoying; it would be addressed.

Lieutenant Colin and Mrs. Gertrude Kingsley headed the welcoming committee for new residents in the block. They had lived on this block in the same house for twenty years. They came to Washington because of the lieutenant's affiliation with the United States Navy. He grew up in Connecticut, and after finishing college, he joined the Navy; and after serving for seven years, he was assigned to the Bremerton Naval Station in Bremerton, Washington, across the Puget Sound from Seattle. He has moved up in the ranks, now holding the title of naval commander. Their only son, now aged thirty-six, had chosen to stay in their hometown of Hartford and is employed in the school system there as instructor of psychology.

Mrs. Gertrude Kingsley had developed a hobby of growing flowers, basically those grown from bulbs. She and her husband were high school sweethearts, and although the neighborhood where they grew up was predominately White, there were two Black families on their street, and three Black students were in their high school graduating class. It seemed a normal occurrence for them to have contact with Blacks.

At the monthly block meeting on this particular night and on this particular street, the subject of integration became the main topic of discussion because of the fact that Darius and Sage Deavers now occupied a house on their block and because Sage Deavers was Black. And as new residents, the new couple should be made welcome; and because Gertrude Kingsley was part of the welcoming committee, she read the letter that Darius had written. She laid the letter on the table beside her chair and asked for discussion.

"As you see, the letter states that his wife is pregnant, and he's asking that they be allowed to stay until their child is born with no more rocks and trash in the yard."

The entrance of a Black person into their lives and into their block was unthinkable, and the comments were, "What? Are you crazy? Of course, this will not in any way be tolerated. Besides, it's against the law. There is a covenant that is not being followed. Not no but hell no!" one man said.

"But they're not bothering anybody," Gertrude said.

"It's like flies. One comes, and pretty soon there's a swarm of them," a second man said.

"And then there's those Black children who come. I don't know why they're there, but pretty soon, you know, they'll be outside playing in the yard, and they'll expect to play with our children, and that is a definite *no*."

"And I see a Black man coming there too," a third man said.

"Flies, I tell you. They also multiply like alley cats and rabbits," the second man said.

"Well, she's pregnant, and they're asking that they be allowed to stay only until their child is born. I don't think that's so unreasonable," Gertrude said.

"I still say that they're breaking the law because there is a restrictive covenant, so the bottom line is, they should not be living there," the first man said.

"Well, you know, I went to school with Black students, and well, they're no different, only the color of their skin. And it doesn't rub off," Gertrude said.

"What do you say, sir?" one man asked, looking at Gertrude's husband. "You know they're not allowed in the Navy."

"That's not really true, but let's leave the Navy out of this. And besides, I'm not responsible for what happens in the Navy. We just happen to live in a mean and hateful world, even though we're all equal in the eyes God."

"Let's leave God out of this too. You didn't see him going to school with them," the second man said.

Both Lieutenant and Gertrude Kingsley could see that there was no possibility they could reach them. They could see that certain beliefs and certain paths of life had been firmly established here.

"So what do you want me to tell them?" Gertrude spoke softly, as if devoid of breath. Her words were preceded and followed with a sigh.

Then one lady spoke up. "When did you say the child is due?" she asked.

"The letter says the first of April."

"That's not such a long time," another lady said.

"Too long, I say," the first man said.

Mrs. Mayweather, who had asked the question, stood up. She looked at the letter, then at those around the room. "You know, I've seen him, and I can hear him in this letter, poor man, and I've seen her, and she's quite pretty. I've been tempted to go over and meet both of them."

"I surely haven't. And he must be some kind of idiot to marry one of them, and who knows what that baby will look like," the third man said.

"A monkey," another man said. There were a couple of smothered giggles.

"Actually, the way this world is mixed up, you don't any of you know your whole ancestral history," Mrs. Mayweather said.

"Well, I know that I'm not mixed with anything Black. My blood is pure White," the first man said.

"If you don't know it," Gertrude said, "all human blood is red. Dr. Drew proved that in his research."

"Humph. He was Black too, and that's what he wanted us to think. I say let's get them out of here right now."

"So they can't just move overnight, and since they must go, I say at least give them time to find another place. They look like nice people, and please, no more rocks and signs in the yard." Mrs. Mayweather said this, and then she took her purse and left the house. Her husband went with her.

"You know, the world is changing," Lieutenant Kingsley said. "Not only the way we see people but in the way we live. There are changes in transportation. No more horse and buggy. There are changes in household appliances. We now have washing machines, vacuum sweepers, and electric irons. No more washboards, brooms, and heating the iron over a hot fire. We have private lines for the telephone instead of waiting for three or four people to get through talking on a party line. Everything is changing, and we have to change with it or continue to live in the dark ages. It's the same with the Black people. We brought them over here from Africa, kicking and screaming, dying in filthy cargo holes, being beaten and cowed. And we think their brains are smaller than ours and that their blood was black, which isn't true. And they've made progress despite us trying to keep our feet on their backs, so we need to change our thinking too."

"So all of a sudden, you've changed? You're White, and that should mean something to you. I still say that they're greatly inferior. They're ugly and kinky-headed. I know we're superior. Otherwise, why are we White, and they're Black? White stands for purity, and since you're the one who mentioned God, for your information, he is also White. Pure and undefiled. I say put a black mark on all their houses. Don't let any of their kids grow up. Kill all of them before they're two."

"Hey," another man spoke, "kill the boys, but you know, we need the girls to do our work, among other things." There was laughter among the men.

There was a moment of silence. Then Mrs. Kingsley spoke, "Is that the message you want me to give them?"

"Maybe not," another woman spoke. "I say let them stay until the child is born."

"Well, that may be all right," the second man said reluctantly. But he was thinking, *It's your message, but it's not mine.*

"Put a mark on their house? What does that mean?" Lieutenant Kingsley asked.

No one answered.

"I hope you don't truly intend to do anything mean against their house. Remember, I work on a destroyer, and that should tell you something." He smiled inwardly, knowing he wouldn't carry out any threat nor do them harm.

"Another nigger lover," the first man said softly, but everyone heard him.

"Call it what you will, but I call it respect for life," Mrs. Kingsley said, and she left the block meeting with a heavy heart, and her husband felt the tremor in her hand as she held on to his arm.

"We've got to do something," she said.

"Yes, but what?" he asked as they walked down the street to their home. It was a nice, calm night with a sky full of stars and a bright full moon.

"I don't know, but I want to be her friend. I'd like to help her weather this storm because I am well aware that hate and prejudice are so cruel."

"You can't leave him out. They hate him just as much, maybe more than they hate her, for being what they called 'stupid enough to marry a nigger.'"

"Oh, I hate that word."

"I have a feeling that they're not going to let them live there in peace."

"So far, there's only been rocks and trash in the yard, but I wouldn't be a bit surprised if they did something worse."

20

On the day after the block meeting, Lieutenant Colin Kingsley woke up at his usual time with Darius and Sage Deavers on his mind. He remembered the hateful words that came from the men who lived in the block—he could call them neighbors, but not neighborly.

"I'm thinking about Ensign Morgan Gray. You remember him, don't you?" he asked his wife.

"I do. He was unhappy here, and he took his family and left."

They were remembering that Ensign Gray was once stationed at Bremerton Naval Base with Lieutenant Kingsley. He had purchased a house for him and his family. Ensign Gray was Black, and he never really felt comfortable living here. It wasn't so much the city, although it certainly had its prejudices. More importantly to him was his feeling about the Navy. He couldn't look forward to any considerable advancement even though he had a college education. Ensign Gray had kept the house thinking that when the president of the United States desegregated the Armed Forces, which was seemingly in the planning stage, he might consider coming back.

"Are you thinking what I'm thinking?" Gertrude asked.

"Yep. I'm thinking about our friends across the street. Morgan doesn't want a sign in the yard so people will know that the house is empty, so it would be a perfect house for Sage and Darius right now. You know, it looks a lot like their house, and it's in a lovely neighborhood."

"Well, they've got to do something."

"You're right. This is an awful position for them to be in. He's trying to run his own law office, which is going to be pretty hard."

"And then there's those children whom she's trying to help, you know, tutoring them to be better prepared for school." And then suddenly a change came over him, and a smile filled his face, brightening up his eyes and his whole countenance.

"What?" she asked, sensing his joy.

"I'll take them—no, we'll take them on our yacht to the boat show and the boat races over at Bremerton because you know they're not allowed to rent a boat or travel on any of the sightseeing cruises. A trip on our boat might cheer them up somewhat, or it could help to take their minds off their troubles, and it would also let them know that we're friends."

"My darling, I think that is a marvelous idea."

Sage had just finished her morning tutoring session with the children and was sitting leisurely at her desk when the phone rang. It was Major Hawthorne. He spoke hurriedly to Sage.

"It's Miriam," he said. "She's on her way over to see you. Please talk to her and help her with your peacemaking skills. She is so depressed, poor baby, and she really doesn't have any close female friends she can talk to. She's taken a liking to you, and it's almost… well…" He paused, not knowing quite how to describe what he wanted to say.

"I know," Sage said, knowing very well how he wanted to end the sentence, knowing he was reluctant to use the word *weird*. Sage had certainly been aware of Miriam's immediate attachment to her on their first meeting, but now she wondered why she was depressed.

"What about her mother?" Sage asked. "I could always talk to my mother about my problems."

"Right now she prefers you. I hope you don't mind."

"I don't mind at all. I'd be glad to have her come, and I'll see what I can do to calm her down."

"Thanks, Sage. I can always see the good in you."

"The Bible says that the kingdom of God is within us. Even you," she said with a chuckle.

"Ha-ha," he said. "I'm not so sure about that, Sage, but I'll see if I can find it in here someplace."

When the doorbell rang, Sage opened the door and welcomed Miriam with outstretched arms and a lingering hug. Hugs to Sage meant a welcoming not only into her home but into her heart. Touching meant, *I feel you. I feel your pain or your love or your peace, whatever feelings are flowing from you, and hopefully my touch can send some peace and good thoughts to you.*

"I'm happy to see you," Sage said, releasing her and placing her arm around Miriam's waist, feeling her pain.

"You don't know how happy I am to see you too," Miriam said, smiling weakly and trying hard not to break down right then and cry.

"Are you hungry?" Sage asked. "It would be no problem to fix something for you."

"No thanks. I'm not the least bit in the mood for food. I just need to talk to somebody. Well, not to just anybody. I feel that I can talk to you, Sage."

"I'm honored that you feel close enough to me," Sage said. She led Miriam to the sofa and sat down beside her. Sage saw the tears that showed in Miriam's eyes, and she reached over and encircled Miriam's hand in both of hers, and Miriam placed her other hand on top of them.

"I came to tell you that I'm pregnant," Miriam said.

"My word, that's exciting," Sage said, hugging Miriam.

"I'm glad to know that you got some help," Miriam said, noticing Mrs. Johnson in the kitchen. My mother's Mamie speaks well of your lady. What's her name?"

"Her name is Mrs. Johnson," Sage said.

The difference was suddenly recognized by Miriam that her mother's maid was called by her first name, and Miriam was not even aware of her last name. It was as if she didn't have one. And here the maid was called by her last name, prefaced by *missus*. Why was this so? The Black and White thing was hitting her in the face again. These two maids were ladies, and they were people. *Yes,* Miriam thought. *Mamie is a Black lady, and we don't know anything about her*

187

life outside my mother's kitchen while Mrs. Johnson is a Black lady, and she's Sage's friend, and Sage is involved in her life.

"And I understand that we're both expecting at about the same time."

"Really?" Miriam said, seeming to recover somewhat. "My due date is the first of April."

"Hey, and mine is the last of March. I think I'll order a pause in your time so that we deliver on the same date. I'm quite looking forward to it," Sage said.

"It can be such a joyful experience. When Timothy was born, I couldn't imagine that I could accomplish such a miraculous thing. You know, carrying a real person inside my body and then actually seeing him and holding him close to my breast. Oh, Sage, I love him so much."

"He's very precocious. I had to laugh when he got up and did that dance with Charles."

"What in the world is the hokeypokey?" Miriam asked, smiling.

"I have no idea where it originated."

"That just about killed my husband because he really hates Black people, and you can't even imagine what my life is like with him. And since I've met you and Darius, he's really killed what little love I did have for him with his hate. And he's tried to instill that hate in Timothy, but I'm determined, somehow, not to let that man take my friends and my son away from me."

"Your husband does seem a little—what shall I say?—cool."

"Oh, Sage, he's not cool. He's a block of ice. That man is a machine. He doesn't feel. He only reacts, you know, to whatever button is pushed. Everything in our life is programmed. Do this at four o'clock. Do this at five. And would you believe that we have a scheduled night for sex?"

"Of course, you're kidding," Sage said, snickering with her hand over her mouth.

"I am not kidding. We have sex by a schedule." Then she mimicked his voice. "Well, my dear, let's get it on." They both laughed. "My marriage is a show, you know, play pretty for the people. Let them see what a lovely family we are. Bullshit. There are times when I think that I hate him."

Sage listened to Miriam, and she couldn't imagine a marriage surviving without love. From what Miriam was saying, her marriage was not a marriage at all. It was a sham. She tried to comfort Miriam.

"I think being pregnant makes women feel different sometimes. But I'm sure it'll change. You'll be happy when you see that little fuzzy head of blond hair emerge. I'm quite looking forward—" She stopped and saw that Miriam's eyes were wet with tears. She wanted so much to comfort her, but she didn't really know what to say.

"If I knew how, I'd get an abortion. And if I knew how, I'd get a divorce," Miriam said, seeming not to be listening to Sage.

"No, no. That's not the right solution."

"Oh, Sage, I hope your marriage stays happy. Marriages don't seem to last somehow."

Sage didn't want to stress the fact that she was happy with her marriage, and she intended for it to stay that way. After a pause, Miriam sighed. "Did you know that my parents are getting a divorce?"

"I didn't know that," Sage said, although she hadn't looked at them as a happy couple.

"Their court date has already been set for next month."

"What seems to be the trouble?" Sage asked.

"It's that my mom thinks my dad has an illegitimate child floating around out there somewhere."

"Oh my."

"And she somehow thinks the child is Black. She accused him of having sex with—oh well, it's terrible." She didn't want to say "with someone Black."

"You are not serious," Sage said with an audible intake of breath. She moved over closer to Miriam and encircled her in her arms. She let Miriam's tears dampen her sleeve as Miriam's head rested on Sage's arm. Finally, Miriam sat up, wiped her eyes, and blew her nose.

"I'm very serious. My parents' marriage has fallen apart, and so has mine. I don't know what to do."

"I've learned that life doesn't always come in a neat little manageable package. I've learned to live life as it is presented to me, and I know for sure that without love, well, nothing makes sense."

"Nobody loves me," Miriam said.

Sage wanted to say *I love you*, but she wondered if she really did. She wasn't sure of her true feelings for Miriam. Miriam was so closely connected to her mother, who hated Sage, and she had a husband who also hated Sage.

"God loves you. Think about that, and your father and your son love you, and besides that, you've got to learn to love yourself. You're a beautiful person, and as my mother always tells me, don't let anyone steal your joy."

"You can feel happy because your husband loves you. I can see that in him."

"Before my husband even came into my life, my mother taught me to love myself. You don't know how it feels to be Black and to have the world hate you. I do, and I say, I love God first, and me second, and everybody and everything comes after that. And another thing, you've got to stop that infernal crying."

"I know. My husband hates to see anyone cry. He slapped Timothy a couple of times for crying."

"Tears can sometimes give temporary relief, but I repeat, don't let them steal your joy. That little angel inside you already loves you, and you can come over here and talk to me anytime. You can call me anytime you're feeling down, either day or night. I'm"—she paused, and the words automatically came out—"I'm your friend."

"Oh, thank you, Sage, and I love you. I really do. I wish I could give this baby to you, and then I'd go away somewhere and no one could find me."

"Then what about Timothy?" Sage asked. "You can't desert him."

"I'd give him to my dad. He loves Timothy, and Timothy loves him."

"And they both love you, so don't forget that." Sage swallowed hard and hugged Miriam tighter.

"But thanks, Sage. I do feel better. You're such a sensible person. I wish I could be more like you." They lingered for a while longer in their embrace.

"On a brighter note," Miriam said, "I have some books for you. They are for mothers and their first pregnancy, you know, how to get through it. Would you like to have them?"

"I sure would."

"Then I'll stop by in the morning when I take Timothy to school, if that's all right."

"Of course, it's all right, and I'll be right here."

Sage watched Miriam as she left, and she felt such a deep sorrow for her. She remembered her own little friend in grade school who wanted to be White. She said she was very unhappy being Black. *Well*, Sage thought, *Miriam is White, and she's unhappy, so being White is not a panacea for happiness, and being Black is not the prime ingredient for unhappiness.*

The next morning, Miriam came by as she had promised, and Timothy was with her. Soon after she arrived, Mrs. Gertrude Kingsley walked across the street to extend the invitation. She was a little nervous as she had the feeling, and rightly so, that some of her neighbors were watching. "Oh well. Oh well."

Gertrude Kinsley took a deep breath, and raising her shoulders up as straight as she could in a gesture of engaging as much strength as she possessed, she walked up the sidewalk and up to the front door and rang the bell.

"I'm sorry," she said as she entered and looked around. "I didn't know you had company. I'm Gertrude Kingsley. My husband and I live just across the street."

"Yes, I'm Sage, and my husband told me about meeting you and your husband," Sage said. "Come on in. Meet my friend and her son." Turning to Miriam, she made the introductions. "This is our neighbor who lives across the street. Mrs. Kingsley, meet Miriam Withers and her son, Timothy."

"I'm happy to meet you," Mrs. Kingsley said, reaching out and shaking Miriam's hand, and then Timothy's.

"And these are my little students, Jasmine and Jasper."

They were seated at the breakfast table, and Mrs. Kingsley went over to shake their hands. The children rose to greet her, extending their hands. Mrs. Johnson walked over from the stove and gave her a warm handshake and a warm smile.

"Good morning," Gertrude Kingsley said. "What lovely children. Actually, Mrs. Deavers, I've come to invite you and your husband to go with my husband and me to Bremerton for the boat show and the boat races. My husband, you know, is a naval officer."

"That's wonderful," Sage said, "But unfortunately, there are restrictions for us on renting the boats or traveling on the ferry."

"I know, but we have our own means of transportation. We own a yacht. We call it the *King and Queen*. And I want you all to come—your husband, these children, and you too, Miriam and Timothy, and your husband, if he'd like to come. And you too, Mrs. Johnson. There's room for everyone." A ray of delight was present around this lady.

"My word, my word," Sage said in amazement. "That's so kind of you to invite us, and we have another good friend who's very much interested in boating. I hope you don't mind if we bring him too."

"And can we bring our mom?" Jasmine asked.

"As I said, there's room for everyone." Gertrude paused and looked around at them all, and she felt so blessed that she and her husband could do this. She was sure that some of them, especially the Black children, had never been on a yacht.

"Can we go?" Timothy said, looking up at his mom. "Can we, Mom? I've never been on a ship. Please."

"Well, it's not exactly a ship," Mrs. Kingsley said with a smile on her face. "But we'd love to take you on our yacht."

Miriam thought, *What a coincidence that Bertram is away as I know he wouldn't allow us to go. Ha! With these Black people, he wouldn't even consider going himself. Sad for the hate in his heart.*

"Thank you for the invitation," Miriam said, looking at Mrs. Kingsley. "We'd be happy to go with you."

At Miriam's suggestion, Major Hawthorne and his wife were also invited to go. He said he was sorry that his schedule prevented him from joining them, and he said the experience, although promising to be a delightful one, would not be new to him as it would be for some of the others, especially the children, for during his army life, he had traveled by land, air, and water. He was happy, however, that

Miriam and Timothy could go without the permission of Bertram Withers, knowing that he was away on a business trip.

The major's happiness extended to the friendship that had come about between Sage and Darius and Lieutenant Kingsley and his lovely wife, and he was happy because he felt that Darius needed more Whites in his life. Uh-huh. Yes, he did.

Major Hawthorne told his wife, Alicia, that she was invited to go on the trip, but she declined, just only because of her ingrown prejudice against Black people, especially Sage and Charles. Her hate was like an ingrown toenail. She couldn't take it out; it had to be physically cut out by an experienced professional, and she would need patience for the healing process.

Darius Paul Deavers was thrilled about the invitation and for the splendid opportunity it would be for the children to experience such a trip which only the Kingsleys could provide at this time. He was, however, aware that neither he nor Charles nor Sage had family ties here. Miriam had ties to Major Hawthorne and Timothy; Karen had ties to Mrs. Johnson and her children. Darius noted to himself that he was attached to Charles by a cord of friendship, not blood. He was attached to Sage by a golden chain of enduring love, and it was interesting, he thought, that his attachments on this trip were both Black. Then thinking of everyone, including the Kingsleys and Major Hawthorne, he smiled, for he felt very much like this was one big happy family in spite of their color differences.

Ariel Sage Copple Deavers was thinking, *So this is integration. Black and White together socially as friends.* Her only previous experience with being racially integrated had been with Darius and his family, and she had spent time in the home of Paul and Beth Porter, and she was comfortable with all these White people. Feeling equal. And with this group, she was at ease, but she knew this integration was private, not public. She looked at her husband, and it was not, *I'm married to a White man,* as so many people said, but, *I'm married to Darius Paul Deavers, and he is the man I love, and together with whomever, with whatever group of people, I am content.*

Karen Johnson awoke early that morning. She thought about the trip and about what a positive experience it would be for the children. She thought about their father and about their relationship as young adults. Not married. Not knowing very much about life. Him turning out to be unworthy, drinking and taking drugs. Oh well. Unfortunately, she had allowed Randy's promise of love to cause her to get sidetracked; but fortunately, she and the children could go on this trip, and she'd be thankful for the experience she and her children would have. They'd never been on a yacht nor even a boat, and they'd never been swimming. *What a blessing this is for us.*

Miriam Withers regarded the trip as a blessing. She was thinking, *I have been given a pleasure trip, with freedom to relax and freedom to laugh, to cry if I want, hug and kiss my son, dance, even do the hokey-pokey. These are people who won't judge me, people who welcome me as I am, who consider me equal, not above and not privileged because of my skin color. I have a father who loves me. The thought of my pregnancy is with me. A little girl. I want so much to love you, and I didn't mean it when I said I didn't want you as it isn't you that I don't want. It's the situation, the atmosphere surrounding my whole life, and it involves your father, the other part of you. But right now you're inside of me, and you're mine. It's me who gives you nourishment, so let's you and me make a bond this day that we will try very hard to keep him from separating us. I found a friend in Sage Deavers, who encourages me to be strong. I am thankful that I have today, so I won't worry about tomorrow because when I wake up tomorrow, it will be today. La-la-la, tra-la-la.*

Charles Williams, whose interest was more than recreational, wanted to learn about boating and all water activities. He was hopeful that Lieutenant Kingsley could help him in his endeavor to obtain these activities for Black people, especially children who were hampered by racial prejudice. Charles was sad for the children yet happy for this opportunity.

Mrs. Johnson and Mamie, both eternal mother hens, offered to make lunches for everyone, so Mrs. Kingsley took them to her favorite delicatessen, let them purchase whatever they wanted, and she was thankful for their knowledge of food preparation.

"We can buy drinks, candy, and popcorn at Bremerton," Gertrude Kingsley told them.

Although Mrs. Johnson and Mamie were invited and encouraged by Sage to come along, they said, "No. Let it be for the young people, and let love abide."

21

Their destination was Bremerton, Washington, which is well known for its Puget Sound Naval Shipyard. It lies on the west shore of Puget Sound, about twenty miles by ferry from Seattle. It is also a major tourist attraction.

The plan was for everyone to meet at eight o'clock Saturday morning at the Kingsleys' house, and Major Hawthorne offered to pick them up in his van, and he would follow Lieutenant Kingsley in his jeep to the loading dock. The major also offered to pick them up from the dock after the trip and to bring them back. His offer was gladly accepted.

Lieutenant Kingsley was experiencing the greatest happiness because of all the young people who were gathered on their patio. Young adults and young children. Their own son was not very close in distance nor attentiveness, and they saw him only if they went to visit him. He never came to visit them, and he had no children; therefore, Colin and Gertrude Kingsley had not been blessed with grandchildren. Lieutenant Kingsley looked at his wife, who was standing beside him, and he knew she was having the same thoughts. He knew that as soon as she met Sage and Darius, she had fallen in love with them; and in both their minds, they had already adopted them as their children. Now that they had met Miriam and Timothy, Karen and Karen's children, they also made them a part of the family they always wanted. Color didn't seem to matter to either of them. Their lives and their house, empty for so long, was now filled, if only for today. She had read his thoughts.

"I will make sure that it isn't just for today. Not only do we need them, but each one of them has a different need of someone. A father, a mother, or loving grandparents."

The adults each brought something they thought would lend to the enjoyment of the trip.

"I am the captain of this friendship ship," Lieutenant Kingsley said. "And I've brought pins in the shape of a ship for each of you to pin on your jacket. You're now seaworthy."

Mrs. Kingsley brought tulip bulbs, small flower pots filled with the proper soil, and instructions for maintaining and replanting them. Note: the state of Washington produced more flower bulbs than any other place in the world, except the Netherlands.

Major Hawthorne, who had extensive knowledge of the state's orchards, brought a bag of delicious red apples, one for each person in the group. Washington orchards produce more apples than those of any other state.

Miriam, with Karen's permission, bought swimming suits, caps, and towels for the children.

Charles, whose love of swimming was strong, brought small colorful inner tubes that would fit around the children's waist to keep them afloat in the water.

Sage, knowing about quilting, brought scissors, needles, thread, and a variety of gingham material and square pieces of cardboard to be used as patterns for the quilt blocks. Darius brought boxes of chalk for a game of hopscotch to be played in the different ways which he'd learned as a child.

The children enjoyed the ride to the east shore of Puget Sound. Jasmine and Jasper were already bonded as brother and sister, and as is the general way with children, they were drawn to Timothy, and he to them. They played a game of owning the cars that passed, claiming them by color. Jasmine chose white cars, Jasper chose red cars, and Timothy chose blue cars.

"There's a white one."

"I see a blue one."

"There's a red one."

"Well, what about trucks? I see a red truck."

"Trucks don't count."

"Why not?"

"I don't think that there's a lot of trucks."

And so they bonded.

Arriving at the east side of Puget Sound, Lieutenant Kingsley led the way to the yacht, and it was a happy group that boarded the vessel. The yacht was equipped with seats along the edge of the deck so that the twenty-five minute trip to Bremerton was more like a sightseeing trip, and there were many things to see, things that most had never seen before.

They *ooh*ed and *aah*ed as they saw boats of every size which crowned the harbors and bays during the boating season, and they marveled at the hundreds of small pleasure boats that were clustered along the bay. They saw sailboats powered only by the wind and boats driven by a powerful outboard motor. The Kingsleys' vessel sailed close enough for them to wave at the people who were fishing from their rowboats, and they enjoyed the beautiful and interesting boat show.

When they were on the grounds at Bremerton, the lieutenant led everyone on a tour of the shipyard. Next was the playground for the children, where they enjoyed the swings, the turnaround, and the toy cars. Then Charles took Karen and the children wading and on a waterslide. They were all dressed in their swimsuits, caps, and inner tubes. They fished in a large tub of water for prizes.

"It's all right for you to go with them, Karen," Mrs. Kingsley said. "But I'm not going to encourage my two little pregnant mammas to go. I wouldn't want them to slip and fall."

Back on the yacht, there was eating and drinking for everyone. There was quilt-making for the ladies. The men went with Charles to seek information about participating in the boat activities. They learned things that Lieutenant Kingsley already knew and Darius suspected: that Charles was at a disadvantage in his ambitions for water activities here because of racism.

"I'll make some inquiries when I get back to the city, but I don't think things are going to change any time soon," Lieutenant Kingsley said.

Darius suggested his game. "Do you know how to play hop-scotch?" he asked the three children.

"We do," Jasmine said, indicating Jasper too.

"I don't," Timothy said.

"Then I'll show you," Jasmine said this.

"I brought some chalk, and I'll draw the lines on the deck, if that's all right," Darius said, looking at Mrs. Kingsley for permission to mark on the deck. She nodded in agreement.

"So we can have two teams," Darius said. "The children against the adults: me, Charles, and Karen." That brightened the mood as Charles was feeling somewhat down.

After enjoying all the planned activities, they headed back across the water of Puget Sound. Lieutenant Kingsley gave each of the children a time at the helm, steering the boat, with his own hands on the wheel, of course. Mrs. Kingsley took the adults on a tour of the lower part of the yacht.

"Darius, you hold Sage's hand going down these steps because they're steep and somewhat narrow. Charles, you hold Miriam's hand, and Karen and I will lead the way. If you little mothers should stumble and fall, we'll catch you," she said, laughing. "Just kidding, but you do have to be careful."

Charles looked from Miriam to Karen, and he was attracted to both of them, noting they both were perhaps his age, except, of course, they were both married. But he concluded that wouldn't keep him from being their friend.

When they disembarked, Major Hawthorne was waiting for them. They boarded the van and settled down as they were ready to relax, except for the children, who were still full of energy.

"Well, look what I have," Sage said, pulling a ball of string from her bag. "I brought pieces of string for each of you."

"String?" someone asked.

"Yes. I can show you how to put the string on your fingers, and drawing your fingers through in different ways, you can make stars and steeples and all sort of things."

"Oh yes, I've seen that done. It's fun," Karen said.

They had become one big happy family. Their differences had been washed away by the water of sameness among them. With the loving attitude toward them of Lieutenant Colin and Mrs. Gertrude Kingsley, they all felt they were in the closeness of another mother and father; and similarly, the Kingsleys were pleased with their new-found children, and they felt they were surrounded by their own children and grandchildren who were not only appreciated but needed. Jasmine, Jasper, and Timothy had bonded beautifully as new friends, not concerned or bothered by their color difference.

It was the beginning of a beautiful sunset, and Darius, sitting in front beside Major Hawthorne, could see the horizon out both the front and the west side of the van. He remembered from high school that an astronomer, Nicolaus Copernicus, was the first to present a mathematical model supporting the premise that the earth is moving and the sun actually stands still, and sunset is when the last part of the sun is about to disappear below the horizon as the earth makes its rotation.

To Darius, the sun appeared to be a big golden ball full of heat that gave it its light, and it was sitting atop a high wall; and slowly, slowly, it started to disappear. Three-fourths gone. One-half gone. And then only a tip, which left just a little light. Then it was gone, and if there weren't for the streetlights, it would be a dark, dark place.

As darkness came, Darius looked at the stars twinkling, trying to give light and direction. Didn't they follow a star? But the darkness didn't bring sadness and fear, for he thought of it as being God's way of putting his world and his worldly beings to sleep. Darius also knew that there are evil ones everywhere who wait for the dark of night to prey on the helpless. He had no way of knowing how true this was.

Darius looked back at his wife, at the children, at Miriam and Karen and Charles, at Mrs. Kingsley; and their obvious happiness dispelled any dark thoughts. Darius Paul Deavers turned toward the sky and smiled.

And then I looked, and I saw a black horse.

As soon as they reached their street corner, both vehicles arriving at about the same time, their world came crashing down. The exterior of the Deavers' beautiful house had been painted black, every inch—the roof, the windowpanes, the steps, even the front walk and the driveway. The words "YOU LIKE BLACK, WELL, YOU'VE GOT IT" had been painted on a large placard and was stuck in the yard. Not only that, there was a six-foot-high kerosene-soaked cross burning in the Kingsleys' front yard. The evil monsters must have watched until they saw them coming back to light it, for it was beginning to be a roaring blaze when they arrived.

Darius Deavers hung his head and cried, hoping not to die.

It can't be real, he thought. But it only took a moment for him to realize that this was not a scene from a movie, nor was he in the midst of a dream that when he woke up, it would be gone. No, this was real.

Lieutenant Kingsley had presence of mind enough to call the fire department and the police, and by the time they arrived, a crowd had gathered, and he realized that he and his wife were as much a spectacle as was the painted house and the burning cross.

Sage couldn't cry. Standing there looking at their first home, she felt a tremendous chill running through her body; and her heart, soul, and mind felt frozen. *Am I turning to stone or a pillar of salt? What have I done wrong?* she wondered, not even being able to imagine in her wildest thoughts that...that what? That someone could be this cruel? That someone could harbor enough hate to do this? It couldn't have been a spur-of-the-moment action, she concluded, because it would take time and money to purchase the paint, the spray gun, the protective gloves and eye goggles, and the patience to carry it out. The time. The effort. Then they needed kerosene and wood for the cross, and of course, she imagined that they took pride and pleasure in the finished product.

Sage was thinking, *And you imagine you've figured it out, like a difficult mathematics problem, and you know the equation, and no matter what numbers you use, if you work the equation right, you always get the right answer. Like you've formed your basic philosophy for living, based on your beliefs. I won't lie. I'll always speak the truth. I will never purposefully hurt anyone, and good things will happen to me. But I've found out that life is not a mathematics problem, and no matter if you use your philosophy [the equation], it doesn't always comes out right. Seems like bad things happen to good people, and good things happen to bad people, so it's important to live with what is, even when it's not according to the plan you've worked so long and hard in developing.*

Standing there, Darius thought, *At least we still have our furniture.* Not so. Getting his nerve, he walked inside, and when he had thought that his world could not have crashed down any lower, it had. He felt like he was in a netherworld, further down, and he was smothering because what he saw was that the evil monsters had taken away the ladder so that he couldn't climb out. In reality, what he saw was that every piece of furniture—the sink, bathtub, refrigerator, stove, bed, and coverings—had also been painted black. They had opened the closet doors and sprayed their clothes. They had opened the kitchen cabinets and sprayed all the dishes. *How had they gotten in? We had locks on every door. He then saw that they had broken down the back door, most likely with a hatchet, for it was in splinters.*

They had not gotten into the garage, so the cars were not damaged. What could anyone do except stand there in shock until their conscious realization of the awful reality of this scene that was playing out in front of them took hold?

Charles had left his car there, but he had parked it on the street around the corner. Some kind of thought proved his fears to be correct, but they were fears that there might be rocks thrown at his car or raw eggs cracked on it, never imagining or thinking of black paint. He took Karen and her children home, all three crying, the children holding on to their mother. All the time, he was struggling to stay calm.

The Kingsleys offered their home, and it would have been convenient for Sage and Darius to stay the night with them. But if the evil dragons didn't want Sage and Darius in their own house, they most definitely would not have wanted them in their neighbor's house. The burning cross represented a warning: *whatever it is you're doing that involves niggers, stop it, or worse things could happen to you.*

Major Hawthorne, bless his heart, put Miriam and Timothy, also crying, in his van, and he offered to take Sage and Darius to the army base to stay in the officers' quarters.

Sage's wisdom took over. "No, we have a building," she said. "It's in a safe place, and it's ours. We'll stay there. It has a kitchen, bathroom, and a divan that opens out into a bed. We will stay downstairs, and Charles can still stay upstairs, and my husband and I, we can survive this together, and we will decide some things later."

Gertrude Kingsley admired Sage more than ever, thinking, *What a brave, sensible, peaceful person she is.* She couldn't imagine all that Sage had lived through in her life, but she knew that Sage had survived it all, and Gertrude Kingsley felt sure that Sage Deavers would survive this. She gathered sheets, pillows and pillowcases, blankets, towels, and sleeping clothes for the young couple. She hugged them, both of them, and Lieutenant Kingsley hugged them, both of them.

It was not a peaceful night of sleep for any of the participants of the trip. It was like seeing an awesome eclipse of the sun and moon for the first time, or waking up one morning and seeing the first roses blooming in your garden. Like sitting outside on a clear night with your children and someone you love and searching for and finding the Big Dipper in the sky. Then suddenly—a catastrophic happening, like a flash of lightning followed by a loud clap of thunder. And then…and then…no moon, no stars, roses that have died and turned into poison ivy.

Part Three

22

After leaving the black-house disaster, Darius and Sage lay in each other's arms, each with their own thoughts.

Darius thought, *"Until our child is born," they said, but they couldn't wait. Their hearts and their evil minds are like a rattlesnake, waiting, waiting, rattling, striking when something gets too close. Something they are afraid could do them harm. But what can we do? What did we even want to do that would harm them? Not a thing. But hate, like weeds, grows uncultivated, unwatered, unwanted, feeding on itself. Unless the roots are destroyed, the weeds, like the hateful feelings, crop up somewhere else, seemingly indestructible. But how do you destroy the roots? Can you?*

So what am I supposed to do now? Join one of the protesting groups? They really don't seem to be accomplishing much. Just treading water and drowning in their own tears. And where will we live? We can't stay here forever. Well, it's not long, only several more months until our little one is due. Of course, I'll have to send Sage back home and stop subjecting her to all this meanness. Then I'll decide where to work. So, God, whoever or wherever, and if you are, which I'm beginning to doubt, my future is in your hands.

Sage was also thinking, *This isn't the end of the world. It's just another one of those stumbling blocks along our way. All the mean things that have already been done to us didn't stop us, and we're not going to let this stop us. Those who haven't experienced this kind of hateful prejudice can't understand how we who have experienced it could survive it without killing somebody or killing ourselves. But He didn't bring us this far to leave us. His people survived the fiery furnace, the flood, the storm, locusts, and they didn't drown in the Red Sea. None of it touched their bodies, and it hasn't touched ours, and we can't let it destroy our love.*

As she lay there, somehow the thing that occupied Sage's mind was the time she had witnessed the incidence of a tornado. After hearing the warning sirens, you're ordered to move away from the windows and to sit quietly in a corner. It was an eerie quietness. Sometimes a tornado cuts a destructive path, uprooting trees, blowing away houses, setting fires, tearing apart what had once been your prize possession.

Then after the storm was over, the skies became clear; and after a period of time, here comes the sun. You note the damage, and even if you lost all of your possessions, you walk off into the sunshine of your life. You could move your body and your mind elsewhere, knowing that where you are does not determine who you are nor how happy or unhappy you can be, for happiness is not a place, nor is it determined by your possessions. Happiness is a state of mind.

Lieutenant Kingsley awoke early. He kissed his wife on the lips as she lay awake. She sat up and swung her feet to the floor. They dressed and enjoyed their morning coffee. Before he left for work, he wanted to be sure that his wife was awake and aware of the ever-present possibility of more evil deeds being done by the neighbors. He and his wife had been thinking about a place for Darius and Sage to live, and they came to the conclusion that the Ensigns' house would be the perfect residence for them at this time, and it would get them out of that little building until they could decide on a permanent move.

Later that same morning, the police came and knocked on every door in the block and asked questions, but of course, no one knew anything, so no arrests were made. The insurance agents came and surveyed the scene, and they also asked questions, but no one was of any help to them either.

Darius awoke early, and he knew he had to get away and seek some peace. He drove back to the pathway by the park. He had to think. He couldn't think. He couldn't pray. He couldn't even cry. He ran down the path and around the lake until he became tired from running. He stood in one place and stomped the ground. Exhausted, he returned to his car. He screamed, sure no one could hear him. There were some things inside of him that had to come out.

He had just now become aware of how many frustrations, how much anger, how many indecisions he'd been holding inside—how many roads diverged in his forests, his wilderness.

I must think. I must find some peace. I have two options: live or die. If I die, I have two options: heaven or hell. What do I know about heaven? People speak of it as a beautiful home in the sky, a haven of rest, streets paved with gold, earth has no sorrow that Heaven cannot heal, I'll meet him face-to-face, I'm just going home. They speak of hell as being a place of eternal fire and brimstone, and in order to experience either place, I'd have to die; and in order to die now, I'd have to commit suicide. How would I do it? Shoot myself in the head? But I don't own a gun, and that's so messy. Blood everywhere. Pills are another option, but what kind would I take? I could use carbon monoxide, sit in my car with the motor running, or I could drive my car into the water and drown. There are enough lakes around this city, so I wouldn't have to go far. Hmm.

What do I know about death? Not much. But I do know something about life. I am familiar with many of the things that are here on this earth, so think about living. But how should I live? After a long while, he got out of his car and walked down the tree-lined pathway and sat down beneath a beautiful tree. It was a juniper tree, and as he sat there, his thoughts centered on Darius Paul Deavers. *You can't be stronger than yourself, but you can be as strong as you make up your mind to be.*

He thought again of the serenity prayer. "Give me the serenity to accept the things I cannot change." *I cannot change my love for Sage, and I cannot change the hateful minds and hearts of the prejudiced White people.* "Give me the courage to change the things I can." *I can change my thinking from worry to helping where I can.* "And give me the wisdom to know the difference." *The difference in those two situations is peace. Can I have peace being White and living in a Black world? Peace knowing that I'm so much different from my wife and her world. Peace to stop my thinking that integration is our savior.*

But when he thought about the building and how small it was, and of the one small bathroom, he was seized by fear. He could see the devil's long bony fingers pointed at him again, and he could hear the devil laughing. Ha! Ha! Ha! You have never lived in a small house. Then he realized that he was crying.

Arriving back at the building, as he got out of the car, he saw Sage sitting on a stool in the yard with a little shovel in her hand, digging in the dirt. She stood up to greet him.

"Hello, dear," she said, smiling. "Mrs. Kingsley says that I can pull the weeds and cultivate the soil, and then when I'm ready, I can plant some flowers. Won't that be wonderful?"

He hugged her, and the tears ran down his face.

"Don't cry, Darius dear. It's going to be all right."

"My dear Sage, I know about your faith, but I want you to go away from here, from all this meanness. I think you should go home to your mother until our child is born."

She put her hands over his mouth. "My dear Darius, you keep saying that, and don't you even imagine in your wildest dreams that I will leave you and go home. I'm already home. Home is with you."

"But this... I don't want you to have to live like this."

"My dear, I've lived in less than this, and we really won't have to because when Lieutenant and Mrs. Kingsley came by, they offered a solution, at least temporarily, for a place we can live. They know a Black Navy ensign who left here, but he didn't want to sell his house, hoping the segregation laws for the Armed Forces would change, and he would come back. So we can live there temporarily."

"Seems like nothing we try to do turns out to be permanent. I don't know, Sage. I just don't know."

"We can only live one day at a time, so I think we ought to do this, and we'll deal with tomorrow when it comes."

"Have you even seen the house? Do you even know what it looks like?" Darius asked, still in a state of sadness.

"No, I haven't seen it, and I don't know what it looks like. And if you recall, I didn't see our first house before you and your dad bought it. I trusted your judgment and his, and now I think we can trust Lieutenant and Mrs. Kingsley's judgment, so put your arms around me and let His peace surround us, and we can go and live there now."

And so they did.

23

When Bertram Withers learned of the trip and of the destruction at the Deavers' house, told to him in detail by his son, Timothy, as they sat one morning eating breakfast, he turned all his rage toward his wife.

"I told you. I told you not to involve yourself with those people. Now look what has happened. Don't you see that the same thing could happen to us?"

"Why would it happen to us?" Miriam asked.

"For the same reason, my dear wife, that it happened to that damn Marine and his wife—for trying to befriend those Black people."

"He's not a Marine. He's in the Navy," Timothy said this.

"Like what the hell is the difference?" He stomped around in a circle, and Timothy began to cry.

"And you go to your room. This doesn't involve you, and stop that damn crying."

Timothy looked at his mother, quite confused about what the problem was. He had enjoyed the trip, and he really liked Lieutenant and Mrs. Kingsley, and he really liked Jasmine and Jasper, and he hadn't seen them as bad because of the color of their skin. He thought that that's how he'd look with a tan. Miriam waved him on.

"Go," she said, and she listened to her husband as he continued his ranting.

"I'll tell you again. Those Black folk are not our social equal, and for all it's worth, they were not supposed to be living in that house. There is a covenant that forbids it, so I think they deserve what they got."

Miriam was brave enough to look at him, and she didn't like him at all.

"And why are you so friendly with them anyway? I see how that Charles looks at you. That's it, isn't it? You're attracted to him because he's Black like that Sage is, and you really like her, don't you?"

"They're just people," she managed to say.

"They're not people. How could you enjoy being with them?"

"It wasn't only me. Your son enjoyed being with the children too."

"He shouldn't have been there either." He threw his napkin down on the table and began shaking his head *again*. "Miriam, I'm warning you. Let this be the last time you do anything with them. And I think I'll go over and have a talk with Mr. Navy"—he put emphasis on the word *navy*—"and tell him and his wife that I don't want them to include you and my son in any more of their outings with those people."

"It wasn't anything they did wrong, and we don't do any recreational things together, so I went because I wanted to go. I really wish you wouldn't go over there. Please. Don't do that."

"You can't tell me what to do. I'm the head of this household, and I say what I'll do, and I say I'm going over there and I'm going to tell them that Black is Black and White is White, and never the twain should meet."

And that's what he intended to do. On his way to the house, quite adamant about his decision, Bertram Withers decided exactly what he would say to the Kingsleys. He would ask them politely, he said to himself, to please exclude his little family from their integrated outings.

Arriving at the house, he parked and stepped out of his car. He hadn't quite known what to expect, perhaps that some buckets of black paint had been thrown randomly on the Deavers' house from a safe distance. But what he saw was much more deplorable than he would ever have imagined, and turning to the other direction, he saw the remains of the burnt cross, which, for reasons unknown, had been left in their yard.

Bertram Withers stood for what seemed like a long time. His inner self was struggling between the conviction that they deserved it because of disobeying the law, and the desire to abhor this thing that had happened to them. Then his resolve returned, and he walked up to the Kingsleys' door and raised the artful bronze knocker—thinking, of course, they would agree with him, and they would understand that those people could not be friends with his family.

"Let me introduce myself," he said as Mrs. Kingsley opened the door. "I'm Bertram Withers—"

"Oh, you're Miriam's husband and the father of that beautiful little boy. Please come in," she said. "But before you thank us, I'd like you to know that we've adopted them all as our own family."

What? What? What is she saying? Bertram was lost in a wilderness of misunderstanding, and his words were frozen somewhere in his larynx, and he couldn't speak what he was thinking.

"Sit down. May I get you something to drink?"

"No, thank you, but—"

"You see, we only have one son, and he's not very close to us, and he doesn't have any children. So you see, we don't have either children or grandchildren."

"My wife always wanted a daughter," the husband said. "And now she has three."

"Three?"

"Yes, there's Sage, and your beautiful wife, and Karen. And we have three grandchildren. Karen's got a boy and a girl, and there's your son. Oh, we feel so blessed."

"Karen. Who is Karen?"

"She's Mrs. Johnson's daughter."

"And who is Mrs. Johnson?"

"She's Sage and Darius's maid."

"Sage has a maid?" he asked, ignoring that she said Sage and Darius.

"Yes, she does."

"Is she Black?"

"Yes, she is."

"So this Karen and her mother are Black? Does Karen work for them too?"

"Oh no. Sage tutors her two little children, and bless her heart, Mrs. Johnson is like an absentee mother for Sage. So having your wife as our daughter, that makes you our son also, and I surely hope your mother and father won't feel any objection to us loving them— and you."

"My mother and father are...they've passed." He didn't want to share his story, and goodness sakes, the more he tried to dislike them, the more his other self or his same inner self wanted to accept them. And how could they use the word *love*? Love was a foreign word to him, and he felt that it could, in no way, be used in talking about Black people.

It was too much for Bertram Withers to receive all at once, especially since what they were telling him had absolutely nothing to do with his reason for coming.

Lieutenant Kingsley joined in the conversation. "Those two, Sage and Darius, they're so good, and they're trying so hard just to live. And with all the hatefulness that's happening to them, they can think about helping other people. I just don't understand how people can hate them just because Sage is Black."

"It's going to be all right, my dear," his wife said, patting his hand. "They have us, and they have Miriam's father. Thank the Lord for Major Hawthorne."

"Miriam's father? Did he go with you?"

"No, he drove us to the pier in his army van, and we had a really wonderful time. It's too bad you were unable to join us."

Bertram Withers, totally caught off-guard by the couple's words, by their evident support of all those whom he was against, stood in a world of confusion. And when both of them stepped forward to bid him good day, they each put their arms around him, with a hug that further frustrated him, as he hadn't come to thank them as they had imagined.

Leaving the Kingsleys' house, he was angry with himself because he hadn't been able to say what he'd come to say. He sat in his car and looked more closely at the Deavers' black house. Although he didn't like them, he could never do anything this mean and hateful to them. *But, oh well,* he was thinking, *it's too bad about their house, but I'm not the cause of any of it, and I won't alter my beliefs. They are inferior, and I'll still forbid my wife from seeing them.*

Then it started to rain, and as he drove along, the rain got worse. The state of Washington is known for its floods and mud slides.

24

After a few days had passed since the trip to Bremerton, Bertram Withers became concerned about his wife's health. Although she rose in the morning, she didn't get dressed, and she wouldn't eat or talk. She'd sit in the chair by the bedroom window staring out at seemingly nothing in particular. She made no effort to feed Timothy or to take him to school, so Bertram was required to get his son fed and dressed; then not knowing what to do as Miriam refused to answer his questions about what was ailing her, he called her mother.

Alicia agreed to come and see about her daughter; and Bertram, relieved, took Timothy to school and went off to his job. Alicia tried to coax Miriam to take a bath and change her gown, but she refused, and Alicia was not able to get her to eat or to talk. After an hour had passed with the same results, Alicia began to wonder if Miriam's actions or nonactions would cause harm to her unborn child. She couldn't relax. It was as if her daughter didn't even see her, her eyes seeming to look right through her like she wasn't even there, so Miriam's condition was causing Alicia Hawthorne to be gravely concerned.

Deciding to throw off her animosity toward her husband and knowing that he had a closer relationship with Miriam than she did, she called him and asked him to come over, thinking that Miriam would confide in him. She answered the door when he rang.

"Bertram says that she's been like this since coming home from that trip over there, and I say that in her condition, she had no business going out on the water and being jostled on a boat and I can imagine what else they put her through. And Bertram agrees with me, and he also laid the blame for her awful condition on that trip, forbidding her from ever going anyplace with those people again."

Listening to her, Major Hawthorne became angry, but he overcame the urge to react to his wife's words, for he understood fully the reason for Miriam's malaise, and he knew that the trip was not the culprit here. He knew that Miriam had been traumatized by the black house, by it being done to such good people as Sage and Darius and by her husband's mean and awful reaction to her going with them, as Timothy had told him.

"And I think she should see her doctor, but she refuses, and Bertram has to work, and now he's trying to take care of Timothy too. This is ridiculous," Alicia said as they went up the stairs.

When he walked into the room, Miriam, looking up and seeing him, put her hand out to him and began to cry. It was the only real emotion she'd shown since becoming this way. The major knelt beside her chair and took her outstretched hand in his; and looking at her pale sad face and her tears, Marvin was more concerned than he had been when Alicia called.

"What about Mamie?" he asked, turning to his wife. "Maybe you could do without her for a few days, and she could come over and take care of the house and the cooking until our girl feels better."

"I can ask her, but I don't know how she'd feel about coming over here."

"I'll ask her," Marvin said. "I have a pretty good relationship with her."

She was thinking, *Well, of course you do. You seem to relate to all of those people. What do they call people like that? Nigger lovers. And I do mean lovers.*

"Since she refuses to go to see the doctor. I don't know what else to do," Alicia said.

"Well, it might be a good idea to call in a private nurse to take care of her. There are some nurses at the hospital who are on call, and I can check them out."

"Well, then I guess that's the next best thing," Alicia said, looking at them holding hands and becoming envious, sensing that

Miriam had a closer relationship with her father than with her. She felt alienated from them.

After her mother left, Miriam's whole world became a brighter, more cheerful place, and the tears stopped, and she smiled at her father.

Miriam was thinking, *I would like for Mamie to come. Mamie won't judge me, and I can get acquainted with her on a whole new level, like Sage and Mrs. Johnson. Mrs. Johnson understands Sage's dilemma being Black in a White wife's role and the newness of being the employer, the boss lady. Think of it as Mrs. Johnson is Black and Sage is White; Mamie is Black, and I am White, but I'll call her Mrs. Caldwell, and I'll get to know her better. I'm sure she has some words of wisdom to share with me, and hopefully she'll take me into her heart as Mrs. Johnson has taken Sage. I wonder if Mamie has a family. I would like to confide in her as a friend, but I know my prejudiced husband wouldn't understand, and the sky would fall if he ever heard me say Mrs. Crawford instead of Mamie. Sage's mother was Darius's mother's maid, and now she is his mother-in-law, and now Darius's mother, the boss lady, is Sage's mother-in-law. What a complicated world when you're mixing Black and White. And now my husband has forbidden me from ever seeing them again and certainly not taking Timothy to play with the children. So what is the difference, except for the color of the skin and the prejudice that has kept them from progressing further? I can't seem to figure it out to everybody's satisfaction, and my own satisfaction of being their friend would be dissatisfaction to my husband and my mother. Oh dear, I can't continue to live like this because this husband of mine is draining the life out of me, and I don't know what to do. Come, Lord Jesus. Or somebody.*

And as it happened, Miriam's condition did not improve, even with Mamie being there to take care of Bertram and Timothy, so Major Hawthorne hired a nurse. Her name was Helen Kane, and she came highly recommended with all the qualifying papers needed to be in the professional nurses' pool. He had known her only casually at the hospital, but there was something about her appearance and her smile that he liked, and she readily volunteered to work for him as his daughter's nurse. These nurses were on call for doctors and private patients, and they worked with the elite who preferred to remain in their home instead of being in a hospital room.

Alicia came on the nurse's first day, and after spending a few minutes getting acquainted with her, Alicia introduced her to Mamie. Alicia took over at Bertram's bidding, and she explained to Mamie and Helen what their specific duties would be. Mamie was to take orders from Bertram; she was to prepare the food for everyone, including the nurse; and she agreed to stay at the house to be available for them and all their needs. Nurse Kane would take care of Miriam.

Alicia Hawthorne introduced Nurse Helen Kane to Bertram and Timothy. Bertram was confident that the nurse's background had been thoroughly researched, and he was confident that she could be trusted with Miriam. Since his wife refused to talk to him or to answer his questions, he had hoped that since Nurse Helen was a professional, she could ascertain the reason for his wife's problem, whether mental or physical, and could help her get over it. He didn't expect that his wife was really physically ill, but he had it in his mind that she had made some ill-advised, bad decisions about the people with whom she and his son should associate. He was thinking, *Of course, I have put a stop to that, and she'll get over it, and I'll continue to keep Timothy in the company of his own kind—White.*

Nurse Helen Kane was White. She was not tall and not short but average height for a woman, five feet six. She wore a plain palegreen cotton two-piece dress, which was trimmed with a white collar and white cuffs. She was not pretty but could be considered very attractive. She had brown eyes, brown hair, pulled back and made into a ball just above her neckline. She was fifty years old.

"What a beautiful person you are," Nurse Kane said as she entered the room and looked down at Miriam.

Miriam raised her head and looked at this person who had spoken so kindly to her, and a little smile could be detected on her usually gloomy facial expression.

"I'm going to take good care of you and our little angel that's inside of you."

Bertram and Timothy came in to say goodbye before going off for their day. Timothy reached over and gave his mother a kiss on the cheek, and Miriam gave him a little smile. It was her second response, but she went right back into her inattentive, sleepy look. Bertram, seeing that it was expected of him, bent down and kissed his wife, but the nurse detected a slight movement of rejection from Miriam. A flinch, if you will.

After Bertram, Timothy, and Alicia left, Nurse Kane turned her attention back to her patient. "If you don't mind, I'd like to make sure your vital signs are normal, you know, your temperature and blood pressure, all right?"

Miriam sat up straight, put her arm out, and nodded yes.

At once, on seeing Nurse Helen Kane, Miriam was especially drawn to her, and she sensed by some seeming inward instinct that Nurse Kane was patient and kind and that she not only liked her but wanted very much to help her. Nurse Kane recommended that Miriam occupy the guest bedroom and that she sleep alone, not with her husband, and she offered to stay a few nights with Miriam to try and determine firsthand the extent of her illness. She would sleep on a foldaway bed on the other side of the room as special thought was also given for the safety and emotional status of the child within her patient. It was a common belief that the temperament of the mother during pregnancy could affect the fetus: happy, sad, angry, peaceful.

When Major Hawthorne came, Miriam heard the doorbell, and her head came up as she recognized her father's voice speaking to Mamie. Major Hawthorne was fond of Mamie, but he had not been able to be very friendly with her in his own house, except when away from the presence of his wife. He knew within his heart that Mamie would take care of the needs of this family and that she would also look after Miriam in a most special way.

"Hi, Daddy," Miriam said, reaching her arms out to him. "I'm so glad to see you."

He knelt down beside his daughter and kissed her hand.

The nurse took special notice of this happy greeting as it was the most joyful emotion Miriam had shown since the nurse had been here. The major, holding one of his daughter's hands, stood from his kneeling beside her and spoke to Nurse Helen. He had seen her at the hospital briefly, but he didn't know her personally.

"Allow me to formally make your acquaintance. I'm Major Marvin Hawthorne, United States Army, retired." He gave her a salute, and she gave him a chuckle. The major felt that this person whose face bore a friendly smile would be a perfect companion for Miriam. He had always known that his daughter needed someone close, someone whose head matched their heart, someone with an interest in the whole person. The major knew his daughter's ailment was mental because she had been ordered to tear herself apart from the new friends she'd found, and her heart was broken. It seemed that Nurse Helen's big smiling eyes looked at Miriam with love.

"Yes," the nurse said, "and you're the father. I'm happy also to make your acquaintance, and our dear little daughter is obviously happy to see you. It's the first real emotion she's shown since I've been here, except she gave a little smile to her son, but I can see that she loves you."

"And I love her," he said, and he kissed Nurse Helen's hand and reached down and kissed Miriam on the forehead.

"Will you be coming every day, and will you be staying at night too?" he asked, looking kindly at the nurse.

"I can come Monday through Thursday, and yes, I can stay with her at night, but Friday and Saturday, I work with the wounded Black soldiers and veterans who are gravely ill. And of course, most of them who are stationed here are away from their homes, so I feel that they need someone who cares about them."

"Aren't there any Black nurses who can take care of them?" he asked.

"Not many, and not enough to fill the need, so I volunteer, but I reserve Sundays for church."

Major Hawthorne was impressed with this knowledge about his daughter's nurse, and there was also something that had readily attracted him to her as a person. He watched as she continued her examination.

"Well, what do you think, Miss Helen?" he asked. "I surely hope that this doesn't have anything to do with the wee one."

"Oh no. You know, she really doesn't seem to be physically ill at all. Her temperature and blood pressure and heart rate and all the vital signs are normal."

"That's good to know. Now, let's see what a few days' rest and some good food and loving care from you and Mamie will do. I'm sure that's all she needs right now." He didn't want to talk in front of Miriam, but something about this nurse pleased him, and he thought that in a few days, it might be all right to share some things that were causing his daughter's depression. He knew why she was suffering.

When he came the next day, he sat with Miriam for a while and finally coaxed her to eat half a sandwich and to drink a cup of warm chicken broth that Mamie had prepared. Nurse Helen wiped Miriam's face with a warm cloth and bade her to lie down. Miriam obeyed, and she was immediately asleep. It was surely that she became relaxed just seeing her father, and she felt contentment with her nurse.

The next day, Major Hawthorne came at the same time, and his presence produced the same positive results. He brought a couple of books, one of Miriam's favorite poems and one of short stories. He and Nurse Helen took turns reading to the patient, and Nurse Helen, laughingly, sang the "Good Morning to You" song, and Major Hawthorne joined in. Their actions put Miriam in a much happier mood.

When he came the next day, the major suggested that they get Miriam out of the house, and he'd take the two of them for a drive.

"I think that some fresh air will make her feel better."

"I agree," Nurse Helen said, being quite pleased with his help, for his presence seemed to be speeding Miriam's recovery from whatever was bothering her.

He drove down to the wishing well, and the three of them walked across the little bridge to make a wish.

"What should I write?" Miriam asked.

"Well, you should write something you love that you want to prosper in the future."

Nurse Helen wrote, "Love."

Major Hawthorne wrote, "Life."

"I want love and joy and peace for everyone," Miriam said, but she didn't write anything.

On the long ride back, Nurse Helen sat in the back seat with Miriam, and Miriam lay her head over on Nurse Helen's lap and went to sleep.

"I like my little patient," Nurse Helen said.

"I think she likes you too," Major Hawthorne said, and after a pause, he said, "And so do I."

The next morning, when Mamie came up to bring their breakfast, Miriam was impressed all the more by the same friendly and amicable way that Nurse Helen showed to Mamie. She complimented Mamie on the lovely breakfast tray she'd prepared for Miriam, and after seeing that Miriam was eating, Nurse Helen went downstairs and shared the breakfast table with Mamie.

"Mamie is such a nice lady," Nurse Helen said to Miriam. "I enjoy her conversation, and she gives off an aura of peace. She says it's because of her faith, and coming from someone who's been—well, you know. Her people have been treated so badly."

This made an impression on Miriam because she wanted to be friendly with Mamie, and she vowed that she'd talk to her as a friend the first chance she got to be alone with her.

That night, after she'd gotten Miriam tucked in for the night, Nurse Helen was sitting as usual in the rocking chair singing softly to her, and as she was singing, the door opened, and Timothy tiptoed in.

"What in the world are you doing out of bed?" Nurse Helen asked. "Come here. I know she's happy to see you, but we don't want to tire her out. Come and sit with me, and we'll sing together."

"Can't I just lie there with her for a little while?" he asked. "I'll be very still."

"It's all right," Miriam said. "He won't bother me."

"I miss you, Mommie."

"Okay, but just for a little while. I don't want your father to be upset with me."

Nurse Helen was pleased to hear Miriam talking.

Timothy curled up beside his mother, and he put his hand on her tummy. When he said good-night to her, he also said good-night to his baby sister. "I'll be so glad when I can see you," he said. Nurse Helen sang softly to them, and soon they were both asleep. Not wanting to disturb them, she pulled the coverlet up over them and whispered a prayer, "Bless them and keep them in your care. Thank you for allowing me this experience with them, and I love both of them. Amen."

The next morning, Nurse Helen woke the child early. Timothy gave Nurse Helen a hug. "Thank you," he said. "You're a nice nurse."

She led him to his room, being careful not to wake his father.

Having tended to Miriam for a week, the nurse found nothing physically in her examinations that could cause concern for Miriam's well-being nor the safety of her unborn child; and since Miriam was eating better and sleeping more soundly, Nurse Helen knew there was nothing more she could do for her. Miriam, however, looked to Nurse Helen's presence when she awoke every morning, and she had become quite fond of her. She liked her face, her patience, and her manner. *What is it in her that gives me peace? I wish my mother were more like her. I wish I could feel as comfortable and trusting with my mother as I do with her. I love her. I love her being here. Even saying nothing, her eyes tell me that she feels the same about me.* These were her thoughts.

Thursday was Nurse Helen's last night to attend Miriam, and Friday morning, she took both Miriam's hands in hers. "Whatever it is that bothers you is not physical. You've let something take over your thinking, and I know that what you have in your mind has a way of controlling your body. Stop telling yourself that you're sad. Speak good things to yourself: 'I am created strong. I love myself. I believe in myself.' I suggest that you talk to Mamie because she has such strong faith, and I know that is how people like her survive. And you are very fortunate to have a father who loves you. Don't forget that."

After listening to Nurse Helen's words about dedication to herself, Miriam knew that it would be all right to love people regardless of their color. She'd found a friend in Sage but had been made to feel this was repulsive, but now Miriam decided it was all right for her to feel as she did. She began to feel better about herself and about her life.

The next morning, after Bertram and Timothy left, Miriam went down to say goodbye to Mamie as she was returning to Alicia.

Mamie advised her to pray and ask God to clear the way for her to find peace.

It was Sunday. It was Nurse Helen's day off, and Major Hawthorne couldn't clear his mind from thinking about her, so he called and invited her to take a trip to the Peace Arch with him. She agreed to go after morning worship service. As they sat in the beautiful park, amidst rows and rows of flowers looking across the waters, they talked.

"I don't understand what's going on with your daughter. She and Timothy seem to be afraid of something. Where do you fit into this puzzle, and what in the world is this about?"

Major Hawthorne ran it down to her from the beginning, point by point. "Well, first, I am not Miriam's birth father. Miriam was adopted, but she doesn't know that."

Nurse Helen looked down at her hands, but she didn't say anything.

"It's all about Black and White," Major Hawthorne continued. "A young White man who was formerly in my unit came to live here. Why? Because he was engaged to a young Black girl, and the law where he lived didn't allow Black and White to marry. The young man's father came here with him to prepare for the wife's coming. His father, an ordained minister, is a rich oil man from Oklahoma where the young man and his fiancée grew up. Well, he purchased a house as a wedding present for the young couple, not aware that the house was in a restricted area. Meanwhile, I received a phone call from an anonymous person who threatened that he'd tell my wife that I was the father of a Black child if I didn't give him a large sum of money, and my wife had picked up the phone upstairs, and she only heard these few words: 'You are the father of a Black child.'

"The young White man, his name is Darius Deavers, and he is a lawyer. Well, together we figured out how to pay this caller a sum of money. Meanwhile, when Darius's family came for the wedding, Miriam immediately liked the Black girl, and they became friends. Her name is Sage. My wife figured wrongly that the reason I was so friendly with Darius is because Sage is my Black child, and my wife hates Black people, and so does Bertram. Then Miriam tried to help the Black man who came with Sage and Darius, and Bertram accused her of being too friendly with him and forbids her to see any of them again.

"My wife asked Bertram to research Sage's background to find out where she came from to see if I can, in fact, be her father. She also suggested that I invite them over to our house for dinner so she could get a good look at the girl. They come, and Bertram treats them badly, and Alicia shows me the result of Bertram's research and Sage's birth certificate, and she insists that she is my child. I was thoroughly disgusted with her, and that's when I left home. The White neighbors who live across the street from Sage and Darius invite them to come on their yacht for a pleasure trip to Bremerton across Puget Sound. They invited them all: Sage, Darius, Miriam, Timothy—Bertram was out of town—Karen, the daughter of Sage's Black maid, and her two young children, Jasmine and Jasper, and the Black friend Charles. They all became closer as friends.

"And damn! Damn! When they return from the trip, there is a cross burning in the Kingsleys' yard, and the Deavers' house had been painted black, inside and out, and there was a sign in the yard: YOU LIKE BLACK, WELL, YOU'VE GOT IT. Timothy tells his father about the trip, and Bertram reads the Riot Act to Miriam, and he goes over to chastise the Kingsleys', and that's when my daughter got sick. She experienced shock, mental and physical, and when you came, she hadn't spoken since."

Nurse Helen took his hand and kissed it. "I have something to tell you about Miriam too.

"What could you tell me about her that I don't already know? I've known her since birth."

"But you don't know anything about her real birth parents, do you?"

"No, I don't." It now crossed his mind that this nurse might have some knowledge about Miriam's parents, and he wasn't sure that he wanted to know what it was. The look on her face bespoke of something ominous. Still holding his hand, she looked up and gave a sigh.

"The truth is that I am Miriam's birth mother."

Since her response to his confession was also a confession, Major Hawthorne could not at once assess his feelings. This woman whom he had begun to love had rendered him *numb*. With having gone through and gotten over so many traumatic happenings lately—the threat, Alicia's accusation concerning Sage, the black house, Bertram's meanness—Major Hawthorne wondered if this lady was telling the truth. But he rationalized that she wouldn't have any reason to lie about such a serious matter. Then he wondered about the father. Would he also come forward and claim his daughter? Claim them both, Miriam and Helen Kane? Oh, where is my Little Green Man?

Sitting there together yet alone in their own present state of mind, they looked up and turned to face each other, almost simultaneously. He put his arm around her shoulder, and still holding his hand, she moved closer. Mother and father.

25

Darius had come to Washington because it was open to interracial marriage, and he was still very much in love with Sage as his wife and would have traveled to the ends of the earth (wherever that is) to be her husband.

However, the moment he stepped outside their house, instead of the feeling of a warm breeze on a winter's day, Darius felt the icy chill of the world's unpleasantness, the world's movie screen that featured their differences. Black and White don't mix. There were so many places they couldn't go together. The places where they were allowed and went together, they had become accustomed to the sideways glances and the outright stares. What was their relationship?

Added to his displeasure, Darius had begun to feel unhappy and out of place at the Black church. Instead of the one-hour service to which he was accustomed, more than two hours was the norm. Instead of announcements being printed in the church bulletin, they were read aloud by a person called the announcement clerk, who seemed to enjoy her role and who took an unnecessary (so it seemed to Darius) amount of time in delivering them. There was an opening prayer, a call-to-worship prayer, the deacon's prayer, and all those praying seemed to say the same words of both petition and thanks. "Thank you for waking me up this morning and starting me on my way. Bless all the sick and afflicted in the world. Bless all the churches that are open in your name. Bless all those who are under the sound of my voice, etc. etc." Then there was always a personal message to the Higher Power. "Oh, Lord, I love you so. You've been so good."

Two collections were taken: one was the general collection, and one was for missions. It was not at all unusual for another collection to be taken for such and such a need and another prayer of thanks for each one. There was a rather long sermon from the pastor, interspersed with, "Somebody should say amen. Let's say, thank you, Lord," etc., etc.

Darius was accustomed to fifteen minutes of praise and worship, which meant quiet singing of some favorite hymn and a prayer by one of the deacons. There was one anthem by the choir, the minister's message, never longer than thirty minutes. And then as you entered or departed, you dropped your donation in the collection basket which was placed at the door; or if you desired, you could mail it in. Announcements were printed in the church bulletin. *Well,* he said to himself, *Sage is doing what she loves, tutoring children, and bless her heart, she is driving her car, something she never did before we were married, and the racial climate has not killed her spirit. So now it is most definitely time for me to think about the direction I would like to go.*

On this particular Sunday, as they were winding down from the day's activities, Sage could sense a tension coming from her husband as they were so attuned into each other's persona.

"What is it, my dear? Is something bothering you?" she asked.

"I'm not happy at our church," he said without hesitation, knowing he had to tell her the truth since they had said they would worship together. "I don't feel fulfilled because it's so much different from the worship service I'm accustomed to. I—"

"I know, dear," Sage said, interrupting him. "I suppose it's time we realized that, unfortunately, there are some things we won't be able to share."

"I don't see that it will create a rift between us if we worship at different churches as long as we worship somewhere and as long as we continue to pray together," Darius said.

"I don't want you to be unhappy," Sage said as she had already sensed his unhappiness at the Black church. "So, my dear, if you want to join a White church, go," she said, kissing his hand.

And on the next Sunday, he did.

26

Arriving at his office on Monday morning, Darius was somewhat disturbed to see that Miriam was there in the office with Charles, and they seemed to be engaged in a friendly conversation, chatting, smiling, and discussing the contents of a brochure that lay on the desk in front of them. Charles stood and greeted Darius with a handshake and a smile.

"Good morning. It's good to see you." Then turning to her, he said. "You remember Miriam, of course."

"Yes, of course. Good morning. I'm surprised to see you here so early." And as he recalled the warning words of Miriam's father, this pleasantness, this closeness, this seeming comradeship between Charles and Miriam bothered him. And it especially bothered Darius that they were here in this office. He listened as Charles explained that they were discussing the building which had housed the Black Recreation Center.

"I found out that it's for sale, and I also learned that there is an abandoned piece of beach property, formerly used as a place to rent boats. I've thought of the possibility that I can buy both properties, and I can turn them into some much-needed recreational facilities for Blacks. Believe it or not, there are almost no places for my people to swim."

To Darius, it seemed Charles was much more interested in swimming and boating than he was in the business of law.

"I want Black people to be able to enjoy the water sports the same as White people do. We have all this water, and Black people don't swim or go boating or rafting, you know, or waterskiing. Boy, oh boy, I look forward to sponsoring swim meets, boat races, even diving contests, and I can see it all as a thriving business for me. At the same time, I will be introducing Black people, adults and children, to the joy of the lakes and all this water."

Darius noticed Charles's constant use of the term "Black people," and Darius was beginning to feel that Charles saw himself more as a savior of them than as one of them. Now with an obviously growing friendship with Miriam and a lull in his alliance with Darius, it might be causing Charles to love his association with Whites and to see himself as one of them. Darius thought Charles was tottering on the brink of disaster, and he wanted to discuss this with him and to tell him he was treading in deep water, and he could drown.

"There are organizations, you know, that could possibly help you, rather than you trying to do it all alone, especially here in a new city where you don't know the people," Darius said, thinking this suggestion might lure him away from seeking help from Miriam.

"I hear that those organizations are more talk than action," Charles answered. "No, I'll try it my way first, and Miriam knows the city, and she's offered to help."

To Darius, there was something gentle in the way she looked at Charles, and he was thinking, *She is beautiful, I must admit, and it would be easy for Charles to form an attraction to her, and her actions are definitely those of a flirting nature. Oh, how ridiculous. Of course, Charles knows better. She's White, and she's married, and she has a very bigoted husband. Someone could get hurt, or even killed.*

"I'd like for you to come along with us to look at these properties," Charles said to Darius, rising and closing the brochure.

"Yes, do come," Miriam said. "Your opinion would be very much appreciated." She held out her hand to Charles as she stood, as if she needed his support.

"No, I'll stay here. I have a lot of work and planning to do. But thanks for asking," Darius said.

He watched them as they left, Charles going to his car and Miriam to hers, and he was thankful that Charles had sense enough not to ride with Miriam, and he knew that he really should talk to him. *But what would I say? You're getting too close to Miriam. Mixed couples, Black and White, are sure to create a problem—oh, oh, Think, Darius. Think about what you're thinking. Well, Miriam is married. Think about that.*

27

The next Sunday morning, Sage and Charles attended the Black Baptist church, but she missed Darius, and now that he wasn't attending anymore, people began to wonder about her relationship with Charles. Where was the White guy? At the same time, Darius was experiencing some jealousy seeing Charles and Sage seemingly enjoying being together at church without him; and Charles, sensing some tension with this situation, after a couple of weeks, stopped attending church with Sage.

The people at the White church, thinking Darius was a young single and eligible bachelor, were happy to have him as a member, and they began including him in their young adults' activities.

"Of course, you're eating dinner with the young adults today. I see that Evelyn Prentiss signed you up, and then we're going to the annual choir concert," one of the male members said to Darius. His name was Blaise McCaslin, and he had been especially friendly toward Darius. Blaise was a very successful executive at the Amster Shipping Company in the small suburb of Henderson.

"Yes," Darius said, "that sounds like a good idea."

After the service, Blaise introduced him to Evelyn Prentiss. Evelyn was president of the Young Adult Pioneers, as they called themselves, and she was private secretary and administrative assistant to one of the executives at the same shipping company where Blaise worked. She was a rather attractive, very outgoing, very well-dressed, and obviously a well-educated lady.

"I've wanted to talk to you as I understand that you're a lawyer," Blaise said.

"Yes, I am," Darius answered, but his mind was still centered on Blaise's statement about the young adult dinner and the choir concert and about being signed up by Ms. Evelyn Prentiss, and he wondered if Sage would be upset if he spent the day away from her.

"We're in need of a legal representative for our company, and I'd like to sit down sometime and talk to you about the position," Blaise was saying.

This brought Darius back from what he was thinking about Sage to what Blaise was saying about his company. "The position?" Darius asked. "Well, right now I'm focused on getting my own law firm established, but yes, of course, we can talk about your company sometime." Darius didn't want to immediately refuse the offer, even though it wasn't in his mind to devote his energies to anything except his own law firm.

"How about today?" Blaise asked. "There's an hour lapse between dinner and the time of the concert. We could talk then," he said, and then he paused, seeming not to have all of Darius's attention. "You are going to the concert, aren't you?"

"Yes, of course," Darius said. He was thinking, *I might as well. I'm sure she won't mind, and I might need to hear what this man has to say about his company, thus leaving my options open. There is the possibility it could be more profitable than struggling with a new business in a new city where I'm not a native son and I'm not known, and Charles doesn't seem as interested as I had hoped. And what kind of clients will we attract in our firm? Hmm. Poor Black, all with issues of child support and domestic violence, etc., etc., etc. Blah, blah, blah.* His thoughts rambled on.

"Then we'll talk after dinner," Blaise said, interrupting Darius's thoughts.

"That will be fine," Darius said.

Darius enjoyed the dinner and the concert. He sat with Blaise and Evelyn, and it was not unnatural to stop after the concert and have a couple of drinks with them, and it was obvious that Evelyn

Prentiss was interested in more than a casual friendship with Darius Deavers. Before he left them, Darius accepted Blaise's offer to make an appointment for Darius to interview with the head of the shipping company's legal department.

Although Darius was later than usual getting home that night, and Sage recognized the smell of alcohol, she didn't chastise or ask questions. Darius told her about the dinner and the concert and the potential for an appointment at the Amster Shipping Company.

"I'm glad you enjoyed yourself, and I think that's a good thing about the interview," Sage said.

He didn't tell her about Evelyn.

Arriving at the entrance gate of the shipping company for his scheduled appointment, Darius was met by Blaise McCaslin, who gave him a VIP sticker and accompanied him to the special VIP parking lot. After parking and exchanging friendly greetings, they entered the lobby of the main building which housed the executive offices, and Blaise took Darius to the office of the president of the legal department.

Blaise had previously described Darius to the president and had highly recommended him as a very likely candidate to become a corporate lawyer in their legal department.

"This is our president, Mr. Lawrence Cartwright," Blaise said.

Darius greeted the president with a warm smile and a warm handshake. The president was a small man, barely five feet tall, with dark eyes and dark hair, thick eyebrows seen just above his thick dark eyelashes. He was very businesslike, but at the same time, he was also very charming.

"Have a seat, Mr. Deavers, is it?"

"Yes, it is. I'm Darius Deavers."

"That's a pretty name. Darius is one of my favorite biblical characters," he said with a nod.

Darius didn't know whether to say thank-you or nothing, but he gathered that Mr. Lawrence Cartwright was familiar with the Bible. Darius nodded, smiled, and sat down. Blaise sat in the chair beside Darius, both directly in front of the president's large mahogany desk.

The president gave Darius a description of the job and a verbal overview of the plant.

"Our shipping company uses trucks, large shipping containers, transport trailers, transport planes, and helicopters. The position requires an advanced degree, which I understand you have. Your job, basically, would be to provide advice on labor relations, employee contracts, tax issues, lawsuits against the company, like employee injury, and complaints. You would be responsible for keeping the company out of trouble." He continued to describe the duties of the position, and Darius wondered if this could be a place and a position where he would be content.

"Well, I've talked quite enough," the president said after a few more comments, smiling with his lips and his eyes. "And now Mr. Blaise here can give you what we call the grand tour of our facility. I'm sure you'll be happy here, and I'm pleased that you're interested in our company. Our application process is a little lengthy, but from what Blaise tells me, you'll not only qualify, but he promises that you'll fit right in." He didn't mention salary, but Blaise had already made Darius aware of their pay scale for lawyers.

"Thank you, sir," Darius said.

"Thank you for coming in," the president said, and Darius knew that he had been dismissed.

"I'm glad you came," Blaise said when they were outside in the hall. "What do you think?" he asked.

"Well, I'll certainly give it some serious consideration. It's a handsome offer."

"Yes, it is."

The tour of the facility was interesting, and the plant was huge.

"Let's go in here," Blaise said, opening the door to an office with a name and title on the door, which didn't mean anything to Darius because he didn't recognize the name; but as soon as he entered the reception area of the office, he knew why Blaise had chosen to come here. Sitting behind a desk in an office to the left of the large reception area was Evelyn Prentiss.

"Good morning," she said, rising to greet them. "I'm glad you came. So what do you think?" she asked, her bright eyes matching her pleasant smile.

"It's a handsome offer," Darius said. "And this is a beautiful office. It fits you perfectly. You're a beautiful person."

Whoa, Darius! Wrong direction. Just what are you saying? Come back to reality. Don't you see what's happening here? These two people, Blaise and Evelyn, both members of the church you joined, are now anticipating that you will become a member of the same work force, and well...

"Thank you," Evelyn said, "and so are you."

"Let's go out and have lunch," Blaise said. "There are some nice eating places around here. We can talk a little more about the company and about the church. You are free for lunch, aren't you?" he asked, turning to Darius.

Darius's mind was telling him that it would be all right to go and that to go would mean acceptance of their ideas about him, which would lead him in a direction that was dangerous. He could see the devil's bony finger beckoning him to *come, go.*

"No," he said, gathering his wits about him. "Maybe some other time." And looking at his watch as if time mattered, which it didn't, he said, "Thanks for everything."

"We'll stop by the office and pick up an application, and you can take it with you. Call me if you have any questions," Blaise said.

"I will do that," Darius said.

"Here's my card," Evelyn said, giving him a card. "Call me sometime." She reached out and took Darius's hand for a handshake, but she held his hand a little longer than was needed, giving him her most come-on smile.

It was a clear day, and after getting the application, Darius and Blaise walked outside. Bidding him good-day, Darius walked to his car. He was thinking, *So, Darius, you can't get much higher than this nor make a salary this high in your own business or as a professor at the university. So what's the harm in thus directing your life? Who am I? And what am I? I'm White, and I'm comfortable worshipping at a White church, and I'm certainly qualified for this high-class position, rubbing shoulders with my own kind, rich and White. It's not as if I'm aban-doning Sage and her Black life, for she's free to attend her Black church, tutor those Black children, and we can still spend our Friday nights and Saturdays together.*

It seemed such a plausible plan.

28

Darius sat in his car and thought about the events of the day, and he had to ask himself some questions. *Why am I here? I am so confused. Wouldn't this be a repeat of Boston?* He thought of where he was and where he had come from, which brought him always to Sage. He had to think about Sage. *She was such an even-tempered, brave person, unafraid of the world. Or knowing that when the world stepped into her path, she relied on her guardian angel to take charge of the situation. She seemed to be content all the time.* He had an urgent need to hug her, hold her, and feel her love. He also felt that he could rely on those divine beings that sat among the tree branches to lead and guide him in the right direction. It was both these things, his love for Sage and his divine beings that sent him home—home to a calamitous situation where he was needed, and one in which Sage was not able to control.

Sage opened the door as he reached out to put his key in the lock, and as he walked in, he could see Mrs. Johnson pacing the floor with silent tears running down her cheeks. He took Sage into his arms, knowing that whatever this was, it was serious, and he didn't want her to have any worries, especially in her condition.

"I knew you would come," she said, holding him tightly around the waist. "I called for you in my mind."

"Yes, my dear," he said. "I felt it in my soul, and now, my dear, I'm here. What's wrong?"

"It's Randy."

"Randy?" he asked, for he didn't recognize the name.

"He's Mrs. Johnson's son-in-law. He's Karen's husband and the father of the children."

"He is the father of the children, but they're not married," Mrs. Johnson said. "And oh, Mr. Deavers, I hate to involve you and Miss Sage in this mess, but I don't know what to do."

"All right," Darius said. "Let's sit down, and we'll talk about it." He put his hand out to her and motioned her to the couch.

"Sir, he don't live with us anymore. Karen put him out about a year ago. That's when she went to work at that shop, bless her soul. You know, sir, she tried to make it with him but—" She was overcome with her emotions.

"Tell him what he's doing now," Sage interrupted her, feeling the immediacy of the present situation.

"Karen saw him coming up the street, and she knew that he was drunk, and she was scared, 'cause whenever he got drunk, he would always want to fight, so she ran to the drugstore and called me. Last time he came over when he was drunk, he wanted money, and she gave him the little we had in a jar. This time, he threatened to kill her and her daddy—you know, my husband—if she didn't give him money. Poor Mr. Johnson. He's sick, and he's scared of Randy. I hope he don't have another heart attack, and, O Lord, I don't know what to do."

Darius didn't know what to do either, but he knew that if Randy was threatening to kill them, he certainly would have some kind of weapon; and if they went there, they could be walking into a deadly situation.

"How about the police? Did you call them?" he asked.

"No. When he's like this, he tells Karen that if she called them, he'd kill her for sure, but you know, sir, most of the time, the police won't even go down there when Black folk are fighting with each other."

His other person began talking to him. *Well, Darius Deavers what are you going to do now? You've been moving closer to the White side. You've joined a White church. You've been offered a position at a large profitable White company. You don't seem to be making it with Charles. Now the pendulum has swung you over into an eddy of the Black side.*

He looked at Sage, and he looked at Mrs. Johnson, and he was back in the kitchen of his home in Proctor with Sage and her mother, and he remembered the riots when his father tried to integrate Sage into his White school, and realizing he couldn't, he had weathered all the frightening things that happened because of it. Mrs. Johnson became Mrs. Mary Jane Copple, Sage's mother. The children became Sage, and Randy became the evil Whites threatening to kill them, and his father was defying everyone and becoming their savior. Now these two Black ladies, his wife and Mrs. Johnson, didn't have anyone else to look to.

I, like my father, must take the same role and become their savior. We survived the riots in Proctor, and we will survive this.

"Then let's go," Darius said. "If it's money that'll save everybody, that's no problem. We'll just pay him." His mind said, *If I perish, I perish.*

"Oh, Lordy, sir, I hate to—"

"Don't worry about it. Let's go. We'll figure out how to diffuse the present situation, then later maybe we can get some help for Randy."

"I don't know if he can be helped," Mrs. Johnson said.

"Sage dear," Darius said, "you stay here. I don't want you involved, especially in your condition."

"But, love, I'm already involved," Sage said. "I have to go. Otherwise, I'd worry myself sick wondering what was happening to you and Mrs. Johnson. Randy doesn't know you, and he hates all White people."

"That sure is right, sir. He blames the White man for his problems," Mrs. Johnson said.

"Sage, dear, what do you think you can do that I can't?" Darius asked.

"Darius, remember, I'm Black. This is a Black situation, and more than likely I can talk to him better on his level than you can."

"You know, honey," Mrs. Johnson said, turning to Sage, "your husband may be right. That crazy boy hates you as much, maybe more, because you're married to a White man, you know, like you think you're better than us. Maybe you oughtn't to go."

"Listen. I am going," Sage said, putting her hands on Darius's shoulders.

Darius looked at her, and he remembered all the times she had diffused seemingly impossible situations with her olive branch. How could he defy her now? He couldn't. Besides, he realized that what she said was right, and now, at this moment, he felt more at ease with her by his side, her being Black and him being White.

"All right, my dear, we'll go together."

Mrs. Johnson, wiping the tears from her eyes, gathered the children together and thanked the Lord for Sage and Darius Deavers.

On the way to her house, Mrs. Johnson told them about Randy and Karen. "They went to high school together, and they were gonna get married when they got out of school, but you know how these young people are, they can't wait, and yes, she got pregnant. She went on and got through high school, but he quit, saying he needed to get a job. I guess he tried, and he worked at the hospital as a janitor for almost a year. And then another baby came, and they tried living with Randy's folks, but it seems that his old man wasn't nothing but a drunk, and his mother wasn't any better, and neither of them could keep a job, including Randy, so the people they were renting from put all of them out 'cause they wasn't paying the rent.

"That's when Karen and Randy and the children come to live with me. And, O Lord, then my husband got hurt and he got so sick and he couldn't work no more. By then, Randy had got with some lowlives, and they started stealing drugs from the hospital, you know, pills and things they could sell on the street. Then they started taking the drugs, and that poor boy, he just seemed to go from worse to worser, poor thing, and it seems like the whole world is against Black folk. Sorry, Miss Sage, I keep forgetting that you're Black, but you just managed to rise above it somehow. Might have to do with your mamma being such a Christian lady. Then the Lord let you meet this young man—bless your soul, sir—and it don't even seem like you're White. I mean, you know, you're so good."

All the while, these words were with Sage: *And He will give His angels charge over you.*

At the same time, Darius was wondering, *Where is God? Like the police, does He avoid this neighborhood too?*

As they walked in the house, they saw Randy holding Karen around the neck with one arm and he held a knife in his other hand. Karen wasn't crying, but there was fear and there also seemed to be some kind of determination in her eyes. Mr. Johnson lay on the floor beside his overturned wheelchair, and his moans were heart-wrenching to hear.

"Oh yeah," Randy said to Mrs. Johnson, "you think you something riding around with this rich White man, but he don't care nothing about you. You just a slave, washing they dirty draws. And Ms. Blackie here," meaning Sage, "she trying to be so high and mighty. Shit, you a nigger just like us. Don't you stand there looking down on me, Black cunt, that's what you are. And Mr. Whitey, he gonna dump you soon as he get him some White pussy."

"Hold on, Mr. Randy," Darius said. "Whatever color we are, we're here to help you, and that lady you're choking is the mother of your children. Do you want to make them an orphan?"

"They my children, and I can do whatever I want with them. Come over here, you all. Come here, Jasper. You too, Jasmine. I'm your daddy, and uh-huh, this your mamma, and this old lady here, call herself your grandma, but she don't mean you no good."

"Take it easy, Randy," Sage said. "Go on, children. Go on over there."

Although the children were in a deep quandary between loving their mother and wanting to love their father, it was Sage's words that were their guide, and they obeyed her. They loved her, and they knew that she loved them.

"Now, Randy, tell me what it is that you want us to do. We're not against you, and believe it or not, we want to help you. Please. What can we do? Right now. What can we do?" Sage asked, holding her hands and arms extended and open, hoping to indicate a non-threatening position.

"Money, Ms. Bitch. That's what you can do is give me some money."

"All right, let her go. Here's some money," Darius said, putting some bills on the table. "But let her go."

Randy was a handsome young man, but he had a head full of uncombed, disheveled hair. He was wearing cotton pants, even though it was cold outside, and he reeked with the smell of alcohol and stale cigarette smoke. He was apparently moved by Sage's softness and seeming absence of fear, and he hesitated and looked at her, but only for a moment. Then he pushed Karen away from him, and he swayed as if she had been his support. He walked unsteadily over to the table where Darius had put the money. He grabbed it up and stumbled to the door.

"This ain't the last you gonna hear from me, Mr. Whitey." He looked back and laughed as he went out the door.

"Daddy, wait," Jasper said, but his little plea landed on deaf ears, for Randy was already walking unsteadily down the street. In his present messed-up life, money was more important to him than his children, or anything else.

Karen gathered the children into her arms, and as if she was waiting for the moment, she began to cry.

"Thank you, sir," she said. "Thank you a lot. But I don't think he would've really used that knife on me. But that alcohol and the drugs that he takes just seem to make him crazy. I sure hope he can find some help."

"So do I," Mrs. Johnson said.

"And Miss Sage, thank you so much for coming. My mother loves you, and my children love you."

"And I love your mother and your children," Sage said.

29

Then everyone's attention was drawn to Mr. Johnson as he lay on the floor.

"Right now we need to see what we can do for your father. I think he needs to be in the hospital," Sage said.

"You're right, my dear," Darius said. "Let's go somewhere and call an ambulance."

"Oh, Mr. Darius," Mrs. Johnson said. "We don't have insurance, and the ambulance company is just like the police. They hardly won't come to this part of town for no sick Black folk because they know that we can't pay."

"Then we'll just take him ourselves. He needs help," Darius said. He knelt down beside Mr. Johnson and put his hand on the poor man's thin arm, more like bones covered with skin. "Can you sit up, sir?" he asked, but the poor, pitiful man looked up at Darius and mumbled some words about dying.

"We're not going to talk about dying. You'll feel a lot better at the hospital," Darius said.

In a weak voice, between gasps of breath, Mr. Johnson begged them not to take him to the hospital.

"He don't want us to take him there," Mrs. Johnson said, "because the last time he was there, it was because he fell on the street and the police had to come, and they were the ones who called the ambulance, and they took him to the hospital."

"What happened then?" Darius asked.

"A policeman came that evening and rang the bell. He told me that my husband was in the hospital, and they took me there. And we sat in the waiting room for a long time, and then they put him in a big room with ten other sick men, and they just left him there until another long time, and then somebody came and asked us a lot of questions, some of them we could answer, and some we couldn't. The next day, they sent him home with a lot of pills, but I think they was just pain pills. I guess it was because they can't do a lot of free stuff for us poor people."

Darius and Karen managed to get Mr. Johnson up from the floor, and they sat him in a chair.

"I'll see that they take better care of him this time," Darius promised.

When they got to the hospital, it was almost exactly as Mrs. Johnson had said. For half an hour, they sat in the waiting area with all the other destitute-looking men, women, and children. When Mr. Johnson's name was called, Darius stood at the counter with Mrs. Johnson as she answered their questions. When was he born? What was his home address? What kind of medicine was he taking? What was his complaint?

Darius was overcome by the confusion, and he realized that the place was understaffed and most likely underfunded, and most of the people who came there were unable to pay. Mrs. Johnson explained to them that besides his work-related back injury, her husband suffered from a weak heart. She told them that they couldn't afford all the medicine that was ordered for him to take, and they couldn't get him to a clinic on a regular basis. Darius took over and said he'd pay the costs.

Then they put Mr. Johnson in a ward with eight other patients, and it was another half hour before a nurse came to examine him. She gave him some medicine to ease his pain, and in a few minutes, he was asleep. No doctor came.

Darius wanted to stay with Mrs. Johnson, but when he looked at Sage, he had to make a decision. He couldn't sacrifice her well-being and the tiredness which he could see in her, and he decided he had done all he could do to help Mr. Johnson at this time.

When they got outside that dismal place, as Darius called it, and got into the car, Darius looked over at the beautiful woman beside him, with her head lying over on his shoulder, asleep. He began to question himself if he wanted her to be delivered there.

Darius again asked some questions. *Who am I? What am I? And why am I here? Why was I compelled to go over there into a poor Black neighborhood, to a poor Black broken family, a poor Black hospital—a totally different situation from the smooth, peaceful world I had been raised in and even how I expected that I would continue to live? Hmm. Right now I will deal with what is and not what I hope I'll see down the road, which is how to fight this awful poverty, this inequality.*

Well, I'm Darius Paul Deavers, rich, White, and I don't want to be otherwise. And with Sage's soft breathing, her hand on his leg, the faint scent of her hair pomade filling his nostrils, he began to reassess what was happening to him. *Hmm, wherever I am is exactly where I'm supposed to be.*

God, he prayed, *this is your world, and we are all your children. Tell me what I can do to help change things especially for my Sage and— ha!—as Charles says, for Black people. And can I do that and remain in my White world? If you are listening, please help me.*

He helped Sage into the house, ran a warm bath for her, put in bubbles and bath oil, lighted some candles, washed her back, dried her off, turned down the covers on her bed, watched her smile as she closed her eyes. As he kissed her on the forehead, she put his hand on her belly, and together, they felt the movement of their new life.

Early the next morning, Darius went back to the hospital to check on Mr. Johnson, also hoping to give Mrs. Johnson whatever help she needed. The hospital ward where Mr. Johnson had been placed was relatively clean. The floors had been freshly mopped and the bedsheets freshly changed. Mr. Johnson was wearing a blue striped hospital gown, and there was a needle in his arm for the medication he was being given. One nurse and one intern and one clerk sat at a desk at the entrance to the ward. Mrs. Johnson sat dozing in a chair beside her husband's bed. Darius walked over to her and gently placed his hand on her shoulder. She opened her eyes, and recognizing him, she sat upright and smiled.

"Good morning, sir," she said, trying to stand and having a difficult time, probably due to a degree of tiredness and a need of sleep. "You needn't to have come back. I know you're a busy man."

"Don't you worry about me," he said. "And don't get up. I know you're tired." He knew she had spent the night right there at the bedside. He pulled a chair from the other side of the bed and sat beside Mrs. Johnson. He looked at the pitifully thin body which lay on the bed covered with a blanket, spittle coming from his mouth.

"So how is he?" Darius asked.

Mrs. Johnson shook her head from side to side. "It don't look very good. He's needed care for such a long time, and the Lord knows, we did the best we could seeing after him. But, sir, it's been kinda hard on all of us, me and Karen and the children, and on him, 'cause he didn't want to be pitiful. The Lord knows he was a strong man when he was well."

Darius took a paper towel from the table and wiped Mr. Johnson's mouth, and as he performed that simple task, he felt a sense of pain because of his own world of plenty and this family's world of need. Then it came to him that all the material things he had weren't completely filling his needs, like the need of equality for his wife and peace for himself and Sage in their striving to be content in spite of the hate that surrounded them, in spite of his need to be gainfully employed. And he rationalized that each person's pain, although different from another person's pain, is still pain.

When Mrs. Johnson looked up at him and said thanks, that look in her eyes, that expression of hope on her face, became a seed that began to grow as a living bond between them. She became, somehow, his strength, even though her world was falling apart. For a moment, he didn't know what to say, and he didn't know exactly how he felt, but something had come over him, and it was like a piece of joy and a piece of sorrow had taken possession of him together and at the same time.

Darius offered to pay for a private room, but Mrs. Johnson refused the offer, and Darius didn't know if her refusal was about the money or if, with her womanly and God-given intuition, she knew that death was near. Her refusal put him in another state of mind, and he could feel her peace. Money didn't buy that for her, and his money couldn't buy it for him, like a can of soda or a house even. He knew it came from within.

They sat quietly and looked at the sick man. Darius had expected Mrs. Johnson to be overcome with sadness from knowing she was losing her husband, someone who had been near and dear to her for many years, and he was surprised to see that she was smiling. Mrs. Johnson knew that she, the doctors, and Darius had done all they could do for her husband.

Then Mr. Johnson briefly opened his eyes and looked around. Then he closed his eyes, and they heard a soft sound coming from his mouth. He was singing. "O Lord, have mercy. O Lord, have mercy." And the words, they knew, were more for them than for him.

They listened in utter amazement, and Darius looked over and saw that now Mrs. Johnson was crying. Then like the unfolding of a new bolt of colorful cloth, with each yard becoming a new and beautiful pattern, Darius could see the heavens opening up with new and different scenery, and Mr. Johnson's soft singing grew and presently became a choir of many voices, accompanied by many instruments—harps, pianos, horns, organs, violins, violas, and cellos. Then he saw a movement upward, and he was blinded by a bright light shining through the trees. Then slowly there was darkness as Mr. Johnson's physical body floated back down to earth's reality.

Death. Darius's inner voice said, *I've never experienced the death of a relative nor a close friend. I've heard it spoken of by Sage. Her father and her sister had been taken by it, but I was not there to witness either of their passing. I have become aware of the beginning of life with my wife's pregnancy, and I am now witnessing the end of life here with this man's death.*

He looked at Mrs. Johnson, and she was smiling through the tears that ran down her face, like the time he saw that the sun was shining, and it was also raining at the same time.

His mind was asking questions, *What is death? Is it the cessation of everything? Is there such a thing as afterlife? It's something I don't understand and cannot explain.*

And his other voice said, *But you're still alive, so don't worry about it. You're still strong and healthy. You can plan for tomorrow, but you can't see tomorrow. So just live your life the best you can and let your work speak for you. Let people be your focus. Help where you can. The darkness will disappear, and the light will shine again.*

Darius Paul Deavers paid for a casket, burial clothes for the deceased, and the burial. Mrs. Johnson wanted a simple private funeral with just herself, Karen, Darius, and Sage. Major Hawthorne, learning of the death and learning that his maid, Mamie, knew Mrs. Johnson, went with her to give support.

30

Darius and Sage were so in touch with each other and so extraordinarily intimate that their thoughts were now flowing together like two drops of water from the same container: *How can we help Mrs. Johnson and her family?*

Sage thought, *When it became certain that I would be living in a new city and meeting new people, I wondered about being able to find a close Black friend here. Then my angel spoke to me, "Karen is Black, and being about the same age, you two can become friends, and you can offer her the same kind of encouragement that you received from your father to get an education and the kind of financial help you received from Reverend Deavers so you could stay in college. You can make it possible financially for her to attend college, and you can tutor her if she needs help with her studies, which will help her succeed at college. She would no longer have to sweep up hair off the floor of the White folks' shop. You can continue tutoring the children, which will better prepare them for life."*

When all this became definitely set in her mind, she spoke to Darius about helping Karen. He agreed.

After the funeral, Sage told Karen that she wanted to talk with her, and when Sage went on Monday morning as usual to pick up Mrs. Johnson and the children, Karen came with them. Sage knew from her own experience and from her personal knowledge of the Black employment situation that it was an absolute necessity, a requirement, for a Black person to have an education in order to get a decent job.

Mrs. Johnson was in the front seat beside Sage. Karen and the children had scrambled into the back seat. The children very much enjoyed riding in a car, and today was more pleasant because their mother was with them, and Sage felt a wonderful closeness to everyone in the car. She glanced back and smiled. *God has given me a Black family here in BeachSide, Washington. A mother, sister, niece and nephew.*

On entering the Deavers' home, Mrs. Johnson and the children knew the schedule. Mrs. Johnson put on her apron and began preparing the meal. She let the children help with a few things. Jasmine got the silverware from the drawer and placed it beside the plates, and Jasper took care of the napkins. They liked helping.

As Sage sat with Karen on the sofa, Karen couldn't help looking around the room and admiring the beautiful furnishings, the largeness, and the spaciousness. She looked at Sage and smiled, and then she turned her face away. Sage could sense that she was somewhat nervous, and Sage wanted so much for Karen to feel at ease.

"Well. We can talk while your mom is getting our breakfast."

"Our breakfast? Are you going to eat with us?" Karen asked.

"Yes. We all eat together. I usually fix breakfast for my husband, and I sit with him and have a cup of coffee while he eats. But I like to eat with the children because it seems that we get to know each other better over a meal."

"Oh, Mrs. Deavers, you don't seem real to me. I mean you don't seem like a real Negro. I think of you as being rich and White, you know, and my mother is your maid. I thought you would be so different and like, you know, so much above us. All the White people I have ever had anything to do with, you know, those people I work for, even the mailman and the police, they're all White, and they treat us like..." She paused, and Sage detected the tears forming in her eyes.

"I know," Sage said, reaching over and taking one of Karen's hands in hers. "I know what you're feeling because I've experienced the same kind of treatment, but I never allowed myself to feel inferior."

"Why would you?" Karen asked. "You have everything. You're married to a White man. A rich White man too."

"My life wasn't always like this. Even before I met my husband, I didn't feel inferior."

"How in the world did you get over it, you know, that feeling?"

"It was my mother who kept telling me not to let them steal my joy. She said that we're all God's children and that He loves us all the same, and that it's the world and the mean people in it that try to defeat us. And my father always made us promise that we'd get an education. And Darius's father kept telling me the same things that my mother told me. So I'm telling you not to let people, Black or White, make you feel less of a person. And please don't feel like I'm your superior because I'm just me, and what I want to be is your friend, not your superior. Our only inequality is in our education and our worldly possessions, and by the grace of God, we're going to change that."

"How?" Karen asked.

"By making sure that you go to college and earn a degree."

"What about my mother? Will she always be a maid?"

"Karen, your mother is a maid because she never had the opportunity to get an education and better herself. That's where you come in. When you're educated and employed with a good salary, you can stop her from working. That's what my sister and brother did. After they graduated from college and got good jobs, they stopped my mom from working."

"I promise you that I'll do that."

Sage looked over at Mrs. Johnson, and she knew it was the Lord who had placed her on that corner that awful day. *And although she's considered to be my maid, she's also my absentee mother.* She looked at Karen, and she also felt a warm closeness to her, thinking, *She really could be my sister.*

"I sure do hope that your husband can help Randy too."

"So do I," Sage said.

"All right, you two, breakfast is ready."

"Come on, Mamma, I set a plate for you too," Jasper said this.

The attraction was immediate, and just as a magnet is able to attract iron, Sage was at once a magnet that drew Karen into the circle of her strength. At the same time, Karen was the magnet that drew Sage into her open arms of a strong friendship. Each crystal-lized into their seemingly preordained place with each other.

Mrs. Johnson thanked her Maker for the blessings Sage and Darius had already brought into her life, and now she felt an over-flowing of blessings into the lives of Karen and the children. She saw that Karen and Sage each had something the other needed, and she could see in their eyes and in their smiles that it would be given freely.

Thus, Sage asked Mrs. Johnson if she would allow her to help Karen, trusting that Darius could help Randy.

"Allow you?" Mrs. Johnson asked. "I will get down on my knees and thank you. You are such a blessing."

"Mrs. Johnson," Sage said, "I don't think you understand what it means to me having a sweet, sensible person like you in my life. It's different being married to a White man. I should, by all rules of the world, be a White lady. But I'm not, and by all the world's catego-rization, I should be poor, but I'm not. And you're not beneath me. You're my friend, my absentee mother, my..." She stopped talking and looked down because she felt so humble. She felt a tear some-where in the back of her tear container wanting to come out, but she was able to keep it in.

"Miss Sage, I know all that. I know just exactly how you feel, and I know how you've lived, and I know just how this old world sees you. Honey, it's not only the White people who hate you and envy you, but it's Black people too. But, darling, I'm who I am, and I'm what I am, and that's your maid. I'm your servant, and I respect you as the person I work for, but I know your heart. Probably wouldn't no White person work for you, and not a lot of Black ones either, but I need this job, and you need some help, and I thank the good Lord for making it happen. And Karen needs you, and you are a role model for her and her children. So you just be who you are. You're levelheaded and you're educated. And, sweetie, you are rich, and that husband of yours, bless his heart, he needs you too. He's kinda lost in this old hateful world, but long as you two love each other like you do—for Lordy, I sure do see it, I see it plain as day—that's going to carry you above all this."

"Thank you, Mrs. Johnson. I know that I'm surrounded by love," she said, and she walked over and hugged Mrs. Johnson, and Mrs. Johnson hugged Sage with her arms and her love.

Sage and Karen went the next day, and they were successful in getting Karen enrolled in some freshman college classes, and Karen smiled.

Darius thought, *Even though Mr. Johnson had not written the great American novel nor invented anything new and useful, but like the fruit trees which grow and each produces its own fruit (peaches, figs, or apples), this man produced a living specimen of himself. It was Karen, and the fruits that had fallen from her life tree were Jasper and Jasmine, which were also from the seeds of Randy. And if any of them were left alone on the ground of life, they would die and become rotten.*

I remembered the man who invited me to join a protest bus ride against segregation in state transportation, which if successful would change the laws for all Black people. But remembering the warmth of Mrs. Johnson's smile, her hand on mine, her peace, the angelic music, it was revealed to me, Darius Paul Deavers, that I cannot change the hearts of the populace of this city nor the laws against segregation for all minorities. You have been given many talents, many riches, and now you can use them to help others. Start with the most needful in this family. It is Randy.

Of course, Randy's hateful attitude toward White people made Darius cringe, and he had to fight the negative feelings within himself about people like Randy because of their laziness, drunkenness, and neglect for their family. All these things Randy blamed not on himself but on the White man. So Darius wasn't sure that Randy would allow him to help, but he would try, and Darius spoke to Sage about helping Randy. She agreed.

Darius made an appointment with Randy for nine o'clock Monday morning of the next week, and at five minutes after nine, Randy Davis was standing before the desk in the office of DEAVERS AND WILLIAMS. This area had been designated for a receptionist, which Darius and Charles planned to hire when things were a little more in place and profitable.

Darius greeted Randy with a smile and a handshake, being impressed with Randy's neat appearance. His clothes were clean and pressed, his hair was freshly cut, not uncombed and a tangled mass as it had been at the house.

Darius didn't want to sit behind his desk like a boss, so he sat on the sofa beside Randy. Like friends. Darius was aware that Randy was nervous, and he tried to make him feel at ease.

"Did you have any trouble finding the place?"

"No, not at all. This is a nice place you got here," Randy said, looking around.

"Thank you. We don't have everything in place yet, but we're working on it," Darius said. He looked at Randy, and Randy looked out the window, and Darius was a little unsure how to start the conversation.

"Would you like a cup of coffee?" Darius asked.

"No, thank you. I don't drink coffee," Randy said.

"Well," Darius said after a moment, "tell me something about yourself."

"You know, sir," he said with an attitude of, *Yeah. Mr. White man, sir.*

Darius waited.

"Tell you something about myself. Well, I'm twenty-four, and I got this far by myself. My parents never was any help to me. My old man was a lush head, and he was mean as hell to us. I got so many slaps and fists upside my head that I for sure wanted to kill him. My mother wasn't much better than him. She drank with him, and we hardly ever ate a regular meal. I tried going to school every day, but it was too hard. I met Karen at a high school football game, and I guess you know the rest. We tried to make it, but it was just…well, it was hard, and I know it was my fault." He paused and looked out the window. "But I didn't know nothing about having a family, you know, and I guess you're wanting to know about my work. The only work I've done is being a janitor. That's what I did when I worked at the hospital, and that's what I did when I worked downtown in a store."

"I'm sure we can change that."

Darius could see that this young man was uncomfortable, but it seemed he was trying to be strong, and he was having a hard time because telling about himself had the effect of calling up all the bad times, and it was causing him to look at himself. And like most people, he didn't want to do that. It was too painful.

"I think the first thing we should concentrate on is for you to finish high school. I can help you with that," Darius said.

"Right, right. That's what I want to do." He was nodding as if he really approved of that option.

At that moment, Charles entered the office from his upstairs abode, and although he was scheduled to spend his mornings in the office, he informed Darius that he had other plans and that he would be out of the office this morning. Normally, Darius would be disappointed about Charles's absence, but he was somewhat relieved that he wouldn't be here today. Darius didn't want to go into any negative descriptions at this time, so he introduced Randy as a friend whom he was trying to help with employment, and that was the truth.

"Well, I'm out of here," Charles said. "Don't you all work too hard."

"We won't. Have a good day," Darius said.

After Charles left, Darius and Randy continued their conversation, and Darius began to feel more comfortable, sensing that Randy was a little more at ease. Darius made an appointment for Randy to come the next day, and they would see about getting him enrolled in some high school classes.

The next morning, Darius went to his office at the usual hour. The riots that so frightened Sage, the destruction of their house, the moving into another house, and the death of Mr. Johnson had put him in a somber mood.

Darius Paul Deavers stood and put his hands up over his head and brought them down the length of his body, and as he did, he spoke these words, "Let this somber mood, this feeling of hopelessness, pass from me." Looking out through the window, he saw that the sky was murky and overcast, and it looked like rain. He thought that the weather did not help him out of the mood that enveloped him. His thoughts then turned to Randy, and he was concerned about him getting here in the rain. *Maybe I should have offered to pick him up.*

Charles came down, and he was again dressed to go out. "I'm really excited about today," Charles said. "I'm meeting with the president of the Black Boating and Fishing Club, and I have an appointment with the city council. Good, huh? And hopefully they will take me into their confidences, you know, and I'm sure hoping they can help me in my recreational endeavors."

Although Darius was perturbed about Charles's change in their schedule, he was pleased that Charles would not be here again today. His presence might not be good for Randy. He was hopeful, however, that Charles would soon commit more of his time to the law firm.

After Charles left, Darius thoughts immediately turned back to Randy. His appointment was for nine thirty. Darius waited. It was ten thirty. Then it was twelve o'clock. Still hoping he would come, Darius thought it would be well to offer to take Randy to lunch, get better acquainted, have a casual conversation, and try making Randy feel comfortable with him before talking about work or education or even his personal development. He also thought about taking the young man shopping for school clothes and supplies. He was looking forward to helping Randy, one person at a time, he thought, instead of going after the ninety-nine.

He busied himself by opening some mail, answering a few letters, but it was difficult to keep his mind focused on anything except Randy.

It was now twelve thirty, and Darius was thinking that there was no point in waiting any longer for evidently Randy wasn't coming. But he wasn't able to keep his mind on his work, and he began pacing the floor. Thoughts swirled around him like a sudden flash flood or a small tornado that appeared in front of him. *Am I interfering where I'm not wanted? Since Randy had not asked for my help, it might be true that he doesn't really want it.*

Then he heard the door opening, and as he turned, he recognized the definite scent of stale alcohol and the lingering odor of cigarette smoke. Then he saw that Randy was wearing the same clothes he'd worn yesterday, and they looked like he'd slept in them. Darius had been hoping that Randy would be clean and sober the same as he was yesterday, and he would be ready to visit a high school.

Despite his feeling of disappointment, Darius greeted Randy at once as if nothing was wrong. He remembered the song they sang in church when the invitation to discipleship was given: "Just as I Am."

"Hello, Randy," he said, extending his hand to him. "I'm glad you came."

Randy reached out and took the extended hand, and to Darius's complete surprise, he apologized for being late.

"It's just that I've been, uh, I've been sick." This pitiful-looking and sounding man stood there, looking around like one who is either lost or who is surveying the place. "But I'm ready now. Yep. I promised her."

Darius didn't know to whom he was referring, but he was almost sure it was Karen and not Mrs. Johnson, because Darius knew that Randy had strong feelings of animosity about his mother-in-law.

Randy continued, "Yes, sir, I'm ready now. Yep. I promised her, and yep, there's a lot of things I can do. I'm sorta a good driver. And I could, uh, maybe, and I stopped drinking. I promised her that I would stop. And I can quit, you know." He emphasized the word *can* as if it was all up to him if he did or didn't drink.

"All right, all right," Darius said, leading him to the couch. "Let's sit down, and we can talk about it." Although, he was at a loss how to proceed or what to say because it was obvious that Randy had been drinking, and he really did look sick, more like he had a hangover. Darius couldn't rouse any anger at him as he was overcome with pity. He couldn't chastise him for drinking, for what good would that do? *What can I do? Lunch.* He realized that he himself was hungry, not having eaten since breakfast, and he had already planned to invite Randy to have lunch with him.

"Have you eaten? How about we go out and have some lunch, for I think that thoughts come forth better with a full stomach." He tried to eke out a laugh.

"Yep. Yep. That sounds good. But first I'd better use the….uh, the facility." He laughed, and Darius also wanted to laugh at his use of the word *facility*.

"Sure, it's right here," Darius said.

After leading him down the hall where the bathroom was located, Darius went back and sat on the couch. His thoughts prevailed. *Is this a Black thing? Is Randy the perfect example of why the Black man has been held down? Has Randy tried and failed? He says that he can stop drinking. But can he? And how can he? Trying to overcome addictions on your own is like trying to climb a mountain without equipment. It can't be done, and it can't be done in one day. Overcoming a bad habit or an addiction is a lifetime endeavor and commitment. But first, Randy must want to stop, and he has to be committed to doing it, and he needs professional help. So is there anything I can do?* he asked himself.

Sitting there waiting for the bathroom door to open and for Randy to emerge, Darius heard the familiar sound of vomiting, and his previous suspicions were confirmed. He was at a more grievous loss as to what he should or could do to help this poor man. He was happy when the doorknob turned, but he was fearful when he saw this pitiful form of a man standing before him. trying to focus on something. Realizing that here was a miserable lost soul, Darius led him to the couch; and instead of sitting, Randy lay down and was immediately asleep.

Darius was in unfamiliar territory, and he knew it. He thought of Charles and Sage, and he tried to reverse the roles and compare them to Randy. Both Charles and Sage were born Black and poor, but Charles had an uncle and a mother who encouraged him toward getting an education. And Sage, like Charles, had some encouragement from her mother and father and from Darius's father. Both Charles and Sage graduated from college. Randy's life didn't include any of those positive aspects. *And here I come, White, educated, and wrongly putting Randy in the same place as I did Charles and Sage.* Not true. They could receive help, but Darius wasn't sure that Randy could.

Darius's thoughts were to let him rest while he cleaned up the mess he left in the bathroom. *Ha-ha! This is the maid's work. Normally I would leave it for the maid, but we don't have a maid for this building. Oh well, Sage taught me how to do this kind of work.* So he got the bucket, water, soap, rag, mop, and he cleaned it. And when he'd finished the cleaning, emptying the water out back, and returned to the front room, Randy was gone.

Darius felt guilty and defeated, and he knew that both he and Randy were out of their element, out of their comfort zones, and they both were at a loss how to come out and present themselves up front and honest.

When he arrived home, Sage recognized his low spirits, but she wasn't surprised. She had personally felt that any success with Randy would be difficult. Perhaps impossible.

31

As Darius had tried and was now seemingly adjusting to his life, to the house he still did not call home, his one abiding consolation was his wife, her constant smile, her strong faith. Yet he was still beset with questions. *How can I have faith in a God who is said to always maintain a perfect order in the world when my life is filled with disorderliness?* He felt a constant pressure that he was not even a person, doing nothing and accomplishing nothing.

So were his thoughts on this November morning when he was dressing to go to his nonproductive office, and the doorbell rang. He answered and found Lieutenant and Mrs. Kingsley there with news that pushed him down further into his dismal pit of pity.

"Since President Harry S. Truman had addressed the NAACP in July, and he had spoken quiet forcefully about civil rights, it seems that now he was encouraged by A. Philip Randolph and others who planned a movement which would be designed to pressure the US government into desegregating the Armed Forces. So Ensign Gray was encouraged that some upward movement would soon be possible for African Americans in the Navy, and I'm sorry to tell you that now he wants his house."

With this short notice, their only alternative was to return to the office building. And they did.

It was nearing Thanksgiving, and Mrs. Kingsley wanted to invite the young couple for Thanksgiving dinner since they had no family here, but as she thought about it, neither did she and her husband. She was also sure that Sage and Darius would have no desire to come back so close to their ruined home.

Mrs. Johnson invited them to share with her family, Karen and the children (they hadn't seen Randy for a while), but Sage and Darius didn't feel at all in a social mood to share the holiday with other people.

Charles attended Thanksgiving services at the church he'd been attending, and he shared Thanksgiving dinner with a family he'd met there.

Alicia Hawthorne had dinner at her house for the family, and although Marvin was living elsewhere, he came because he didn't want to cloud Timothy's mind with, *Where is Grandpa?* Alicia also had as her guests two couples who were members of the Symphony Society. They engaged in their artificial conversation. They laughed their artificial laughs, and they smiled their artificial smiles.

Miriam was thinking, *Thanksgiving is most often celebrated with only family and close friends, and it is a day to give thanks for them being a part of one another's life.* Miriam felt that these guests were neither family nor friends, and she shared nothing with them, and worst of all, she and Bertram were expected to attend the holiday concert with them. Oh, oh, oh. She ate sparingly. She knew that after Mamie had finished serving the dinner for Alicia, she was going to join Mrs. Johnson and Karen and the children, and she knew that Timothy shared her feeling that they both would much rather be with them. Even Bertram, who was familiar with having boring dinners with his company employees, was bored, and he thought they would have been happier at home with Miriam's home-cooked meal and Timothy helping and him setting the table. Miriam looked at her mother, and it was like looking at a cardboard poster of her. Artificial. Miriam Withers smiled as they did, and she was relieved when the evening was over.

Darius stood looking out the window of their building, and although there was the beauty of autumn, with the fallen leaves, the brown grass, flowers that had endured the weather, not wanting to die, his melancholy thoughts were pointing homeward. *But where is home for me now? I'm quite lost in a land of nowhere, and I quite disagree with Emily Dickinson's poem which included the line, "Where thou art—that—is home."*

"Cheer up, my dear," Sage said.

"How can you be so calm when our whole world has crumbled?"

"Think, if you can, of making a cake that doesn't turn out right through no fault of yours. It could be that the oven didn't heat properly or the baking powder was old, and as a result, the cake fell in the middle, and the texture was gummy. Well then, you can still eat it and give thanks if it's all you have. And today is Thanksgiving. It's a day to give thanks."

"What in the world do we have to be thankful for?" Darius asked, looking at her with disbelief. "We have no house, no furniture, no family."

"We have each other. We have a child on the way, and we have a roof over our heads. Let's be thankful for what we do have."

"My dear, you could find a bright spot in a pool of mud. You're amazing."

"You know," Sage said, putting her arms around his waist and looking out the window with him, "I remember one holiday at school, and those of us who had stayed on campus, well, we got together, and we made a big pot of gumbo. Each person brought something, and we just threw everything into the pot, and it turned out to be delicious. We ate and had a good time. So let's make us some gumbo. Our kitchen is little, but we can make it do. We'll have our Thanksgiving right here. You and me and our little boy, Douglas Darius Fir Deavers."

"Or our little girl, Willow Ariel Mede Deavers." Her bright mood took hold of him, and he laughed with her.

So they went out to the mall and shopped. They made some gumbo, and they ate, and they gave thanks for peace, love, joy, happiness, health, and strength.

When Charles returned from his dinner, he was not in a happy holiday mood, being alone with no family, and seeing his friends' current misfortunes compounded his sad mood. He knew something had to be changed. They all needed help, and it could come from only one positive source. He called Reverend Deavers, who consulted with his wife and with Mary Jane Copple. With no hesitation and with little time-consuming planning, they reacted.

"We'll be there on Saturday," Reverend Deavers said, and when Charles told Sage and Darius the wonderful news, they went to bed thinking happily about Saturday when their families would arrive.

Sage had been so strong for everyone else—Darius, Karen, the children, Miriam—and now her determination was to stay strong and not let this new hole in the dike, this new river to cross, this new problem, break her. No tears. As she had said so often, "Don't cry, Darius." But when she saw her mother getting off the airplane, the floodgates of her stored-up determination opened, and Sage Deavers cried. The thumb of her determination had been removed from the dike, and she didn't know she had so many tears. She had missed her mother without being so aware of it until she saw her. It was like she'd been alone in a foreign land.

"Oh, Mother dear, just let me feel your arms around me," she said, also putting her arms around her mother's waist. For Sage, there was no love like a mother's love, and no matter that the Scripture says to leave your father and your mother, and though it tells a husband to cling to his wife, Sage felt it was the same for a wife. And she had clung to Darius, she had loved him, and she had given him what she thought was all her love. But no. She was now more aware that no one person could hold all the love she had to give, and there was a special part that was reserved just for her mother.

It was a most joyous reunion. Darius and Sage with Darius's parents, Reverend and Lucy Deavers. Darius and Sage with Mrs. Mary Jane Copple, Sage's mother. The love flowed all around, and Major Hawthorne, having picked them up from the airport, was looking on; and although he hadn't met Sage's mother before today, he felt the love. His thoughts were, *What a beautiful lady. It's no wonder that Sage is so beautiful.*

Charles was happy to see them, for to him, they were also his family, as he had adopted Mrs. Mary Jane Copple as his mother.

Then everyone was drawn to the fact that Sage was carrying a new life. The two mothers proudly patted her protruding midsection, a first grandchild for Lucy Deavers and a first child for Mary Jane Copple's baby girl.

How unfortunate that everything had to be decided according to Black and White. But how fortunate that their love and their knowledge of what was allowed and what was not, formed an umbrella of peace. Major Hawthorne again offered to take them to the officers' quarters, but again Sage declined his offer.

"No, no," Sage said. "I need this love. We've been separated by circumstances beyond our control, but for right now, I don't want any of you to leave us. We can all go to our present place of residence, which is the office. We are allowed there, and we can sit awhile and enjoy one another."

After arriving at the little building, Major Hawthorne and Charles went out and picked up food. They purchased sandwiches and lemonade, and for their meal, they also included the leftover gumbo and pound cake.

"Oh dear, I'm so happy," Sage said, and she refused to be separated from her mother, so Darius and Charles slept upstairs, and Sage slept downstairs with her mother. Mary Jane Copple was quite content with that arrangement. These parents had been so very worried after hearing the news of the house being ruined, but they were now thanking God for the safety of their children.

Reverend Deavers said, "Tonight, my wife and I will stay at the hotel, and tomorrow we'll attend church, and we'll pay a visit to your damaged house. Then on Monday, we can plan to meet, and we'll sit down together and make some plans for you and Sage to find another home."

Darius wanted to protest, but Sage put her hand on his arm. "Just be thankful," she said.

When Reverend Deavers said, "Tomorrow we'll attend church," Darius couldn't tell his father that he had no desire now to deal with attending church. First, he hadn't told his parents that he and Sage attended different churches. Second, he hadn't told his new friends Blaise and Evelyn that he was married and that his wife was Black. His previous thoughts were that they could live both lives, with him being White in a White church and Sage being happy attending a Black church.

But since Darius had all his life been truthful, when he and his father attended the White church, Darius confessed to his father, who, of course, suggested that he tell Blaise and Evelyn the truth.

"We already knew that," Blaise said with a shrug of his shoulders. "It was revealed in the company's background check. It was a routine procedure."

"I must confess," Evelyn said, hugging Reverend Deavers, "that I had wanted to know your son better as I recognized his inner beauty, and now I can see where that beauty comes from. I'm very happy to meet you, Reverend Deavers, and I'm looking forward to meeting your lovely wife, and also your wife, Darius."

"We read what happened to your house, and I prayed for you and your wife," Blaise said.

"I understand that it was in all the newspapers," Darius said.

"That day, after I read the article, I stopped every hour, and I asked God to stay with you and to give you and your wife strength to stay strong," Evelyn said this.

"May I take the liberty to invite you and Blaise to go with us to see the ruined house?" Darius asked. "My father has planned a prayer vigil there after church to release it all to God. Our wives and Sage's mother will meet us there."

"I would be honored," Evelyn said.

"And I as well," Blaise said.

Mrs. Lucy Deavers, not wanting to leave Sage, went to the Black church with her and Mary Jane Copple, and Sage felt very much at ease going with her two mothers. And when Charles joined them, she smiled. Sage had attended the church, and she had enjoyed good fellowship with the people she met there, but she hadn't joined any of the organizations, mostly because of her pregnancy and her energy level. She didn't want to tax her strength.

After church, they gathered on the front lawn of the black house: Sage and Darius Deavers, Reverend and Lucy Deavers, Mary Jane Copple, Lieutenant and Gertrude Kingsley, Blaise McCaslin, Evelyn Prentiss, Charles Williams, and Major Hawthorne. For five minutes, there was quiet and observation, each with their own thoughts about the minds of the perpetrators that could harbor so much hate. So-called civilized people.

"Love those who hate you," Evelyn said.

"Pray for those who despitefully use you," Mary Jane Copple said.

"I think of today as being beautiful and highly productive of good," Gertrude said.

"It's a new day, let us rejoice and be glad in it," Colin said.

"And He will give His angels charge over you to protect you in all your ways," Sage said.

"The Lord is my light and my salvation," Blaise said.

Reverend Deavers led them in saying the Lord's Prayer.

Darius, however, was thinking, *I feel like I'm in a maze, and every time I take a step, I run into a brick wall.*

Charles was thinking, *I've witnessed worse. I've seen hangings and lynching.*

Major Hawthorne took them all to dinner at a restaurant that received both races.

Note: Since they also owned the land on which the house stood, it would be their responsibility to take whatever action they wanted to take concerning the house, and they were painfully aware that they couldn't leave it here forever.

32

On Monday, as Reverend Deavers had suggested, they agreed to find a new residence for the young couple. Together with their parents, they looked at the beautiful homes on the east side, overlooking the hills, not far from the waters of the Puget Sound. Finding one that they liked and making sure there was no restrictive covenant, Reverend Deavers purchased it. The house was beautiful. There was a large grass covered yard front and back, a drive-in garage, living room, dining room, sitting room, kitchen, breakfast nook on the first floor, three bedrooms upstairs, two baths, large windows, and carpeted floors. There was a front porch that extended across the front of the house and around several feet on the side, much like Mary Jane Copple's house in Oklahoma. Sage remembered the many hours she had spent sitting there with her mother.

"Now we'll furnish it fully. Money is no problem. We have it, and what better way to spend it than on our children. Oh, I'm so happy," Lucy Deavers said.

Everyone had a shopping list. The ladies: Sage, Lucy Deavers, Mary Jane Copple, and not wanting to leave her out, they invited Gertrude Kingsley. She selected and placed several house plants. The men had their list: Darius, Charles, Reverend Deavers, Major Hawthorne, and Lieutenant Kingsley. What a variety of choices. But Sage, knowing that everyone had a preference, had decided on a color scheme, which was the only specific order.

Soon after they took possession, Sage and Darius sent out invitations to their Christmas celebration. It was at Christmastime last year that they first said "I do" at their mock wedding ceremony in Oklahoma, and they had decided to celebrate at this time every year. The invitation read as follows:

MR. AND MRS. DARIUS AND SAGE DEAVERS
INVITE YOU AND YOUR FAMILY
TO A CELEBRATION OF
OUR NEW HOME
MEET OUR PARENTS
ONE-YEAR ANNIVERSARY OF OUR PROMISE
AND
THE BIRTH OF JESUS THE CHRIST

NO GIFTS

DATE: DECEMBER 24, 1947
TIME: 5:00 p.m.

Bring something that represents
your hope for the future or your belief,
small enough to be hung as an ornament on our
TREE OF HOPE AND LOVE

Dinner will be served at six o'clock.
We thank you for your presence.

* * * * *

When the invitation arrived at the Withers' home, there were some very adverse reactions. Miriam decided immediately that she would attend, and she told herself that it would be a more enjoyable way to spend Christmas Eve than how she'd unhappily endured Thanksgiving Day. But then she turned her attention to her husband, certain of what his answer would be: *Those are not people I will*

associate with, and I will not allow you to go there and take my son.
That's what he would say, and she was right; for when they sat down
to dinner at their home that evening, she laid the colorful invitation
beside his plate.

"Look at this," she said. "What a wonderful way to spend
Christmas Eve, with all those charming people. I think it would be
so nice for us to go."

"And I can see Jasmine and Jasper again. They're my new friends.
So can we go, Daddy? Can we?" Timothy asked this.

Bertram picked up the invitation, read it, got up, and placed it
on the serving table behind him. Sitting back down, he held out his
hands, the right hand to Miriam and the left hand to Timothy, as
usual, for the blessing.

"Shall we say grace?" he said.

So together they said, "Lord, we thank you for the food we are
about to receive, which will nourish our bodies, and we thank you
for our family. Amen."

Bertram picked up his fork and began eating his salad. Their
conversation then consisted of each person answering the usual question, which Miriam knew was only meant to promote conversation
and not to give any real information.

"Well, Timothy, how was your day?" Bertram Withers said.

"We went outside today, and since it was cold, we had to put on
our coats and hats and gloves, and when we went in for lunch, well,
they gave us hot chocolate. But one boy, his name was Jonathan, and
he knocked his cup over, and his legs got burned, and he had to go to
the nurse. And his mom came to school, and she fussed, and so the
lady said, 'No more hot chocolate.'"

"Yes, it is not sensible to allow young children to have something
hot, and most definitely without personal one-on-one supervision,"
Bertram said this. He put another fork of salad in his mouth, chewed
for a few seconds, and Miriam and Timothy knew to wait until he
asked them to speak. "And you know," he said after a moment, "this
period from now until the first of the new year is a busy time for me.
The tedious year-end reports for the department are due, with every
i dotted and every *t* crossed and every penny accounted for, every

employee evaluated, and all written down in detail. And you know, it is so frustrating that those typists are not as accurate as you want them to be"—and on and on and *I* and *I* and blah, blah, blah.

He finished his salad, picked up his napkin, and slowly wiped his mouth before he spoke again.

"And you, my dear, how was your day?"

She was well aware, from past experience, that he was not interested in how her day had gone, and she always gave the same answer. "It went well." But today she had said to herself, *This evening, I will speak my mind. I will clip the strings from this puppeteer who sits at the head of this table, and I will let him know that I am not his puppet. I am a person. I have a mind, and at this particular stage in my life, things I had clung to before have fallen apart. My mother and father are getting a divorce, my marriage is not a marriage, so why should I concern myself about trying to keep the peace? I'm pregnant, and I must stay with him until my child is born, and then I know that I will make some changes. The changes will be mine and mine alone, for my present unhappiness must end, or I will surely die. This man is slowly and painfully killing me.*

"Well," she asked, calling upon her newfound bravery and looking him in the face, "what about the invitation?"

"Of course, we're not going. Those are not people I will associate with, and I will not allow you to go there and take my son, and we'll let that be the end of that." He said this without looking up at her.

"I want you to know," she said, still looking at him, "that I'm going, and I plan to take Timothy. Those are genuinely good people, and I like them, and so does Timothy. I was hoping you could see it in your heart to go with us, but if not, so be it." She was holding the salad fork in her hand, but she wasn't eating.

For Bertram, this was shocking behavior, and he was forced to look at her, and her eyes and her unwavering stare told him that here beside him was not the person he'd been married to all this time. He didn't like what he saw, and he attributed her behavior to "those people," as he called them. Not having any idea how to answer her, he finished his dinner in silence and left the table. For the rest of the evening and for the next few days, he was cool to her and to his son, and he did not mention the invitation.

On a Saturday morning, later in December, Bertram, Miriam, Timothy, and Major Hawthorne were having their usual breakfast at Alicia Hawthorne's house. Major Hawthorne was there, despite the strained relationship with his wife and their pending divorce, because of Timothy and, of course, Miriam.

Although they talked of other things, the prevailing thought on everyone's mind was the Christmas invitation. Sage and Darius, not wanting to exclude Alicia, had addressed an invitation to Major Marvin and Mrs. Alicia Hawthorne.

"I'm sure you're already aware of this shindig they're throwing," Alicia said as she handed the invitation to her husband.

"Oh yes, I am aware of the celebration, as Sage and Darius called it, not a shindig, but I haven't seen the actual invitation." He opened the envelope, and being impressed with the design of it and the activities included, he smiled. "I guess we'd better start thinking about our ornaments," the major said.

"That means that you think we're going," Alicia said, and she laughed. "No way."

"And why not?" he asked.

"Have you forgotten that they're colored?" she asked.

"Would you please tell that to my wife. She insists on going, and I say the same thing. No way," Bertram said this.

"They're not both colored. Darius is White," Marvin said.

"But that other one is colored. What's his name?"

"You mean Charles. What's he got to do with it?"

"Well," Alicia said, hitting her hand on the table, "I don't like him either."

"Well, it doesn't matter to me what you say. I'm going," Marvin Hawthorne said.

"Good for you, Daddy," Miriam said. "And I say, so am I."

"And I say, no, you're not. I'm head of my household, which fact you might have forgotten, and I say this association with the colored Sage Deavers and Charles Colored Williams has to end. We're not going."

"Colored doesn't mean they're not human. Sage is a lovely person," Miriam said.

"Sage is a very lovely person, and I'm sorry you feel that way about her. And I like Darius, and I'm looking forward to going to their celebration," Marvin said.

"Of course, we know why you're so intent on staying close to her," Alicia said, emphasizing the word *her*.

"Oh, Mom," Miriam said. "Why do you keep saying that as if it's true, and my word, what if it is? I love her. She's my only friend." She couldn't control her tears. She put her hands over her face and cried. Timothy, to everyone's surprise, went over and put his arms around his mother from the back of her chair.

"Don't cry, Mommie," he said, tears rolling down his cheeks.

The tears were too much for Bertram, and he was totally overcome. He couldn't bear to see people crying. And here were his wife and his son crying. His thoughts swirled around and around, and even his body became unstable, and he shook his head and wiped the perspiration from his forehead. Now as he looked at her and at his son, he thought about them. *My wife is sitting here crying, and she is pregnant, and I have refused to think about her condition and her wishes and her ideals and even about her life. Evidently, she is not happy, and neither is my son, and neither am I. So damn it, I'll have to think this over. Maybe I can look at Sage in a different way.* Those were his thoughts.

"Stop it," he whispered. "Just stop it with the tears. And now my son is crying. Don't you know that men don't cry?"

Miriam looked up at him. "I can't understand what is happening in this room. This whole room is filled with selfishness, and it is frightening me. Daddy," she said, "please take me home." And looking over at her husband, she said, "No, don't take me to that cave of horrors, for that's what it is, and my husband is the evil dragon. Take me with you. Take me anywhere but there."

"You will not," Alicia said. "Bertram is right. He's head of his house. Oh damn, this is all because of that little Sage witch." She threw her glass against the fireplace, and it broke into pieces.

There was a noticeable moment of quiet. Then Miriam took Timothy by the hand, walked over, and put on their coats. Marvin followed them, and as they approached the door, Bertram walked in front of them.

"All right. I won't let those people break up my home, especially now that we're expecting a baby, for goodness sake. And I do love you, Miriam, and I love you, Timothy, so…well, we'll go to the shindig, whatever it is," he said, looking over at his wife.

"It's a celebration, and I'm going," Marvin said.

"Well, we'll all go," Bertram said.

And they did.

"I still won't go," Alicia Hawthorne said. And she didn't.

Mamie, who was also invited, had listened from the kitchen. "And, of course, I'm going," she said. And she did.

Since the passionate manner in which her husband had agreed to accompany them to the Christmas celebration, Miriam had not mentioned it to him. To those who did not know him, it would appear that he had changed and that his biases and his prejudices toward "those people" had waned, if not left him altogether, and he would accept the Deavers as friends. But knowing him as she did, Miriam felt that Bertram Withers had agreed to go with her and their son only in an effort to create some peace at the moment and also with consideration for her condition. But she felt in her heart that his consideration was temporary, and he and her mother still harbored the same bitter feelings of animosity toward "those niggers." Miriam knew that was how they labeled them in their minds.

33

THE CELEBRATION. There was a large lighted Christmas wreath with red and green ribbons and pine cones sprayed with gold hung outside the house just below the roof above the front door.

Darius and Sage stood at the entrance to greet the guests. Charles stood beside them, giving out name tags.

The invited guests were Bertram and Miriam Withers and Timothy; Major Marvin and Alicia Hawthorne; Lieutenant Colin and Gertrude Kingsley; Randy and Karen Davis, Jasmine, and Jasper; Mrs. Johnson; Mrs. Caldwell; Blaise McCaslin, and Evelyn Grayson. Miraculously, with the exception of Alicia Hawthorne and Randy Davis, also present were Reverend and Mrs. Deavers and Mrs. Mary Jane Copple, everyone who was invited came. When Timothy saw Jasmine and Jasper, he ran to them with a happy smile. Then happy hugs and giggles were exchanged.

After everyone was seated, Darius and Sage stood beside the beautiful, brightly lighted Christmas tree. Sage was wearing a white satin-and-lace maternity dress sewed by her hand, and Darius looked especially handsome in his white tuxedo.

Darius began, "Good afternoon. We are Darius and Sage Deavers, and we welcome you to the celebration of our new home. We ask forgiveness for those who destroyed our first home, and we express thanks to our friends, Lieutenant Colin and Mrs. Gertrude Kingsley, for providing us with a temporary home. And a very special thanks to my parents, who purchased this lovely home for us. Now meet my parents, Reverend Paul and Mrs. Lucy Deavers."

Sage added, "Now meet my mother, Mrs. Mary Jane Copple. My father, Isaac Copple, is deceased."

Darius then informed them, "Although we were legally married in April at the Peach Arch Park here in Washington, we are celebrating this day, the one-year anniversary when we first said "I do" in a mock wedding ceremony in Oklahoma, and we now renew our pledge." He took Sage's hand. "I, Darius Paul Deavers, do again pledge my love to you, Ariel Sage Deavers. I will never leave you nor forsake you as long as I live."

Sage answered him, "I, Ariel Sage Deavers, do again pledge my love to you, Darius Paul Deavers. I will never leave you nor forsake you as long as I live."

They kissed, and Darius addressed their guests, "We are also elated to celebrate the birth of our Lord and Savior Jesus the Christ. In the book of Matthew, we read, 'Wise men came from the east to Jerusalem saying: Behold, a virgin shall conceive and bear a son.'"

Sage followed, "In Luke, we read, 'The angel said, Do not be afraid Mary, for you have found favor with God and behold, you will conceive and bear a son and you shall call his name Jesus. He will be known as the Son of God.'"

Darius said, "The next agenda for the evening is the sharing of your name and an explanation of your ornament, which you will give to Charles, who has the pleasant task of hanging it on our tree of hope and love. I will make the first sharing. The number on your name tag is the order in which you will make your presentation.

"My name is Darius Paul Deavers, and I am a licensed attorney. I bring this tree. I believe in trees. Trees shed foliage, which helps feed them for the coming new season. Trees give us much-needed food and shade. Trees are divine as only God can make a tree, and my hope is that God will guide my steps to a productive growth for the future of those who come after me and also love for one another. The bringing of gifts symbolizes that the Magi brought gifts to the newborn Christ child. Now come and decorate our tree of hope and love. Let your ornament represent something you hope for the future, something you love."

Sage came next. "My name is Ariel Sage Deavers. I've brought both an angel and a sprig of garden sage. I believe in angels. Psalm 91 says, 'For He will give His angels charge over you to guard you in all your ways.' There is also a garden plant named sage. Sage tea, made from the plant, is said to relieve indigestion, to improve memory, and to strengthen the nervous system. A sage is also defined as a very wise person. So I trust my angels to show me how to use my wisdom for teaching children." She gave Charles a small white angel and a sprig of green sage, which he hung on the tree.

It was now Major Hawthorne's turn. "My name is Marvin Hawthorne. I am a retired major in the United States Army. I am the father of Miriam Hawthorne Withers and the grandfather of Timothy Withers. I bring for the tree a small United States flag, sometimes referred to as Old Glory. The flag represents my patriotism to this country, and my hope is that we can get rid of our hate and our separation and replace them with love and togetherness, and we can truthfully become the United States of America." He gave Charles a small US flag, which he hung on the tree.

Lieutenant Kingsley spoke next. "My name is Colin Kingsley. I am a retired lieutenant from the United States Navy. I am married to Gertrude Kingsley, and we own a private yacht. My ornament for the tree is a white dove of peace with an olive branch in its mouth. As God caused a flood, I would like to see a flood that would wash away the mean and unfair laws that exist against people of color, and when I send a dove out from my yacht, it would return with an olive branch in its mouth. An olive branch is a symbol of peace." He gave Charles a small white dove with an olive branch in its mouth, which the latter hung on the tree.

Mrs. Kingsley followed. "My name is Gertrude Kingsley, and I'm married to Lieutenant Colin Kingsley. My ornament is a book. I devote a good deal of my time to growing flowers, but I also devote my time to growing fruits and vegetables. Now I would like to write a book that explains the preparation and the nutritional benefits of all growing plants. I know that a healthy diet produces a healthy brain and a healthy body. My hope is that my book will be helpful as a guide to healthy eating." She gave Charles a small book, which he hung on the tree.

It was now Bertram's turn, and he said, "My name is Bertram Withers. I am Miriam's husband and Timothy's father. I am a professor at the university. I love life, and I want to live a successful existence. I have brought for the tree a ladder. My hope is that it will always be there for me to climb to my highest level in life. Keep a ladder close, and as you contemplate your goal, it will be a useful tool. A necessary tool for climbing." He gave Charles a small ladder, which Charles hung on the tree.

Miriam spoke next. "My name is Miriam Yvonne Withers. I am the daughter of Major Marvin Hawthorne and Mrs. Alicia Hawthorne. I am the wife of Professor Bertram Withers and the mother of Timothy Withers, and soon to be the mother of another beautiful child. A mother's heart is full of love, so I bring to you a mother's heart, and my hope is that every child will be blessed with a loving mother." She gave Charles a small red heart, which he hung on the tree.

Then Blaise spoke, "My name is Blaise McCaslin. I don't have a family here. I am a lawyer, but I have a primary interest in banking. Growing up, I had a piggy bank, and I remember that my father worked hard, and my mother was a homemaker. And every week when my father brought his money home, Mother would put a dollar in a jar and a penny in my piggy bank. She told me that pennies make dollars, and a dollar is your very best friend. My hope is that you will teach your children to work hard and to save some of their money. I bring for the tree a piggy bank." Charles hung it on the tree.

Karen followed. "My name is Karen Johnson. I am the daughter of Mrs. Erma Johnson and the mother of Jasmine and Jasper. I was never married to their father, Randy Davis, but we have high hopes for his future. My ornament for the tree is a tassel. I read about Pandora and her box, and like Pandora, I was carrying a bag of evil things, like poverty and worry, and I was told never to open it. But beautiful Sage Deavers came along and opened it, and we let all those evil things out, and she helped me to close it, and only a tassel was left. A tassel means that I've graduated college, and my hope is that I can use my education to lift as I climb. My ornament is a tassel." She gave Charles a gold tassel, which he hung on the tree.

Evelyn was next. "My Name is Evelyn Prentiss. I believe in God. My husband, my mother, and my three-year-old child were killed in a car accident. I was lost, and I didn't want to live. I was just twenty-seven years old. My pastor told me that I was saved for a reason. He said, 'If you really want to live, get acquainted with God.' He gave me a leather-bound Bible, and I studied it, and now I teach a Bible class at my church every Wednesday night. You're all invited to attend, and my hope is that you will teach your children about God. For the tree, I've brought a little matchbox Bible." She gave the book to Charles, which he hung on the tree.

Jasper, Timothy, and Jasmine stepped forward. They said in unison, "We are three wise men who followed a star."

Jasmine said, "We are two wise men and one wise lady." There was laughter.

Jasper continued, "My name is Jasper Davis. I am the son of Karen Johnson and Randy Davis and the grandson of Mrs. Johnson. My gift is a hammer and some nails. I hope to study building, and the first thing I will build is a house for my family. Miss Sage and Mr. Darius took us to their house and showed me about living in a nice house." He gave Charles a small hammer and some nails, which he hung on the tree.

Jasmine was next. "My name is Jasmine Davis. I am the daughter of Karen Johnson and Randy Davis and the granddaughter of Mrs. Johnson. My gift is a needle and some thread. I hope to study sewing, and I will make some pretty dresses. The first will be for my mom and my grandmom. It was Miss Sage who taught me about sewing." She gave Charles a needle and a spool of thread, which he hung on the tree.

Timothy then said, "My name is Timothy Withers, and I am the son of Mr. Bertram and Mrs. Miriam Withers and the grandson of Major Marvin and Mrs. Alicia Hawthorne. My gift for the tree is a doctor's black bag. My hope is to study medicine and become a doctor, and I will build a strong heart for my mom that can't be broken." He gave Charles a small black bag, which he hung on the tree.

They all said, "Will you help us sing:
O star of wonder, star of night,
Star with loyal beauty bright
Westward leading, still proceeding,
Guide us to thy perfect light."

"My name is Lucy Yvonne Deavers," Lucy said, stepping forward. "I am Darius's mother and the wife of Reverend Michael Paul Deavers, and Darius is our only child. For the tree, I've brought a sprig of alfalfa. The alfalfa plant requires pollinators when flowers are in bloom. But pollination of the alfalfa plant is somewhat problematic as the pollen-carrying keel of the plant trips and strikes the pollinating bees on the head. The bees didn't like being struck on the head, so they learned to get the nectar from the side of the flower. So here comes Sage, my little honeybee, trying to get close to me, and I'm hitting her upside her head with my prejudice. But she and my son, Darius, the king bee, kept figuring out ways to get close to me. And they've produced something sweet in me—love and kindness. And my hope is that everyone will decide how to defeat the hateful prejudices that are hitting us all." She gave Charles a sprig of alfalfa, which he hung on the tree.

Mrs. Mary Jane Copple, Mrs. Erma Johnson, and Ms. Mamie Caldwell stepped forward.

Mary Jane Copple said, "My name is Mary Jane Copple. I am Sage Deavers's mother, and I bring you faith. In Hebrews, we read, 'Now faith is the substance of things hoped for, the evidence of things not seen.'" She gave Charles a yellow ball with the word *faith* on it, which he hung on the tree.

Mrs. Mamie Caldwell said next, "My name is Mamie Caldwell. I bring you hope. In Psalm 16, we read, 'Therefore my heart is glad, and my flesh shall rest in hope.'" She gave Charles a green ball with the word *hope* on it, which he hung on the tree.

Mrs. Erma Johnson said, "My name is Erma Johnson. I'm Karen's mother and Jasmine and Jasper's grandmother. I bring you love. In First Corinthians, we rea, 'Though I speak with the tongues of men and of angels, and have not love, I am become as sounding brass, or a tinkling cymbal.'" She gave Charles a purple ball with the word *love* on it, which he hung on the tree.

The three ladies joined hands and said, "And now abideth faith, hope and love. These three. But the greatest of these is love."

Reverend Deavers stood up. "I am Reverend Michael Paul Deavers. I am the father of Darius Deavers, and my beautiful wife is Lucy Deavers, and my beautiful daughter-in-law is Ariel Sage Deavers. By profession, I am a minister of the Gospel, which means that I am an agent assigned to lead people to know and to follow the teachings of Jesus the Christ and thus to become Christians. My ornament is a bright and shining star. The star is defined as a pentagram, and the five points of the star represent the five earthly and heavenly materials: spirit, earth, air, fire, and water. In the Scriptures, the Magi followed a star, which led them to the baby Jesus, who is a bright and shining star and the light of the world. So we each can follow Jesus and thus glorify God, who is in heaven." He gave Charles a lighted star, and he hung it at the top point of the tree.

Charles stepped in front of the tree. "My name is Charles Williams. I have brought a piece of lamé [pronounced la-may]. Lamé is a sheer brocaded fabric with tinsel filling threads of gold and silver. I will wrap it around the tree and thus enclose all of your ornaments, which represent your beliefs and hopes. My hope is that you will stay together in peace and love. I am standing outside this tree because I won't be here to find my peace with you. I came to Washington with Darius and his beautiful wife, Sage, to what I thought was a better place than where I lived in Georgia. I had high hopes of making a difference in the racial climate here. But for me, none of my hopes and dreams have been attained here in Washington, so I've decided to return to Georgia, where I'll take my education and my ambitions and where they are also needed. I'll be leaving right after the new year with my adopted mother, Mrs. Copple, and with my other adopted mother and father, Reverend and Mrs. Deavers, all of whom I have come to love. My hope is that you will stay in peace and love one another as our Lord and Savior Jesus Christ loves you, and you will be a help to someone in need."

Then Darius announced, "Dinner is served. Now my beautiful wife will bless the table."

Sage entreated them as she prayed, "I ask that you join hands with the persons next to you. Bow your heads and receive some words of thanks. Dear Lord, we thank you for the food we are about to receive. We thank you for the hands that prepared it. We thank you for the fellowship of friends who will partake of it as it is for the nourishment of our minds, our souls, and our bodies. Amen."

As they left for the evening, each person received a calendar for the new year with space for their new year's resolutions. The children received a dictionary, an orange, an apple, and a box of Christmas candy.

On January 1,1958, the family and friends of Darius and Sage enjoyed the traditional New Year's dinner: Reverend Deavers, Lucy Deavers, Darius and Sage Deavers, Mary Jane Copple, Charles Williams, Erma Johnson, Karen, Jasper, Jasmine, and Mamie Caldwell. On January second, Reverend Deavers, Lucy Deavers, Mary Jane Copple, and Charles Williams left BeachSide, Washington, each to return to their hometown.

Part Four

34

On January 5, Darius Paul Deavers awoke early. It was Monday morning. He sat up, turned his covers back, and quietly got out of bed. Sage opened her eyes and looked dreamily at him. He walked around to her side of the bed, kissed her on the forehead, and said, "I love you." She gave a nod of her head in response and closed her eyes. Although their usual routine was to arise at the same time, get dressed, have coffee together, and then he would go off to work and Sage would go about her routine of picking up Mrs. Johnson and the children, since it was the last trimester of Sage's pregnancy, she slept as late as she wanted as she no longer went to pick up Mrs. Johnson. She had given Karen her car to use, and Karen brought her mother and the children over. Karen attended her classes at the university, and she came back at three o'clock and picked them up. Sage spent two hours with the children, and she spent the remainder of the day sewing curtains, coverlets, and sheets for the nursery. Oh, what joy that filled her soul.

Darius arrived at his office at nine o'clock, and it was his first day back since the holidays, and thoughts of the celebration were still with him, including Charles's announcement that he would be leaving. Although he would miss Charles as his friend, Charles had not been very beneficial to the law firm, and Darius knew that he had to focus on new beginnings for himself. He looked at the old calendar on his desk, and he replaced it with a new one. He opened it to January, and his eyes fell on the line for "new resolutions." He realized, *It's a new year. I have a new house, new furniture, and a new law firm. No more Deavers and Williams.* He was momentarily overcome by the possibility of making it alone, and the voice of his old life was saying to him, *You couldn't make it with a partner. What makes you think you can be successful alone?* Then his other voice said to him, *The past is over, but the present is here, and the future is before you, waiting for you to take a step forward to meet it. Think positive.*

He stood and began doing some exercises to get himself started. He opened the first file drawer and took out all the files. He did this with the firm determination to work with what he had. He would take care of those cases, no matter how trivial. He would send out new flyers; he'd change the sign outside to "DARIUS DEAVERS, Attorney at Law." He thought of Burnett and the fact that he was a success. Alone. Then his other voice said, *But Burnett is Black, and his office is in an all-Black neighborhood. And although your office is in a Black neighborhood, you are White, and Burnett's slogan is* HELP. *Yes, that's exactly what I need. Hmm, I'll hire an office clerk to answer the phone, type cases, and write letters. So I'll need a typewriter. Oh dear, those things will take time and money. Or perhaps I should contact the man from the protest group and offer my legal services there.*

Like a pendulum swinging back and forth, his thoughts went one way and then another, and he was engaged in an internal dispute with what he wanted to do, what he could do, and what he should do. He had asked those who came to the celebration to bring an ornament that spoke of their personal desires and their hopes for the future, so he knew that he had to focus on his own personal hopes and desires and how he could accomplish them.

Then he remembered his mother's ornament. It was so relevant. A piece of alfalfa and the difficulty of being pollinated. Hmm. He decided that he must become the king bee and figure a way to keep the evil deeds, the evil prejudices of life, from deterring him and hitting him where it hurts—which, of course, brought him back to his original purpose in choosing law. It was to help people solve their legal problems, which at that time included and was involved with people of his station in life, White and rich, his own security, finding his rightful place.

Then along came Sage and the obstacles of race and the issue of Black versus White. And Karen's mention of Pandora's box. The myth was that Pandora had been warned not to open the box. He was warned not to leave his profitable, rich law firm for the reason of marrying Sage. But Pandora had opened the box, and all the evils of the world were released. And like Pandora, he opened the box when he married Sage, and all the evils of inequality of the races surrounded them. But Pandora was able to close the box, and only hope was left.

"So I'll strive to close it, and hope will be left to save me, hope for success as a White lawyer in a Black environment," he said aloud.

He stepped away from his desk, looked around at his lonely office, went out, and got in his car. He drove home with a clear vision of how he would program the future.

Sage met him at the door with her usual pleasant smile, a hug, and a kiss. When he felt her love, he was overcome with joy as a breath of fresh air, and he realized that he had not included her pregnancy in his decision. This thought brought him up out of his indecision, of all uncertainty and doubt, and he knew he had to survive.

"I'll go to the office every morning, and I'll accept whatever cases come. I'll strive to accept my life, and I'll love my beautiful wife, and I'll look forward to the birth of our child. I can make it if I try, and I will try."

35

It was April 1, 1948, and Alicia Hawthorne was alone in her house. Her marriage had fallen apart, but she still had Miriam, Timothy, and Bertram in her life; and every morning, she called to see if her expecting daughter and her grandson were all right. Besides the call each morning, she stopped by every other day to see them. They were her life. They were her happiness.

Alicia Hawthorne looked forward to the new baby with enthusiasm, and she planned to spend the first few weeks after the birth with Miriam. Even though Mamie would be there, Alicia wanted to take care of Miriam and the new arrival herself. She had bought little gowns and shirts and socks, all white, as she had dressed Miriam in all white for the first year of her life.

Alicia had helped Miriam decorate and furnish a nursery, and she regretted that she and Marvin weren't working together. She couldn't, however, erase the hate and racial loathing for him, thinking he had had sex or an affair with a Black woman, and she had the same ill feelings for Sage, blaming her for the breakup of her marriage. She was very unhappy that Miriam chose to be Sage's friend, and she was also very angry that Bertram had gone to the little Christmas shindig, as she called it—and cursed and be damned, they took Timothy, which allowed him to associate with those Black children again.

She was thinking, *Now that I'm divorced, I don't have to be concerned about Marvin. I'll love this baby, and I'll continue my efforts to keep my grandchildren White. I'm sure I can steer Timothy and Miriam away from those people and teach them the advantages and the privileges of being White. Superior.* She waited with eager enthusiasm for the arrival of their child.

All that day, Miriam sat in the big comfortable lounge chair in their living room. She could hear Mamie going back and forth in the house doing her chores. When her husband came home from work, he greeted her warmly with a kiss on the forehead.

"How are you two feeling, my dear?" he asked, patting her belly.

"I'm a little tired, and I'll be glad to have my body back," she said.

"I know, dear, but it can't be too much longer. After dinner, I'll give you a nice body rub with that special oil your mother brought. You'll feel better."

"Thank you, Bertram. That'll be good," she said, not really being taken in by his kindness, which came across to her as being very false. Maybe it was that he had changed. Maybe all the love and joy he experienced at the Deavers' Christmas celebration had brought about a change in him. Normally, he could not be called an affectionate husband, and he was never a very friendly person. He had no intimate friends. He was connected to many people at his job, at their church, but he hadn't developed any close relationship with any of them. Since the Christmas celebration, he had accepted Miriam being friendly with Sage. He had become friendly with Evelyn at her Bible study on Wednesday nights, and seemingly, he was listening more closely to Evelyn's teaching from the Scriptures about faith and love.

At dinner that evening, the conversation was the same as usual; and at eight o'clock, after Miriam had read to Timothy and kissed him good-night, he asked, "Mommie, when will I have a little sister?"

She told him that she was sure that it wouldn't be long.

"And I'm sure I'll love my little sister," he said.

Getting herself ready for bed, she knew from remembering Timothy's birth what her backache meant. Mamie agreed to stay with Timothy while his daddy took his mommie to the hospital, and she promised she'd call Alicia and Major Hawthorne and inform them.

It was April 1, 1948, and Mary Jane Copple and Lucy Deavers had come for the birth, and they were sitting in the living room with Sage and Darius.

"Well, Sage dear," Darius said, patting her belly, "you weighed 125 pounds when we got married, and now you weigh 145. Whew! We're going to have a twenty-pound baby."

"No," Sage's mom said, laughing. "A lot of that is water. You always gain some extra weight during pregnancy, but it'll go away after the little one gets here."

"I can't remember exactly how much I gained with this one here," Darius's mom said, touching Darius on the shoulder. "But I know he was so pretty, and when they laid him down beside me, I said, 'Is this what was causing me all that pain?'" She laughed. "But you know, that's really not what you remember because when they get here and you look at them, it's love at first sight, and you forget all about the pain."

"I don't think we have much longer to wait. When we were at the doctor's office yesterday, he said 'any day now,'" Darius said.

"I was hoping it would be the thirteenth," Sage said.

"Sage thinks thirteen is her lucky number, but most people think of the thirteenth, especially Friday the thirteenth, as unlucky," Darius said.

"Yep," Mary Jane said. "People have always said that's when the black cats roam around at night, and witches and goblins creep out from their dark places and eat up little girls."

"And my sister thinks that if a black cat crosses your path, you'll have bad luck. And boy, if one came along in front of her, she'd turn around and walk backward and go the other way," Sage said.

"And there are those who warn you not to ever break a mirror because if you do, you'll have thirteen years' bad luck," Lucy Deavers said.

"Hey, why are we talking about all that bad stuff?" Darius asked. "Nothing bad is going to happen, and it's not even the thirteenth. It's the first, and it's a lovely, lovely day."

So they sat on the couch eating popcorn and drinking lemonade. All three of them put a hand on Sage's belly, and they sang a happy song.

Pretty soon, Sage knew that it was time, so they gathered in a family hug. Mary Jane said a prayer, and Sage and Darius left for the hospital, both filled with joy about the birth of their first child.

On this day at the beginning of April, the city of BeachSide, Washington, was blessed with moderate temperatures, very different from the cold temperatures and ice storms of the state of Oklahoma. At that time in BeachSide, Washington, however, the racial climate was cold as ice. Hospitals were segregated, but there were a few where Negroes were admitted, only if they paid for a private room and brought their own private doctor and nurse, which was what Darius had done. His experience at the colored hospital with Mr. Johnson had convinced him that he didn't want Sage to be delivered there.

When they arrived at the hospital, Sage was placed in their reserved private room. Nurses and doctors went by the door and looked in and passed on. When their private doctor and nurse arrived, both White, Darius began to feel at ease. Knowing the conditions and the feelings of the White people, Sage had learned the way to peace, and she knew how to be comfortable with her surroundings. And no matter how she was ignored and looked down upon, she did not let it create hate, fear, or depression in her being.

She was thinking, *It is such a comfort having Darius here with me, and also knowing that my mother and his mother will be at home to help me when we are released from here with our new little bundle of joy is an added comfort.*

When her pains were close, Sage was placed in their segregated delivery room. Major Hawthorne had brought Nurse Helen to the hospital with him, and not wanting to sit with Alicia and Bertram in the White waiting room, they waited in the segregated room with Darius. Major Hawthorne introduced Nurse Helen as Miriam's nurse. Just that. After Sage's delivery, Darius waited until they brought his little bundle in and laid her in Sage's arms, and he cried. Nature is so perfect, and giving birth is so amazing, he thought; for there, wrapped in a little blanket, lying in his wife's arms, was a pure White infant with a little fuzzy head of light-brown hair. Her eyes were slightly open, and she was crying loudly. He could see her blue-green eyes, so much a mixture of his light-blue eye color and Sage's light

293

green. Looking under the blanket, he was relieved that she had all her fingers and toes. He thought about how she would be classified on the birth certificate in the space for "race." He knew they would classify her as Black because that's what Sage was, but he and Sage weren't concerned about how the world, the United States, this hospital, would classify their child. To them, she wouldn't be half-White, half-Black, one-fourth Indian. She would be 100 percent human, an angel to be loved and cherished as such. They had decided before she was born that if a girl, her name would be Willow Mede. Willow for a beautiful sturdy tree, and Mede from the same chapter in the Bible where Darius's named was found.

Wonder of wonders, the two expectant mothers, Sage Deavers and Miriam Withers, went into labor around the same time. They were delivered at the same hospital, which had gravely upset Alicia Hawthorne; but Bertram Withers, knowing Sage would be in a separate part of the hospital, had accepted it.

In the White waiting room, there were two expectant fathers, Derrick Brandler and Bertram Withers, and one lady, Alicia Hawthorne. They introduced themselves.

"I'm Derrick Brandler, and this is my first, and I'm really worried about how my wife is doing. But I'm still excited, and I wonder what our little one will look like. You know, no abnormalities, all fingers and toes. But I'm sure we all go through that."

"We do," Bertram said. "I'm Bertram Withers, and this is my wife's mother, Mrs. Alicia Hawthorne."

"I'm glad to meet you," Derrick said.

"Likewise," Alicia said.

"I'm a little nervous too, but this is my second," Bertram said. "We have a six-year-old son, but my wife is calm, so it makes me sort of calm too."

"Well, blessings to us both," Derrick said.

After birth, the White newborns were placed in the nursery behind a glass partition in what was called the showroom, each in their own little bassinet, which was labeled with the parents' name.

Alicia and Bertram waited for their expected arrival as skaters who have finished their routine await their scores. Bertram was happy that his first child was a boy, as is normal, for most fathers are happy for a male offspring. They could perhaps look forward to the son becoming a great person, maybe president of the United States. Miriam wanted a girl. She already had a boy. Alicia Hawthorne wanted a girl grandchild.

36

"If you can keep your head when all about you are losing theirs and blaming it on you...," Rudyard Kipling wrote it, and Darius Paul Deavers had to call it up among so many other thoughts within his brain at this time.

It turned out to be one of the worst nights we've known so far. This was worse than the cross-burning on our neighbor's lawn, the painting of our home, and the burning of my father's clubhouse in Oklahoma where we were planning to have our mock ceremony.

Standing outside the glass partition, the White parents and family waited patiently for the nurses to bring out the newest addition to their family, smiling in anticipation. All the little hospital bassinets were there to be filled with small new entries into the world. They came wrapped ever so tightly in the White hospital baby blankets.

At once, all the smiles of anticipation were instantly replaced with shock. The hospital officials had closed and sequestered the nursery so that no one was allowed to enter or leave. The nurses and doctors were questioned, and one could see and feel the evil in everyone's heart. As long as it was an all-White thing, everyone was fine, but there might have been some rational thought or even acceptance that a mistake had been made, for a child with an olive-skin complexion, dark-brown hair, and brown eyes was placed in the bassinet labeled "Withers," so Bertram and Alicia decided that the child in their bassinet definitely belonged to Sage, and they were sure that a mix-up occurred because this was a restricted hospital, and their child should be in a separate room and not here with the White babies.

"Hell and damnation! Of course, there's been a mix-up. You've most likely given us the Deavers's child," Alicia said.

"What have you done?" Bertram shouted, banging on the glass partition. "Surely, there's been a mix-up," he said, repeating Alicia's words.

Mr. Derrick Brandler, with the attention momentarily diverted from his own little arrival, looked around, wondering, *Has there really been a mix-up? Have they mixed up our child?*

What followed was like an unreal dream. A nightmare. And thankfully, there was a glass partition, which Bertram tried to go around. When he was unable to get into the nursery, Bertram yelled and screamed obscenities. He pounded on the glass, and when Darius came out to see what was causing all the commotion, Bertram confronted him.

"Look at this child. She's colored. This is obviously your child, you and your colored wife. Damn you. Get that little nigger out of my bassinet," he shouted.

Darius knew it wasn't their child because little Willow Mede had been delivered in a segregated delivery room, and she was placed with her parents in their segregated hospital room, and she looked White. But since there were no other people of color in this hospital, he knew, somehow, that it was Miriam's child. But how? He thought about the loving feeling he had seen in Miriam and Charles.

There was pandemonium. The security personnel came and ushered everyone out of the hall. Everyone had to return to the waiting room, "until the whole thing could be sorted out and evaluated," they said. Hospital guards, city police, counselors—all were called.

Back in their room, Darius found Sage lying peaceful as could be in her bed, propped up on two pillows, holding their newborn girl. She had heard the voices, and she knew that the child she held in her arms was hers. She wondered about the brown child.

Darius felt that he and Sage and Willow Mede were alone in this hospital with all the confusion about a mix-up and Sage being vilified as the culprit. But his thoughts prevailed. *We were alone together, and as the tears came into my eyes and ran down my cheeks onto my lips and fell on my shoulders, I could hear Sage say, "Don't cry, Darius. It's going to be all right." How many times had she said that to me, calm as you please?*

I knelt down beside the bed and put my hands up on top of Sage's hand, and I prayed. I didn't know exactly what to say, for there were so many things that had gone wrong since we came to the state of Washington, so I started with the Lord's Prayer, and I ended my prayer with, "Thou knowest." I squeezed Sage's hand, and we said, "Amen."

Everyone involved was involved. Accused. Shocked. Amused. Afraid of repercussions. The nurse who brought the Withers's infant in to be placed in its labeled bassinet checked the labels matching the infant's wristband to be sure that she had not made a mistake. Major Hawthorne waited with them for the doctor's reports, although he already knew what the reports would reveal, and he remembered what Helen Kane had told him.

It was three o'clock in the morning when the doctors came, and each confirmed the characteristics of the child each had delivered. The private doctor, having delivered Sage's child, confirmed that he had delivered a beautiful, healthy six-and-one-half-pound girl. He smiled to himself while telling them that he had delivered what was supposed to be (as was designated on the birth certificate beside the word *race*: "Black") a Black child. But he confirmed that the infant he had caught in his hands from between the Black woman's thighs was White as the driven snow. Certainly not Black. Light eyes. Light-brown hair. White skin.

Miriam's doctor was also sure of the delivery of the Withers's child. Between those White thighs, he had pulled a beautiful curly-haired, brown-eyed baby girl. He was sure of what he saw, but at the same time, he was apprehensive of the aftermath of this, seeing the father was White. He had informed the mother that she had delivered a beautiful girl, only that, and he had confirmed to everyone else that the baby girl with the olive skin belonged to Miriam Withers.

"Well," Bertram said, trying to recover from the doctor's report, "if that is our child, then I knew it. I knew it. My wife really was having an affair with that nigger Charles. Oh hell, I could kill them both. Why in the hell did those people have to come here?"

Major Hawthorne, who had also come out into the hall, knew what he had to do. "You wait here," he told Helen Kane. "I don't want Bertram and Alicia messing with you." He went immediately to the waiting room, thinking, *I might as well get this over with now.* He tried to tell Bertram why the one in his bassinet was really his.

"No, it's not Charles's baby. Let me explain the situation to you and Alicia. One, Miriam was adopted. Two, Helen Kane is Miriam's birth mother, and her real father, now dead, was a Black man, so Miriam is part Black."

That information rendered both Alicia and Bertram speechless. The shock to their bodies and minds was like a sudden earthquake, a sudden tsunami, a devastation so horrible it couldn't possibly be happening.

With the information they received, with the verification they'd received from both doctors as to the child each had delivered, Alicia put her hand over her mouth to try and cover her feeling, her crying, her shock. Then her whole body crumpled, and she fell to the floor. She had fainted, and Bertram had already decided to give the child up for adoption.

The most difficult part of this problematic situation was still ahead for Major Marvin Hawthorne. Although he had faced many life-threatening battles in his years of army life, and although he didn't think that what he was about to do meant the possibility of death, it did mean a very heavy burden for him and a very traumatic thing for his daughter to hear and to digest. He decided to take Nurse Helen Kane with him, hoping the fact that Miriam had met her and liked her might make it easier for Miriam to accept her as her birth mother.

Helen Kane was nervous, but she was in control, as she always was when she was beginning a new assignment with a new patient. Although this was a new and different assignment, the person who was lying in this hospital bed was not new to her.

Miriam Withers, half awake and half asleep, and hearing the door to her room being opened, looked toward the door, expecting to see the nurse bringing her baby.

"Hello, Daddy. Hello, Nurse Helen," she said.

"Hello, baby," the major said, kissing her on the forehead. "Congratulations. You have a beautiful baby girl."

"Oh, I'm so anxious to see her, but I guess they wait a while after the birth to give us mothers some time to rest."

"I know, but we're here to tell you something else."

"What, Daddy? Is there something wrong with my baby?"

"No. No, your baby is perfect in every way, and she's beautiful."

"And where is Bertram? And my mother, where is she?"

"They'll probably come soon, but, well, first, we have to tell you something else."

"You two are going to get married. That's it, huh? I expected as much, and you don't need to worry about me. I'll just have two mothers."

"We'll talk about that later, but now, baby," Major Hawthorne said, taking her hand in both of his, "I have to tell you something that I ought to have told you before."

"Daddy, you're scaring me. Before what? Is something the matter with your health or my mother's health?"

"No," Nurse Helen said, sitting on the other side of the bed. "It's about me."

"What could anything about you have to do with me and my baby, except that you'll be my stepmother?" Miriam, already weak from her delivery, felt that there was something in the room that was threatening her, like a million flies or bats, and she wasn't getting enough air into her lungs. So she took a couple of deep breaths and lay back on her pillow, trying to relax.

"Miriam, what I have to tell you is that," Major Hawthorne said, and he paused and took a deep breath, "is that you were adopted."

As she slumped down farther, trying to digest this, it seemed as if the noise of the insect's wings fluttering and the bats screeching was more threatening. She began to cry, tears rolling down her cheeks.

"Why are you telling me this now, after all these years?"

"Well, we're stepping forward and telling you now because… well, the truth is that I'm your real mother," Helen said. "I birthed you. And your baby is my grandchild, and I'd really love to see her once in a while. I'm not asking to take Alicia's place, and she doesn't even need to know. I just want a place in your life and in our baby's life."

"I guess I ought to have told you sooner," Marvin Hawthorne said, taking Miriam into his arms.

"And that means that you're not really my father, or are you?"

"Not on paper, but in my heart, you know that I love you."

"And I love you too," Helen Kane said.

Miriam's heart was not beating with regularity, but it was fluttering. It was breaking, and she didn't know what to do. Finally, she looked at Helen Kane, hate showing in her eyes.

"I honestly don't care what you say now, but you're not my mother. No. Alicia Hawthorne is my mother. You gave up the right to call yourself my mother when you gave me away. A real mother doesn't do that no matter what the circumstances. I'd never give my child up for adoption. Thanks for stepping forward, as you say, Ms. Kane, but you can just take two steps back. No, take twenty-eight steps back because that's how old I am and how many years you've deserted me. Please go and don't ever come near me again. I hate you. Go. Go now."

Helen Kane stood up and left the room. She too began to cry.

"Oh, Daddy," Miriam said, laying her head on his shoulder.

"You're right, I am your daddy, and I love you."

"Well, do I have a real daddy?" she asked.

"Yes, you do, and he's dead," Marvin said.

"He's dead?" Miriam asked. "So I'll never get to meet him."

"We can talk about that later, but you ought to rest now."

"Don't leave me, Daddy."

"I'll stay right here with you, and I'll never leave you, for the rest of your life."

Miriam lay in his arms, and he let her cry.

Finally, when Miriam was quiet and being sure she was asleep, Major Hawthorne kissed her hand, rose, and went to see how Helen Kane was faring. She was sitting quietly in the waiting room, seemingly deep in meditation. She looked up at him and smiled, and he loved her more than ever to see how she had accepted this painful situation.

It was later that Miriam's doctor, knowing that she had not been told about the reason for all the confusion, went with the nurse to present the beautiful little brown child to her mother. As would be normal in such a situation, the news of the birth of a Black child to a White mother, the reaction of the child's father and grandmother, known and talked about throughout the obstetrics floor, had also reached Miriam. Amazingly, perhaps mental telepathy and remembering all the past happenings concerning race, Black and White, including the phone call, learning she was adopted, Miriam was not completely surprised when the nurse placed the little brown-eyed girl in her arms.

"So I am the child whose father was Black."

It took her a few minutes to take it all in, but the infant noise from her newborn called her attention from herself to her child, and the cord that had linked her to this squirming little individual was still attached, if only mentally, and the relationship of this child to her was certain, and immediately they loved each other. The doctor was relieved when Miriam smiled, realizing that no explanation was necessary.

"Your little girl is perfect in every way," he said. "No abnormalities of any kind. She weighed in at six and one-half pounds, eighteen inches long, and with very strong lungs. Congratulations."

"Thank you," Miriam said as the nurse began showing her how to present the little one with the breast.

When Major Hawthorne returned, prepared to tell her about her birth father, he was surprised to see her holding her infant and smiling.

"It's all right, Daddy, I know."

"Who...who told you?"

"I figured it out for myself. I thought back to the phone call, and I didn't think anybody would just make up such a story that couldn't possibly have any truth to it. And since I knew Sage wasn't your child, as my mother thought it had to be, and knowing that you weren't my real father, and you weren't guilty of committing adultery, then it was easy for me to determine that I am the Black child. So now I have to accept that Helen Kane is my real mother, and my real father was a Black man, and he's dead. True, Daddy?"

"Yes," he said softly and slowly, and tears filled his eyes. His body and mind became relaxed, knowing that all the secrets had been revealed to her, and obviously, she was content with herself and her child. But she hadn't been told of the reactions of Bertram and Alicia, but well, she had figured that out also.

"No matter," she said, reaching for his hand. "I know this presents a problem for my mother and my husband because they've always hated Black people, but you know, we'll deal with one thing at a time."

He was amazed at her strength. Peace through strength, and her love for him caused his most comforting and relaxing peace at this time.

"Oh, I love you so much, and I will love this little angel. Have you thought of a name for her?" Marvin asked.

"I'll call her Felicity Esther. *Felicity* means 'one that can bring happiness,' and *Esther* means 'star.'"

"How beautiful. I like that name."

"Do Sage and Darius know?"

"Yes, I told them."

"And what did they say?"

"Of course, they still love you, and Darius said he would talk to Bertram."

"Bless their hearts."

"And they're coming to see you before they leave the hospital," Major Hawthorne said.

"Do you think Bertram can love me as Darius loves Sage, knowing that I'm Black?" she asked. Then she answered herself, "I doubt it, Daddy."

"Well, I'm going to talk to Bertram and Alicia again, and I'll try to reason with them. Two wide rivers to cross."

"I hope you can swim, Daddy."

"Maybe I'll rent a boat."

"You'll need an ocean liner to cross that raging water."

They smiled. They hugged. He kissed her on the cheek, and he kissed Felicity Esther on the cheek.

Darius had paid for only three days of recuperation for Sage in their private room. The time required for White patients was nine days. She and Darius spent most of the three days admiring little Willow Mede. Sage's heart knew only love for people, and it overflowed to those around her who had been waiting with open arms and open hearts for what the birth produced, and everyone was thankful for the safe arrival of the child and for the well-being of Sage.

Creating a pall, however, a little dark cloud over the sunshine of their happiness, was the pity and sorrow they felt for Miriam. Sage had become so accustomed to having Darius's love and so sure of it that she couldn't imagine trying to live without it, and Black didn't enter into her equation. Miriam was being defined by something she didn't create and couldn't get rid of. *Don't they know that she is the same person she has always been? Poor Miriam.*

Before leaving the hospital, Sage and Darius went to visit Miriam, despite the fact that Blacks were not allowed in that section of the hospital.

"They'll just have to arrest us," Sage said as she and Darius walked into Miriam's room.

After hugs and kisses and looking at and sharing each other's baby, they all three—Darius, Miriam, and Sage—tried hard to hold back their tears.

"Isn't it something?" Miriam said when she was able to become calm. "My Black father didn't want me because I looked White, and now my baby's White father doesn't want her because she looks Black. I guess it's like they say, history repeats itself. And you know, now that I'm Black, that means that Timothy is also Black. So I guess my mother and my husband will hate him too. Oh, Sage, what am I going to do? I can't see my way out of this."

"There's always a way out of any situation. You'll just have to take some time and figure it out for yourself. Decide what it is you want to do and do it, and don't think about anybody else except you and your children," Sage said.

"And we're here for you, no matter what you decide," Darius said. "I'm going to have a talk with your husband. I'll try and make him see that, well, you're still his wife, and you're still the same person that he fell in love with years ago. And no matter, these are his children. You don't mind if I talk with him, do you?"

"Of course not. Thank you, Darius. You're one in a million."

Darius left Sage and Miriam with the intention of going to have a talk with Bertram, only to find that he and Alicia had already left the hospital. When he told Sage and Miriam, Miriam was not surprised; and Sage, sensing Miriam's disappointment, with her wisdom, consoled Darius and Miriam.

"My dear, you may not have been successful in reaching Bertram because it was not the right time. You and Bertram are two totally different people. You didn't decide to love me, despite the fact that I'm Black. You fell in love with me without even thinking about what the word meant. Bertram, on the other hand, was taught to hate all Black people, and I don't think you can change that. Some people need more than talk, more than words, you know. Like some mentally disturbed people, they're given shock treatment."

"Bertram needs a swift kick in the head to shock him into changing his attitude," Darius said.

"Or a kick in the behind," Sage said.

"I know that's right, and I do love both of you, and thanks for your kiss to my head, which helped me think differently," Miriam said. Hugs and kisses were in order.

Bertram Withers was not thinking with a rational mind, and he left the hospital without seeing Miriam. Every day, however, Major Hawthorne went to see his daughter and her baby. One day, Sage and Darius went with him. One day, Lucy Deavers went with him. They wanted Miriam to know that they loved her.

It was the day for Miriam's release from the hospital, and Bertram knew he was the only one to release her and take her home.

"Please, Daddy, can I go with you?" Timothy asked. "I want to see my little sister."

"I'll be bringing them home this morning, and you'll see her then."

All the while, Bertram was wondering what he would tell him about the color of the baby's skin, but he didn't know that the color of her skin would be of no concern to Timothy.

Bertram left his house at eight o'clock without having slept at all and without drinking his usual two cups of coffee. Mary Jane Copple had told Mrs. Erma Johnson of the births, and Mrs. Johnson had told Mamie. Mamie, standing beside the kitchen table, said a silent prayer. She could see a heavy curtain being drawn, which shut out all the brightness, and some dark thoughts kept pushing their way through.

After entering the hospital, and in spite of his overwhelming contempt for the brown-eyed girl asleep in her crib, Bertram Withers stood outside the glass partition in the hospital and looked at her. This was the first time in his entire life that he ever had occasion to pay any attention to a child of another race, and she looked so much like Timothy he had to turn away. But turning away didn't erase the fact that Timothy was also a mixed-race child, and since his wife hadn't been unfaithful to him with the Negro, these two biracial children were his. He was their father. He knew that he should congratulate his wife on carrying and giving birth to a healthy infant, but what would he say to her? *It's all right. So you're Black, so what? I still love you, and we'll work this out together.* He couldn't call up the courage he needed to say those things. He kept saying to himself, *But they're Black. I have a Black wife and two Black children. Biracial doesn't take precedence over Black.*

On entering her room, Bertram saw Miriam sitting in the hospital's wheelchair, and a nurse came in cuddling the little one in her arms. The rule was to see that the mother and the newborn were safely out of the hospital after their release.

Words came from other patients, nurses, and hospital staff for Miriam: "Congratulations," "Stay safe," "God bless you," "Take care of that little angel."

As he drove along after leaving the hospital with his two occupants in the back seat, Bertram was thinking, *What do I do now?* His fears were getting in the way of his driving, and he had to slow down and ask for some calm. It should have been a happy feeling for this father with a new child, but with every minute came a new fear, and he had to strive to keep his mind on where he was going. Home. Could their present house still be their home? Could he love these people who made up his family?

Bertram thought of the people in his life and wondered what they would think of him. Could they accept this other side of his life? His mother-in law couldn't. His employer couldn't. The homeowners association couldn't. The White schools wouldn't, and his church wouldn't. He felt so alone. He felt like a man on a sailboat, caught in a flood and being thrown from his boat into the water and crying to those people who were standing on the bank, laughing and watching him drown.

What could save him? He thought of Darius, who he now felt was in the same boat with him, in the same flood with him, having a Black wife, but Darius did not drown but was saved and helped and supported by…by what? He claimed it was by love. *Can I still love them? Some say by trust in God. What a joke. I've attended church, Bible study, and I learned what it says about trusting God, but God, whoever he is, and even if he is, he cannot save me.*

Nothing made sense to him, and he thought of actually driving the car into one of the lakes that surrounded them. That would solve the problem for him, Miriam, and the baby. What was her name? He didn't know. But then what would happen to Timothy? Timothy could still claim White, and he could live with his White grandfather, who wasn't really his grandfather, and Bertram had totally erased Helen Kane from his mind. Oh, woe!

Drawing closer to the house, he looked in the rear-view mirror and was momentarily captivated by Miriam's smile as she looked at the bundle in her arms. He knew that she was happy within herself and with that little bundle, which was still his child, so innocent, so free of guilt, and he wondered how Miriam could be content knowing that she was Black.

A few minutes later, he drove into his driveway. As he followed his wife into the house, he was being totally ignored by Mamie and

Timothy, who were waiting with such happy anticipation for this baby. For a few seconds, he too was overcome with pleasure, but soon his misery and unhappiness returned, and he sat alone on the sofa.

Bertram Withers accepted as settled in his mind that it would be in the best interest of everyone that he leave his wife and his two children since all three of them were Black. He was so lost, and as hard as he tried to reconcile himself with the situation, he couldn't reach any conclusion that seemed satisfactory. He had already suffered through finding about her Blackness. He had tried to be a good husband, above reproach, and it had now blown up in his face, and he was hurt, disgraced, all through no fault of his. Life, he concluded, is unfair, and then you die, and that was more than likely his best solution. Death.

In her condition, Alicia Hawthorne could not be left alone; and after Major Hawthorne had made the arrangements for her to be admitted to a special rehab center, he went to visit her, and he took Miriam and Felicity with him.

"You wait here in the lobby, and I'll see if it's all right for you all to visit. There might be some restrictions." He knew that there was no reason she couldn't visit, but he wanted to prepare Alicia, wondering now about her feelings. He wasn't sure. As soon as he entered her room and she looked up and saw him, Alicia quickly put her hand up, palm facing him.

"Go away," she said. "I know why you're here, and you are wasting your time because I hate you."

"I know. I know that you hate me," he said, trying to call up some peace. "But I've brought your daughter and your new granddaughter. That little baby is so beautiful, and your daughter is so alone, and they both need you, and when you're well—"

She didn't let him finish. "In the first place, she is not my daughter, is she? No, she isn't. So that means that little Black child is not my granddaughter, and she's not yours either."

"That's not true. We're the only parents Miriam has ever known, and she's the only child we've ever raised as our own. I'm still her father, and—"

"No, you're not, and I'm not her mother," she interrupted him. "And if you had been a little more concerned about her background, and most surely if I had known, I would never have allowed you to adopt her, so will you please go away."

With a pained look on his face, and a pain in his heart, this man looked at this lady he had married, whom he had loved at that time and who he thought loved him, and she began to look like a giant spider: her fingers spread out before her like a web, her eyes looking at him like poison darts, and he became afraid of her. And now, looking at her, not only was he afraid of her, but he was afraid of what evil she could wish on Miriam and Timothy and Felicity, even on him. She had turned out to be a vile, disgusting, ugly woman.

When he thought of Miriam, Timothy, and Felicity, his heart opened wider, and he was thinking, *I've never known love like this. And as I look at my wife, I know that I can't erase all the hate that is in her heart, but I know that I can dedicate the rest of my life to loving Miriam and her two children. I still see them as my daughter and my two grandchildren.* And as he walked out of her room and out of the building, all the ugliness he'd felt there left him, and the warmth of the sunshine filled his soul with beauty. Peace. The look on his face was enough for Miriam. She knew that this lady had turned against her because she was Black, and she knew how this lady felt about Black people. She steeled herself against the hate, but she didn't cry.

Bertram Withers wanted to protect his position at the school's law department and to keep open the possibility of becoming president of the university. Therefore, in order to keep his mind clear of family problems, he took up residence in one of the apartments on campus reserved for faculty.

Sitting alone in the early evening, looking out the window from his third-floor living room, he felt completely at ease, even a little happy. First, as he had decided, *I cannot be distracted by the awful situation I've been put in. My job comes first, and I've been diligent in maintaining a high rating there and also in my personal life. I've provided well for my family, attended church as a family, and given fatherly attention to my son, and there must be ways out of this present family predicament.* Deep breaths. A glass of wine. A warm bath. Directing his thoughts to his work, he slept well and arose early the next morning and went to his office.

What now? What about my family? All at once, he felt himself driven into a corner. Driven into two corners, one-half of him into the corner of his professional interests and one-half into the corner of his personal interests. His professional interests required being cold and methodical, and for his entire life, he had been in preparedness for his professional career. His personal life required warmth, love, and compassion, but he couldn't come up with a solution that would integrate the two. Thus, he felt like he was arm-wrestling in a contest where winner gets all his desires; loser walks away with nothing. It was professional against family, and the university's policy of not admitting Black students meant his own children, being Black, would not be admitted. He must surely remain in his profession, at his present position, but how could he get rid of the family that was labeled Black? How could he get rid of his two children, his home, his wife? Would divorce be the answer? The obstacle in the whole of it was that this child, who very definitely looked Black. Did she have a name? He hadn't thought to inquire as the birth certificate hadn't been signed—on purpose.

I'll just calmly present Miriam with this solution. He wrote,

Dear Miriam:

After doing much thinking and much intense soul searching, I know that I cannot allow my life to be turned around and changed by the awful set of circumstances that I've been put in, through no fault of my own.

It would be in the best interest of all of us if we stop and realize exactly what constitutes our problem and what our solution must be. A very definite obstacle has been placed in the way of our continued success as a family, and that obstacle is this child, who very definitely

310

looks Black, because she is Black and the fact of her Blackness would affect our whole lives. We would be forced to move into a restricted neighborhood, the children would be required to attend colored schools, and we would be barred from our church. And I cannot abide that. The solution: you, Timothy, and I could go on living as before, being White, because we look White, but we will quietly give this child up for adoption. Now. We'll pretend that our family is the same, living and being respected as White, and after a reasonable amount of time, I will grant you a divorce because if the fact of your being Black becomes known, it would create the same set of problems, and more than likely, I would lose my job. After the divorce, I will go my way, and you and Timothy can go your way.

I will always provide for you financially, but I am White, and I cannot live in a Black world. You will have to decide soon, at least by tomorrow, in order for the adoption to be carried out before we place our names on the birth certificate. I have the adoption papers here, and I just need your signature.

Bertram Withers

37

Today was Saturday, and Timothy didn't have school. Bertram had returned to the campus, and Miriam was again reading the harshness of his words and digesting exactly what he had written. Amazingly, she didn't cry. She was thinking, *It seems that no matter how good you try to be, your fate is sealed by things you didn't create and can't control. So now I'm Black. I'd never really looked at Black people as people until I met Sage and Charles, and Karen and her children. Now I have to look at Timothy, my own son, and my beautiful daughter, Felicity, as something different. How can the world separate people by their skin color? We're all the same inside. Although they say that Black people have black blood, that is not true. All human blood is the same. The same color. red. Even though now I'm Black—ha, ha!—nothing has happened to me that changed me, like being struck by lightning or washing in the pool seven times. I'm still the same Miriam, although my husband and my mother, my adoptive mother, see me now as something ugly and stupid and Black. Not White.*

Who can love me now? I've been White all my life. How can I change now? I don't know who or what I am. And what about my children, one looking White and one looking Black? Mamie speaks of having a spiritual life, but I only see and feel my personal life. She speaks of our internal being, and other people only see me externally. We grow up with a belief in who we are, and we are trained to be that kind of person, and then we learn that that's not who and what we are at all. Sage says she owes her dignity and peace to her mother, who always told her that she was beautiful. She told me not to let them defeat me, and don't let your husband and your mother fill your heart with the kind of hate they have. She says that each one of us has our own brain, and that's what we must use to think with. You can't think with anyone else's brain so that their thoughts become yours. But unfortunately, I am forced to consider Bertram's thoughts.

She was depressed, but she didn't realize that there was a normalcy in postpartum depression. Bertram didn't come home that night, and Miriam didn't sleep at all, but she lay awake, trying to think.

It was Sunday. She dressed herself and her children in their Sunday's best as she thought about church, but as soon as she left the house, she changed her mind. She wasn't sure where she was going, but she knew she had to get out of that house. She couldn't think positively in those gloomy rooms, filled with his presence. And she didn't think he would change his mind, for he'd said that the Negro was a direct descendant of the ape and no smarter or prettier. So he must see her as ugly and ignorant. Black.

As she drove by the black house, she was thinking that it might be as Bertram said: that this could happen to them. It made her sad looking at it, and she thought, *It really can't stay here like this forever. It should be destroyed, and I can't stay like this forever. This dark mood must be destroyed. But how?*

Miriam decided she could talk to Gertrude Kingsley, and hopefully she could get some help with her decision. She rang the bell, and Gertrude was so happy to see them, but somehow Miriam couldn't seem to open up to her. She didn't think she knew her that well, and she didn't want to talk to her against Bertram.

"Would you mind keeping them for a while so I can do a little shopping?" she asked Mrs. Kingsley (which wasn't true). "It's easier without them," she said.

"Miriam, I'd be honored," Gertrude Kingsley said. At the same time she was thinking, *She is such a beautiful little lady, but she seems lost. I wonder if she's happy.* She stood in the door with the baby in her arms and holding Timothy's hand. She looked at Miriam as she got in her car and drove off.

Miriam was thinking, *I'm on the road of life, and I don't have a road map, and I'm lost. Marriage—what is it? Growing up, I thought that my parents had a happy marriage, but now they have grown apart. I can't compare my marriage to the seemingly happy marriage of Sage and Darius because Darius is loving, accepting, and he admires his Black wife. How can I stay on top of the lily pond when my everyday life is filled with brambles and dead leaves which are weighing me down? Pulling me down. Bertram thinks that his way of life is how it should be. It doesn't matter that his family is unhappy. He does what he has to do to be happy, which is what makes me unhappy.*

Her thoughts prevailed. *I'll take my children, and I'll leave him. But where will I go? To my father who loves me, but who is really not my father? And now he is with Ms. Helen Kane, who says she is my mother by blood and says she loves me. But I do not love her. I hate her for giving me away and for staying away all these years and for coming forth now to claim me and totally disrupting my life. But even so, I love my little ecru piece of life, and although her entrance did disrupt our lives, it was a blessing for them to know that I hadn't been unfaithful with Charles. But which was worse, being unfaithful with Charles or being Black? Maybe that would be better because Charles would not desert me. We all, me and my children, could be happy with him. Maybe. And now this man that I married has given me an ultimatum. I could stay with him and let him suffer the consequences and try to maintain this marriage and pray for his acceptance of my child. My children. Would he accept counseling?*

No, I must go. Where? I could seek a home with Lieutenant and Mrs. Kingsley, and maybe they could talk to Bertram and help steer his thoughts in a different direction, one of accepting us. No. They don't have any close life experience with Black people. I think my best avenue to take is talking to Sage and Darius. Black Sage. White Darius. Hmm. Maybe Darius could talk to Bertram now as a White man married to a Black woman as I am. She gathered up her courage and went to see Sage and Darius.

"Where are the children?" Sage asked.

"They're with Mamie," she lied, not wanting to give an explanation for where they actually were. Darius was not home, so she sat with Sage. She wanted to show her Bertram's letter but unable she was to do so. Sage's intuition told her that Miriam was not in calm spirits and that she was unhappy and on the verge of tears.

"What's wrong?" Sage asked.

"Wrong?" she said, bending her head in an effort not to cry. "You're so blessed, Sage," she said, not looking up. "Everything in your life is good, but I'm sure it's because you're so good and so clearheaded."

"No, I'm not that good. It's that I just try to deal with life, with people, with problems as they come so they aren't able to destroy me. Now tell me what's wrong, and I'll see what can I do to help. I don't like seeing you like this." Sage took Miriam's hand in hers.

"I guess it's just one of those after-birth blues," Miriam said, deciding not to show her the letter and thus to burden her friend with her problems, which Sage surely couldn't solve for her. And still in the same unsettled mood that she'd been in since reading the letter and thinking about his ultimatum, she stood up and, releasing her hand, hugged Sage.

"Miriam, you are a beautiful person, and I'll always be your friend. But even if I'm not, you can't always depend on people. Put your hand in the hand of, you know, the one who stilled the waters."

"Just remember this, Sage. I appreciate knowing that I can come to you because I consider you to be my best friend, and I love you. Goodbye, my friend."

Sage knew that Miriam's low mood was directly from knowing that she was Black, and other people knowing that she was Black, those people who couldn't accept Black. She thought about Randy and what Darius said about him: "It's like being an alcoholic. You want to stop drinking, but you don't know how, and you imagine that no one can really feel your pain if they haven't experienced the same problem. So you suffer alone."

Unable to shake the mood, Miriam got back in her car and drove through the city streets. She was bothered by the steady downpour that came on suddenly, and she was distracted by the sound of car horns being honked by impatient motorists. She wanted to think and to get it settled in her mind what to do. Abide by his wishes? Give up her precious baby as her mother had done? Who would take her? Would they be kind and loving parents or mean and prejudiced people, hating White people and teaching the hate to her child?

Should I give her to Sage? I know she would love her. Or should I take both my children and go live in the house I'd known as home all my life since my mother and father won't be living there anymore? But it's in an all-White neighborhood. Maybe I'll try to stay with Bertram even though he hates Black. How do I feel about being Black? That's the question I have to answer. I don't know. I can't think right now. Give my children to Karen because Timothy loves Jasper and Jasmine, but she isn't financially able to take on such a burden. It's sad that Felicity is drowned in a sea of hate. She's so pretty, and Timothy loves her so much, and when he kisses her, she smiles already. And wouldn't you know it? Sage's little girl is pure White, and mine is not. Maybe we could exchange children.

She drove off the main street and parked. She felt her body tingle, then stiffen. She was struggling to breathe, not getting enough air. She rolled the window down, and the chill and dampness overtook her. She closed the window and drew one of the new baby blankets that she'd left in the car over her knees. She tried to relax. Then falling asleep, she had a dream. She was in a basket being held up with a strong cord which was attached to a helicopter, and she was afraid that lightning would strike it, or somehow the cord would break, and she'd fall into the black water below. But she woke up before that happened.

Miriam drove to the same place where they had gotten on the Kingsleys' yacht for the trip to Bremerton, and she sat in her car by the waters of Puget Sound. It was so peaceful there, and the rain had stopped, and the skies were clear. It was near the time of day when the sun was slowly disappearing, and the temperature was dropping.

She thought, *Just relax. Think peaceful thoughts. You have two beautiful children whom you love, and thank the Lord, I know that they love me. And there are people in my life who love them.* She kept thinking this, but each time she said it, instead of peace, the same little dark cloud full of evil was sitting up there, and she always came back to the same opposing message: *But we're still Black.*

As she looked up, another message came bright and encouraging: *In Sunday school, they taught us that God is love, and love overcomes all human sorrows, and no sorrows are too insignificant for God's compassion. But where is God? I can't find him, and he can't seem to find me either because I'm not real. I'm invisible.*

She looked at the water and at the boats in the water. She looked at the sandy shore and imagined herself only one little grain of sand amid the thousands; and if she were washed away, she would not be missed, and some other grains would immediately fill her empty space.

I should never have been born, but I was, and now I must live or die. Whatever I do and whatever anyone else does, it will all end the same. We will all die at some time. All my married life, he was sapping my strength, smothering my dreams. He never loved me. I was a necessary object to be used only when he needed me for his satisfaction. I don't have a mother. Alicia is nothing to me, and Nurse Helen has come into my life too late. Where has she been all these years? My real father is dead, and Major Hawthorne has done the best he could to raise me as his own, but I am not his. I belong to no one.

Her mind said, *You have to make a decision. Anything will be better than how you are now living. And what will change in your favor? Your husband? The laws? Your supposed-to-be mother, Alicia? Your blood? No, none of that is likely to change.*

She had not eaten today, and she thought to drive to the delicatessen and get a sandwich, but when she got there, she wasn't hungry anymore, and she thought of her plan. She bought a jar of pickles. She got back in her car and drove to the same spot by the lake. She emptied the pickles out beside the water and took a paper from her glove compartment, a pen from her purse, and she wrote some words and put them in the jar. She held her hands around the jar and closed it tightly. She looked down the hill at the Puget Sound, and she remembered that it flowed out into the water and into the deep blue sea. She released the emergency brake, put the car in neutral, and she smiled as it began its descent. She took a deep breath, lay her head back, and went to a watery sleep.

In the jar, written on a slip of paper, was her name, address, her husband's name, their phone number, and the words, "Take care of the children."

Part Five

38

The day of her suicide, Miriam had left Timothy and Felicity with Gertrude Kingsley, and being allowed to help with the Withers's children was tantamount to Gertrude having a family, and she was elated as she assumed the role of their grandmother. But after the memorial service (Bertram did not want a big funeral), the children went home with their father; and with Bertram's pitiful crying, his drooping shoulders at the service, it was obvious that he was in no condition, mentally, to make any decisions or to take care of his children. Even though no one had asked her, Mamie stayed at the Withers's house because she felt that God had placed her there at this particular time to take care of Timothy and Felicity, and also to watch over and pray for Bertram.

Every Saturday since Miriam's death, the major went by to see the children; and as usual, Mamie let him spend a few minutes holding and cuddling Felicity and giving her the bottle, and she allowed him to take Timothy out for a ride, sometimes getting ice cream or going to the park.

This Saturday, as they were riding along, Major Hawthorne looked at Timothy, admiring his blue eyes, light-brown hair, and bright smile, and he loved him, as always. He realized that Timothy and Felicity needed him, and he needed Timothy and Felicity, and he experienced the marvelous feeling of grandparental love. He had felt parental love for Miriam, and now he was thinking, *Whoever is up there beyond the clouds, I thank you for filling the void in my life left by Miriam's demise and Alicia's mental and physical absence with these children. Oh, Miriam. Sad for the hate.*

Every time he saw Timothy, the child asked him the same question: "Can you take me to see my friends?"

"What friends?" he asked.

"Jasmine and Jasper. We could get Felicity, and we could go and live with them. Their mother could be our mother since we'll all be Black together."

Marvin Hawthorne was not a crying man, but Timothy's plea filled his heart with pain, and he was forced to fight back the tears. "I think it's best that you stay with your dad. He needs you."

"No, he doesn't. He doesn't even eat with me, and he doesn't tuck us in at night. Miss Mamie feeds us, and she puts us to bed, and she stays with us at night."

"Your dad is still grieving about your mother. Give him a little time, and he'll…well, he'll let you know how much he loves you." This was certainly his abiding hope, but at the same time, his mind was occupied with some questions. Who will finally take custody? Who would want to? Then at once his mind focused on Helen Kane and he remembered that, other than Bertram, she was the only blood relative of these two children. And with Bertram acting such a nonexistent, noninterested, nonloving parent, she could claim her right to them, if she had the desire to do that.

Arriving back at the Withers's house, Major Hawthorne kissed Timothy on the forehead and gave him a hug. "Be good now, and I'll come to see you next Saturday. I love you."

"I love you too, Grandpa."

Now three months had passed since Miriam's death, and Bertram Withers was being gradually swallowed in a quicksand pool of pity, and everyone knew that if he didn't try, he would be completely swallowed up, and death would be his fate. For the past week, he hadn't even gone to work.

Mrs. Gertrude Kingsley offered to go each morning and pick Timothy up and take him to school and to go and pick him up after school and take him home. This day when she went to pick him up from school, the teacher gave her a note to take to his parents. The note said, "Timothy is not doing well in school. He just sits, he doesn't pay attention, and he doesn't do his homework. He got into a fight with one of the girls who called him a dummy, but this was no out-of-the ordinary thing as children often called each other names."

The teacher requested a conference with Timothy's parent. Today was Friday, and Gertrude asked Major Hawthorne if he would intervene as Bertram was not communicating with anyone.

On Monday, Major Hawthorne called and made an appointment to see the teacher on Tuesday, but Monday afternoon, when Gertrude Kinsley went to pick Timothy up after school, she waited outside in the car for a long while, and he didn't come out. Concerned, she went inside to his classroom, and the teacher found a note on the young boy's desk, and Gertrude shrank a little inside when she read it: "I'm going to find my friends Jasmine and Jasper. We can go and get my little sister from my daddy 'cause he doesn't want us, and their mom can be all of our moms."

Gertrude Kingsley didn't want to call the police, so she called Major Hawthorne and gave him the news. She called the Withers's house and gave Mamie the news. Knowing that Mamie was there taking care of Felicity and the house and knowing that Bertram was—what? She didn't know. Wanting to support Mamie, she and her husband decided they would go to the Withers's house. Thus, the news rang through the friendship line: "Timothy has run away."

When Major Marvin Hawthorne received the phone call from Gertrude Kingsley, he was again thrown into a state of total despair. Some time ago, his peaceful life had been agitated by his wife's deceitful moves against Sage, only because Sage was Black. His beautiful daughter had taken her life only because she learned that she was Black, and her husband and her mother were very prejudiced against Black people. Now his grandson had run away because he thought his father didn't love him because he was being labeled as Black. Damn. Damn.

For several minutes, he sat motionless in his big comfortable chair, and then he moved only by a mechanical course of procedure. *Get up out of your chair. Walk. Get in your car. Drive.* He was preoccupied with fear for Timothy, being only seven years old and out there alone on the unfamiliar streets, and he knew there was absolutely no way his grandson could find the way to his friends' house; and without precognition, Timothy wanted a replacement for his mother. He had chosen Karen.

Only after driving about five minutes, and perhaps going five miles, did the major calm down enough to think. It was now five o'clock, and it would be dark soon. He was hopeful that Timothy would be found before darkness had fallen. Then there was a spirit of, *I must overcome any fear. I must believe in my heart that he is safe. I must somehow become the needed pillar of strength for Timothy, so I can't let myself fall apart.*

His first stop was the police station. He told them that his seven-year-old grandson was out there somewhere. "I'm sure he's lost." He gave them a description and the approximate time that Timothy had left school; and as he would be out combing the streets too, he gave the police some numbers to call if they found Timothy: Gertrude and Colin Kingsley, the Withers's house, and Sage and Darius.

It was Monday evening. During the past week, people had called the Withers's house, but Bertram had refused to speak to anyone and would only eat, just sparingly, if Mamie took his food up to his room. He also refused to see any of those who came to visit: Major Hawthorne, Darius, Gertrude Kingsley, the pastor of their church.

When Evelyn Prentiss got off from work this day, she went by to check on Bertram, for she felt that she knew him well enough to give him some comfort. She had met him at the Deavers' Christmas celebration, and he had attended her Bible study on Wednesday nights.

Mamie told Evelyn of Bertram's pitiful condition, so Evelyn insisted that she be allowed to see him, and with Mamie remembering from the Christmas celebration that Evelyn was a Christian and hoping she could talk to him, she admitted her.

Evelyn was a rather tall woman with a beautiful bright complexion and dark-brown eyes that seemed to look right inside you and see all the way to your soul, and her claim of being a Christian was not a put-on. It was real, and she hoped that by teaching the Word, she was helping people to believe and to love the Lord. Evelyn, however, always wanted to be married as she was not content living a single life, and she had met several men whom she examined as prospective life mates. Unfortunately, she had placed Darius in the category of being a satisfactory prospect, only to learn that he was married.

When she first met Bertram, she liked him, but she did not consider him a prospect because he too was married; and although he was now single, that was not her main motive for visiting him. She thought that he needed a friend.

Evelyn walked into Bertram's study unannounced and stood for a moment looking at him and shaking her head in pity for how pathetic he looked. He was sitting with his head down, his arms clasped in front of him as if he was cold.

"Good afternoon, Bertram," she said softly.

Hearing her, he raised his head a little and opened his eyes, which had been closed as if he was asleep, but he wasn't. "How did you get in here?" he asked, frowning. "I gave specific orders—" He stopped and took a deep breath as if he had no energy; then he continued, "I told her I would not see anyone."

"It wasn't her fault. I insisted, and she didn't know how to refuse me." She pulled up a chair beside him and, sitting down, placed her hand on top of his arm.

"If you've come to preach to me about God, you might as well leave," Bertram said.

"My dear friend, I didn't come to preach to you. I just came to see how you're doing."

"Yes, and to pray for me. Oh, I know you believe that I ought to pray and ask your precious Lord to give me the answer to my disease."

"Disease?" Evelyn asked.

"Yes, because I'm ill, and if there is such a thing as a Supreme Being, which I doubt, he or she or it can't help me. What I have is incurable."

"Most diseases can be cured with treatment."

"Mine can't, and surely not with your holy water or some spit and clay. Yuck! How about laying on of hands? Well, you've got your

325

hand on me, but I don't feel any better. So please go and leave me alone."

"That's why I'm here. I don't want you to be alone. It's not good just to sit here all by yourself and hibernate. That won't solve anything, and Mamie says that you're not eating. My dear Bertram, if you don't eat, you'll die."

The mention of death aroused a morbid irritation which caused him to think of his wife. He raised his head, and his eyes were filled with tears.

"She chose death. I gave her a choice, and oh God, oh God… she chose death for herself." He was evidently unaware that he had called on God.

"But you're not responsible for her death," Evelyn said.

"Oh yes, I'm totally responsible. I gave her an ultimatum, and she…and she…" He looked around as if he was in a daze, and he was searching for something.

"I don't know what ultimatum you gave her, but she had a choice, and we can't go back and change what happened, so let's just start from today."

He tried to respond, but the words wouldn't come, and he could see Miriam when he went to identify her and claim her body, and he could see the words she wrote as her last wish: "Take care of the children." Suddenly his body began to shake convulsively, and he burst into tears.

Evelyn, with her womanly instincts, knew that his tears were a breakthrough and an indication that he was feeling some emotion. This was good because he had been as one comatose.

She stood, put her hands on his shoulder in a gentle massage, and let him cry. She had not forgotten his pitiful weeping at Miriam's burial, and she was wondering what she could do now to help him when she heard a knock at the door and saw Mamie standing there looking quite distraught. But before Evelyn could ask her anything, Mamie spoke.

"Timothy has run away," she said, repeating the words just as Gertrude had said them to her.

"Oh no," Evelyn said, keeping her hands on Bertram's shoulders; this was in order to steady herself as she felt rather faint.

Bertram Withers, on hearing those terrible words, spoken so softly yet clearly by Mamie, felt a cruel pain in his chest, and he wanted desperately to be alone, and *I need to think* were the words that commanded him to insist that Evelyn leave him.

"Go, please. Go," he said, gently pushing her out and closing and locking the door.

Feeling frustrated, Evelyn called her friend Blaise McCaslin. He was sitting at his kitchen table eating a salmon salad sandwich when he received her phone call.

"Timothy Withers has run away," she said.

"Oh dear, how awful," he said, trying to digest her terrible news and also his sandwich.

"Can you come?" she asked.

"Where are you?" he asked also trying to stay calm.

"I'm here at the Withers's house, and I need you. Please come."

And right away, he left his house, took his half-eaten sandwich, and drove to the Withers's house,

On the way, he was thinking of the Withers's family from the Christmas celebration. *Bertram had seemed to be happy, and it was a joy watching Timothy with Jasper and Jasmine as the three wise men, but Miriam had seemed to be unhappy. Then came her suicide after she heard that her biological father was Black, which meant that she was part Black. Part Black means that you're Black, and she was despised by her husband and her adopted mother. Lesser than. I would like to have the ability to call her back. I'd be her companion, for I was made so aware of the racial clime when I met Darius and Sage. Sad for the hate.*

He arrived at the Withers's house at almost the same time as Lieutenant Colin and Gertrude Kingsley. They sat at the kitchen table in shock and confusion. Not knowing what to say to one another, Evelyn reached over and took Mamie's hand, and they all closed their eyes and prayed silently.

Whether it was the negative reaction to her attempts to reach him and trying to give him some hope or her natural woman's intuition, Evelyn wondered what Bertram was doing now. Perhaps he felt that suicide was the answer, or death, as Miriam had chosen.

"I'm worried," she said, looking over at Mamie. "It's awfully quiet up there. Come with me and let's see if we can get him to talk to us."

"I'll go up with you," Mamie said. "But I know that he won't talk to me."

Leaving the others downstairs, she and Mamie walked slowly up the stairs and stood outside the door to his room. Evelyn spoke words of encouragement to him, hoping in her heart that he could hear her. "May the Lord bless and keep you. May he make his face to shine upon you and give you peace." Mamie prayed silently, *Not my will but Thine be done.* Their thoughts were interrupted by the sound of Felicity crying, and their concern turned from Bertram to the baby.

Meanwhile, Major Hawthorne, not finding Timothy, went to the Withers's house to see if there was any news. He sat quietly with Lieutenant Colin and Gertrude and Blaise.

After locking the door, Bertram sat down, closed his eyes, and tried to think. From time to time, he opened his eyes and looked around in the unlighted room, but he couldn't gather his thoughts together in any one direction. His thoughts seemed to jump in and out, and it was not possible for him to concentrate on his plight. *What is happening? Where am I?*

Then he had a clear vision which focused on his children. First it was Felicity, and why was she Black? And then it was Timothy, and why was he White, and why did he run away? He stood up and started to pace back and forth from the chair to the window, then around the chair where he'd sit but for only a few seconds. He was thinking, *I gave my wife an ultimatum, and if she had made the right decision, to give Felicity up for adoption, it would have set things right, and we could have gone on with our lives. But she had chosen...she had chosen...oh, she had chosen to kill herself.*

So now that a totally new situation had arisen with Timothy, Bertram didn't know how to rectify it. If he satisfied himself, it would be to give both the children up and to separate himself from all the Black people and those White people who loved the Black people. He was thinking, *Woefully, all this attention has been focused on me because Timothy has run away, and it is the consensus of everyone that I should be concerned, not only about Timothy but about that little girl who is crying in my house. Crying. Why couldn't she have run away with her brother?*

He felt that he was in an impossible place, like a man on water skis holding on to a tow rope which was being pulled by a boat, enjoying himself, when a storm had arisen. He could call out for help from those in the boat, hoping they could hear him. He could try holding on to the rope through the turbulence, or he could turn loose the rope and try swimming to shore. In either case, he was facing the possibility of death. So thus was his dilemma. Call out for help? Hold on to the rope and ride out the storm? Turn loose the rope and swim to shore or sink and drown?

In reality, this storm that had arisen was the Black lives that had been thrown into his life. He now could open the door and call for help. Walk out and face—what? Who? He could turn loose of everything he'd been holding on to—his house, his family, and his reputation—and try making it to another place, alone. Either way, he could fail. He sat down and cried. He heard the voices of those downstairs. He heard the front door opening and closing. He heard footsteps on the stairs. He heard the baby crying. Then he heard nothing.

Later in the evening, after hearing the news of a runaway child, while making their rounds, two city policemen noticed that the light was on in the phone booth on the corner. They knew that the light came on when the door was closed and went off when the door was opened. On investigating, they found a little boy who was there on the floor of the booth, fast asleep. Taking the paper from the child's hand, one of the officers saw a phone number and an address and the names Jasmine and Jasper. Timothy had been too short to reach the dial, and he hadn't been aware that he needed money to make a call; being very tired, he had fallen asleep. When the officers went to the address, it was Karen who opened the door.

"Timothy. Oh, Timothy," she said, looking at the weary child, then up at the policeman. "You've found him. Thank the Lord."

Timothy went immediately to her, and Karen, reaching down, hugged him, both crying.

"Is this your child?" the officer asked.

"No, he really isn't, but I know who he is, and I know his father."

Karen went with the policemen, taking Timothy, over his loud protestations—"Don't take me there, he doesn't want me"—to the Withers's house. There was joy on seeing the child who had been lost. But there was also concern for his father, who was upstairs, locked in his room. Being told all the particulars of the situation and of Bertram's seclusion, the officers decided to investigate. Receiving no answer to their knock or loudly calling his name, they asked Mamie if she had a key; and when she used her key to open the door, they found the unconscious Bertram lying across the bed. He was taken to the hospital by ambulance.

The people sitting here seemingly had more love for one another than some people who were blood relatives. Instead of chaos in this house, there was peace, and this unrelated group of people became as family. The two heads of this household, Miriam, the mother, had taken her own life; and now Bertram, the father, had attempted the same. One child, a product of this pair, had run away in an attempt to find solace with another family. The other child, an infant, innocent, not yet knowing that the color of her skin was the cause of the present upheaval, was asleep in her crib.

Evelyn, not wanting Bertram to be alone, went with him to the hospital; and Major Hawthorne, feeling that Evelyn needed support, went with her, knowing that Evelyn would try giving the dying man some reason to live. And being the closest to Bertram as a relative, he also felt that he would be the one to take responsibility for the house and the children during Bertram's incapacitation.

Gertrude Kingsley, having assumed the role of grandmother, offered to stay at the house until the fate of the father was known; and Mamie, being familiar with the household and the baby, agreed to stay, wanting no disruption for Felicity. Lieutenant Kingsley, feeling the gravity of the situation, knew he couldn't leave the two women, his wife and Mamie, alone in the house.

"Yes, we'll stay here tonight," he said, kissing his wife on the cheek. "Tomorrow is another day, and we'll decide what to do then."

And just as various plants, ground cover, flowers grow from once fallow ground, now enriched feelings of a loving family sprang up from previously emptiness of relationships—father, mother, grandmother, grandfather, sister, brother, friend—future bonds of love. So arrangements were made for the moment, and they were made by each person, not from feelings of responsibility but from sincere feelings of love.

Blaise McCaslin looked at Timothy, and he remembered Karen at the Deavers' Christmas celebration with Jasmine, Jasper, and Timothy calling themselves the three wise men, and he understood Timothy's attachment.

"Can't I please stay with you and my friends, Miss Karen, please?" he pleaded.

"Maybe later on," she said, kneeling down and giving him a hug, not wanting to give him a definite *no*.

Blaise was impressed by the kindness and patience in Karen toward Timothy, not one of her own, and he found himself looking more intently at her. He remembered holding her hand as they gathered in the circle at the Christmas celebration, and he had been somewhat surprised by her warm smile and her gentle hug as each person hugged the persons who stood beside them.

Lieutenant Kingsley, seeing Timothy standing there holding Karen's hand, shivering from the cold, and realizing how tired Timothy was, took him in his arms and consoled him. The child was almost immediately asleep, so he helped Mamie put him to bed. Karen, relieved that here was another friend, thanked him. Then Blaise saw her standing alone, tired and confused. Responding to his feeling of, *I must help her,* he offered to take her home. And Karen, also remembering him and not wanting the policemen to take her home—more questions, nonattachments—accepted his offer.

There was little conversation as Karen and Blaise rode along with each one being tired but also reluctant to engage in normal lines of conversation with each other, two people from different backgrounds and together, alone, for the first time. Their thoughts were also along different lines.

Blaise thought, *She seems like such an intelligent, calm lady, and even with only a few words being spoken, I feel drawn to her, all the while trying to guess her thoughts.*

Karen was thinking, *How nice and kind of him to do this. I didn't want the policemen to take me home, and I didn't want to bring Timothy with me. So much trauma. I've seen enough hate lately expressed between people who are supposed to have love, and I wonder where this young man, this young White man, fits into the picture. Oh well, relax and enjoy the peace here.*

When they arrived at her house, Blaise was surprised at where she lived, never having been on this side of town, and just now realizing that this was where most of the poor Black people lived. He walked to the door with her, wanting to see her safely inside.

"Thank you so much," she said.

"You're quite welcome. I could see that you were tired, and I felt you were anxious to get home."

As he was talking, Mrs. Johnson opened the door.

"Oh, Karen, I'm so glad you're back. I was worried sick about you," she said.

"I'm all right, Mamma. This nice young man was kind enough to bring me home."

"Oh, I remember you from the Christmas party," Mrs. Johnson said with a pleasant smile on her face. "Thank you. Why don't you come in and get warmed up. I usually give Karen and the children some hot chocolate when they've been out in the cold."

He stepped inside, again intrigued by this kind lady as he remembered the Christmas presentation of faith, hope, and love given by her and her two friends. "Thanks for the offer, but I need to be getting on home. I'm Blaise McCaslin, in case you forgot my name."

"And this is my mother, Blaise, and these are my two little ones," Karen said as the children had also entered the room, being happy to see their mother and full of questions about Timothy.

Blaise was feeling warm in Mrs. Johnson's presence and aware of the humble although neat and clean house. He wondered how they all fit into such a small space.

"We'd really like for you to stay," Karen said, also obviously experiencing a liking for him and also appreciating his kindness.

When she reached out her hand, he felt welcome here. At the same time, he also felt some fear caused by the Black-White mixing. He hesitated. But the warm welcome he received from all of them and the sincere, cordial greeting, the hot chocolate, and also the steam pudding, which he had never known of or tasted before, gave him a feeling that it was all right for him to be here.

The conversation centered around Timothy, Timothy's father, and the happiness of the children.

When he was home, Blaise thought more about it. He thought about Darius and how pleased he and Evelyn had been to welcome a new, successful young man to their church, at the same time, not knowing that Darius had come alone because he was married to a Black lady, who would not have been welcome at their White church. He remembered what had happened to their house, and he was momentarily beset with, *Well, if you marry this Black lady, the same could happen to you.* Then he laughed and told himself that he was not contemplating marriage. It was just that he could feel her need, and he wanted to help. Lying in bed, he thought more about it. Since he had very much enjoyed the evening in their small house, he concluded that it might be all right for him to like that little family. Especially Karen.

After Blaise left, Karen also sat with her thoughts. How nice to feel a man's attention. She'd been in such constant stress, first with Randy and his inability to get his life together and to do something positive with it. Then there was more stress from working at such a hard, low-paying, low-self-esteem-producing job and the pain of her father's death. Then along came Sage and Darius with a new life for her, for her children, and her mother. Now here came Blaise, and she knew he was attracted to her, and she was attracted to him. But— *Hmm, he's White. He's never been married. He doesn't have children, and he seemed to like her children. Oh, Karen. It's such a new feeling.*

It's such a new possibility. Can I love a White man? Sage does. But, oh well, I'm not Sage, and he's not Darius, and tomorrow is another day. She slept soundly.

39

At the hospital, the doctors determined that Bertram Withers had overdosed on sleeping pills, but they were able to cleanse his body of the poison, and the prognosis was that he would survive.

Gertrude and Colin, knowing that Mamie did not want the responsibility of the Withers's house, had taken her and the children to their house. Blaise McCaslin had returned to work. Major Hawthorne checked on the Withers's house every night, and Evelyn Prentiss checked on Bertram every day.

After three days, Bertram Withers was released from the hospital, and not wanting to ask anyone to pick him up, he called a cab. He wanted to be left alone.

Entering his house, he relaxed. He stood and looked around, and the memories caused him a moment of unhappiness and loneliness. However, that moment soon passed, and he was thinking, *I don't need any of this anymore. I'm free to make a totally new start. First, I'll sell the house and all the furniture. There are too many memories and no real need since I will be living in the faculty housing. Second, I'll enlist the help of Mamie to gather up Miriam's things. She can take whatever she wants, and we can give the rest to charity. I will give the children's belongings, clothes, and furniture to whoever they will be living with. It will be either a temporary arrangement until I decide, or I might just give both of them up for adoption.*

I feel that all my actions now should be for my personal contentment. Time heals all wounds, and even though I've lived through some painful moments, I can erase all traces of my former life, and I don't really need a family. I won't attempt to form any friendship with Marvin Hawthorne because, actually, he is not my relative. Being president of my prestigious and, thankfully, all-White university, I will be free.

Having carefully and fully considered everything, with his determined ambition, he could let worry and guilt pass away from him, and he could become interested in pleasure, maybe taking up skiing or golf. He had come home with joy in his heart.

There were several pieces of mail awaiting him. One was from the university. He sat down, breathed a sigh of relief, and kissed the envelope, knowing that herein was his passport to happiness. Being president of the university would allow him all the desires of his heart, and he could start a new life.

Then came the bombshell that blew it all apart. On opening and reading the letter, he was stunned. The letter contained this message:

Dear Professor Withers:

We regret to inform you that the selection for president of the university is Professor Franklin Woods Holliman. Your position as head of the law department has also been reassigned. Your position as instructor, however, is still available if you choose to keep it.

Sincerely,
Mary B. Overton,
Department of Personnel

Feeling very weak and faint, Bertram Withers sat down to keep from falling. He was very sure that he had been denied the presidency because his wife and children were Black. He knew they did not want to fire him, but he was positive he would not want the position he was offered. He was angry with everyone, with the world and with the law of the land. As the doctor had cleansed the poison he had swallowed from his body, could he now cleanse this hate for Black people from his mind? Did he really want him to?

I should have died. The poison should have killed me. I had been so sure of myself and my position and the possibility of becoming president at the university, and I had placed it uppermost on the shelves of my mind. It was what I wanted, and I was willing to get rid of any imagined obstacle—of course, which included my family, my Black wife, my Black children.

Well, I wasn't successful on my first attempt at suicide, and I think if I really want to kill myself, I should get a gun. That's a sure way. The only person to be considered is me. My former mother-in-law, Alicia Hawthorne, who really is not my mother-in-law, is out of my life. Marvin Hawthorne has assumed the role of a relative, which he isn't, and I can forget Evelyn with her holier-than-thou philosophy.

Bertram Withers took his revolver out of the case where it was kept. He loaded it and put it on the table beside him. He was thinking, *I can do this.*

Since Evelyn Prentiss had resolved to stay close to him and to continue her attempts to encourage him to want to live, when she got off from work that afternoon, she drove to the house and parked. Knowing that Major Hawthorne came every evening to check on the house, she waited, hoping she hadn't missed him. When she saw his car approaching, she was relieved. She opened her door and waited for him to come over. They walked up the sidewalk to the front door and rang the bell. They waited a few minutes for Bertram to answer the bell. Then they heard the gunshot.

Major Hawthorne used his key, and he and Evelyn Prentiss cautiously yet alarmed, not sure what they would find inside, entered the house. They were very bewildered and surprised when they saw Bertram Withers sitting in the chair, the gun still in his hand. They were then very relieved when they heard him speak, knowing that he hadn't fatally injured himself.

"I tried. I tried, but I couldn't do it. I aimed at my chest, then my head, and I… I… I guess my hand was shaking so."

Evelyn was intent on taking care of Bertram and trying to convince him that it was just another unfortunate accident, and "this too will pass." However, from the moment Marvin entered and Bertram saw him, Marvin felt unwelcome. Marvin and Bertram had never been in complete peace with each other, and Marvin now felt a message coming from Bertram: *You are not welcome here.*

"Can I get you something?" the major asked, still hoping for some civility with the man.

"No. No, and please go. I want very much to be left alone."

And Major Hawthorne, hearing the negative tone and knowing this was Bertram's house and then being assured that Evelyn was not afraid of the bewildered, unhappy man, he placed the keys on a nearby table and left the house.

Evelyn stood beside Bertram's chair and took his hand. "I was concerned about you," she said. He looked so pitiful and helpless, and her heart went out to him. Her presence seemed to bring a calming spirit that came over him, but as quickly as it came, the feeling left him. He pulled his hand away and turned his head, for his eyes had filled with tears. He hated tears in anyone, but what he was beginning to realize was that tears have a life and a will of their own. Even for him.

"I am your friend, and I want you to believe that. I'm here for you, but you would get stronger, and you would find your way much faster if you let someone help you. I'm willing to try."

"No thanks. I want to believe in myself."

"And that's a good thing, but there is strength in believing in God. Honestly, he can help you."

"How can you believe in God, and you don't even know if such a person exists?"

"There is such a thing as faith," she said, and she pulled up a chair and sat beside him.

"Faith, Higher Power—words that don't mean anything to me."

"Faith means that if you pray for something and you turn it over to God, and you believe that he exists, it will come to pass."

"Sounds like children who believe in Santa Claus. If they ask him for something, and if they're good children, they will get what they ask for. Well, just like Santa Claus doesn't exist, neither does this imaginary God. I don't believe any of that stuff. It's just words.

I believe that if I work hard and concentrate on what I'm doing, I'll be just fine."

"Man is not autonomous. You didn't get here by yourself, and you haven't made it this far by yourself."

"I will find my way, and I'll find it by myself."

"Well, 'so a man thinketh, so is he.' Every morning when I'm first awake, I speak good words over my day and my life. Will you try that?"

"I might as well. Nothing else seems to be working."

"I have some cards with positive thoughts printed on them," she said, taking a few small cards from her purse. Again taking his hand, she pressed it and gave him the cards.

After she left, he looked at the cards, and shrugging his shoulders, he threw them in the wastebasket.

Evelyn Prentiss sat in her car, and she knew she had failed to help him to believe in God as she had so wanted, and she had also hoped that they could have possibly developed a love relationship, even being married and being a mother to his children, for she had always longed for a family. At home, she lighted a candle and tried to relax, sitting for a long while, thinking. Finally, she came to a firm conclusion: *I can't remake him, and I don't need three children—him, Timothy, and the baby—to try and raise. It would be more of a burden than a saving grace. I have my church, my Bible study group, and I will get in closer communication with Sage and Darius. And I still have my friend Blaise, so I'll stay close to him.*

40

Helen Kane had been introduced into Miriam's life before anyone knew who she was, and now that Miriam was no longer here, her major concern was for her grandchildren, and she wanted to be a part of their lives. Marvin Hawthorne loved Helen Kane, and he knew that compassionate care was a part of the training to be a nurse; and the closer he came to her, the more he was aware of her natural compassionate nature. The more time he spent with her, the more his heart overflowed with her presence.

They both knew that a decision had to be made concerning the future of the children, so they went to visit Bertram. Major Hawthorne remembered that the last time he visited Bertram, he had left with an unsavory taste in his mouth. And now, approaching the Withers's house, he felt nervous and afraid.

During Bertram's marriage to Miriam, Marvin had tolerated him, and he was very aware of Bertram's very deep bias against Blacks. Then, Lord have mercy, for him to come to hate Miriam, that was terrible. Marvin now felt very sure that this stupid (he called him) man would also hate the children.

"I don't hate the children," Bertram said. "It's that I don't see how I can take care of them and also work full-time. And then there's the house. Can I still live here, you know, with a Black child? The world is so strange, you know…" He went on and on.

Major Hawthorne had actually stopped listening to Bertram, and when there was a pause in his ramblings, he spoke. "Would you be willing to allow us to legally adopt both the children? Nothing

340

temporary. It would have to be a permanent adoption," he said, and he was thinking that with a legal, permanent adoption, Bertram couldn't change his mind somewhere down the road and come to take them back.

"Us?" Bertram asked.

"She is their true grandmother, and I am their grandfather, and we can do this together," Major Hawthorne said.

From Bertram's face and from the shocked look in his eyes, his open mouth out of which no words came, Marvin knew Bertram had not thought about Helen Kane as their real grandmother nor that she would actually want the children. Bertram was occupied with what was good for him and how he would go forward with his life. But then it hit him, square between the ears. Those words. That question. *Would you be willing to allow us to legally adopt both the children?*

Marvin and Helen looked at each other, and they noticed that Bertram's eyes, though not full of tears, were moist.

"Could we talk more about this some other time?" he asked, turning away from them. "I'm very tired and confused right now, and I need some time to think. How about tomorrow? Yes, come back tomorrow. I'll know then, and I'll tell you my decision tomorrow."

As Marvin drove away, he was also confused and sad, for he wondered if he was doing the right thing. Indeed, the only thing he could reproach himself for was loving too much. He had loved Miriam and also Timothy, and now there was Felicity. Dear, sweet little Felicity.

"Well, given more time to think, it might be that Bertram would find it in his heart to take the children."

"I wonder," Helen Kane said.

As Marvin Hawthorne thought more about Bertram, he pitied him. Where could he go for help? Alicia was not able in her condition to help him. Evelyn had not been able to help, and the ones who were willing, mainly Lieutenant Colin and Gertrude Kingsley, had been thought of by Bertram as lovers of those Black people, those people whom Bertram hated.

Then following his instincts, he stopped his car beside the beautiful waters of the lake. He stepped out of the car, walked around to the passenger's side, took Helen Kane's hand, escorted her out of the car, and then he walked to the edge of the lake. Holding her hand, he knelt down beside a poplar tree and proposed to her.

"Helen Kane, beautiful, loving, caring, patient lady, will you marry me?"

Her heart was already overflowing with a sense of belonging, being Miriam's mother and the children's grandmother and loving Major Hawthorne, who truly considered himself to be the children's grandfather, she said *yes*.

41

After his visitors left, Bertram Withers sat and began looking around the room. The pictures on the walls, on the mantle above the fireplace, the white lace curtains that Miriam had sewed by hand, the floor lamp with the gold plated trimming, all these things, everything he looked at reminded him of Miriam and Timothy—the family picture of the three of them, the spinet piano that sat beside the lamp. He had watched Timothy sitting there practicing his beginning lessons. He tried not to think of either of them or of his surroundings, or Major Hawthorne's request: "Would you allow us to adopt them?"

He asked himself and answered the question, *Adopt them? Well, why not? Timothy loves the major as the only grandfather he has ever known, and this nurse, if what she says is true—and of course, it is—she is the children's real grandmother. And I don't know if I could take care of an infant.*

Bertram's head was full of clutter, and his thoughts rambled on, *Well, I'll give them my answer, my decision, tomorrow. No, the day after, both the major and the university. Nothing is working for me. Nothing is fitting into the mold I was trying to make for my life.* He sat down at his desk and began to write. After a while, thinking and reading over what he'd written, he went out and got into his car.

It was a clear, cold day, and a dusting of snow was on the ground. It was five o'clock, and the streets were heavy with traffic, people going home from work. He drove to the foothills of one of Washington's mountains, parked, and started hiking up. They say that the higher up you are, the closer you are to that infinite space where it's easier to communicate with whatever Supreme Being there is. Then he stopped, for instead of the voice of some imagined Supreme Being, the words that came to him were from Miriam: *Take care of the children.*

Then without consciously deciding to do it, he turned and walked down. He got back into his car and drove to the spot where Miriam had been found. He began talking to her as if she were really there, "I did love you, Miriam. I really did, and I loved our son, but I was so filled with myself, so full of ego, self-pride. I never stopped to imagine that I could love someone else. Oh, Miriam, I did love you, and I did love Timothy, but my ego pushed it aside, and my prejudice against Black people pushed you. It pushed you into that lake. I should have been able to take care of Timothy and the baby. What's her name? Felicity. Who in their right mind would name a child Felicity? I should have been able to make them love me. The Kingsleys say they love me. Evelyn loves me, but do I love them? No, I don't love any of them."

And Bertram Withers wept. "I have no reason to be here. I wasn't successful with the pills nor the gun, but I can do this." He got out of his car and walked along the edge of the water, the tears uncontrolled. He wanted to walk into the lake and drown, but somehow he couldn't do it. He got back into his car and spoke to her.

"Miriam, I'm sorry for how I treated you. Can you hear me? Can you see me? Yes, I think you can, and I know that you forgive me, and I hear you, and don't worry, the children will be with people who love them and will take care of them, like you said. Miriam, I love you. I'll see you soon." He closed his eyes and bowed his head.

Major Hawthorne and Helen Kane waited all the next day, but they didn't hear from Bertram. "Come back tomorrow," he had said. But he also said, "Maybe the next day." Then knowing what kind of uncertain thoughts Bertram Withers was expressing and what their hopes were for the custody and care of his grandchildren, they went to check on the unhappy father. Not getting an answer after he rang the doorbell, Marvin tried and found that the door was unlocked. They entered and called his name, and receiving no answer, they realized that Bertram was not there. There was an envelope on the mantle in the living room addressed to him. After reading its contents, he had to sit down in order to compose his mind and evaluate his feelings. The letter read thus:

> To Major Marvin Hawthorne, my late wife Miriam's adoptive father, the only father she ever knew, and the only grandfather my children have known. And to Helen Kane, Miriam's birth mother, the true grandmother of our children:
>
> I hereby leave you full custody of Timothy and Felicity Withers.
> I hereby leave you with all the money in my bank accounts.
> I hereby leave to you my two children; this house, located at _____, all its furnishings, my life insurance policies; these to be available and controlled by them until the children reach the age of eighteen. Timothy, reaching the age of eighteen before Felicity, will share his half of everything with her, and Major Hawthorne and Helen Kane will still have custody and care of Felicity until she reaches the age of eighteen.
> Any salaries owed to me, insurances from my employment, are for your use. All of Miriam's possessions, insurances, assets, were left to me and are now included in my possessions.
>
> Signed this day: (date)
> Attorney Bertram G. Withers

Written on a second sheet was another message.

To Major Marvin Hawthorne:

> I, Bertram Withers, have gone to be with my wife, Miriam Withers. I realize how much I loved her, and I want to tell her that, and I want to let her know that I share her bidding to take care of the children, and I humbly ask that it be carried out. I also thank you for the care and support you give to my mother-in-law, Alicia Hawthorne. She needs you, and I thank you for your love and for your dedication, and your devotion that you also gave to Miriam and our children.

> Bertram Withers.

When he was home, Major Marvin Hawthorne received a call from the police telling him that Bertram had been found. It was at the same lake where Miriam had entered the water, and Bertram's hands held a jar. The jar held a note. The note read, "Take care of the children. I've gone to meet my sweet, kind, and loving wife. Please inter me close to her, and we will be forever together as one. Thank you. Bertram Withers."

Part Six

42

Little Willow Mede Deavers had been the center of attention for Darius Deavers for the first three months of her life. Darius was in awe marveling at the miracle of life, a life which came from his seed. He had reveled in the love he received from the two grandmothers, Mrs. Mary Jane Copple and Mrs. Lucy Deavers, and he had watched the miracle of them becoming closer as friends, one Black and one White, one rich and one not rich, one college educated and one not, smiling as they were happily sharing their grandchild, who was his child, his precious first child.

Darius had spent those three months enjoying the abundance of love which surrounded him, but when his mother and Sage's mother left, he had to turn his thoughts again to his own life and his work. He had hardly gotten over the distressing news of Miriam's death, and not only had there been great sorrow about her, there was a greater concern about the children. Then they received the heart-wrenching news: "Timothy has run away."

"Why would he do that?" Darius asked.

"I'm sure that poor little boy feels like his father doesn't want him and his little sister because he now considers them to be Black, and naturally, Timothy is suffering from losing his mother," Sage said, her wisdom speaking to her.

Then the happy news reached them that Timothy had been found. Almost immediately, however, Darius and Sage were again overcome when Major Hawthorne called with the more distressing news that Bertram had overdosed on pills. Not accidently but on purpose. And he was taken to the hospital, and later he took his own life by drowning as Miriam had done.

Consuming Darius's mind was the reason for all these awful happenings, and he was forced to ask himself some questions. *Why are people Black, and why are they the cause of so much hate?* Darius never had any Black history in school, and he never had any reason to question the origin of the Black race. Wanting some answers, he searched through numerous books, including the encyclopedias, also the Bible, the laws, and the Constitution. His thoughts were, *Help me to understand this. When I look at all those who I know and love— my dear wife and her family, Mrs. Johnson, Karen and her children, and my friend Charles—I don't see how there can be any negative thoughts about them. Even Randy, who fit the description most people have of them as less-than, is still a person, not a creature.*

In his research he came across an article from a "creation" magazine which stated, "Concerning the origin of the races, the Bible records that: 'All men are descendants of the first created man Adam, and the line of all human ancestry passes through Noah. Only Noah, his sons, and their wives survived the flood which destroyed all other men living at that time.'" He asked, *Weren't Adam and Noah White?*

Another bit of information from the encyclopedia stated:

> In 1871, Charles Darwin published *The Descent of Man*. This book outlined Darwin's theory that man came from the same group of animals as the chimpanzee and other apes. Another book by Darwin, *The Origin of the Species*, states that by means of Natural Selection, or preservation of Favored Races in the struggle of life, were facts on which Darwin had based his concept of evolution.

Another article stated, "Many persons object to the theory of evolution because it conflicts with their religious belief that the account of Creation in the Bible is a historic fact."

But to Darius, even reading about the separation of the languages at the Tower of Babel and the Creation, Adam and Noah, and about Darwin's theory of evolution, he did not understand how the Black race came to be and why Blacks were so despised. Even reading about the history of slavery and Blacks being brought here as slaves didn't solve the problem for him.

That evening, Darius was sitting on the couch with his face in his hands, being beset with questions for which he had no answers. *Why am I here? What am I going to do here? Will the Black situation be the cause of my downfall? Am I stupid trying to make it alone when my office is in a Black neighborhood and I am White?*

Sage came and sat beside him and began feeding Willow. Sensing that he was unhappy, she asked, "Darius dear, what is bothering you?"

"I don't know what to do. I feel so lost in that office by myself, and I don't know anything about the neighborhood. At one time, I considered teaching law at the university, and I considered taking a job at the shipping company. Both are in the category of law. Should I reconsider either of them and give up this idea of being independent when I'm confused about all the hate that surrounds us?"

In her life, Sage had also been strapped with problems caused by being Black, trying to teach in Colorado where she wasn't allowed to have a contract, so she decided that the system was flawed, and she went home and considered a teaching position in Oklahoma's all-Black school system. Was that the answer? Yet, now living in BeachSide, Washington, she had to make herself content. Evidently, Darius couldn't.

"I would suggest that you move away from your office for a while and stop trying to be so independent and so strong by yourself—and stop fighting the system. You know that I'm with you whatever you decide, but I don't like seeing you so sad. My dear, I suggest that you take a position with one of the established law firms for a while as an intern, and you can learn a lot about the court system. You have the education, but you don't have very much actual experience as a lawyer. There are times when it's best to start at the bottom. Use your education and all your other assets for upward mobility while you're also learning, and then you'll know where you fit in and where you'll be useful. And by the way, you're also very handsome." She took his hands from his face and kissed them, one and then the other.

"Bless your heart," he said, and he did as she suggested. He applied and was accepted as an intern at the law offices of Marshall, Lewis & Allen. White lawyers. White clients. A White neighborhood.

On Monday morning, the first day of his internship at Marshall, Lewis & Allen Law Firm, which occupied the entire eighth floor of the twelve-story building, Darius Paul Deavers reported to the office on time. His modern office was equipped with all the necessary items: a desk, desk chair, three chairs for clients, a bookshelf with several rows of law journals, a wall clock, and a phone.

During the week, a couple of phone calls were directed to an intern, which he answered and which didn't result in any appointments. One call was from an unhappy wife, not seeking a divorce but wanting answers about separate maintenance. Then a man who was asking for information: "What can I do about children playing on my lawn? I've put up a fence, but they keep throwing their ball over and then climbing over my new fence to get it. They trample on my grass and my flower garden. If I shoot them, could I be charged since I would just be protecting my property?"

Hmm. Are these the kinds of things I will be dealing with here? I am discouraged.

Darius talked with the other intern who was employed there. His name was Norrell Ivers. He was a recent graduate. He had passed the required bar examinations. He was married with one child. Norrell was White, and he exuded an extremely pleasant personality. He had been employed at the law firm of Marshall, Lewis & Allen for little more than a year, and he was content here. Even though Darius Paul Deavers was comfortable in the office setting, especially since there were only three employees in the intern's office (Norrell, a secretary, and himself), contrary to Norrell's ambition only to always work for someone else, Darius was unquestionably looking forward to having a law firm of his own, making his own decisions, and working for the betterment of those who were classified as minorities. Norrell's attitude was toward himself and for himself. He was committed to trying the seemingly trivial cases to the best of his ability, but he had no intention of becoming interested in the clients personally, only in their ability to pay.

He and Darius talked about politics, about the current cases, and just as he had done before in Boston, Darius mentioned the racial disparity here in the city and in this office. "There are no Black employees and no Black clients here," he said.

The intern looked at Darius and frowned, wondering about Darius's concern. "That's just the way it is, you know. They have their lives, and we have ours. But I'm here for a reason."

"What reason?"

"I'm here to learn. I don't have any actual experience as a lawyer in the courtroom, in administration, or procedures, and neither do you, so I suggest that we work together. One morning, I go and observe in the actual courtroom, and you stay here and take care of the intern's duties. And the next day, you go, and I stay here. We alternate, and we can both learn."

"Then what?"

"That depends on what you want to accomplish. I just want to be a part of an established law firm where I can earn a decent salary instead of being on my own. You know, these little cases we take now might seem insignificant, but we can learn something from them and also establish a reputation. All the time, we're earning a salary."

Norrell always seemed to be satisfied. He never complained about anything, and in answer to "Good morning, how are you today?" he always said, "I'm blessed."

What? As Darius looked at Norrell, he was thinking, *You're poor, just starting out. You use public transportation, and you live in a rented apartment. How can you say that you're blessed?* Darius concluded that it was just a statement Norrell had decided to use as an answer to the much-asked question.

Well, Darius Deavers thought, *I'm not poor. I drive an almost-new car, and I am not a renter, and this position pays a decent salary. But I still don't feel that I'm blessed.*

One day, the young Black lady who cleaned the offices of Marshall, Lewis & Allen stumbled over some books that were on the floor as she was emptying the wastebaskets, and she fell and broke her arm. There was a clinic on the first floor of the office building, and Darius took her there. The nurse and doctor looked at her and suggested that he take her to the Black hospital, for they didn't treat broken bones. When he took her to the Black hospital, it was the same situation all over again as when he brought Mr. Johnson there, and Darius knew that she would need help. Her husband was at work, and she couldn't call him. But he couldn't come and get her anyway because they didn't have a car, so Darius stayed with her until after she was treated.

"You don't have to stay with me, Mr. Deavers," she said, crying from her pain. "You don't know how it feels to always be in need. It's different being Black," she said.

Darius had to think about Sage. "Yes, I'm quite aware of the difference, but I'm here to help you," he said.

"I sure do thank you, and I know that they'll probably fire me, you know. They don't want us to be a problem."

"Well, maybe you could get a different job."

"I wish. But that job at the office, it's all I could get, and a different job at any other place would be just the same: hard work and little pay."

"Where does your husband work?" Darius asked.

"He works on the loading dock, and that sure is some hard work. Before that, he worked in the hospital's laundry, and that wasn't any easier, but he gets paid a little more on the dock. It's still not much, and we're both so tired when we get home we—" She paused and looked at Darius. "But, sir, I'm sorry, I'm not intending to be complaining because we are surviving."

By the time she had been treated and he took her home, her husband was off work, and he was home. They were Bridget and James Parker, both in their early twenties. Darius told him that he would pay the bill for her, and since she was hurt on the job, perhaps they'd reimburse him.

James thanked Darius, and at the same time, he looked at him, someone he had never met, who was offering to pay his bill. Someone White. An anomaly.

After Darius left them, the things she said stayed on his mind. One was, "It's different being Black." The other was, "This is the only kind of job we can get." So Darius decided to do some research on the duties involved in their jobs. He learned that the three jobs she mentioned—at the loading docks, the laundry, and cleaning the building—required the ability to be on your feet for an extended amount of time; the ability to lift, push, and/or pull fifty pounds, sometimes more, depending on the contents of the bags or boxes; the ability to do excessive bending and physical movement; and the knowledge or willingness to learn the use of all the powered equipment.

Darius concluded that all those jobs included labor which required every ounce of a worker's strength with long hours and low pay.

Bridget worked the evening shift from five in the afternoon to two in the morning. James worked the early-morning day shift, reporting to work at six in the morning until three in the afternoon. James got home in time for Bridget to leave for work, and she got home before time for him to leave for work. This allowed them to keep their two-year-old son, Jordan, at home, him tending the child while she worked and her tending the baby while he worked. They were both off on Sunday, but he worked every other Saturday. Bridget was off on Saturday and Sunday every week. Little Jordan took his skin coloring, a shade of chocolate between his light-skinned mother and his medium-to-dark-skinned father. He was a beautiful child.

It was rather amazing to Darius that, as she told him, they were a happy couple, and they managed to spend their free time together, and each took responsibility for some of the cleaning, cooking, shopping, and laundry.

"Well, sir, I'll probably see you tomorrow," she said.

"Even with a broken arm, you can't take a few days off for the healing process?" Darius asked.

"I'm sure they'd fire me if I took even one day off."

This is your opportunity, Darius Deavers, to experience one part of being Black.

With Sage's permission and agreement, he went to work with Bridget, doing her work while she instructed him what to do and while she rested as much as possible, trying to let her arm heal. Bridget was responsible for emptying the wastebaskets on the entire eighth floor, the fifteen offices, each with inner offices, reception room, and coffee room. Darius counted; there were no less than five wastebaskets in each office. Each wastebasket was emptied into a large container that was pulled along as you moved. There were two restrooms in each of the four halls with three stalls, three washbowls, and a large wastebasket in each. She cleaned the bathrooms.

They stopped twice to sit and rest, and they each drank a can of soda that Darius purchased from the machine. They stopped for Bridget to eat lunch or dinner, whatever you wanted to call it. Bridget had brought two sandwiches and two cookies. They filled the empty pop cans from the water fountain and drank.

Darius moved slowly at first, but when he thought of how much had to be done in the course of eight hours, he began to get the feel of it, and he worked faster. But when they sat down to rest, he began to feel that he wouldn't be able to make it through; and a couple of hours later, he felt that he had no strength left. But his determination was strong, and his compassion for Bridget helped him to continue working the entire eight hours. But thinking that doing this hard work would make him know how it felt to be Black was not true. He still only knew how it felt to work this hard, and although this was the only kind of job Bridget was allowed to get, one didn't have to be Black to do it. He was still White, and his color was not the determining factor in being able to do it.

Darius got into his car, took Bridget home, and went home. He couldn't find a way to work on the dock with James, but he went as close as he could, parked his car, and watched him work. Now, more and more, he was beginning to realize that being Black and uneducated, this was their life. Had to be. He thought about Mrs. Johnson and Miss Mamie, and then he thought about Sage and Charles and the difference in the kind of jobs they had. Sage had a college education, and she was a teacher. Charles had a college education, and he was a lawyer. Hmm. But even though they were still Black and tethered and segregated in so many other ways, being educated made a difference.

Back at the law office the next week, Darius spoke to Norrell about Bridget, telling him how very stressful and tiring her job was and the awful prejudice that existed against Blacks which kept her in this kind of job.

"Darius, your concern is misplaced," he said. "Somebody has to do it. We've worked hard getting an education, and they haven't, and I can't say that it's because of prejudice because they've got Black colleges that they can go to. But hey, that's all some people can do. It's all they want to do, and you can't change that"—blah, blah, blah.

Darius Paul Deavers listened, and he asked himself the same question: *What can I do to change that?*

He didn't tell Norrell Ivers that his own wife was Black, and he never accepted Norrell's invitation to bring Sage and have dinner with him and his wife, and Darius never invited him and his wife to his house.

Still trying to come to some definite conclusion about how he would proceed with his life, needing to definitely decide on some employment, Darius invited Blaise to have lunch with him. "Is the shipping company where I should work?"

Blaise had become intensely aware of the Black situation in the world since meeting Darius and Sage, and Karen and her family, and he wanted to program his life outside his work area in a helpful way. Somewhere. Perhaps in employment. He wanted to stay close to Darius, but sitting and sharing lunch with him, Blaise sensed that something was amiss.

"I am lost," Darius said. "I am in a quagmire of doubt, trying to find my place, and I'm sure I know what is causing this dilemma. I love my wife, but the world hates her. Sage can't live peacefully in my White world, and I can't find my way to live in hers. What do you think I can do to change this?"

"I think," Blaise said, after a pause, having a good idea what his problem was, "that if you stay close to your wife, she'll help you make a sensible, rational, comfortable decision. Sage seems to believe that she'll find her way and her place in life and that she'll be content there."

"I need to find my place too, especially in employment. What about working here? Do you think I could be happy here?" he asked.

"You could most definitely work here, and I'm sure you would be an asset to this company, and I will be right here to help you along the way until you've gained the knowledge you need to move forward on your own. But you have to ask yourself if this is where you want to be for the rest of your life. This is not a temporary position, and you'll be expected to make this your career, and somehow I don't see you in the position of working for someone else and following someone else's job descriptions. You know, I have been thinking that you and Sage have so much knowledge and experience about the needs of minorities. Perhaps you should take some time in deciding and listen to your heart and see what it says about what you and Sage should be doing in the future, where you'll be happy, because it's obvious you're unhappy where you are. And speak to your father about your life and your place in it. He seems like such an inspired, levelheaded person, and I'm sure he'd tell you to pray to be led to your high calling, for I'm sure you have one."

As Darius was leaving, Blaise stopped him at the door. "By the way," he said, "tell me about Karen."

Darius was not in the right frame of mind to talk about Karen, and he didn't know why Blaise was asking. "That's something I can't answer. You'll have to ask Karen." He left it at that, thinking no more about it. He drove home with gloomy thoughts that this talk with Blaise had not really helped him to make a decision. Again, he felt defeated.

Holding the baby in her arms, Sage met her husband at the door with her usual pleasant smile, a hug, and a kiss. When Darius felt her love and when he saw their little bundle of joy they had called Willow, he was overcome with love for them, yet that little cloud of doubt and despair still hovered over him. He looked at his beautiful Black wife, and he was reminded of his restricted neighborhood, his failure to develop a meaningful law firm in a Black area, his inability to attend church with his wife, to be satisfied at Marshall, Lewis & Allen Law Firm, and the destruction of their first home. All this told him that happiness in this city was impossible.

Sage was beginning to feel that Darius was not the same loving husband he had been when they were first married. He seemed to have lost interest in her, in Willow Mede, in his career, and Sage was beginning to feel that he had lost all interest in living. She thought about Miriam and Bertram and of them letting life defeat them, and she feared for her husband.

"She's already beginning to look like you," she said, looking over at Willow, but he was engrossed in his pitiful thoughts and wasn't able to receive his wife's obvious contentment, joy.

"Please forgive me, my dear, but I don't feel…" He paused. How did he feel? Sad? Ill? "I don't feel well. I'm going upstairs and lie down for a while."

"All right, dear. I'll call you when dinner's ready."

After he had left the room, Mrs. Johnson, with her motherly instincts, knew that Sage was troubled by Darius's behavior. She came and sat beside her. For a minute or two, there was only Willow's baby sounds as the two ladies said nothing, yet Sage felt the comfort of Mrs. Johnson's presence.

"What is the matter with him?" Sage asked, talking more to herself than to Mrs. Johnson. "He's changed so much, and it's as if he's so unhappy. I can bear his inattention to me, but Willow, he hardly ever holds her anymore."

Yet she knew that to be able to deal with any and all situations, she had to remain calm. When he didn't come down at the usual time that they had a predinner drink, both she and Mrs. Johnson became more concerned than when he went upstairs saying he didn't feel well.

Sage could feel Mrs. Johnson's love and concern, and although Mrs. Johnson's concern was for Sage, she also had compassion and caring for Darius. He had been very kind to her and to her family, both to Mr. Johnson and Randy; but being Black and having lived in a White-controlled world all her life, she was quite conscious of the difficulty both Darius and Sage were trying to overcome. Darius was trying to live in Sage's Black world and still maintain his Whiteness, and Sage was trying to tolerate his White world and their rules, which never allowed her to forget that she was Black, and still love him, even though he was White.

"Should I call him to come down?" Sage asked.

"Well, he said he didn't feel well. Poor baby, he's in such a lot of confusion," Mrs. Johnson said.

"Well, so is everybody. We were relatively happy, knowing there was this Black-White thing hovering over us, but we were so in love it was like we knew we could overcome it. But now it has hit Miriam, Bertram, and Alicia, and they came to a fork in the road, and none of them knew which way to turn, to the Black way or to the White way, so they just sat there in the dust and died. And my husband seems to be at that same fork in the road, dying."

"Baby, you don't have to sit here and die, and he don't either."

"But what can I do?" Sage asked. "It's like he can't even look at us anymore. We're this Black thing that has now entered into every inch of his life, and he thought he had conquered it. He only allowed himself to think about how much he loved me, me as a person, but now the world, this city—the church, schools, jobs, hospitals, every-where—they have made him see me as that ugly Black thing and him as Mr. Beautiful White."

"You're not ugly, and don't you even let being Black make a dif-ference in how you feel about yourself. What do you think made me and your mother and Mamie just keep on keeping on?"

"I don't really know, being strong, I guess."

"It was our faith and our determination to survive in spite of the hate, and that's what's going to save you."

"Oh, I don't know. Right now I'm so confused." Sage tried to smile, trying to keep her spirits up, although she felt like crying.

"Well, baby, if you really feel that you are at the fork in the road, then you have to get up and do something. So go up there and see about your husband. Tell him how much you love him and that you understand what he's going through. He needs you right now." She took the sleeping baby from Sage.

"Why does everybody always expect me to be the strong one?"

"Because you are, and it's your faith that keeps you strong."

"I think Darius has lost his faith. He's lost faith in everything, even himself."

"Come on, honey. I know you haven't lost your faith, so you've got to take charge. Go on up there and talk to him."

"All right," she said with a sigh, but after some minutes, Sage came down without him.

"Well, Mrs. Johnson, that didn't work. My husband wants me to go home. He says that I'd probably be better off at home."

"Home?" she asked. "This is your home. You're already at home."

"No, he means home to my mother, to my Black family, away from this White world I'm trying to live in."

"What about your baby? She's also White."

"What about her?" she asked. "Of course, I'll take her with me. Evidently, he doesn't love her either. I think he's sorry he married me." Sage Copple Deavers didn't cry.

Mrs. Johnson was also feeling Sage's pain, but what could she say? What could she do?

"I'll clean up the kitchen, then I'll go home, and I'll pray for you and Mr. Darius and this beautiful child." But she was thinking, *I know how she feels, and there's been so many times in my life that I felt like I just couldn't go on. But there wasn't this mixing with Black and White then, and we were making ourselves content with just us Black folk. Our own church. Our own friends. But these young Black people now, well, they want more, but the evil Whites and the awful laws are still holding them down. And Lord, I don't want life to get the best of them, especially Miss Sage and Karen and even Mr. Darius. He's suffering too.*

After Mrs. Johnson left, Sage called her mother. "This marriage isn't working out, and my husband wants me to come home, so that's what I'll do."

"Oh, baby, are you sure?" Mary Jane Copple asked.

"Yes, Mamma, I'm sure. So I'll let you know when we'll be there so you can have somebody to pick us up. Willow and me."

43

The year was 1948. It was the middle of August, perhaps the hottest time of the year in Oklahoma, and Reverend Paul Deavers was busy with his involvement in FABCS (Financial Aid for Black College Students), the organization whose main purpose was helping to promote higher education for the Black students in this city. He had been instrumental in forming this organization after becoming aware of the prejudices against Black people through contact with their maid, beautiful half-Black, half-Indian Mary Jane Copple and her daughter, beautiful green-eyed, brown-skinned Sage Copple, who was struggling to stay in college because of lack of money. These two had made an impression on Reverend Deavers, and they made him much more aware of the plight of minorities and the debilitating prejudice against them.

At the church where Reverend Deavers belonged, he was assistant to the pastor as head of the Department of Education, and included in his duties was teaching theology to young men and women, boys and girls. His church in Oklahoma, as were most churches in the United States, was segregated, so all of his members were White. And since there was no concern for Blacks, he did not mention his involvement with the organization FABCS. A few of his acquaintances knew of his liberal views, but they didn't talk about them with him. He had to accept the laws of the land and their prejudices, but that didn't deter him from his determination to help potential Black college students. Right now, however, his help was needed in his own family.

This was also a time in America, in all forty-eight states, when Blacks were segregated and denied equal rights in every aspect of their lives, especially in education. Many schools across the South closed rather than integrate. Blacks seeking equal rights in employment sparked race riots in many cities: Detroit's riot in 1943 was caused by resentful Whites who were against employment of Black auto workers. Thirty-four people died, and hundreds were injured. There were race riots in Los Angeles, California; Beaumont, Texas; and Columbus, Tennessee. A group of Whites in some Southern states who called themselves Dixiecrats broke off from the Democratic Party because they were opposed to racial integration, and they wanted to keep the Jim Crow laws that were for segregation in place. In 1942, a group of Blacks who believed that that they should have equal and fair rights in every facet of their lives the same as Whites created the Congress of Racial Equality (CORE).

It was during the time of all this turmoil in the United States concerning racial prejudice that Reverend Deavers's White son, Darius Paul Deavers, defied tradition, laws, and family for the right to marry Ariel Sage Copple, who was Black, and Reverend Deavers had warned his son that the life he had chosen would not be an easy one. At the same time, however, Reverend Deavers had developed a strong liking for Sage and her mother, and he did not oppose the marriage. Sage and her mother had also, just by being themselves—loving, kind, confident—won the admiration of Darius's mother, Mrs. Lucy Deavers, who had been taught all her life to honor segregation for Black people.

Now, surprising to his father yet expected from some members of both families, Darius had allowed the world's hate and BeachSide's hostile atmosphere of separation to overcome his ability to cope. And his inability to cope had placed a burden of sadness over Sage's normal peace of mind, and she wasn't willing to sit idly by and allow Darius's attitude and despondency to destroy her love for him nor his love for her nor her life.

The phone call from Sage to Mary Jane Copple prompted a call to Mrs. Lucy Deavers, who relayed the message to her husband that Darius was unhappy and he wanted Sage to leave and come home.

Nothing else needed expression, and despite his total dedication to FABCS, and especially during this time when he was busiest with the organization, the reverend, a dedicated father, felt that his major concern now was his children, Darius and Sage.

"I'm going to Washington. I need to see what's happening out there. I need to find out what Darius is doing, or not doing, that makes him want Sage to come home," Reverend Deavers said.

"I'm going with you. I need to see about Sage," Lucy Deavers said.

"No. This is something I want to do alone, but if I see that Sage needs you and her mother, I'll call you. And, my dear, do you remember that I haven't seen our first little grandchild?"

Mary Jane Copple was also concerned about her daughter, but she felt within her heart that the presence and the love of Reverend Deavers and of Mrs. Erma Johnson would supply the props and encouragement which Sage needed.

As he prepared for the trip, not wanting to barge in on Sage and Darius unannounced, Reverend Deavers put in a call to Major Marvin Hawthorne, hoping he could shed some light on the situation. He was aware that the major had been in close contact with Darius and Sage, and Reverend Deavers trusted the major's judgment.

"What do you see as the problem with my son?" Reverend Deavers asked.

Major Hawthorne hesitated in answering because he didn't want to betray Darius, yet he decided that it would be more beneficial for him to say what he really felt. "It seems that Darius hasn't been able to find his place in the employment world, especially since the absence of Charles, and he hasn't been able to deal with the pressures, you know, of all the mean things that have happened because of Sage being Black. It has kinda gotten the best of him, and we know that Sage was a bright spot in the whole of it, her friendship with Miriam, trying to help her, her support for Karen, her love for Mrs. Johnson and the children kept her spirits up. But now that she's unhappy, it just seems like a dark cloud has even blocked out her sun."

"Well, I'm coming out there, and I'll talk to Sage. I know how strong she is, and I'm praying that together, all three of us, we can help my son to develop a permanent agenda that will show him how to cope with all the evil deeds and prejudices, which, of course, can't be eliminated."

"You know that he was a savior for me when I was threatened and needed someone in my corner. Oh..." He paused and covered his eyes, but he quickly recovered. "I'm so glad you're coming. You just can't imagine what a relief it is to know that you'll be here, and I know you can figure it out because you're exactly the blessing we all need."

"And you're a blessing to me, and I thank you," Reverend Deavers said.

After talking to Reverend Deavers, Major Hawthorne thought a visit to his two young friends was needed, even though it was hard for him to imagine that there was trouble between them because he had thought of Sage and Darius as being an example of the perfect, coping, loving couple.

When he arrived at the Deavers' home, it was Sage who answered his ring. Darius was at his office. Sage greeted him with a smile and a hug and invited him to come in. She sat on the couch and invited Major Hawthorne to sit beside her. Willow was lying peacefully in her bassinet.

"I heard from your father-in-law," he said, sitting down beside her. "And I came to tell you that after you called your mother, you know, to say that Darius wanted you to come home, well, she called Darius's mother."

"I didn't know she did that," Sage said.

"And of course, Darius's mother told her husband, and he called me, and—" He stopped and breathed a sigh. "And he said he's coming out here to see what he can do to help."

Sage didn't say anything, but she was thinking, *So now everybody knows, and I guess everybody is concerned. Oh well, we'll see how it plays out.*

"The reverend, he loves you so much as if you were his own daughter, so you'll have to stay here, and I know that this can only have a happy ending. It's just that Darius's mind is on vacation right now, and I feel sure that his dad is the one who can give it a ticket back home where it belongs." He smiled as he looked at Willow. "That is a cute little wiggly thing," he said as Sage pulled the blanket back to reveal more of her child.

"I don't know if my husband can find himself in all this hate. It has not helped him to cope with our situation, you know, me being Black and him having to suffer from all the restrictions and hate because of me. So he's thinking that maybe if I went away for a few months, it would allow him to get his head on straight."

"Well, you can't do that now since your father-in-law is coming," he said, and Sage smiled. When she thought what would happen if she went to Proctor, she could hear them: "I told you so," and pointing fingers and clapping hands over the seeming truth of their predictions.

"You didn't tell me when he's coming," Sage said.

"I'm picking him up this afternoon, and I'm sure he will want to talk to you first."

"What he most likely wants to do first is to see his grandchild because you know that he hasn't seen her yet. Thanks for coming, Major. You've always been a good friend."

"I hope you won't mind if I go and talk to your husband, you know, try and get him a little prepared for his father."

"Of course, I don't mind. If anyone can get to him, it'll be you—and, of course, his father."

And that was that.

44

When Major Hawthorne walked into the office, Darius greeted him with a handshake and a smile.

"What brings you here, my friend?" Darius asked, and then assuming a businesslike voice and demeanor, he bowed. "Do you have a pressing legal problem, sir, that I can assist you with?"

"No," the major said, laughing, and then changed his demeanor to one of seriousness. "It's not legal. It's friend to friend."

Darius realized that the Major was serious. "Well then, let's sit down and talk about it." Darius led the major to the couch, and they sat facing each other.

"I've just come from talking to your dear wife, and she tells me that you want her to go home to her mother, away from all this strife, you said."

"And that's the truth."

"Well, of course, I don't agree with you."

"And that's your privilege," Darius said.

"Then why? What seems to be the problem?"

"It's that I'm unhappy, and I haven't been able to keep her happy, and that causes me to feel like a complete failure. But you probably don't understand because you've already been successful in your career, and I haven't. You've already worked out the unhappy situation with your grandchildren, and I haven't decided about how to raise Willow, looking White, yet she will be called Black. I'm lost, out in the wilderness, but you're safe and sound in your own peaceful environment."

"Okay. Let's talk about you and me and where we are in our present situations. Yes, I'm older than you and the days of building a career are over for me, but I remember that when I was in trouble and didn't know where to turn or how to solve my problem with something that was threatening me, it was Attorney Darius Deavers who unselfishly came to my rescue, and I saw you as a wonderful problem-solver, a willing helper, and a friend."

"Thank you," Darius said.

"You're welcome. At the same time, you had a problem stemming from a similar set of circumstances. I was being threatened by strangers with having a Black daughter, and you feel threatened because you have a Black wife. I felt sure that my problem had been solved by your money and by the people leaving who were making the threats, and you felt sure your problem had been solved by having your White parents and other White people to welcome your Black wife, me included.

But then the world came along and dumped both of us White men over the fence into another kind of world altogether. Back to Black. For me, the discovery that Miriam's father was a Black man, which meant my daughter was Black, and which automatically labeled her children as Black. It was a setback. For you, the evil Whites destroyed your honeymoon home because your wife is Black. In the White world in which I lived, it was just a fact of life for me and my family that there were two kinds of people, superior and inferior—and the superior were White, and the inferior were Black.

"And now here I am, White, with two Black children to raise. Yes, Felicity looks Black, but even though Timothy looks White, by virtue of having one Black parent, he is Black. That means that I've got to leave my White world and live in a Black-restricted neighborhood, take the children to a Black school and a Black church. And my friend, although Willow looks White, but because her mother is Black, you will be required to do likewise."

"What are you saying? I can't be successful or content as a White man even though that's what I am?" Darius asked. "I am still an educated White man, and I haven't changed."

"You haven't changed, my friend, but the situation has changed, so now it's really not about you."

"What do you mean it's not about me?" he asked. "It most definitely is about me. If I'm going to live a successful life as anything—lawyer, husband, father—I have to come to some peaceful terms with myself and who I am. I'm White, and the woman I love is Black, and because of that, everything around me is falling apart."

"No, that's not true. It's falling apart because you trust in the fact that you're White to save you, and seemingly you love being White, and in order to live in your precious White world, you think you should get rid of your wife, which to you is a Black albatross. You're listening to your head instead of your heart, and your head says, 'I am White,' and your heart says, 'I love Sage.' I don't think you're going to be happy without her or Willow. And I know that you think that I'm all for Sage and against you, but you know that I love you and Sage the same."

He left it, and Darius, with that.

The Wise Counselor said the words from a century-old proverb: "One ought to hold on to one's heart, for if one lets it go, one soon loses control of his head too."

Major Hawthorne, neatly dressed in his uniform, with his usual happy smile, met the reverend at the airport. Despite the fact that he was comfortable with this man as a friend, Major Hawthorne still respected the reverence that emanated from Reverend Michael Deavers as a man of peace.

"What is our destination, sir? Would you like to go to the base for housing or to your son's house?"

"No, neither one. I'm going to stay at the hotel. I don't want to burden my children with the inconvenience of having a houseguest right now, so I'll get checked in at the hotel, and then I want to talk to Sage and Mrs. Johnson before I talk to my son. I assume that he's still at his office."

"Yes, he is."

"And you know that I haven't seen my precious first granddaughter, and I'm certainly looking forward to that."

When Reverend Deavers and Major Marvin Hawthorne drove into the driveway, Sage was sitting by the front window watching for their arrival. She opened the door even before they rang the bell, and she walked out on the porch to meet and greet them. She gave a lingering hug and a kiss to her beloved father-in-law, and thankful that the major had picked him up, she gave Marvin a hug as well. Sage was sure that Major Hawthorne had given Reverend Deavers all the information that he knew about Darius's feelings, and Sage was looking forward to telling the Reverend some of the actions and feelings about Darius of which the major wasn't aware.

Major Hawthorne greeted Mrs. Johnson with a handshake and a kiss on her hand. Little Willow Mede had been bathed and fed, and she was lying in her bassinet wearing a pretty pale-yellow and white outfit, with a white and yellow ribbon in her hair. She was born with a head full of straight hair, eyes green and brown, seemingly a mixture of both colors. She was awake.

Although he was anxious to get introduced to his granddaughter, Reverend Deavers, always respectful to those around him, greeted Mrs. Johnson with a warm handshake before turning to Sage. "What a beautiful granddaughter," he said, looking at Willow. "May I pick her up?"

"Yes, do. Willow, darling," she said, "this is your grandpa. Now, you be nice and give him one of your best smiles." Lifting Willow and placing her gently in his arms, Sage saw the tenderness and love that showed on this grandfather's face.

"I think she knows who I am," the reverend said, kissing her on the forehead.

"Of course, she does," Sage said, putting her arms around them both. "I'm so, so glad you're here. Now come and sit down in this rocking chair. She likes being rocked."

"She's a good baby," Mrs. Johnson said, placing a cloth on the reverend's shoulder. "But she does spit up sometimes. I don't want her to mess up your nice clothes."

"Thank you, but I'm sure I don't mind. Whatever she does is fine with me."

Major Hawthorne knew this was a private family meeting, and his presence was no longer needed. "I'll be leaving now, but you call me if you need me," he said.

Reverend Deavers, still sitting, thanked the major for picking him up and for his willing support. Mrs. Johnson walked him to the door, and then she went about her duties in another part of the house, leaving Sage and Willow and Reverend Deavers in the living room.

"Blessed are the peacemakers," Sage said, smiling at her father-in-law, "for they shall be called the sons or children of God, and that's exactly what we need here, someone who can bring about some peace. And what does the song say?" she asked. "There shall be peace in the valley, and that's exactly where Darius has taken us, for we are down in the valley."

"Do you know what's troubling him?" Reverend Deavers asked. "The major thinks that he's disappointed because he hasn't been able to make his law firm work, and he doesn't know how to keep the evil White wolves away because of you."

"That's a part of it, but I think he has lost his faith. He says if there is a God, how can He let there be so much hate for Black people. He's read and read, and he wonders how Black people were created in the first place and why they are the target of so much prejudice. He came here feeling so strong and thinking, you know, since he was so happy with his marriage, that he could heal all the evils and all the prejudices out here."

"No one person can accomplish all of that, but there are a number of good things he can do."

"He totally discounts all the good things he has already done. He helped Major Hawthorne when he was in trouble, he stood by Mrs. Johnson until her husband passed, and he paid for his hospital and burial costs. And later, he spent some time trying to help Randy."

"Who is Randy?"

"He's the father of Karen's children."

"You mean, her husband?"

"No, they were never married. It was one of those high school romances, and Randy never seemed to get himself or his life together."

"What was his trouble? No education?"

"Well, that, and then he got into alcohol and drugs."

"Like a lot of young people do these days when life gets hard for them."

"You're right, and just last month, a young lady who does the cleaning where Darius works fell and broke her arm, and just like he did with Mr. Johnson, he took her to the hospital, and he paid for her care. And believe it or not, he went to work with her that night and did most of her work so she wouldn't have to use her arms so much. Her employers should have paid her bills, and they should have given her time off so her arm could heal."

"They didn't?"

"You know it's still very unfair for my people, and now my husband calls himself *useless*"—she emphasized the word and mocked Darius's voice—"because he can't fix everything that confronts him here. Seems like he thinks the whole world is nothing but pitfalls, and he can't be happy or successful here."

"Sage, you and I know that it's not just this city. It's everywhere. And not just Black people, we have all been in deep quandaries in our lives. I worked at several jobs, unhappy all the while, until I turned to the place where I always knew I belonged. But for what seemed like an eternity, I didn't know how to get there."

"You mean your ministry."

"Yes, and it was your mother"—he paused, as if recalling the moment—"well, I was talking about my feelings one day, and your mother, bless her heart, she walked over from doing the dishes and put her hands on my shoulders, and somehow I was filled with her spirit, and I knew how to direct my life, my thinking, and my actions." He paused and looked at Sage as if seeing her as her mother. He patted her hand. "I had just the same feeling when our ranch was burned, just before your mock wedding, and I was also very discouraged, even angry with God, and I remember that your mother walked over to me then and placed her hands on my shoulders, and the air was miraculously filled with her peace. It was so moving that my wife was moved. You remember, don't you?"

"Yes, I remember. It was a very miraculous moment for all of us who were there, especially your wife, for it was at that moment your wife's heart was changed, and we both know it was nothing but the Lord."

"And it is the Lord who sent me here. Maybe I have honestly been sent as a peacemaker for you and Darius." He paused again and took a deep breath. "But you know, Sage, God puts the strength and the will in all of us who believe, and now Darius has to figure out a way to work from inside himself. That's where his strength is."

Reverend Deavers paused and looked around. He felt a soft breeze of peace through the room. He looked, and Willow Mede was fast asleep. "She really does like me, doesn't she?"

"We all do," Sage said.

"Sage," he asked after a few moments of quiet, "what would make you happy?"

"Sir, I'm not unhappy. I'm confused."

"But confusion is on the road to discontentment, and that leads to complete unhappiness."

"It's not that I'm so confused that I don't know how to deal with my life. It's that my husband is unhappy with everything—this marriage, his employment, and the hate that seems to surround us. We promised our love to each other, and I thought that would sustain us, and I don't know why that isn't working for him."

"What would sustain you?" he asked. "Of course, I'm just as worried about you as I am about him."

"What I want to do is teach Black children some things. First, I want to teach them to love themselves, and that comes from inside. I learned that from my mother early in life. She said that bad things will happen all around you, and maybe bad things will happen to you because you're Black, but don't let those things control what happens inside of you. She said that God gave each one of us our own brain to think with, and the Word says, 'So a man thinketh, so is he.'"

"Of course, all those things she told you are true," Reverend Deavers said.

"The other thing is, I want to teach Black children to read early in their young lives. Reading is basic to knowledge, and knowing how to read can lead to much more knowledge. So even if it should happen that my husband and I don't make it together, wherever I am, that's what I'll be doing. I'll be teaching Black children to love themselves and to love knowledge, and of course, to love God."

"My dear Sage, those are lofty and sensible thoughts for you, but you and Darius are only going to find your peace together. I know that, and everybody who knows you knows that. And what did the ladies say at the Christmas celebration? It's faith in God, hope for the future, and love, and the greatest of these is love. That means love of God, of yourself, of your children, and love of your fellow man. And I know that you have those things, and that is what needs to be transferred to your husband. Touch him with your thoughts, give him your peace, which I've come to know is colorless. You know, I believe in laying on of hands, and you may not know it, but you're a replica of your mother."

"I do know that all those who love us are so sure that we should be together—that includes you and your wife—and it's such a blessing, you know, that with your wisdom and your knowledge, to hear you say it makes me realize that it is true, and now somehow, we have to plant that truth inside my husband. But if he can't abide that, well, I... I..." She paused. "This is what I'm thinking, and this is what I'll do."

He listened to her words about her future, her wisdom about her life, and his heart fell a little as her words were shocking to him. She reached over and kissed him on the cheek, taking the sleeping infant from him.

"I'll take her up and put her in her bed, and you can chat with Mrs. Johnson for a while."

Reverend Deavers stood by the door where Mrs. Johnson was polishing silver, and although Sage's words stayed with him, he directed his thoughts to Mrs. Johnson.

"I want to thank you so much for your care and compassion for Sage. She's so brave, so if she calls for help, it must be pretty bad out here," he said.

"Well, sir, I knew it wouldn't be the right thing for her to leave right now. Your son may not realize it, but he needs her with him, and I wonder that he can't see that."

"It's been hard for him too, coming to a new city, getting married, and trying to assume the role as head of a household. He's always lived in a protected environment, and he wasn't ever required to take control of things. I know that all of this is new to him."

"Yes, sir, and it's new to her too. She's in a new place too. She was brought up all her life thinking of us coloreds as being the maids and cooks and servants, and that included her own mother, so she really didn't know how to act being a Negro and having one of us as her maid." She smiled. "It was sorta funny, and I knew I had to make her comfortable in her role and treat her like she was the wife of a rich White man, which she really is."

"We all know that you're special to her, and a great number of people would not be able to work for her, White or Black. We are very thankful for you."

"She's been a lot of help to me too and to my family. When I first met her, it was when she needed help, and I was there at the right place and at the right time to help her."

"She told her mother how she met you, and it wasn't really a coincidence."

"No, sir, we know it was the Lord, and when she cried and said I reminded her of her mother, well, my heart just opened up to her. And bless her heart, she was so scared. But, sir, you know that Mr. Darius have sure enough helped me too, you know, because when my husband was sick, your son took him to the hospital, and he stayed right there with us, until my husband died, Lord have mercy, and he paid for everything. He took care of the hospital bill and for the funeral bill—he just took care of everything. And that little wife of his, she is helping my daughter go to college, and she was teaching the children how to read 'cause that's what they need is a good education."

"That's what I'm trying to do for young Black students who want to go to college. I began to realize the problem when I met Sage. She was struggling to pay for her education."

"Well, sir, that sure is what we need. We need for White folks to come and help 'cause we just can't do it by ourselves because the row gets too hard for us to hoe, if you know what I mean."

"I know exactly what you mean, and we do need to furnish a plow, and we'll pray for God to send the rain and soften the soil."

"Oh, sir, we've got to be her plow, and his too. They don't know how beautiful they are, and now with that little one—and, sir, I had to smile when she came home with that child, pure White. But you know, I believe that that baby's a sign, and her being part Black and part White, I just believe she's here to help Miss Sage and Mr. Darius to see the light 'cause that's what she is. She's a bright shining light. And I believe that they are chosen too. What does the Bible say, 'some of us are called, and some of us are chosen, and those He calls, he helps them get through.'"

"Yes, and those He called, He also justified. And those he justified, he also glorified." Reverend Deavers was moved and also amused hearing her say Miss Sage and Mr. Darius and hearing her paraphrase the scripture.

"So, Mrs. Johnson, how did you make it through with all the hateful things that were brought against you?"

"Well, it just took a lot of courage and a lot of praying, and we just learned how to live through it. But a whole lot of our people couldn't take it, and so they just gave up. We can march and carry signs, but the only thing that's going to make things change is that some of you good Christian White folks come to help us."

"You're so right. That's what my son is, and we'll pray that the Good Lord will show him the way to help."

There was a warm spirit of something good taking place within him, and the whole house and the whole air around him was filled with it, and there was no way it could be ignored. He could see how this lady reminded Sage of her mother because they both seemed to have something that White people didn't have, even those who were rich and healthy and seemingly happy. It was peace, it was faith, and it was acceptance of not only themselves but of those who mistreated them. Here was a friend, an inspiration, hated only because of the color of her skin.

"May I hug you?" he asked, putting out one hand toward her.

"Oh, sir, that would make me feel honored," she said taking his hand and joining him in a hug. Peace. Their smiles created the sunshine which lighted up the room.

45

Taking Sage's car, Reverend Deavers went to see his son.

"I'm sorry that I've disappointed you and Mom," Darius said to his father, sitting on the couch with him. "Everything I have, I owe to you and her. You've given me an expensive education, a car, two homes, a huge bank account, and still I can't seem to establish myself."

"We gave you all those things because you're our child, and you don't owe us anything. It was our responsibility to take care of you until you were prepared to take care of yourself, and I don't understand why you are having problems doing that."

"I know that I am not the son you want me to be."

"What we want you to be is a decent person, a loving husband and father, and a good Christian. It wasn't that we gave you so much because we wanted to dictate what you did with your life, because once you give something to someone, it belongs to them, and how they use it is up to them."

"And I sincerely want to thank you for coming out here to prop me up and to help me fix my problems."

"Oh no, you've got it all wrong. I didn't come all the way out here to help you fix your problems or to prop you up. Oh no."

"What? Then why did you come?"

"Well, before I can help you to fix anything, I have to first find out where it's broken, and I can't prop it up if I don't even know what it is. So I came out here to find out what the hell is wrong with you."

Darius looked up quickly, showing his shock, thinking, *Is this man of the cloth cursing because of me? Oh my.*

"Don't be shocked. I know you think hell is only a curse word, but the word *hell* is also a noun, and the dictionary defines it as any place or state of torment or misery, and you seem to have put yourself right in the middle of that, and I'd like to know why."

"It's because I'm a failure," Darius said, bowing his head. "I haven't been successful in my own law firm, and I was at the lowest level in someone else's firm, and I can't seem to protect my wife from all the prejudice and hate because she's Black. And now I have another heavy responsibility to worry about. I have a child who looks pure White. So how do I raise her? Black or White? By the one-drop rule, she's Black, and she'll be treated just like her mother is treated."

They sat for a while in silence, Darius waiting for his father's thoughts and his father deciding how to answer his son's negative and pitiful-sounding feelings.

Finally Reverend Deavers said, "I'm sure you aren't aware of how many times you said the word *I* in a very negative way. 'I'm a failure,' 'I can't,' 'I haven't been successful,' 'I don't know how to raise my child.' Son, your thinking is all wrong. It's not always about you."

"Seems I've heard that before."

"And what has happened to your faith? Do you still have a prayer life? Don't you believe in God anymore?" he asked.

"When I think about God, the world, and the infinity of space, I am only one little dot, one little organism likened to the size of an ant or a grain of sand. There are thousands and thousands of churches and millions and millions of people with prayers and petitions and needs, so I am much too small for any God or Supreme being to be the least bit concerned about me."

"Think about the mustard seed," his father said. "It is the smallest seed in the world, but under God's provisions of sunshine and rain, it grows to become a tree, large enough for the birds to come and lodge in its branches."

"I'm not a seed. I'm a living, breathing person," Darius retorted.

"In the Gospel of Saint Matthew, we also find this parable: If a man have a hundred sheep, and one of them has gone astray, wouldn't he leave the ninety-nine and go and seek that one which is lost? You're as important to God as that little grain of sand and as that one little lost sheep."

"That's a parable, and a parable is allegorical," Darius again retorted.

"Darius, you have an earthly father who is here beside you, and you have a Heavenly Father, who is in heaven, and He is always with you, and neither of us want you to get lost."

"Well, I'm totally lost, and I feel like an insignificant little piece of clay," Darius said, turning and looking away from his father. "If I'm gone, nothing will stop. The world will go on just the same. Night will follow day, and day will follow night. Businesses will open their doors, and people will go about their daily routines the same—you and Sage and everybody else. So why am I even here? You and Mom have supplied me with all I have, so if I die, what do I have to leave my children? Nothing. Because I am nothing. Evil White people and their evil laws will always prevail. Can't eat here, can't stay at this hotel, can't go to school here, can't teach here, and on and on. And, Lord have mercy, the churches are segregated so I can't even worship God with my wife. You and Mom probably made a mistake with me, giving me such an easy life."

"We didn't make a mistake with you by giving you such an easy life, but you're making a mistake by throwing it away. This is a new life for you, and you have everything you need to make it work. Let's turn that negative *I* around and make it a positive *I*. 'I can,' 'I have a good education,' 'I'm White,' which by the world's standards, you're superior, and all that gives you some advantages."

"A few, I guess," Darius said, still in his negative mood.

"More than a few, I'd say. You have a lovely educated wife, who, by the way, is not a hindrance to you, and sending her away will not remove her from your mind or cure your imagined problems. You probably think that when she and Willow are gone, then you can construct your life as you want it to be, but I know that's not true. You need them. And you can't change the prejudiced people or their evil minds. They're like the billy goats whose goal is to climb until they reach the top, wherever they think that is, kicking everything good or bad out of their way, and that includes minorities and even some of their own kind. But it's all inspired by a quest for power, and money defines their power. What they call love of self means hate for everyone else. And Darius, dear, you cannot change their hearts."

"How about their prejudiced laws?" he asked. "If the laws could be changed, I think integration would soon follow."

"There will never be total integration because groups, people with like habits, like beliefs, even those of a certain skin color, will always separate themselves, and trying to change man's unequal laws would require a lot more people and a lot more time. And right now you don't have either. And for your information, you can worship God anywhere. You don't have to be in a White church or a Black church. So let's get rid of your *I* problem."

"But I have to be concerned about me and about how I can make a success with my life. Otherwise, why am I here?"

"Well, first you're here because we brought you here. Actually, you didn't have anything to do with being here, but by the grace of God, you can choose what you do here."

"Yes, and that's to take care of my life."

"That's true, but don't forget about the dying message that Miriam and Bertram left. Their message was to take care of the children. And it is true that your children will be classified as Black. Therefore, your ability, your strength, your duty, your first obligation, and yes, your contract with infinity, is to take care of the children."

"Of course, I'll feed my children and clothe them, and…" He paused, for his father put his hand up and interrupted him.

"They didn't say to take care of your children. They said take care of *the* children. There's a difference. And it would serve you well to have some purpose in life that is beyond yourself, for no man should live such a life of selfishness. You know, Sage already has the right approach, and that is to teach the children to read, for the ability to read is the basis for all learning and for eventual freedom. And a fight for freedom doesn't just include your own children, but it should include all Black children. With a firm foundation in the three Rs—reading, writing, and arithmetic—then as adults, they will be equipped to demand better jobs, and then they can take care of themselves and their children. They can fight for freedom and equality, regardless of the unequal laws. Those of us who are White have always been free, so we should fight to remove the chains from those who are bound, for as long as some of us are not free, then none of us should feel that we are free. So let this be an awakening for you to see this as your true purpose in life."

These two men, so much alike, yet one further along the paths and experiences of life than the other, sat for a time, saying nothing. The father was wondering if his words had reached his son. The son, previously so set in his decision, was torn. Finally, Reverend Deavers took his son's hand and looked him straight into his face.

"Have you thought about how life will be for Sage and Willow if Sage goes back to Oklahoma?" he asked.

"It will only be until I get my own life figured out, and then I'll bring them back."

"Well, think about this: Willow will be in an all-Black home, all-Black environment with no father, and that is not a normal family structure. Of course, everyone will love her, that's true, and she won't be mistreated. But Sage told me that if she leaves you now, with you having no definite plans for her return, she will never come back to you."

There was an audible gasp from Darius.

Reverend Deavers continued, "She says that she will divorce you, and she will give Willow to us because she thinks that Willow would feel more like she belonged if she were raised in a White home. She says that you could come to visit with Willow anytime you wanted, and when the divorce is final, she says that you'd then be free to marry someone White, and Willow would never know she had a Black mother."

Shock and pain. Darius's mind traveled back to Miriam, and like Miriam, Willow would be raised in a White environment, living as a White person, then being swallowed up in the avalanche of lies that had been building up around her, then falling down, smothering from the truth. "Your mother is Black, therefore, you are Black."

"What? What are you saying? Divorce me? Never to see me again?" Darius was totally thrown to the ground. "Oh, Lord have mercy," Darius said.

"Yes, that's who can help you," his father said, aware of his son's exasperation and shock. "Think of Esther and Mordecai. In the book of Esther, the scripture tells us that God prepared the place and the opportunity, and Esther and Mordecai chose to act for Him. It would be such a blessed thing if you would plan to be God's servant in your place and time and with your abilities, for who knows? It may be that you and Sage were put together by God, and you have been sent out here, for such a time as this."

Reverend Michael Deavers left, and feeling his own need to spend some time in meditation and prayer, this man of God did not kneel. He stood at the edge of a nearby park and let the beginning drops of rain fall on his face as he looked upward. He prayed,

"O God, our God from ages past, our hope for years to come. You have been our shelter from the stormy blasts and our eternal home. You were here before the earth, and water stood, and earth received her frame. So from everlasting to everlasting, we will praise your name. Spirit of the living God, fall fresh on me. Spirit of the living God, fall fresh on us. You are the Potter, and we are the clay, so mold us and make us as you want us to be. I ask that you make your presence known here. Set guard over our family and keep watch over the doors of our homes. Hide my son and his wife behind your cross and use him simply as a vessel to bring forth your word and your will, for you are real. I love you, Lord, and it is in your most humble name that I do pray. Amen."

46

Darius stood looking out the window, listening to the sound of the rain and watching as the storm intensified and the clouds covered the sun so that it was getting dark and the trees across the way were swaying and bending from the harsh wind. The intermittent flashes of lightning blazed across the sky, and the roar of thunder followed. The changes from light to dark, from the sounds of the storm to a quiet lull, to only the heavy rain pounding on the roof and washing down on the sidewalk, seemed to cause him to change with it. His thoughts swayed as the wind—right, left—and he was changed from Darius Deavers to a big Washington Elm tree, tossed and controlled by forces outside himself, and forces over which he had no control.

His father's words were ringing in his ears: "Your obligation, your duty, is to take care of the Black children. The main drawback for them is in education, so your responsibility is to educate the children. And this is not about you." He remembered that Major Hawthorne had also said, "This is not about you. Miriam's and Bertram's dying messages were to take care of the children, and those two parents died because of how the world classified Black children—inferior, unable to learn." He thought about Charles Williams and his disappointment that he had not been successful in getting freedom and equality for Black children in recreation.

At first, Darius was in total disagreement with what his father was saying as his state of mind had been in an extremely negative mode. But then his thinking changed. *This is the father who has been with me all of my life, one who has supported me and taught me the difference between in right from wrong, good from bad, belief in God from dependence on myself, and who has direct communication with my Heavenly Father.* Listen to their words.

Darius began to realize that he had been selfish all his life. Even when he met and fell in love with Sage, he was not thinking about the injustices heaped upon Black people and what kind of struggles he might have put her through being married to her. He had not thought of her as being Black. She was the person whom he loved. He realized, *I loved her against reason, against all discouragement that assailed me. My feelings were much stronger than my reason. For most of my life, I lived in my White world, and all the White people of my age and of my contacts, my friends, lived as I lived. And like blind men, we did not see anything wrong in the way we lived. White was White and Black was Black. White was superior, and Black was inferior. White was smart, and Black was ignorant. White was rich, and Black was poor. I have always had money without having to worry about how to get it. Oh dear.*

He was compelled to think about all the millions and millions of Black people who had no idea where their next meal was coming from or how to pay the rent and utility bills. Prejudice, hate, and ignorance had held them down, and it seemed that no matter how hard they tried, they couldn't seem to rise above the poverty level.

The children. The children. Take care of the children, then the dawn, the light, the message from above: all of these children among us now are classified as Black because all their mothers are Black: Jasmine, Jasper, Jordon, Timothy, Felicity, and Lord have mercy, Willow Mede Deavers. All those Black mothers have struggled with prejudice, and so will their children.

He was mentally and physically knocked off his feet. His strength was gone, and he found himself lying on the floor, on his back. He looked up, and his thoughts went to Charles. *Are you upstairs? No, he's not here to help me.* He managed to stand up, and Charles was standing beside him. He was right there in the office with him, smiling, and a realistic presence came drifting in on a breeze and stood beside Charles. It was Iola, Sage's friend, and Darius knew that Iola and Charles had been reunited, and his thoughts turned to her, and he heard her words: "My sister and I have a school. We teach our children while they're young to read and count." A school. He felt himself changing, and his other voice came from somewhere in the trees, *This is not about you. With an education, Black children, as adults, will be qualified for better jobs, and they can know how to fight the unequal laws. Start a school.*

What? The voice, the words, became louder and louder, and he couldn't turn them off. He was filled with newness. His old person and his old way of thinking had left him, and he felt that he was a seed, small as the mustard seed, but fed and watered with faith in God. He would be helped to grow, his branches spread out wide and strong, and giving life and help to those who needed it and could receive it. *Start a school. Start a school. Start a school.* And as your father said, "There are some things you are not expected to do alone. Think of those who were at the Christmas celebration and of the gifts they brought which represented their hopes and love. They love you, and they can help you with a school."

The storm seems to be growing weaker. The trees are no longer tossed and driven by the wind, and neither am I. I can see it clearly now. Most of the buildings in this block are unoccupied, mostly empty store fronts, one- and two-story buildings. Buy them for a school. A name? A name? Burnett had said "Help." Yes. HELP: Healing, Education, Legal aid—praise from above.

He got into his car with his mind partly on the wet streets and greatly on seeing Sage, holding her, reassuring himself and her that he couldn't exist without her, without Willow Mede. Mrs. Johnson met him at the door, showing concern.

But Mrs. Johnson's concern was not for Sage; it was for him, wondering if he was safe out there in the raging storm.

He began speaking, out loud, hoping that God could hear him, "Sage? Is she gone? Oh dear God, please forgive me, don't take them away."

Sage, bless her heart, was sitting peacefully in the rocking chair, having fed Willow and watching the little one falling asleep. She knew exactly what his thoughts were. They had been communicated to her mentally by her angels.

Darius Paul Deavers fell on his knees beside her. Darius Paul Deavers bowed his head and wept, but they were tears of joy, tears of enlightenment. He knew that he couldn't let his precious Sage go. He couldn't abandon his precious Willow Mede. His father had asked, and he now asked himself, *What in the hell is the matter with you?*

"Don't leave me. Don't leave me. I'm not the same as I was with my thoughts, my color, my aspirations—they were all misplaced. I can see it clearly now. Most of the buildings in that area are not occupied. My Sage, we can start our own school. You teaching, me providing legal counsel. We can purchase all those buildings in the block. A school and an office. I—"

She put her hand on his face, lifting it upward. "Don't cry, Darius," she said. "I understand, and it's going to be all right. I heard your thoughts when my angels spoke to me, and you must know that Black, White, green, blue, we three, we are one."

She stood and placed her hands on his shoulders, and a new and joyful feeling came over him, surrounding him with peace. The curtain, the clouds that had kept his mind closed, hidden, were opened, and the true light engulfed him—the Way, the Truth, and the Light.

I can continue to be who I am: a White man with a purpose, a White lawyer as a legal helper, an advocate, a father, loving husband with a Black wife, both of us with a purpose, a teacher, a helper. And a biracial child.

Their lingering hugs, their kisses, their laughter and joy were genuine and they knew—whatever, wherever, they were one.

The Wise Counselor reminded him, and Darius remembered the passage from James Baldwin's *The Fire Next Time*:

> The very time I thought I was lost
> My dungeon shook
> And my chains fell off.

THE CHRISTMAS CELEBRATION

Y<small>OU ARE INVITED TO</small>

<small>A CELEBRATION</small>

<small>A RENEWAL OF THE WEDDING VOWS OF</small>

D<small>ARIUS AND</small> S<small>AGE</small> D<small>EAVERS</small>
T<small>HE</small>
<small>CELEBRATION OF OUR SCHOOL</small>

T<small>IME: FIVE O'CLOCK</small>
D<small>ATE:</small> D<small>ECEMBER TWENTY-FOURTH</small>
<small>NINETEEN HUNDRED FORTY-EIGHT</small>
<small>AT THE</small> D<small>EAVERS' HOME</small>

A huge Christmas tree, with many colored lights and gold and silver tinsel, stood in a corner of the living room. A large lighted star glowed at the top of the tree. Paper flowers had been strung on a cord and laid at the edge of the carpeting, and fresh-cut red roses filled the vases, which were placed all around the room.

Darius was wearing a white silk tuxedo, and Sage was wearing Mrs. Lucy Deavers' beautiful white wedding dress. Willow Mede was dressed in yellow and white lace.

Those invited were as follows:

Reverend Paul Deavers, Mrs. Lucy Y. Deavers
Mrs. Mary Jane Copple, Burnett Copple, Kay Lee Copple,
Beth and Paul Porter, Mrs. Mamie Caldwell
Mrs. Irma Johnson, Blaise McCaslin, Evelyn Prentiss
Major Marvin and Mrs. Helen Hawthorne, Timothy and Felicity Withers
Lieutenant Colin Kingsley, Mrs. Gertrude Kinsley
Karen, Jasmine, and Jasper Davis

Charles Williams and Iola Lewis
Bridget, James, and Jordan Parker
Willow Mede Deavers

After the celebration, they all joined hands in a circle, and Darius said, "Go in peace, go in joy, go in love."

EPILOGUE

Randy Davis arrived early on Christmas Eve at what had been his home. Mrs. Johnson answered the ring. Randy was driving a large delivery truck, and he asked if he could come in.

"I've brought Christmas presents for the children," he said.

Mrs. Johnson was surprised to see him, and her mind went back to the last time they saw him. It was not a pleasant memory, but her faith, hope, and love opened up to him.

"I haven't come to stay," Randy said, sensing her hesitation in inviting him in. "And I don't want to disrupt you all's life. I just wanted to do this for Christmas since I'm able at this time."

Karen had walked in behind her mother, and she went in front of her and opened the screen door and invited him in.

"It's good to see you, Randy, and you're welcome to come in. The children will be happy to see you and, of course, to get some presents."

Still standing, he put the bag of presents beside the tree; then he turned and put out his hand to Karen.

"I want to ask you and your mamma to forgive me, you know, for, well, for everything I did wrong when I was here. And I'm hoping that from time to time, when I get a little extra money, I can come by and help you all some."

Karen was moved by this as it was something she had been hoping for since she met Randy. She wanted him to apologize, especially to her mom. And she sensed, somewhere in the air of his presence, that he was trying to change; and in his change, his kind thoughts were for his family. His children. For her and her mom. She took his outstretched hand and went closer and gave him a hug. They sat on the couch, and he told her more about his present life.

"I work for a moving company on weekends, and I also use my truck during the week for deliveries. I'm buying it, and I think I can make a pretty good living with it. I live in a community building, with people like me who are having problems with addiction and who don't want to be loaded down with the problem of trying to have a house, but we want a clean place to call home. I'll help you as much as I can, and I'm going to go over there and thank Darius and Sage for trying to help me, but I knew that I wasn't able to stick to no constant, everyday program at that time. It wasn't something I could do right then, and I didn't want to interfere in your life and try to act like a idiot in front of the children and for nobody to feel sorry for me. This life I'm living now, I feel safe, you know, but I'm trying as hard as I can to get off that stuff, and I'm doing pretty good."

He got up to leave, and he handed her an envelope, and he handed one to Mrs. Johnson. "It's just a little something to help you with some of the bills, you know."

Karen stopped him before he got to the door. "If you want, you can say hello to the children. They'd like that." And they did. They liked it a lot. He was still their daddy, the only one they had ever known, and children have a way sometimes of loving where adults have problems with their feelings.

"I hope you all have a happy and a merry Christmas. I'm sorry I can't be a good husband to you and a father to my children right now, but I'm trying real hard to be a better person."

Tears fell from Karen's eyes and rolled down her cheeks. She hugged him and tried to smile. Mrs. Johnson, who had been taking it all in, also gave him a hug. "Thanks, Randy," she said. "I'll be praying for you."

On New Year's Eve, Randy Davis stopped by to see Sage and Darius. Willow Mede had been bathed, fed, rocked, kissed by her mother and father, and she was asleep for the night. Mother and father were thankful that now she slept through the night and having mended all the broken pieces of their lives, they were looking forward to tomorrow, with resolutions and promises for a better start. Their peace was interrupted by the sound of the doorbell. Darius answered and was surprised to see, there at the door, Randy. It was a moment before Darius recognized him as he had quite a different appearance than when he last saw him. Neat. Clean. Smiling.

"I'm sorry to come so unannounced, but I wanted to come and thank you for being so good to me, you know, when I was here before." He reached out for Darius's hand, and Sage, recognizing his voice, came to the open door. It was obvious that Randy had not been sure how they would receive him; but Darius, not holding any grudge and having been told by Mrs. Johnson that he had visited them on Christmas Eve with presents for the children, took his hand and invited him in, well aware that there was no lingering smell of alcohol on his breath.

Sage was also impressed by his appearance, for here was a very good-looking, clean, well-dressed Black man, and since Charles left, there were no Black men in her life. She stepped closer and held out her hand. Darius looked at his wife, and he saw that she had an expression of serious pleasure as she looked at Randy's clean-shaven, now handsome appearance. He was jealous. But to give credence to jealousy, he understood that it had to be a one-way street. Randy could like his wife, and she could like him, without intruding on her love for her husband. And when Sage drew them close, Darius on one side and Randy on the other, it opened Darius's eyes that there was kinship here. It was Randy's sincere appreciation and his sincere respect for Sage which brought on a kinship with Darius, Darius who had tried to help him not because he was White and felt superior to uneducated Black Randy but a kinship with people, which had of course been planted by his love for Sage and her colorless feelings for people. Randy and Darius recognized it clearly.

The jealous feeling was quick and short-lived, and Darius was glad to let his wife enjoy the real friendship of this young man as she had no opportunity of fellowship with a male of her race. Sage felt this, and she reached over and kissed Randy on the cheek.

"I have to apologize to you, Miss Sage," Randy said, "for all those mean and stupid things I said to you. You are a real beautiful lady, and I want to make my peace with you and with your husband before I leave town." He told them of his present living conditions and employment.

"And I saw what they did to your house, and I might be able to help you get it tore down. I work sometimes with a wrecking company, and I do a lot of the hauling, and I know you don't want to leave it like that. And what about you all's insurance?"

Darius told him that the insurance company didn't pay for that kind of damage, just natural disasters.

"Does that include fire?" Randy asked.

"Yes, it does," Darius said.

And as Randy was leaving, Sage said, "We both pray for your future and the future of a relationship with your children."

Leaving them, Randy felt a sudden inspiration that he was a worthwhile person. He couldn't be all that he was expected to be—a good husband, a constant father, a churchgoing Christian—but he could be a better person, a good person as opposed to a bad, mean, ornery nobody; and he was determined to try, to think his own thoughts and not those produced by alcohol and drugs, and he was determined not to associate with lost people who had no direction to follow.

If I can help somebody along the way, then my living will not be a total barrel of garbage.

Listening to the horns being blown, the guns being fired, and all the noise of the New Year's Eve celebrations, Sage and Darius were not aware of the sirens from a fire truck answering the call to a house on fire at 121 Layton Street. The residents of the same block were very much aware. Randy Davis was very much aware. He smiled.

ABOUT THE AUTHOR

Madestella C. Holcomb is a writer in many genres including plays, editorials, poems, and stories. She is a retired editor from the US government. She is a mother, a grandmother, a great-grandmother, and a Christian. She lives in Denver, Colorado. This is her second novel, which continues the storyline started in her first, *Therefore Choose Life*.

CPSIA information can be obtained
at www.ICGtesting.com
Printed in the USA
BVHW030817090820
585844BV00001B/2